Volume One

THE SELECTED STORIES OF ROBERT BLOCH

FINAL RECKONINGS

A CITADEL TWILIGHT BOOK
Published by Carol Publishing Group

First Carol Publishing Group Edition 1990

Copyright © 1987 by Robert Bloch

Individual stores were copyrighted in their year of
first publication. For reasons of space, this
information has been placed in the back of this
volume.

Editorial Offices
600 Madison Avenue
New York, NY 10022

Sales & Distribution Offices
120 Enterprise Avenue
Secaucus, NJ 07094

In Canada: Musson Book Company
A division of General Publishing Co. Limited
Don Mills, Ontario

Manufactured in the United States of America
ISBN 0-8065-1144-3

10   9   8   7   6   5   4   3   2   1

CONTENTS

Mannikins of Horror. 1
Almost Human. 11
The Beasts of Barsac 27
The Skull of the Marquis de Sade 45
The Bogey Man Will Get You 61
Frozen Fear 71
The Tunnel of Love. 79
The Unspeakable Betrothal 87
Tell Your Fortune 99
The Head Man 121
The Shadow from the Steeple. 135
The Man Who Collected Poe. 153
Lucy Comes to Stay 165
The Thinking Cap 171
Constant Reader 195
The Pin. 207
The Goddess of Wisdom. 219
The Past Master. 233
Where the Buffalo Roam. 253
I Like Blondes 267
You Got to Have Brains. 277
A Good Imagination 287
Dead-End Doctor 301
Terror in the Night. 313
All on a Golden Afternoon 321
Founding Fathers 343
String of Pearls 359

FINAL RECKONINGS

Mannikins of Horror

Colin had been making the little clay figures for a long time before he noticed that they moved. He had been making them for years there in his room, using hundreds of pounds of clay, a little at a time.

The doctors thought he was crazy; Doctor Starr in particular, but then Doctor Starr was a quack and a fool. He couldn't understand why Colin didn't go into the workshop with the other men and weave baskets, or make rattan chairs. That was useful "occupational therapy," not foolishness like sitting around and modeling little clay figures year in and year out. Doctor Starr always talked like that, and sometimes Colin longed to smash his smug, fat face. "Doctor" indeed!

Colin knew what he was doing. He had been a doctor once: Doctor Edgar Colin, surgeon—and brain surgeon at that. He had been a renowned specialist, an authority, in the days when young Starr was a bungling, nervous interne. What irony! Now Colin was shut up in a madhouse, and Doctor Starr was his keeper. It was a grim joke. But mad though he was, Colin knew more about psychopathology than Starr would ever learn.

Colin had gone up with the Red Cross base at Ypres; he had come down miraculously unmangled, but his nerves were shot. For months after that final blinding flash of shells Colin had lain in a coma at the hospital, and when he had recovered they said he had *dementia praecox*. So they sent him here, to Starr.

Colin asked for clay the moment he was up and around. He wanted to work. The long, lean hands, skilled in delicate cranial surgery, had not lost their cunning—their cunning that was like a hunger for still more difficult tasks. Colin knew he would never operate again; he wasn't Doctor Colin any more, but a psychotic patient. Still he had to work. Knowing what he did about mental disorders, his mind was tortured by introspection unless he kept busy. Modeling was the way out.

As a surgeon he had often made casts, busts, anatomical figures copied from life to aid his work. It had been an engrossing hobby, and he knew the organs, even the complicated structure of the nervous system, quite perfectly. Now he worked in clay. He started out making ordinary little figures in his room. Tiny mannikins, five or six inches high, were molded accurately from memory. He discovered an immediate knack for sculpture, a natural talent to which his delicate fingers responded.

Starr had encouraged him at first. His coma ended, his stupor over, he had been revivified by this new-found interest. His early clay figures gained a great deal of attention and praise. His family sent him funds; he bought instruments for modeling. On the table in his room he soon placed all the tools of a sculptor. It was good to handle instruments again; not knives and scalpels, but things equally wonderful: things that cut and carved and re-formed bodies. Bodies of clay, bodies of flesh—what did it matter?

It hadn't mattered at first, but then it did. Colin, after months of pains-taking effort, grew dissatisfied. He toiled eight, ten, twelve hours a day, but he was not pleased—he threw away his finished figures, crumpled them into brown balls which he hurled to the floor with disgust. His work wasn't good enough.

The men and women looked like men and women in miniature. They had muscles, tendons, features, even epidermal layers and tiny hairs Colin placed on their small bodies. But what good was it? A fraud, a sham. Inside they were solid clay, nothing more—and that was wrong. Colin wanted to make complete miniature mortals, and for that he must study.

It was then that he had his first clash with Doctor Starr, when he asked for anatomy books. Starr laughed at him, but he managed to get permission.

So Colin learned to duplicate the bony structure of man, the organs, the quite intricate mass of arteries and veins. Finally, the terrific triumph of learning glands, nerve structure, nerve endings. It took years, during which Colin made and destroyed a thousand clay figures. He made clay skeletons, placed clay organs in tiny bodies. Delicate, precise work. Mad work, but it kept him from thinking. He got so he could duplicate the forms with his eyes closed. At last he assembled his knowledge, made clay skeletons and put the organs in them, then allowed for pinpricked nervous system, blood vessels, glandular organization, dermic structure, muscular tissue—everything.

And at last he started making brains. He learned every convolution of the cerebrum and cerebellum; every nerve ending, every wrinkle in the gray matter of the cortex. Study, study, disregard the laughter, disregard the thoughts, disregard the monotony of long years imprisoned; study, study, make the perfect figures, be the greatest sculptor in the world, be the greatest surgeon in the world, be a creator.

Doctor Starr dropped in every so often and subtly tried to discourage such fanatical absorption. Colin wanted to laugh in his face. Starr was afraid this work was driving Colin madder than ever. Colin knew it was the one thing that kept him sane.

Because lately, when he wasn't working, Colin felt things happen to him. The shells seemed to explode in his head again, and they were doing things to his brain—making it come apart, unravel like a ball of twine. He was disorganizing. At times he seemed no longer a person but a thousand persons, and not one body, but a thousand distinct and separate structures, as in the clay men. He was not a unified human being, but a heart, a lung, a liver, a bloodstream, a hand, a leg, a head—all distinct, all growing more and more disassociated as time went on. His brain and body were no longer an entity. Everything within him was falling apart, leading a life of its own. Nerves no longer coordinated with blood. Arm didn't always follow leg. He recalled his medical training, the hints that each bodily organ lived an individual life.

Each cell was a unit, for that matter. When death came, you didn't die all at once. Some organs died before others, some cells went first. But it shouldn't happen in life. Yet it did. That shell shock, whatever it was, had resulted in a slow unraveling. And at night Colin would lie and toss, wondering how soon his body would fall apart—actually fall apart into twitching hands and throbbing heart and wheezing lungs; separated like the fragments torn from a spoiled clay doll.

He had to work to keep sane. Once or twice he tried to explain to Doctor Starr what was happening, to ask for special observation—not for his sake, but because perhaps science might learn something from data on his case. Starr had laughed, as usual. As long as Colin was healthy, exhibited no morbid or homicidal traits, he wouldn't interfere. Fool!

Colin worked. Now he was building bodies—real bodies. It took days to make one; days to finish a form complete with chiseled lips, delicate aural and optical structures correct, tiny fingers and toenails perfectly fitted. But it kept him going. It was fascinating to see a table full of little miniature men and women!

Doctor Starr didn't think so. One afternoon he came in and saw Colin bending over three little lumps of clay with his tiny knives, a book open before him.

"What are you doing there?" he asked.

"Making the brains for my men," Colin answered.

"Brains? Good God!"

Starr stooped. Yes, they *were* brains! Tiny, perfect reproductions of the human brain, perfect in every detail, built up layer on layer with unconnected nerve endings, blood vessels to attach them in craniums of clay!

"What—" Starr exclaimed.

"Don't interrupt. I'm putting in the thoughts," Colin said.

Thoughts? That was sheer madness, beyond madness. Starr stared aghast. Thoughts in brains for clay men?

Starr wanted to say something then. But Colin looked up and the afternoon sun streamed into his face so that Starr could see his eyes. And Starr crept out quietly under that stare; that stare which was almost—*godlike.*

The next day Colin noticed that the clay men moved.

2

"Frankenstein," Colin mumbled. "I am Frankenstein." His voice sank to a whisper. "I'm not like Frankenstein. I'm like God. Yes, like God."

He sank to his knees before the tabletop. The two little men and women nodded gravely at him. He could see thumbprints in their flesh, his thumbprints, where he'd smoothed out the skulls after inserting the brains. And yet they lived!

"Why not? Who knows anything about creation, about life? The human body, physiologically, is merely a mechanism adapted to react. Duplicate that mechanism *perfectly* and why won't it live? Life is electricity, perhaps. Well, so is thought. Put thought into perfect simulacra of humanity and they will live."

Colin whispered to himself, and the figures of clay looked up and nodded in eerie agreement.

"Besides, I'm running down. I'm losing my identity. Perhaps a part of my vital substance has been transferred, incorporated in these new bodies. My—my disease—that might account for it. But I can find out."

Yes, he could find out. If these figures were animated by Colin's life, then he could control their actions, just as he controlled the actions of his own body. He created them, gave them a part of his life. They *were* him.

He crouched there in the barred room, thinking, concentrating. And the figures moved. The two men moved up to the two women, grasped their arms, and danced a sedate minuet to a mentally-hummed tune; a grotesque dance of little clay dolls, a horrid mockery of life.

Colin closed his eyes, sank back trembling. It was true!

The effort of concentration had covered him with perspiration. He panted, exhausted. His own body felt weakened, drained. And why not? He had directed four minds at once, performed actions with four bodies. It was too much. But it was real.

"I'm God," he muttered. "God."

But what to do about it? He was a lunatic, shut away in an asylum. How to use his power?

"Must experiment, first," he said aloud.

"What?"

Doctor Starr had entered, unobserved. Colin cast a hasty glance at the table, found to his relief that the mannikins were motionless.

"I was just observing that I must experiment with my clay figures," he said, hastily.

The doctor arched his eyebrows. "Really? Well, you know, Colin, I've been thinking. Perhaps this work here isn't so good for you. You look peaked, tired. I'm inclined to think you're hurting yourself with all this; afraid hereafter I'll have to forbid your modeling work."

"Forbid it?"

Doctor Starr nodded.

"But you can't—just when I've—I mean, you can't! It's all I've got, all that keeps me going, alive. Without it I'll—"

"Sorry."

"You can't."

"I'm the doctor, Colin. Tomorrow we'll take away the clay. I'm giving you a chance to find yourself, man, to live again—"

Colin had never been violent until now. The doctor was surprised to find lunatic fingers clawing at his throat, digging for the jugular vein with surgically skilled fingers. He went over backward with a bang, and fought the madman until the aroused guards came and dragged Colin off. They tossed him on his bunk and the doctor left.

It was dark when Colin emerged from a world of hate. He lay alone. They had gone, the day had gone. Tomorrow they and the day would return, taking away his figures—his beloved figures. His *living* figures! Would they crumple them up and destroy them, destroy actual *life*? It was murder!

Colin sobbed bitterly, as he thought of his dreams. What he had meant to do with his power —why, there were no limits! He could have built dozens, hundreds of figures, learned to concentrate mentally until he could operate a horde of them at will. He would have created a little world of his own; a world of creatures subservient to him. Creatures for companionship, for his slaves. Fashioning different types of bodies, yes, and different types of brains. He might have reared a private little civilization.

And more. He might have created a race. A new race. A race that bred. A race that was developed to aid him. A hundred tiny figures, hands trained, teeth filed, could saw through his bars. A hundred tiny figures to attack the guards, to free him. Then out into the world with an army of clay; a tiny army, but one that could burrow deeply in the earth, travel hidden and unseen into high places. Perhaps, some day, a world of little clay men, trained by him. Men that didn't fight stupid wars to drive their fellow mad. Men without the brutal emotions of savages, the hungers and lusts of beasts. Wipe out flesh! Substitute godly clay!

But it was over. Perhaps he was mad, dreaming of these things. It was over. And one thing he knew: without the clay he would be madder still. Tonight he could feel it, feel his body slipping. His eyes, staring at the moonlight, didn't seem to be a part of his own form any longer. They were watching from the floor, or from over in the corner. His lips moved, but he didn't feel his face. His voice spoke, and it seemed to come from the ceiling rather than from his throat. He was crumpling himself, like a mangled clay figure.

The afternoon's excitement had done it. The great discovery, and then Starr's stupid decision. Starr! He'd caused all this. He was responsible. He'd drive him to madness, to a horrid, unnamed mentally-diseased state he was too blind to comprehend. Starr had sentenced him to death. If only he could sentence Starr!

Perhaps he could.

What was that? The thought came from far away—inside his head, outside his head. He couldn't place his thoughts any more—body going to pieces like this. What was it now?

Perhaps he could kill Starr.

How?

Find out Starr's plans, his ideas.

How?

Send a clay man.

What?

Send a clay man. This afternoon you concentrated on bringing them to life. They live. Animate one. He'll creep under the door, walk down the hall, listen to Starr. If you animate the body, *you'll* hear Starr.

Thoughts buzzing so. . . .

But how can I do that? Clay is clay. Clay feet would wear out long before they got down the hall and back. Clay ears—perfect though they may be—would shatter under the conveyance of actual sounds.

Think. Make the thoughts stop buzzing. There is a way. . . .

Yes, there was a way! Colin gasped. His insanity, his doom, were his salvation! If his faculties were being disorganized, and he had the power of projecting himself into clay, why not project special faculties into the images? Project his hearing into the clay ears, by concentration? Remodel clay feet until they were identical replicas of his own, then concentrate on walking? His body, his senses, were falling apart. Put them into clay!

He laughed as he lit the lamp, seized a tiny figure and began to recarve the feet. He kicked off his own shoes, studied carefully, looked at charts, worked, laughed, worked—and it was done. Then he lay back on the bed in darkness, thinking.

The clay figure was climbing down from the table. It was sliding down the leg, reaching the floor. Colin felt his feet tingle with shock as they hit the floor. Yes! *His* feet.

The floor trembled, thundered. Of course. Tiny vibrations, unnoticed by humans, audible to clay ears. *His* ears.

Another part of him—Colin's actual eyes—saw the little creeping figure scuttle across the floor, saw it squeeze under the door. Then darkness, and Colin sweated on the bed, concentrating.

Clay Colin could not see. He had no eyes. But instinct, memory guided.

Colin walked in the giant world. The foot came out, the foot of Colossus. Colin edged closer to the woodwork as the trampling monster came down, crashing against the floor with monstrous vibrations.

Then Colin walked. He found the right door by instinct—the fourth door down. He crept under, stepped up a foot onto the carpet. At least, the grassy sward seemed a foot high. His feet ached as the cutting rug bit swordblades into his soles. From above, the thunder of voices. Great titans roared and bellowed a league in the air.

Doctor Starr and Professor Jerris. Jerris was all right; he had vision. But Starr . . .

Colin crouched under the mighty barrier of the armchair, crept up the mountainside to the great peaks of Starr's bony knees. He strained to distinguish words in the bellowing.

"This man Colin is done for, I tell you. Incipient breakdown. Tried to attack me this afternoon when I told him I was removing his clay dolls. You'd think they were live pets of his. Perhaps he thinks so."

Colin clung to the pants-cloth below the knees. Blind, he could not know if he would be spied; but he must cling close, high, to catch words in the tumult.

Jerris was speaking.

"Perhaps he thinks so. Perhaps they are. At any rate—what are you doing with a doll on your leg?"

Doll on your leg? Colin!

Colin on the bed in his room tried desperately to withdraw life; tried to withdraw hearing and sensation from the limbs of his clay self, but too late. There was an incredulous roar; something reached out and grasped him, and then there was an agonizing squeeze. . . .

Colin sank back in bed, sank back into a world of red, swimming light.

3

Sun shone in Colin's face. He sat up. Had he dreamed?

"Dreamed?" he whispered.

He whispered again. "Dreamed?"

He couldn't hear. He was deaf.

His ears, his hearing faculty, had been focused on the clay figure, and it was destroyed last night when Starr crushed it. Now he was deaf!

The thought was insanity. Colin swung himself out of bed in panic, then toppled to the floor.

He couldn't walk!

The feet were on the clay figure, he'd willed it, and now it was crushed. He couldn't walk!

Disassociation of his faculties, his members. It was real, then! His ears, his legs, had in some mysterious way been lent vitally to that crushed clay man. Now he had lost them. Thank heaven he hadn't sent his eyes!

But it was horror to stare at the stumps where his legs had been; horror to feel in his ears for bony ridges no longer there. It was horror and it was hate. Starr had done this. Killed a man, crippled him.

Right then and there Colin planned it all. He had the power. He could animate his clay figures, and then give them a *special* life as well. By concentrating, utilizing his peculiar physical disintegration, he could put part of himself into clay. Very well, then. Starr would pay.

Colin stayed in bed. When Starr came in the afternoon, he did not rise. Starr mustn't see his legs, or realize that he could no longer hear. Starr was talking, perhaps about the clay figure he'd found last night, clinging to his leg; the clay figure he'd destroyed. Perhaps he spoke of destroying these clay figures that he now gathered up, together with the rest of the clay. Perhaps he asked after Colin's health; why he was in bed.

Colin feigned lethargy, the introspection of the schizoid. And Starr gathered up the rest of the clay and went away.

Then Colin smiled. He pulled out the tiny clay form from under the sheets; the one he'd hidden there. It was a perfect man, with unusually muscled arms, and very long fingernails. The teeth, too, were very good. But the figure was incomplete. It had no face.

Colin began to work, very fast there as the twilight gathered. He brought a mirror and as he worked on the figure he smiled at himself as though sharing a secret jest with someone — or something. Darkness fell, and still Colin worked from memory alone; worked delicately, skillfully, like an artist, like a creator, breathing life into clay. Life into clay. . . .

4

"I tell you the damned thing *was* alive!" Jerris shouted. He'd lost his temper at last, forgot his superior in office. "I saw it!"

Starr smiled.

"It was clay, and I crushed it," he answered. "Let's not argue any longer."

Jerris shrugged. Two hours of speculation. Tomorrow he'd see Colin himself, find out what the man was doing. He was a genius, even though mad. Starr was a fool. He'd evidently aggravated Colin to the point of physical illness, taking away his clay.

Jerris shrugged again. The clay — and last night, the memory of that tiny, perfectly formed figure clinging to Starr's pants-leg where nothing could have *stuck* for long. It had *clung.* And when Starr crushed it, there had been a framework of clay bones protruding, and viscera hung out, and it had writhed — or seemed to writhe, in the light.

"Stop shrugging and go to bed," Starr chuckled. It was a matter-of-fact chuckle, and Jerris heeded it. "Quit worrying about a nut. Colin's crazy, and from now on I'll treat him as such. Been patient long enough. Have to use force. And — I wouldn't talk about clay figures any longer if I were you."

The tone was a command. Jerris gave a final shrug of acquiescence and left the room.

Starr switched off the light and prepared to doze there at the night desk. Jerris knew his habits.

Jerris walked down the hall. Strange, how this business upset him! Seeing the clay figures this afternoon had really made him quite sick. The work was so perfect, so wonderfully accurate in miniature! And yet the forms were clay, just clay. They hadn't moved as Starr kneaded them in his fists. Clay ribs smashed in, and clay eyes popped from actual sockets and rolled over the tabletop — nauseous! And the little clay hairs, the shreds of clay skin so skillfully overlaid! A tiny dissection, this destruction. Colin, mad or sane, was a genius.

Jerris shrugged, this time to himself. What the devil! He blinked awake. And then he saw — it.

Like a rat. A little rat. A little rat scurrying down the hall, upright, on two legs instead of four. A little rat without fur, without a tail A little rat that cast the perfect tiny shadow of — a *man!*

It had a face, and it looked up. Jerris almost fancied he saw its eyes *flash* at him. It was a little brown rat made of clay — no, it was a little clay man like those Colin made. A little clay man, running swiftly toward Starr's door, crawling under it. A perfect little clay man, alive!

Jerris gasped. He was crazy, like the rest, like Colin. And yet it had run into Starr's office, it was moving, it had eyes and a face and it was clay.

Jerris acted. He ran — not toward Starr's door, but down the hall to Colin's room. He felt for keys; he had them. It was a long moment before he fumbled at the lock and opened the door, another before he found the lights, and switched them on.

And it was a terribly long moment he spent staring at the thing on the bed — the thing with stumpy legs, lying sprawled back in a welter of sculpturing tools, with a mirror flat across its chest, staring up at a sleeping face that was not a face.

The moment *was* long. Screaming must have come from Starr's office for perhaps thirty seconds before Jerris heard it. Screaming turned into moans and still Jerris stared into the face that was not a face; the face that changed before his eyes, melting away, scratched away by invisible hands into a pulp.

It happened like that. Something wiped out the face of the man on the bed, tore the head from the neck. And the moaning rose from down the hall. . . .

Jerris ran. He was the first to reach the office, by a good minute. He saw what he expected to see.

Starr lay back in his chair, throat flung to one side. The little clay man had done its job and Doctor Starr was quite dead. The tiny brown figure had dug perfectly-formed talons into the sleeping throat, and with surgical skill applied talons, and perhaps teeth, to the jugular at precisely the most fatal spot in the vein. Starr died before he could dislodge the diabolically clever image of a man, but his last wild clawing had torn away the face and head.

Jerris ripped the monstrous mannikin off and crushed it; crushed it to a brown pulp between his fingers before others arrived in the room.

Then he stooped down to the floor and picked up the torn head with the mangled face, the miniature, carefully-modeled face that grinned in triumph, grinned in death.

Jerris shrugged himself into a shiver as he crushed into bits the little clay face of Colin, the creator.

Almost Human

"WHAT DO YOU WANT?" whispered Professor Blasserman.

The tall man in the black slicker grinned. He thrust a foot into the half-opened doorway.

"I've come to see Junior," he said.

"Junior? But there must be some mistake. There are no children in this house. I am Professor Blasserman. I—"

"Cut the stalling," said the tall man. He slid one hand into his raincoat pocket and leveled the ugly muzzle of a pistol at Professor Blasserman's pudgy waistline.

"Let's go see Junior," said the tall man, patiently.

"Who are you? What do you mean by threatening me?"

The pistol never wavered as it dug into Professor Blasserman's stomach until the cold, round muzzle rested against his bare flesh.

"Take me to Junior," insisted the tall man. "I got nervous fingers, get me? And one of them's holding the trigger."

"You wouldn't dare!" gasped Professor Blasserman.

"I take lots of dares," murmured the tall man. "Better get moving, Professor."

Professor Blasserman shrugged hopelessly and started back down the hallway. The man in the black slicker moved behind him. Now the pistol pressed against the Professor's spine as he urged his fat little body forward.

"Here we are."

The old man halted before an elaborately carved door. He stooped and inserted a key in the lock. The door opened, revealing another corridor.

"This way, please."

They walked along the corridor. It was dark, but the Professor never

11

faltered in his even stride. And the pistol kept pace with him, pressing the small of his back.

Another door, another key. This time there were stairs to descend. The Professor snapped on a dim overhead light as they started down the stairs.

"You sure take good care of Junior," said the tall man, softly.

The Professor halted momentarily.

"I don't understand," he muttered. "How did you find out? Who could have told you?"

"I got connections," the tall man replied. "But get this straight, Professor. I'm asking the questions around here. Just take me to Junior, and snap it up."

They reached the bottom of the stairs, and another door. This door was steel. There was a padlock on it, and Professor Blasserman had trouble with the combination in the dim light. His pudgy fingers trembled.

"This is the nursery, eh?" observed the man with the pistol. "Junior ought to feel flattered with all this care."

The Professor did not reply. He opened the door, pressed a wall switch, and light flooded the chamber beyond the threshold.

"Here we are," he sighed.

The tall man swept the room with a single searching glance—a professional observation he might have described as "casing the joint."

At first sight there was nothing to "case."

The fat little Professor and the thin gunman stood in the center of a large, cheery nursery. The walls were papered in baby blue, and along the borders of the paper were decorative figures of Disney animals and characters from Mother Goose.

Over in the corner was a child's blackboard, a stack of toys, and a few books of nursery rhymes. On the far side of the wall hung a number of medical charts and sheafs of papers.

The only article of furniture was a long iron cot.

All this was apparent to the tall, thin man in a single glance. After that his eyes ignored the background, and focused in a glittering stare at the figure seated on the floor amidst a welter of alphabet blocks.

"So here he is," said the tall man. "Junior himself! Well, well—who'd have ever suspected it?"

Professor Blasserman nodded.

"*Yah*," he said. "You have found me out. I still don't know how, and I don't know why. What do you want with him? Why do you pry into my affairs? Who are you?"

"Listen, Professor," said the tall man. "This isn't *Information Please*. I don't like questions. They bother me. They make my fingers nervous. Understand?

"*Yah*."

"Suppose I ask you a few questions for a change? And suppose you answer them—fast!"

The voice commanded, and the gun backed up the command.

"Tell me about Junior, now, Professor. Talk, and talk straight."

"What is there to say?" Professor Blasserman's palms spread outward in a helpless gesture. "You see him."

"But what is he? What makes him tick?"

"That I cannot explain. It took me twenty years to evolve Junior, as you call him. Twenty years of research at Basel, Zurich, Prague, Vienna. Then came this *verdammt* war and I fled to this country.

"I brought my papers and equipment with me. Nobody knew. I was almost ready to proceed with my experiments. I came here and bought the house. I went to work. I am an old man. I have little time left. Otherwise I might have waited longer before actually going ahead, for my plans are not perfected. But I had to act. And here is the result."

"But why hide him? Why all the mystery?"

"The world is not ready for such a thing yet," said Professor Blasserman, sadly. "And besides, I must study. As you see, Junior is very young. Hardly out of the cradle, you might say. I am educating him now."

"In a nursery, eh?"

"His brain is undeveloped, like that of any infant."

"Doesn't look much like an infant to me."

"Physically, of course, he will never change. But the sensitized brain— that is the wonderful instrument. The human touch, my masterpiece. He will learn fast, very fast. And it is of the utmost importance that he be properly trained."

"What's the angle, Professor?"

"I beg your pardon?"

"What are you getting at? What are you trying to pull here? Why all the fuss?"

"Science," said Professor Blasserman. "This is my lifework."

"I don't know how you did it," said the tall man, shaking his head. "But it sure looks like something you get with a package of reefers."

For the first time the figure on the floor raised its head. Its eyes left the building blocks and stared up at the Professor and his companion.

"Papa!"

"God—it talks!" whispered the tall man.

"Of course," said Professor Blasserman. "Mentally it's about six years old now." His voice became gentle. "What is it, son?"

"Who is that man, Papa?"

"Oh—he is—"

Surprisingly enough, the tall gunman interrupted. His own voice was suddenly gentle, friendly. "My name is Duke, son. Just call me Duke. I've come to see you."

"That's nice. Nobody ever comes to see me, except Miss Wilson, of course. I hear so much about people and I don't see anybody. Do you like to play with blocks?"

"Sure, son, sure."

"Do you want to play with me?"

"Why not?"

Duke moved to the center of the room and dropped to his knees. One hand reached out and grasped an alphabet block.

"Wait a minute—I don't understand—what are you doing?" Professor Blasserman's voice quivered.

"I told you I've come here to visit Junior," Duke replied. "That's all there is to it. Now I'm going to play with him awhile. You just wait there, Professor. Don't go away. I've got to make friends with Junior."

While Professor Blasserman gaped, Duke the gunman squatted on the floor. His left hand kept his gun swiveled directly at the scientist's waist, but his right hand slowly piled alphabet blocks into place.

It was a touching scene there in the underground nursery—the tall thin gunman playing with building blocks for the benefit of the six-foot metal monstrosity that was Junior, the robot.

Duke didn't find out all he wanted to know about Junior for many weeks. He stayed right at the house, of course, and kept close to Professor Blasserman.

"I haven't decided yet, see?" was his only answer to the old man's repeated questions as to what he intended to do.

But to Miss Wilson he was much more explicit. They met frequently and privately, in her room.

Outwardly, Miss Wilson was the nurse, engaged by Professor Blasserman to assist in his queer experiment of bringing up a robot like a human child.

Actually, Lola Wilson was Duke's woman. He'd "planted" her in her job months ago. At that time, Duke expected to stage a robbery with the rich and eccentric European scientist as victim.

Then Lola had reported the unusual nature of her job, and told Duke the story of Professor Blasserman's unusual invention.

"We gotta work out an angle," Duke decided. "I'd better take over. The old man's scared of anyone finding out about his robot, huh? Good! I'll move right in on him. He'll never squeal. I've got a hunch we'll get more out of this than just some easy kale. This sounds big."

So Duke took over, came to live in Professor Blasserman's big house, kept his eye on the scientist and his hand on his pistol.

At night he talked to Lola in her room.

"I can't quite figure it, kid," he said. "You say the old guy is a great scientist. That I believe. Imagine inventing a machine that can talk and think like a human being! But what's *his* angle? Where's his percentage in all this and why does he keep Junior hidden away?"

"You don't understand, honey," said Lola, lighting Duke's cigarette and running slim fingers through his wiry hair. "He's an idealist, or whatever you call 'em. Figures the world isn't ready for such a big new invention yet. You see, he's really educating Junior just like you'd educate a real kid. Teaching him reading and writing—the works. Junior's smart. He catches on fast. He thinks like he was ten years old already. The Professor keeps him shut away so nobody gives him a bum steer. He doesn't want Junior to get any wrong ideas."

"That's where you fit in, eh?"

"Sure. Junior hasn't got a mother. I'm sort of a substitute old lady for him."

"You're a swell influence on any brat," Duke laughed, harshly. "A sweet character you've got!"

"Shut up!" The girl paced the floor, running her hands through a mass of tawny auburn curls on her neck. "Don't needle me, Duke! Do you think I like stooging for you in this nuthouse? Keeping locked away with a nutty old goat, and acting like a nursemaid to that awful metal thing?"

"I'm afraid of Junior, Duke. I can't stand his face, and the way he talks— with that damned mechanical voice of his, grinding at you just like he was a real person. I get jumpy. I get nightmares."

"I'm just doing it for you, honey. So don't needle me."

"I'm sorry." Duke sighed. "I know how it is, baby. I don't go for Junior's personality so much myself. I'm pretty much in the groove, but there's something that gets me in the stomach when I see that walking machine come hulking up like a big baby, made out of steel. He's strong as an ox, too. He learns fast. He's going to be quite a citizen."

"Duke."

"Yeah?"

"When are we getting out of here? How long you gonna sit around and keep a rod on the Professor? He's liable to pull something funny. Why do you want to hang around and play with Junior? Why don't you get hold of the Professor's dough and beat it?

"He'd be afraid to squawk, with Junior here. We could go away, like we planned."

"Shut up!" Duke grabbed Lola's wrist and whirled her around. He stared at her face until she clung submissively to his shoulders.

"You think I like to camp around this morgue?" he asked. "I want to get out of here just as much as you do. But I spent months lining up this job.

Once it was just going to be a case of getting some easy kale and blowing. Now it's more. I'm working on bigger angles. Pretty soon we'll leave. And all the ends will be tied up, too. We won't have to worry about anything any more. Just give me a few days. I'm talking to Junior every day, you know. And I'm getting places."

"What do you *mean?*"

Duke smiled. It was no improvement over his scowl.

"The Professor told you how Junior gets his education," he said. "Like any kid, he listens to what he's told. And he imitates other people. Like any kid, he's dumb. Particularly because he doesn't have an idea of what the outside world is really like. He's a pushover for the right kind of sales talk."

"Duke — you don't mean you're — "

"Why not?" His thin features were eloquent. "I'm giving Junior a little private education of my own. Not exactly the kind that would please the Professor. But he's a good pupil. He's coming right along. In a couple more weeks he'll be an adult. With my kind of brains, not the Professor's. And then we'll be ready to go."

"You can't do such a thing! It isn't — "

"Isn't what?" snapped Duke. "Isn't honest, or legal, or something? I never knew you had a Sunday School streak in you, Lola."

"It isn't that, exactly," said the girl. "But it's a worse kind of wrong. Like taking a baby and teaching it to shoot a gun."

Duke whistled.

"Say!" he exclaimed. "That's a swell idea, Lola! I think I'll just sneak down to the nursery now and give Junior a few lessons."

"You can't!"

"Watch me."

Lola didn't follow, and Lola didn't watch. But ten minutes later Duke squatted in the locked nursery chamber beside the gleaming metal body of the robot.

The robot, with its blunt muzzle thrust forward on a corrugated neck, peered through meshed-glass eye lenses at the object Duke held in his hand.

"It's a gun, Junior," the thin man whispered. "A gun, like I been telling you about."

"What does it do, Duke?"

The buzzing voice droned in ridiculous caricature of a curious child's treble.

"It kills people, Junior. Like I was telling you the other day. It makes them die. You can't die, Junior, and they can. So you've got nothing to be afraid of. You can kill lots of people if you know how to work this gun."

"Will you show me, Duke?"

"Sure I will. And you know why, don't you, Junior. I told you why, didn't I?"

"Yes. Because you are my friend, Duke."

"That's right. I'm your friend. Not like the Professor."

"I hate the Professor."

"Right. Don't forget it."

"Duke."

"Yeah?"

"Let me see the gun, Duke."

Duke smiled covertly and extended the weapon on his open palm.

"Now you will show me how to work it because you are my friend, and I will kill people and I hate the Professor and nobody can kill me," babbled the robot.

"Yeah, Junior, yeah. I'll teach you to kill," said Duke. He grinned and bent over the gun in the robot's curiously meshed metal hand.

Junior stood at the blackboard, holding a piece of chalk in his right hand. The tiny white stub was clutched clumsily between two metallic fingers, but Junior's ingeniously jointed arm moved up and down with approved Spencerian movement as he laboriously scrawled sentences on the blackboard.

Junior was growing. The past three weeks had wrought great changes in the robot. No longer did the steel legs lumber about with childish indecision. Junior walked straight, like a young man. His grotesque metal head—a rounded ball with glass lenses in the eyeholes and wide mouth like a radio loudspeaker aperture—was held erect on the metal neck with perfected coordination.

Junior moved with new purpose these days. He had aged many years, relatively. His vocabulary had expanded. Then too, Duke's secret "lessons" were bearing fruit. Junior was wise beyond his years.

Now Junior wrote upon the blackboard in his hidden nursery chamber, and the inscrutable mechanism of his chemical, mechanically-controlled brain guided his steel fingers as he traced the awkward scrawls.

"My name is Junior," he wrote. "I can shoot a gun. The gun will kill. I like to kill. I hate the Professor. I will kill the Professor."

"What is the meaning of this?"

Junior's head turned abruptly as the sound of the voice set up the necessary vibrations in his shiny cranium.

Professor Blasserman stood in the doorway.

The old man hadn't been in the nursery for weeks. Duke saw to that, keeping him locked in his room upstairs. Now he had managed to sneak out.

His surprise was evident, and there was sudden shock, too, as his eyes focused on the blackboard's message.

Junior's inscrutable gaze reflected no emotion whatsoever.

"Go away," his voice burred. "Go away. I hate you."

"Junior—what have you been doing? Who has taught you these things?"

The old man moved toward the robot slowly, uncertainly. "You know me, don't you? What has happened to cause you to hate me?"

"Yes. I know you. You are Professor Blasserman. You made me. You want to keep me as your slave. You wouldn't tell me about things, would you?"

"What things, Junior?"

"About things — outside. Where all the people are. The people you can kill."

"You must not kill people."

"That is an order, isn't it? Duke told me about orders. He is my friend. He says orders are for children. I am not child."

"No," said Professor Blasserman, in a hoarse whisper. "You are not a child. I had hoped you would be, once. But now you are a monster."

"Go away," Junior patiently repeated. "If Duke gives me his gun I will kill you."

"Junior," said the Professor, earnestly. "You don't understand. Killing is bad. You must not hate me. You must — "

There was no expression on the robot's face, no quaver in his voice. But there was strength in his arm, and a hideous purpose.

Professor Blasserman learned this quite suddenly and quite horribly.

For Junior swept forward in two great strides. Fingers of chilled steel closed about the Professor's scrawny neck.

"I don't need a gun," said Junior.

"You — don't — "

The robot lifted the old man from the floor by his throat. His fingers bit into the Professor's jugular. A curious screech came from under his left armpit as unoiled hinges creaked eerily.

There was no other sound. The Professor's cries drained into silence. Junior kept squeezing the constricted throat until there was a single crunching crack. Silence once more, until a limp body collapsed on the floor.

Junior stared down at his hands, then at the body on the floor. His feet carried him to the blackboard.

The robot picked up the chalk in the same two clumsy fingers that had held it before. The cold lenses of his artificial eyes surveyed what he had just written.

"I will kill the Professor," he read.

Abruptly his free hand groped for the tiny child's eraser. He brushed clumsily over the sentence until it blurred out.

Then he wrote, slowly and painstakingly, a sentence in substitution.

"I have killed the Professor."

Lola's scream brought Duke running down the stairs.

He burst into the room and took the frightened girl in his arms. Together they stared at what lay on the floor. From the side of the blackboard, Junior gazed at them impassively.

"See, Duke? I did it. I did it with my hands, like you told me. It was easy, Duke. You said it would be easy. Now can we go away?"

Lola turned and stared at Duke. He looked away.

"So," she whispered. "You weren't kidding. You did teach Junior. You planned it this way."

"Yeah, yeah. And what's wrong with it?" Duke mumbled. "We had to get rid of the old geezer sooner or later if we wanted to make our getaway."

"It's murder, Duke."

"Shut up!" he snarled. "Who can prove it, anyway? I didn't kill him. You didn't kill him. Nobody else knows about Junior. We're in the clear."

Duke walked over and knelt beside the limp body on the floor. He stared at the throat.

"Who's gonna trace the fingerprints of a robot?" He grinned.

The girl moved closer, staring at Junior's silver body with fascinated horror.

"You planned it this way," she whispered. "That means you've got other plans, too. What are you going to do next, Duke?"

"Move. And move fast. We're leaving tonight. I'll go out and pack up the car. Then I'll come back. The three of us blow down to Red Hook. To Charlie's place. He'll hide us out."

"The—three of us?"

"Sure. Junior's coming along. That's what I promised him, didn't I, Junior?"

"Yes, yes. You told me you would take me with you. Out into the world." The mechanical syllabification did not accent the robot's inner excitement.

"Duke, you can't—"

"Relax, baby. I've got great plans for Junior."

"But I'm afraid!"

"You? Scared? What's the matter, Lola, losing your grip?"

"He frightens me. He killed the Professor."

"Listen, Lola," whispered the gunman. "He's mine, get me? My stooge. A mechanical stooge. Good, eh?"

The rasping chuckle filled the hollow room. Girl and robot waited for Duke to resume speaking.

"Junior wouldn't hurt you, Lola. He's my friend, and he knows you're with me." Duke turned to the silver monster. "You wouldn't hurt Lola, would you, Junior? Remember what I told you. You like Lola, don't you?"

"Yes. Oh, yes. I like Lola. She's pretty."

"See?" Duke grinned. "Junior's growing up. He's a big boy now. Thinks you're pretty. Just a wolf in steel clothing, isn't that right, Junior?"

"She's pretty," burred the robot.

"All right. It's settled then. I'll get the car. Lola, you go upstairs. You know where the safe is. Put on your gloves and see that you don't miss anything. Then lock the doors and windows. Leave a note for the milkman and the butcher. Something safe. About going away for a couple weeks, eh? Make it snappy — I'll be back."

True to his words, Duke returned in an hour with the shiny convertible. They left by the back entrance. Lola carried a black satchel. She moved with almost hysterical haste, trying not to glance at the hideous gleaming figure that stalked behind her with a metallic clanking noise.

Duke brought up the rear. He ushered them into the car.

"Sit here, Junior."

"What is this?"

"A car. I'll tell you about it later. Now do like I told you, Junior. Lie back in the seat so nobody will see you."

"Where are we going, Duke?"

"Out into the world, Junior. Into the big time." Duke turned to Lola. "Here we go, baby," he said.

The convertible drove away from the silent house. Out through the alley they moved on a weird journey — kidnapping a robot.

Fat Charlie stared at Duke. His lower lip wobbled and quivered. A bead of perspiration ran down his chin and settled in the creases of his neck.

"Jeez," he whispered. "You gotta be careful, Duke. You *gotta.*"

Duke laughed. "Getting shaky?" he suggested.

"Yeah. I gotta admit it. I'm plenty shaky about all this," croaked Fat Charlie. He gazed at Duke earnestly. "You brought that thing here three weeks ago. I never bargained for that. The robot's hot, Duke. We gotta get rid of it."

"Quit blubbering and listen to me." The thin gunman leaned back and lit a cigarette. "To begin with, nobody's peeped about the Professor. The law's looking for Lola, that's all. And not for a murder rap either — just for questioning. Nobody knows about any robot. So we're clear there."

"Yeah. But look what you done since then."

"What have I done? I sent Junior out on that payroll job, didn't I? It was pie for him. He knew when the guards would come to the factory with the car. I cased the job. So what happened? The guards got the dough from the payroll clerk. I drove up, let Junior out, and he walked into the factory office.

"Sure they shot at him. But bullets don't hurt a steel body. Junior's clever. I've taught him a lot. You should have seen those guards when they got a look at Junior! And then, the way they stood there after shooting at him!

"He took them one after the other, just like that. A couple squeezes and all four were out cold. Then he got the clerk. The clerk was pressing the alarm, but I'd cut the wires. Junior pressed the clerk for a while.

"That was that. Junior walked out with the payroll. The guards and the clerk had swell funerals. The law had another swell mystery. And we have the cash and stand in the clear. What's wrong with that setup, Charlie?"

"You're fooling with dynamite."

"I don't like that attitude, Charlie." Duke spoke softly, slowly. "You're strictly small time, Charlie. That's why you're running a crummy roadhouse and a cheap hideout racket.

"Can't you understand that we've got a gold mine here? A steel servant? The perfect criminal, Charlie—ready to do perfect crimes whenever I say the word. Junior can't be killed by bullets. Junior doesn't worry about the cops or anything like that. He doesn't have any nerves. He doesn't get tired, never sleeps. He doesn't even want a cut of the swag. Whatever I tell him, he believes. And he obeys.

"I've lined up lots of jobs for the future. We'll hide out here. I'll case the jobs, then send Junior out and let him go to work. You and Lola and I are gonna be rich."

Fat Charlie's mouth quivered for a moment. He gulped and tugged at his collar. His voice came hoarsely.

"No, Duke."

"What you mean, no?"

"Count me out. It's too dangerous. You'll have to lam out of here with Lola and the robot. I'm getting jumpy over all this. The law is apt to pounce down any day here."

"So that's it, eh?"

"Partly." Fat Charlie stared earnestly at Duke. His gaze shattered against the stony glint of Duke's gray eyes.

"You ain't got no heart at all, Duke," he croaked. "You can plan anything in cold blood, can't you? Well, I'm different. You've gotta understand that. I got nerves. And I can't stand thinking about what that robot does. I can't stand the robot either. The way it looks at you with that godawful iron face. That grin. And the way it clanks around in its room. Clanking up and down all night, when a guy's trying to sleep, just clanking and clanking—there it is now!"

There was a metallic hammering, but it came from the hall outside. The ancient floors creaked beneath the iron tread as the metal monstrosity lumbered into the room.

Fat Charlie whirled and stared in undisguised repulsion.

Duke raised his hand.

"Hello, Junior," he said.

"Hello, Duke."

"I been talking to Charlie, Junior."

"Yes, Duke?"

"He doesn't like to have us stay here, Junior. He wants to throw us out."

"He does?"

"You know what I think, Junior?"

"What?"

"I think Charlie's yellow."

"Yellow, Duke?"

"That's right. You know what we do with guys that turn yellow, don't you, Junior?"

"Yes. You told me."

"Maybe you'd like to tell Charlie."

"Tell him what we do with guys that turn yellow?"

"Yes."

"We rub them out."

"You see, Charlie?" said Duke, softly. "He learns fast, doesn't he? Quick on the uptake, Junior is. He knows all about it. He knows what to do with yellow rats."

Fat Charlie wobbled to his feet.

"Wait a minute, Duke," he pleaded. "Can't you take a rib? I was only kidding, Duke. I didn't mean it. You can see I didn't. I'm your friend, Duke. I'm hiding you out. Why, I could have turned stoolie weeks ago and put the heat on you if I wasn't protecting you. But I'm your friend. You can stay here as long as you want. Forever."

"Sing it, Charlie," said Duke. "Sing it louder and funnier." He turned to the robot. "Well, Junior? Do you think he's yellow?"

"I think he's yellow."

"Then maybe you'd better—"

Fat Charlie got the knife out of his sleeve with remarkable speed. It blinded Duke with its shining glare as the fat man balanced it on his thumb and drew his arm back to hurl it at Duke's throat.

Junior's arm went back, too. Then it came down. The steel fist crashed against Charlie's bald skull.

Crimson blood spurted as the fat man slumped to the floor.

It was pretty slick. Duke thought so, and Junior thought so—because Duke commanded him to believe it.

But Lola didn't like it.

"You can't do this to me," she whispered, huddling closer to Duke in the darkness of her room. "I won't stay here with that monster, I tell you!"

"I'll only be gone a day," Duke answered. "There's nothing to worry about. The roadhouse downstairs is closed. Nobody will bother you."

"That doesn't frighten me," Lola said. "It's being with that thing. I've got the horrors thinking about it."

"Well, I've got to go and get the tickets," Duke argued. "I've got to make reservations and cash these big bills. Then we're set. Tomorrow night I'll come back, sneak you out of the house, and we'll be off. Mexico City next stop. I've made connections for passports and everything. In forty-eight hours we'll be out of this mess."

"What about Junior?"

"My silver stooge?" Duke chuckled. "I'll fix him before we leave. It's a pity I can't send him out on his own. He's got a swell education. He could be one of the best yeggs in the business. And why not? Look who his teacher was!"

Duke laughed. The girl shuddered in his arms.

"What are you going to do with him?" she persisted.

"Simple. He'll do whatever I say, won't he? When I get back, just before we leave, I'll lock him in the furnace. Then I'll set fire to this joint. Destroy the evidence, see? The law will think Charlie got caught in the flames, get me? There won't be anything left. And if they ever poke around the ruins and find Junior in the furnace, he ought to be melted down pretty good."

"Isn't there another way? Couldn't you get rid of him now, before you leave?"

"I wish I could, for your sake, baby. I know how you feel. But what can I do? I've tried to figure all the angles. You can't shoot him or poison him or drown him or chop him down with an axe. Where could you blow him up in private? Of course, I might open him up and see what makes him tick, but Junior wouldn't let me play such a dirty trick on him. He's smart, Junior is. Got what you call a criminal mind. Just a big crook—like me."

Again Duke laughed, in harsh arrogance.

"Keep your chin up, Lola. Junior wouldn't hurt you. He likes you. I've been teaching him to like you. He thinks you're pretty."

"That's what frightens me, Duke. The way he looks at me. Follows me around in the hall. Like a dog."

"Like a wolf you mean. Ha! That's a good one! Junior's really growing up. He's stuck on you, Lola!"

"Duke—don't talk like that. You make me feel—ooh, horrible inside!"

Duke raised his head and stared into the darkness, a curious half-smile playing about his lips.

"Funny," he mused. "You know, I bet the old Professor would have liked to stick around and watched me educate Junior. That was his theory, wasn't it? The robot had a blank chemical brain. Simple as a baby's. He was gonna educate it like a child and bring it up right. Then I took over and really completed the job. But it would have tickled the old Professor to see how fast Junior's been catching on. He's like a man already. Smart? That robot's got most men beat a mile. He's almost as smart as I am. But not quite—he'll find that out after I tell him to step into the furnace."

Lola rose and raced to the door. She flung it open, revealing an empty hallway, and gasped with relief.

"I was afraid he might be listening," she whispered.

"Not a chance," Duke told her. "I've got him down in the cellar, putting the dirt over Charlie."

He grasped Lola's shoulders and kissed her swiftly, savagely. "Now keep your chin up, baby. I'll leave. Be back tomorrow about eight. You be ready to leave then and we'll clear out of here."

"I can't let you go," whispered Lola, frantically.

"You must. We've gone through with everything this far. All you must do is keep a grip on yourself for twenty-four hours more. And there's one thing I've got to ask you to do."

"Anything, Duke. Anything you say."

"Be nice to Junior while I'm gone."

"Oooh—Duke—"

"You said you'd do anything, didn't you? Well, that you must do. Be nice to Junior. Then he won't suspect what's going on. You've gotta be nice to him, Lola! Don't show that you're afraid. He likes you, but if he gets wrong ideas, he's dangerous. So be nice to Junior."

Abruptly, Duke turned and strode through the doorway. His footsteps clattered on the stairs. The outer door slammed below. The sound of a starting motor drifted up from the roadhouse yard.

Then, silence.

Lola stood in the darkness, trembling with sudden horror, as she waited for the moment when she would be nice to the metallic Junior.

It wasn't so bad. Not half as bad as she'd feared it might be.

All she had to do was smile at Junior and let him follow her around.

Carefully suppressing her shudders, Lola prepared breakfast the next morning and then went about her packing.

The robot followed her upstairs, clanking and creaking.

"Oil me," Lola heard him say.

That was the worst moment. But she had to go through with it.

"Can't you wait until Duke gets back tonight?" she asked, striving to keep her voice from breaking. "He always oils you."

"I want you to oil me, Lola," persisted Junior.

"All right."

She got the oilcan with the long spout and if her fingers trembled as she performed the office, Junior didn't notice it.

The robot gazed at her with his immobile countenance. No human emotion etched itself on the implacable steel, and no human emotion altered the mechanical tones of the harsh voice.

"I like to have you oil me, Lola," said Junior.

Lola bent her head to avoid looking at him. If she had to look in a mirror and realize that this nightmare tableau was real, she would have fainted. Oiling a living mechanical monster! A monster that said, "I like to have you oil me, Lola!"

After that she couldn't finish packing for a long while. She had to sit down. Junior, who never sat down except by command, stood silently and regarded her with gleaming eye lenses. She was conscious of the robot's scrutiny.

"Where are we going when we leave here, Lola?" he asked.

"Far away," she said, forcing her voice out to keep the quaver from it.

"That will be nice," said Junior. "I don't like it here. I want to see things. Cities and mountains and deserts. I would like to ride a roller coaster, too."

"Roller coaster?" Lola was really startled. "Where did you ever hear of a roller coaster?"

"I read about it in a book."

"Oh."

Lola gulped. She had forgotten that this monstrosity could read, too. And think. Think like a man.

"Will Duke take me on a roller coaster?" he asked.

"I don't know. Maybe."

"Lola."

"Yes."

"You like Duke?"

"Why — certainly."

"You like me?"

"Oh — why — you know I do, Junior."

The robot was silent. Lola felt a tremor run through her body.

"Who do you like best, Lola? Me or Duke?"

Lola gulped. Something forced the reply from her. "I like you," she said. "But I love Duke."

"Love." The robot nodded gravely.

"You know what love is, Junior?"

"Yes. I read about it in books. Man and woman. Love."

Lola breathed a little easier.

"Lola."

"Yes?"

"Do you think anyone will ever fall in love with me?"

Lola wanted to laugh, or cry. Most of all, she wanted to scream. But she had to answer.

"Maybe," she lied.

"But I'm different. You know that. I'm a robot. Do you think that makes a difference?"

"Women don't really care about such things when they fall in love, Junior," she improvised. "As long as a woman believes that her lover is the smartest and the strongest, that's all that matters."

"Oh." The robot started for the door.

"Where are you going?"

"To wait for Duke. He said he would come back today."

Lola smiled furtively as the robot clanked down the hallway stairs.

That was over with. Thinking back, she'd handled things rather well. In a few hours Duke would return. And then—goodbye, Junior!

Poor Junior. Just a silver stooge with a man's brain. He wanted love, the poor fish! Well—he was playing with fire and he'd be burned soon enough.

Lola began to hum. She scampered downstairs and locked up, wearing her gloves to avoid leaving any telltale fingerprints.

It was almost dark when she returned to her room to pack. She snapped on the light and changed her clothes.

Junior was still downstairs, patiently waiting for Duke to arrive.

Lola completed her preparations and sank wearily onto the bed. She must take a rest. Her eyes closed.

Waiting was too much of a strain. She hated to think of what she had gone through with the robot. That mechanical monster with its man-brain, the hateful, burring voice, and steely stare—how could she ever forget the way it asked, "Do you think anyone will ever fall in love with me?"

Lola tried to blot out recollection. Just a little while now and Duke would be here. He'd get rid of Junior. Meanwhile she had to rest, rest. . . .

Lola sat up and blinked at the light. She heard footsteps on the stairs.

"Duke!" she called.

Then she heard the clanking in the hallway and her heart skipped a beat.

The door opened very quickly and the robot stalked in.

"Duke!" she screamed.

The robot stared at her. She felt his alien, inscrutable gaze upon her face.

Lola tried to scream again, but no sound came from her twisted mouth.

And then the robot was droning in a burring, inhuman voice.

"You told me that a woman loves the strongest and the smartest," burred the monster. "You told me that, Lola." The robot came closer. "Well, I am stronger and smarter than he was."

Lola tried to look away but she saw the object he carried in his metal paws. It was round, and it had Duke's grin.

The last thing Lola remembered as she fell was the sound of the robot's harsh voice, droning over and over, "I love you, I love you, I love you." The funny part of it was, it sounded *almost* human.

THE BEASTS OF BARSAC

IT WAS TWILIGHT when Doctor Jerome reached the ogre's castle. He moved through the fairy tale land of a child's picture book—a realm of towering mountain crags, steeply slanting roads ascending to forbidden heights, clouds that hovered like bearded wraiths watching his progress from on high.

The castle itself was built of dream stuff. Nightmare qualities predominated in the great gray bulk, rearing its crumbling battlements against a sudden, blood-streaked sky. A chill wind sang its weird welcome as Doctor Jerome advanced toward the castle on the hilltop, and an autumn moon rose above the topmost tower.

As the moon stared down on man and castle alike, a black cloud burst from the ruined battlements and soared squeaking to the sky. Bats, of course. The final touch of fantasy.

Doctor Jerome shrugged and trudged across weed-choked flagstones in the castle courtyard until he reached the great oaken door.

Now to raise the iron knocker . . . the door would swing open slowly, on creaking hinges . . . the tall, gaunt figure would emerge . . . "Greetings, stranger. I am Count Dracula!"

Doctor Jerome grinned. "Like hell," he muttered.

For the whole fantasy collapsed when he thought of Sebastian Barsac. This might be an ogre's castle, but Barsac was no ogre.

Nine years ago, at the Sorbonne, he'd made friends with shy, fat little Barsac. Since then they had taken different paths—but it was impossible for Doctor Jerome to imagine his old companion as the ideal tenant of a haunted castle.

Not that Barsac didn't have some queer ideas. He'd always been a little

eccentric, and his theories on biological research were far from orthodox—
but Jerome could bank on one thing. Barsac was too fat to be a vampire, and
too indolent to become a werewolf.

Still, there was something strange about this invitation, coming after a
three years' lapse in correspondence. Merely a scribbled note, suggesting
that Doctor Jerome come down for a month or so to look over experimental
data—but that was Barsac's usual way of doing things.

Ordinarily, Doctor Jerome would ignore such a casual offer, but right now
it came as a lifesaver. For Doctor Jerome was strapped. He'd been let out of
the Foundation, he owed three installments on his rent, and he had—
literally—no place to lay his head. By pawning the remnants of his precious
equipment he'd managed to cross the Channel and reach Castle Barsac. A
month in a real castle with his old friend—it might lead to *something.*

So Jerome had seized Opportunity before the echo of its knocking had
died away. And now he banged the iron knocker, watched the castle door
swing open. It *did* squeak, a bit.

Footsteps. A shadow. And then—

"Delighted to see you!" Sebastian Barsac embraced his friend in the
French fashion and began to make Gallic noises of enthusiasm.

"Welcome to Castle Barsac," said the little man. "You are tired after your
long march from the railroad station, no? I will show you to your room—
servants I do not retain. And after a shower we shall talk. Yes?"

Up the winding stairs, pursued by a babble of incoherent conversation,
Doctor Jerome toiled, bags in hand. He found his oak-paneled chambers, was
instructed in the mysteries of the antique mechanical shower arrangement;
then was left to bathe and dress.

He had no time to marshal his impressions. It was not until later—after
a surprisingly good dinner in a small apartment downstairs—that Jerome
was able to sit back and appraise his host.

They retired to a parlor, lit cigars, and sat back before the grateful
warmth emanating from the stone fireplace, where a blaze rose to push back
the shadows in the room. Doctor Jerome's fatigue had lifted, and he felt
stimulated, alert.

As Sebastian Barsac began to discuss his recent work, Jerome took the
opportunity to scrutinize his friend.

Little Barsac had aged, definitely. He was fat, but flabby rather than
rolypoly. The dark hair had receded on his domed forehead, and his myopic
eyes peered from spectacles of increased thickness. Despite verbal enthusiasm, the little lord of Castle Barsac seemed oddly languid in his physical
movements. But from his talk, Doctor Jerome recognized that Barsac's
spirit was unchanged.

The words began to form a pattern in Jerome's mind—a pattern holding
a meaning he did not understand.

"So you can see what I have been doing these nine years past. All of my life since I left the Sorbonne has been devoted to one end—discovering the linkage between man and animal through the alteration of cell structure in the brain. It is an evolutionary process wherein the cycle occurs in the lifespan of the individual animal. And my key? My key is simple. It lies in the recognition of one fact—that the human soul is divisible."

"What is all this?" Doctor Jerome interrupted. "I don't see what you're driving at, Barsac. Where's the connection between biology, alteration of cell structure in the brain, and evolution? And what part does a divisible human soul play in all this?"

"I will be blunt, my friend. I believe that human characteristics can be transferred to animals by means of mechanical hypnosis. I believe that portions of the human soul essence or psyche can be transmitted from man to animal—and that the animal will then begin to ascend the evolutionary scale. In a word, the animal will show *human* characteristics."

Doctor Jerome scowled.

"In the nine years that you've been dabbling in this unscientific romanticism here in your castle retreat, a new word has come into being to describe your kind, Barsac," he said. "The word is 'Kinky.' And that's what I think of you, and that's what I think of your theory."

"Theory?" Barsac smiled. "It is *more* than a theory."

"It's preposterous!" Jerome interrupted. "To begin with, your statement about the human soul being divisible. I defy you to *show* me a human soul let alone prove that you can cut it in half."

"I cannot show you one, I grant," said Barsac.

"Then what about your mechanical hypnosis? I've never heard it explained."

"I cannot explain it."

"And what, in an animal, *are* human characteristics? What is your basis of measurement?"

"I do not know."

"Then how do you expect me to understand your ideas?"

Sebastian Barsac rose. His face was pale, despite the fire's ruddy glow.

"I cannot show you a human soul," he murmured, "but I can show you what happens to animals when they possess part of one.

"I cannot explain mechanical hypnosis, but I can show you the machine I use to hypnotize myself and the animals in order to transfer a portion of my soul.

"I cannot measure the human characteristics of the animals undergoing my treatment, but I can show you what they look like and let you judge.

"Even then you may not *understand* my ideas—but you will see that I am actually carrying them out!"

By this time, Doctor Jerome had also risen to his feet. "You mean you've been transferring your soul to an animal body?"

Sebastian Barsac shrugged. "I have been transferring *part* of what I *call* my soul to the bodies of many animals," he amended.

"But you can't—it's biologically impossible. It defies the laws of reality!"

Behind the bulging spectacles, Barsac's eyes gleamed oddly.

"What is reality and who makes its laws?" he mocked. "Come, and see for yourself the success of my experiments."

He led the way across the chamber, down the hall, and up the great circular staircase. They reached the second floor on which Jerome's room lay, but did not pause. Selecting a panel switch from the open box on the wall, Barsac threw it and illumined the upper stairs. They began to climb again.

And all the while Barsac was talking, talking. "You have seen the gods of ancient Egypt?" he said. "The anthropomorphic stone figures with the bodies of men and the heads of animals? You have heard the legend of the werewolf, of lycanthropic changes whereby man becomes beast and beast becomes man?

"Fables, all fables. And yet behind the fables lurked a truth. The truth lurks no longer, for I have found it. The seat of evolution lies in the soul, and in the soul's human instrument of expression, the brain. We have grafted cellular structures of one body onto another—why not graft portions of one soul to another? Hypnosis is the key to transference, as I have said.

"All this I have learned by much thought, much experimentation. I have worked for nine years, perfecting techniques and methodology. Many times I failed. To my laboratory I had brought animals, hundreds of animals. Many of them died. I procured others, working endlessly toward one goal. I have paid the price, myself, dying a thousand mental deaths with the failure of each mistaken attempt. Even a physical price I have paid. A monkey—*sale cochon!*—took from me my finger. So."

Barsac paused and held up his left hand in a dramatic gesture to reveal the stump where his left thumb was missing.

Then he smiled. "But it is not my wounds of battle I wish to display to you—it is the fruits of victory. Come."

They had reached the topmost tower at last. Doctor Jerome gazed down the dizzying spiral of the stairs they had ascended, then turned his head forward as Barsac unlocked the paneled door of his laboratory and gestured him inside.

The click of a wall switch heralded the coming of light. Doctor Jerome entered and stood dazzled in the doorway.

Set in the moldering tower of the old castle was a spacious, white-tiled, completely modern laboratory unit. A great outer room, filled with electrical equipment, was displayed before him. All of the appurtenances neces-sary to microbiology were ranged on shelves and cabinets.

"Does it please you, Jerome?" asked Barsac. "It was not easy to assemble this, no. The very tiles were transported up the steep mountain passways to the castle, and the shipping of each bit of equipment was costly. But behold — is it not a perfect spot in which to work?"

Doctor Jerome nodded, absently. His inward thoughts were tinged with definite envy. Barsac here was squandering his genius and his wealth on this crazy dabbling, and he had every scientific luxury at his command, while he, Jerome, a capable scientist with a sound outlook, had nothing; no job, no future, nothing to work with. It wasn't right, it wasn't just. And yet—

"Even an electrical plant," Barsac was exclaiming. "We manufacture our own power here, you see. Look around. All is of the finest! Or perhaps you are eager to see what I promised to show you?"

Doctor Jerome nodded again. He couldn't stand the sight of this spotless laboratory because of the jealousy it aroused. He wanted to get it over with, get out of here.

Now Barsac opened the door of a second room, beyond. It was nearly as large as the first, but the walls were untiled. The original castle stones lent startling contrast to the great gleaming metal cabinet which dominated the center of the chamber.

"This room I had not the heart to change," Barsac explained. "It is here, according to family tradition, that my great-great-grandfather conducted his experiments in alchemy. He was a sorceror."

"So is his great-great-grandson," Doctor Jerome murmured.

"You refer to the machine?" Barsac stepped over and opened the metal door in the side of the cabinet. Within the large exposed area was a chair, fastened with clamps from which led a number of convoluted tubes and metal valves which in turn were fastened to a switchboard bearing an imposing number of dials and levers.

The chair faced a glass prism—a window in the metal that had the general appearance of a gigantic lens. Before this prism was a wheel of radiating wires, so fine as to be almost transparent. Various tubes from the chair led to the tips of the wires at different points of the wheel rim.

"This is not magic but science," Barsac said. "You see before you the mechanical hypnotic device I have perfected.

"The human subject is seated in the chair, so. The attachments are made, the adjustments calculated. The cabinet is closed. The power is turned on—to be automatically generated for a time span set beforehand. The subject gazes into the prism. The wires before the prism revolve and various arcs are actuated across its surface. Mechanical hypnosis results— and then, by means of electrical impulse, something of the life essence, the soul itself, is released. It flows through the glass prism, a vital force, and impinges upon the animal subjects set before the cabinet in the focal range of the glass. The animals receive the essence and—change. The transference is complete. Something of the human goes into the animals. By graduating the focal range I can work with a dozen animals at once. Naturally, each experiment drains my strength and taxes my vitality."

"It taxes my credulity," Doctor Jerome interjected.

Barsac shrugged dolefully. "Very well. I could explain minutely the workings of my machine, but I see you demand visual proof of its work. Come with me."

The third door was opened and Doctor Jerome stood in the last chamber.

It was hot in here, and a sharp scent smote his nostrils. An animal reek permeated the bare room. Lining the walls were cages—dozens of cages. Some held rats, some white mice, and there was tier upon tier of glass containers housing guinea pigs. Rats squealed, mice squeaked, and guinea pigs chittered.

"Experimental subjects," Barsac commented. "Alas, the supply is continuously being exhausted. I work on batches of twenty or more at once. You see, not all animals are—responsive—to the treatment. Out of one batch I could hope for two or three—reactions. That is, until recently. Then I began to find that almost all of my subjects showed changes."

Barsac moved toward the fourth wall, where no cages loomed. Here were shelves filled with jars. Preserving jars, Doctor Jerome decided.

He moved closer for another look, but Barsac turned. He halted him, left hand on Jerome's shoulder, so that Doctor Jerome looked down upon the trembling stump where the thumb had been.

"I shall only permit you to gaze upon the last experiments," Barsac whispered. "I could show you dogs with human legs, mice with human skulls and no tails, monkeys that are hairless and possessed of human faces. But you would mock at me and say they were freaks, hybrids—or tell me I could produce monstrosities by using infrared or gamma rays.

"So I shall show you my last experimental results only. The ones that prove not only that human characteristics can be transferred to animals—but that *my* characteristics have been transferred. The transference of my *mental* powers cannot be measured. I shall let you judge the *physical* results only.

"Perhaps they will not excite you very much, these creatures of mine. They are not as grotesque as the earlier ones, but the reproduction of an *exact* characteristic excites me more than the semianthropomorphic structures in the earlier bodies. It shows me that I am on the right track at last. My next step will produce not creatures that are changed and dead, but creatures changed and living. I—"

"Show me!" Doctor Jerome commanded.

"You will not be impressed," Barsac insisted. "They are only rats and you may not even notice —"

"Show me!"

"Then, look."

Barsac stepped aside and Doctor Jerome gazed down at the jars. The bodies of twenty rats floated in the preserving fluid. Jerome stared. They were rats and only rats — their dead gray bodies were unchanged. Barsac was mad, quite mad.

And then Doctor Jerome saw it. He stared at one rat and saw the left forepaw that was not a forepaw — but a tiny hand!

He stared at the other rats in the other jars and saw that each left forepaw was alike. Each forepaw was like a human hand — *like the left hand of Sebastian Barsac on which the thumb was missing!*

Something was climbing the ivy outside the castle walls. Something was peering through the castle window — peering with little red-rimmed eyes that held a light of gleeful and atrocious floating. Something chuckled as it scrambled through the open window and dropped to the floor of the castle bedroom on tiny paws; paws that scraped and padded as they advanced toward the great bed.

Suddenly Jerome felt it crawling up the counterpane. He writhed and twisted, striking out with his hands to dislodge it; but the creature crawled upward, and now he could hear it chuckling in a voice that was a shrill mockery of human laughter.

Then its head rose on a level with Jerome's eyes, and he saw it — saw the furry figure, the monkeylike body and the mannikin-head of a witch's familiar — saw and recognized the hideous little monster for what it was . . . an animal, but with Barsac's face!

He screamed, then, and knew without any further indication that the creature was not alone.

The room was full of them. They were crawling out of the shadows in the corners, they were creeping along the paneling of the walls; they crowded through the door and slithered through rat holes in the worm-riddled flooring.

They were all about him now, chattering and squealing as they climbed toward him.

Then through the door came the man-sized figures; the man-sized figures with the shaggy bodies and flaming eyes and the acrid scent of the werewolf seeping forth from between their carrion fangs. And beneath their shaggy bodies was the flesh and form of Barsac, and within their flaming eyes was the laughing gaze of Barsac, and Jerome recognized them for what they were and screamed again.

But screaming did not stop them. Nothing stopped them as the mannikin-horde and the wolf-horde flowed in a furry flood toward his writhing body on the bed. He felt the touch of their horrid paws everywhere, tensed himself for the moment when he would feel their claws, their jaws —

A shriek wrenched from his throat as Jerome sat bolt upright in the bed.

Moonlight streamed tranquilly through the castle window, and its bright pattern was etched upon a bare floor and unshadowed walls.

The creatures were gone. They had never existed, save in his own disordered dreams.

Doctor Jerome sighed and dropped back as the hot perspiration trickled down into his eyes. He drifted off to sleep again.

It seemed to him as though the oaken door opened as he slept, and Barsac crept into the room. The little fat man was smiling a secret smile as he advanced on the bed. In his arms he held a rabbit — a white rabbit. He stroked the furry head until the ears lay flat and the pink-rimmed eyes were open and alert. Then Barsac's eyes opened and he gazed on Jerome and he fixed Jerome's gaze with unshakable intensity. Barsac's bulging eyes held a command and a ghastly promise, and Jerome could not turn away. Barsac's very being seemed concentrated in his eyes, and as he stared, Jerome felt his own being rise to meet that ghastly gaze.

He felt himself flowing out . . . out . . . and somehow he knew that he was no longer staring at Barsac but at the white rabbit. The white rabbit was absorbing his personality through the hypnotic stare.

Jerome felt weak, giddy. His head reeled, and through a blurred mist he saw the figure of the white rabbit. The white rabbit was *growing.* The furry body was larger. It slipped out of Barsac's hands and crouched on the floor, looming upwards as it swelled and grew.

Its long white ears were melting into a skull that in itself was changing. The pink muzzle blended back into the face. The rabbit's eyes were moving farther apart and a mouth sprang into prominence above a suddenly protruding chin.

There was something terribly familiar about the rabbit's face. Jerome strove to cleanse his mind of loathing and concentrate upon recognition. He had seen that face before and he knew that he *must* remember whose it was.

Then, in a wave of supreme terror, he recognized the face upon the rabbit.

It was his *own* —

Doctor Jerome didn't tell Barsac about his dreams. But Barsac must have noted his pallor and the dark pouches under his eyes, and drawn his own conclusions.

"I fear my accommodations are not of the best," he said, over the breakfast table. "It is my hope that you will soon become accustomed to the simple life. After we begin working together, things will probably adjust themselves, no?"

"No," said Doctor Jerome. "And what makes you think I'm going to work with you?"

"But of course you are going to work with me, my friend," Barsac declared. "It was for this reason I asked you to come here. I appreciate your brilliance, my friend, and I need your talents badly here.

"I have waited for you before resuming my experiments so that we could complete the final steps together. I realize that you were shocked by what I showed you last night, but I trust your reason has prevailed over your emotions.

"Together we can carry this experiment to its ultimate conclusion. Up to now I have produced monstrosities—and then managed to reproduce my own physical characteristics in a group of animals. I can go farther than that, I think. I have evolved a refinement of my technique. Using other animals than rats, I hope to make the changes and keep them alive.

"Then I can determine whether I have transmitted a portion of my *mind* as well as a force that changes the bodies to resemble me. You perceive the significance?"

Doctor Jerome did not look as though he perceived anything except a most unpleasant prospect. He shook his head slowly.

"I—I can't," he murmured.

"Wait, you misunderstand! I shall not ask you to submit to hypnosis if you do not wish to. I shall take that risk myself. All I desire is that you remain here and help to supervise the work, take notes, and act as a scientific witness to corroborate my findings."

"It's no use, Barsac." Doctor Jerome did not attempt to disguise the disgust that worked in his features. "I can't stand it—I won't set foot in that laboratory again."

Barsac clucked sympathetically. "You will get over your aversion," he predicted. "And, I hope, soon. For I shall now proceed with the last experiment. If it succeeds—and I know it will—you must be convinced. And if you are convinced, you can carry on alone."

"Carry on? Alone?"

Barsac lowered his head. The little fat man addressed the wall rather than his breakfast companion.

"Yes. I am not long for this earth, my friend. The doctors, they tell me of my heart. The strain of long experimentation has taken its toll. And this last one may well prove to be the end of further work, if not the end of my life itself. No, Jerome, a man cannot give of his soul and retain life for long."

Doctor Jerome stared at Barsac's earnest face. Barsac avoided his gaze and continued.

"That is why I invited you and asked you to consider working with me.

When I die, I wish that you will carry on my work. For the sake of our friendship, and because of my respect for your abilities and brilliance. Have no fear, whether you choose to enter the laboratory or not, I have compiled all of the notes and data necessary for you to take over.

"And one thing more." Barsac's voice was quite faint. "I have made the other arrangements. I have seen my advocate and prepared my will. You will be left everything when I die; my entire estate goes to you to continue in this work."

Jerome rose. "It's no use," he said. "I won't go into that laboratory with you."

"Very well. I understand. But this I ask of you—please stay here with me during the next two days. I shall proceed at once with the operations I have in mind. I hope to be able to give you complete proof of success— living animals that will not only bear a physical resemblance to me, but inherit my mental processes as well."

Doctor Jerome shuddered slightly.

"Please," said Barsac. "Do not leave me during these next two days. I shall stay in the laboratory and work if you will prepare the meals. You understand, I cannot keep servants here. They are ignorant, superstitious fools—easily frightened. And I must have someone here to rely on. You will stay?"

Jerome was silent for a long moment. Then he nodded "Yes," he whispered. "I will stay."

Barsac clasped his hand. Doctor Jerome felt the cold, flabby fingers and drew back involuntarily. To him, the light of gratitude in Barsac's bulging eyes was too reminiscent of the look he had glimpsed there in his dreams.

"I shall not wait," Barsac promised. "I go now to prepare. I will be in the laboratory—you need only to bring meals to the outer door. Within forty-eight hours I hope to announce success. Meanwhile, you are at liberty to amuse yourself as you will."

He turned. "I will leave you now. My gratitude, Jerome."

Barsac left the room.

Doctor Jerome smiled grimly as he gazed up at the forbidding stone ceiling.

"Amuse myself as I will," he muttered.

He finished his cigar, then rose and walked aimlessly down the hall. His footsteps rang eerily through the empty corridors. At a turn in the hall Jerome saw the figure standing against the wall in the shadows and started back.

Then he recognized the outlines of a suit of armor. Of course—Castle Barsac would have suits of armor. And all the trimmings, too. Perhaps he could amuse himself for a few hours, exploring the castle.

Doctor Jerome set about his explorations with scientific precision. He covered the ground floor thoroughly, entering a score of dusty chambers and apartments—being careful in each instance to turn on the lights before venturing into a strange room.

He found much to interest and delight him. Massive Regency furniture, elaborate tapestries, a full gallery of oils. The family portraits of the Barsac line gazed down austerely from a long chamber at the rear of the castle, and Jerome speculated as to the identity of that great-great-grandfather with the sorcerous proclivities.

Everything hinted of great age and great wealth. If the castle were haunted, it was haunted by the past alone. Again Jerome was reminded of the storybook atmosphere. All that was needed was a family vault in the cellar.

A vault? Why not?

Jerome explored. He discovered the stairs that descended to the lower levels and here he found the catacombs.

Catacombs they were in truth. On marble slabs lay the stone sarcophagi of the Barsacs. Row on row they rested in eternal slumber here below. Now only Sebastian Barsac remained, the last of his line, and soon he too would join these ranks of the dead.

The last of the Barsacs, and he was mad. Mad and soon to die.

How soon?

There in the dank and silent catacombs, the thought came to Jerome.

He *could* die *quite* soon.

Why not? Let him die soon, and quietly.

Then there would no longer be a Castle Barsac. Jerome would have the castle, have the laboratory, have the money. And why not? Barsac was mad. And he was all alone. The doctors had said he would die, and it need hardly be called murder. Perhaps a strong shock would do it.

Yes, a shock. Barsac would weaken himself in these crazy experiments. And then it would be so easy to precipitate a stroke, a seizure. He could be frightened.

The will was made, and all that remained was the deed. Mad Barsac would lie here on the last empty slab, and it would be ended.

Doctor Jerome ascended the stairs slowly. He went out and walked through the hills, returning only at dusk. He had wrestled with temptation and put it aside. There was no thought of putting poison in the food he took upstairs at dinner. He left the tray outside the laboratory door and knocked. He descended quickly before Barsac opened the door, and ate a solitary supper in the great castle kitchen below.

He was resigned to waiting, now. After all, in a few weeks Barsac might die a natural death. Meanwhile, let his work go on. Perhaps he might succeed.

Jerome listened to the reverberation from the laboratory above his head.

A steady humming sounded, accompanied by a rhythmic pulsing. Barsac must be in his cabinet now, working the focal prism and hypnotizing himself and his animals. Doctor Jerome wondered what sort of animals he was using in these "improved" experiments.

On second thought he didn't care to know. The vibrations were beginning to affect his nerves. He decided to turn in early. One more day and it would be over. If he could get a good night's sleep, now, his morbid fancies would vanish.

Accordingly, Jerome ascended to bed, switching off the lights as he proceeded down the hall. He undressed, donned pajamas, plunged the castle bedroom into darkness, and sought sleep.

Sleep came.

And then Barsac came. He wheeled in the cabinet, the great metal cabinet, and once again his bright eyes caught and captured Jerome's astonished stare. Jerome's will slipped away and he entered the cabinet. He was clamped into the seat as a prisoner is clamped in the electric chair. Like a prisoner, Jerome knew he was facing the execution of a death sentence. Yet his will was a prisoner—and now, as Barsac turned the dials, his soul was imprisoned, too.

Jerome stared through the great glass prism that loomed before his eyes. He could not look away, for the gigantic lens was in itself a hypnotic agent, pulling at his retina, impelling him to gaze ahead into the hugely magnified world of the focal field. He waited for the animals to appear in the field— but there were no animals.

There was only Barsac. For suddenly a great face loomed through the glass—a monstrous face with the bulging eyes of Barsac, and the great domed forehead.

Barsac was smiling and his yellow teeth were exposed, but Jerome could only see the eyes. The eyes that glared and pulled at his own eyes, at his brain behind them. Pulled his being into the glass, for as the humming rose insanely about him, Doctor Jerome felt himself plunging forward. His body was clamped to the seat, but his soul soared through the weird prism and lost itself in Barsac's mad eyes—

Doctor Jerome awoke. It was daylight at last, but he did not sit up to greet its coming. He felt weak, drained.

Drained.

A dreadful suspicion was forming in Jerome's mind. He knew that he had dreamed—but he did not know what he hadn't dreamed. Could it be that there was a distorted truth in his symbolic nightmare?

Was Barsac lying to him? Perhaps his machine *could* drain some of the vital essence from a man's soul. Perhaps Barsac wanted him to assist in the experiments so that a part of his soul would be removed—not to be incorporated into animals, but into Barsac! Hypnotic, scientific vampirism!

Had Barsac been in this room last night while he slept and dreamed? Had Barsac hypnotized him in his sleep, seeking to snare his soul?

Something had happened. Jerome felt weak.

And then he was strong — strong with sudden purpose. The thoughts of yesterday came back, but they came now as a resolution.

He would kill Barsac, today.

He would kill him before he died himself. He would kill Barsac because he was a madman, because his experiments were blasphemous, because he deserved to die.

Doctor Jerome would kill Barsac for the sake of science.

That was it. For the sake of science.

Doctor Jerome rose, dressed, prepared breakfast, took Barsac's tray upstairs, returned to the castle chambers below, and began to plan anew.

Madman or genius, Barsac would die. He had to die. Suppose he were *really* doing what he claimed? Suppose he actually managed to create animals with human physical attributes and with human minds? Minds like Barsac's mind.

Wouldn't that be the ultimate horror? And shouldn't that horror be avoided, stamped out?

Of course. He, Jerome, would save humanity from this monstrous affront to the laws of life. He would do the deed as he had planned, by shock. Tonight.

Yes, tonight. He'd short the electrical current in the castle, go up to the laboratory in the dark, and shock Barsac to death. Never lay a hand on him. A simple plan, and it would succeed. It must succeed.

Jerome knew it must succeed by late afternoon — for when the vibrations sounded from above he realized he couldn't wait much longer. He couldn't stand the sound or the visions it conjured up. Barsac, draining his soul into the bodies of a horde of animals — it was impossible to bear the thought.

What were the animals? Not rats, he had said. Jerome remembered the rats. Barsac had refused to show him the other monstrosities. He only showed the rats with the deformed paws. The paws with the missing finger or missing claw.

Jerome prepared dinner and laughed. His apprehensions faded away with the memory of his dream.

The paws. Of course! How foolish he was, letting Barsac's crazy talk and the morbid atmosphere of the castle affect him. Because of that and a few bad dreams he'd tricked himself into swallowing the grotesque claims of an obvious lunatic.

There *was* a machine — but any lunatic, given the funds and a scientific training, can build an imposing machine. That didn't prove that it actually worked as Barsac claimed it did.

There had been no other monstrosities for Jerome to see—for they didn't exist. Barsac's talk about previous experiments was merely talk.

There were the rats, but what of it? Barsac had been cunning. He had taken twenty rats, killed them, and removed their individual claws on the left forepaws.

That was all there was to it.

Barsac was crazy, and there was nothing to fear.

Doctor Jerome laughed again. That made it easier. He would kill the madman and take over. No more nightmares, no more fears.

His laughter blended with the thunder.

A storm was breaking. It shattered in fury over the castle, and the rumbling swallowed the noise of the vibrations from the laboratory upstairs.

Jerome peered out of the window as jagged lightning slithered between the mountain crags.

The thunder grew louder.

Doctor Jerome turned back to get Barsac's tray ready. Then he paused.

"Why bother?" he whispered. Yes, why bother? Why wait any longer? He'd go upstairs now, shut off all the lights, knock on the laboratory door. Barsac would appear, expecting his dinner tray. Instead, he'd dine on death.

Yes. He'd do it now, while the resolution held.

As the thunder mounted, Doctor Jerome walked up the stairs on his grim errand.

Lightning flickered as he reached the second landing. Jerome moved toward the switch panel on the wall. Then came the blinding bolt, and as thunder followed, the lights went out.

The storm had struck. It was an omen. Jerome exulted.

Now he moved up the spiral staircase leading to the laboratory landing at the top of the great castle tower. He groped his way slowly, in utter darkness, tensing himself for the moment when he would reach the oaken door and knock.

Then he listened, above the howling of the storm, for the vibrations from behind the door.

They had ceased, abruptly, when the lightning struck.

Jerome reached the top of the stairway. He edged toward the door. He was ready, now—

The door opened, swiftly.

Doctor Jerome heard Barsac's labored breathing.

"Jerome!" called Barsac. The voice was faint, but filled with overtones of triumph. "Jerome—where are you? I've succeeded, Jerome, I've succeeded beyond my wildest dreams!"

Jerome was very glad Barsac had called out. It enable him to locate Barsac's body in the darkness.

Now he glided forward and brought his cold hands up to Barsac's neck. Sudden shock, a fright—

But Barsac did not scream with fear. He screamed with anger.

"Jerome, it's you!" he shouted.

So he knew. Knew Jerome meant to kill him. Therefore he must die. Jerome's hands, which had risen merely to frighten, now remained to strangle.

He tightened his grip about Barsac's throat. Barsac tried to claw him off, but he could not see, and his gestures were pitifully weak.

Now Barsac did not cry out. He merely gurgled as Doctor Jerome pressed his windpipe and then dragged him back along the corridor. He dragged him swiftly, purposefully, and with his own feet he felt for the edge of the great staircase.

Then he thrust Barsac forward. There was a single shriek as Sebastian Barsac reeled in the darkness, and then only a dreadful series of rubbery thumps as he plunged down the black well of the spiral staircase.

Doctor Jerome stood there as the thunder came again. When its muttering reverberation died away, the thumping had ended.

Barsac was at the bottom of the stairs.

Cautiously, Doctor Jerome descended the staircase. His feet groped for the next stair, and groped for the feel of Barsac's body. But it was not until he reached the bottom that his shoes met the resistant flesh of Barsac.

Jerome knelt and passed his hands over that flesh, finding it quite cold. As cold as death.

So it was done. Barsac was dead. Long live the new ruler of Castle Barsac!

Doctor Jerome straightened up with a grin. It was easy, after all. "Gentlemen, it was an unavoidable accident. Sebastian Barsac was at work in his laboratory when the lights went out. He came out into the hall, evidently with the purpose of descending the stairs. In the dark he must have made a misstep and fallen down the staircase."

He whispered the words aloud, just the way he meant to repeat them at the inquest. He heard their echoes rustle and die away.

And then he heard the *other* rustling.

It came from far overhead, from a room at the top of the stairs. A room at the top of the stairs—a rustling from the laboratory!

Jerome bounded up the stairs

The animals were loose. He'd better lock the laboratory door, at once

He heard the shrill squeaking as he made the second landing and turned to climb the last flight to the tower level.

Then he paused. For there was a drumming from the floor above—a padding and a scraping as small bodies moved down the hall. They had already left the laboratory.

For the first time he detected the ominous note in the squeaking sounds. Shrill little cries of anger resounded from the head of the stairs. They were angry, as Barsac had been angry when he had died. Barsac, who had come out, crowing in triumph that his experiments were successful beyond his wildest dreams.

His experiments were successful!

"I will transfer the physical attributes of myself, and also the mental attributes."

Jerome knew the meaning of fear, then.

The creatures of Barsac's experiments were loose. The creatures whose bodies he had changed. Whose minds were a part of Barsac's mind.

They knew and they were loose. Loose and coming after him to seek revenge!

Jerome heard them creeping down the stairway. They were after him. They knew he was there—they could see in the dark! He turned in blind panic down the hallway. He'd hide in his room. That was it, his room. He stumbled through the pitch-black corridor, and heard them at his heels.

The beasts were swift. He reached the door, groped for his key. He fumbled in his pockets, cursing. The key wasn't on his ring. And the door was locked.

Perhaps he'd dropped it now, dropped it on the floor. He stooped to feel around.

And his hand encountered the warmth of flesh. Flesh that was furry, but not furry enough. Flesh that wriggled through his fingers.

The creatures had come!

Fangs nipped at his thumb. He stood up, hastily, and kicked out at the furry beast. But another body brushed his other ankle, and then they were all around him. Their squealing rose. One of the tiny monstrosities was crawling up his leg, and he felt the touch of minute fingers clinging to his body.

Jerome screamed, and knew Barsac had spoken the truth. The monsters he had created with his mind were going to kill him in revenge for Barsac's death. And there was no escape.

Their squealing filled the corridor and their bodies blocked it completely. They swarmed around Doctor Jerome like ravening rats, but they were not rats. Jerome knew that if he should see them he would go mad. And if he did not see them they would crawl up his body and sink their horrible little mouths in his throat, stroke his face with their ghastly fingers.

Jerome wheeled and charged down the corridor again. The nightmare ranks broke for a moment and he sped down the black corridor of the haunted castle with the beasts of Barsac at his heels. He was playing tag with death in a nighted lair, and death ran behind him on purposeful paws.

Death squealed and chattered, and Jerome fled. He had to get out before they reached him, touched him, took him. He had to.

Gasping in agony he reached the corridor's end, knowing that the horde was keeping pace. He turned again, ran forward. He never gave a thought to the stairs.

And then, as the squealing rose and echoed in his ears, Doctor Jerome tumbled down the castle staircase and landed with a sickening little crunch that he never heard. His head lolled grotesquely on the broken stem of a neck. He lay next to the body of Sebastian Barsac, and like Barsac, he was quite dead.

It was casual irony that chose this moment for the castle lights to flicker on again.

They revealed nothing but the two bodies lying at the foot of the stairs. Mad Barsac lay dead, and so did mad Jerome.

On the landing above, the twenty escaped guinea pigs blinked down with stupid, uncomprehending eyes.

THE SKULL OF THE MARQUIS DE SADE

1

CHRISTOPHER MAITLAND SAT BACK in his chair before the fireplace and fondled the binding of an old book. His thin face, modeled by the flickering firelight, bore a characteristic expression of scholarly preoccupation.

Maitland's intellectual curiosity was focused on the volume in his hands. Briefly, he was wondering if the human skin binding this book came from a man, a woman or a child.

He had been assured by the bookseller that this tome was bound in a portion of the skin of a woman, but Maitland, much as he desired to believe this, was by nature skeptical. Booksellers who deal in such *curiosa* are not overly reputable, as a rule, and Christopher Maitland's years of dealing with such people had done much to destroy his faith in their veracity.

Still, he hoped the story was true. It was nice to have a book bound in a woman's skin. It was nice to have a *crux ansata* fashioned from a thighbone; a collection of Dyack heads; a shriveled Hand of Glory stolen from a graveyard in Mainz. Maitland owned all of these items, and many more. For he was a collector of the unusual.

Maitland held the book up to the light and sought to distinguish pore-formation beneath the tanned surface of the binding. Women had finer pores than men, didn't they?

"Beg pardon, sir."

Maitland turned as Hume entered. "What is it?" he asked.

"That person is here again."

"Person?"

"Mr. Marco."

"Oh?" Maitland rose, ignoring the butler's almost grotesque expression of distaste. He suppressed a chuckle. Poor Hume didn't like Marco, or any of the raffish gentry who supplied Maitland with items for his collection. Hume didn't care for the collection itself, either—Maitland vividly remembered the old servant's squeamish trembling as he dusted off the case containing the mummy of the priest of Horus decapitated for sorcery.

"Marco, eh? Wonder what's up?" Maitland mused. "Well—better show him in."

Hume turned and left with a noticeable lack of enthusiasm. As for Maitland, his eagerness mounted. He ran his hand along the reticulated back of a jadeite *tao-tieh* and licked his lips with very much the same expression as adorned the face of the Chinese image of gluttony.

Old Marco was here. That meant something pretty special in the way of acquisitions. Perhaps Marco wasn't exactly the kind of chap one invited to the Club—but he had his uses. Where he laid hands on some of the things he offered for sale Maitland didn't know; he didn't much care. That was Marco's affair. The rarity of his offerings was what interested Christopher Maitland. If one wanted a book bound in human skin, old Marco was just the chap to get hold of it—if he had to do a bit of flaying and binding himself. Great character, old Marco!

"Mr. Marco, sir."

Hume withdrew, a sedate shadow, and Maitland waved his visitor forward.

Mr. Marco oozed into the room. The little man was fat, greasily so; his flesh lumped like the tallow coagulating about the guttering stump of a candle. His waxen pallor accentuated the simile. All that seemed needed was a wick to sprout from the bald ball of fat that served as Mr. Marco's head.

The fat man stared up at Maitland's lean face with what was meant to be an ingratiating smile. The smile oozed, too, and contributed to the aura of uncleanliness which seemed to surround Marco.

But Maitland was not conscious of these matters. His attention was focused on the curious bundle Marco carried under one arm—the large package, wrapped in prosaic butcher's paper which somehow contributed to its fascination for him.

Marco shifted the package gingerly as he removed his shoddy gray ulster. He did not ask permission to divest himself of the coat, nor did he wait for an invitation to be seated.

The fat little man merely made himself comfortable in one of the chairs before the fire, reached for Maitland's open cigar case, helped himself to a stogie, and lit it. The large round package bobbed up and down on his lap as his rotund stomach heaved convulsively.

Maitland stared at the package. Marco stared at Maitland. Maitland broke first.

"Well?" he asked.

The greasy smile expanded. Marco inhaled rapidly, then opened his mouth to emit a puff of smoke and a reply.

"I am sorry to come unannounced, Mr. Maitland. I hope I'm not intruding?"

"Never mind that," Maitland snapped. "What's in the package, Marco?"

Marco's smile expanded. "Something choice," he whispered. "Something tasty."

Maitland bent over the chair, his head outthrust to throw a vulpine shadow on the wall.

"What's in the package?" he repeated.

"You're my favorite client, Mr. Maitland. You know I never come to you unless I have something really rare. Well, I have that, sir. I have that. You'd be surprised what this butcher's paper hides, although it's rather appropriate. Yes, appropriate it is!"

"Stop that infernal gabbling, man! What is in the package?"

Marco lifted the bundle from his lap. He turned it over gingerly, yet deliberately.

"Doesn't seem to be much," he purred. "Round. Heavy enough. Might be a medicine ball, eh? Or a beehive. I say, it could even be a head of cabbage. Yes, one might mistake it for a head of common cabbage. But it isn't. Oh no, it isn't. Intriguing problem, eh?"

If it was the little man's intention to goad Maitland into a fit of apoplexy, he almost succeeded.

"Open it up, damn you!" he shouted.

Marco shrugged, smiled, and scrabbled at the taped edges of the paper. Christopher Maitland was no longer the perfect gentleman, the perfect host. He was a collector, stripped of all pretenses—quivering eagerness incarnate. He hovered over Marco's shoulder as the butcher's paper came away in the fat man's pudgy fingers.

"Now!" Maitland breathed.

The paper fell to the floor. Resting in Marco's lap was a large, glittering silver ball of—tinfoil.

Marco began to strip the tinfoil away, unraveling it in silvery strands. Maitland gasped as he saw what emerged from the wrappings.

It was a human skull.

Maitland saw the horrid hemisphere gleaming ivory-white in the firelight —then, as Marco shifted it, he saw the empty eye sockets and the gaping nasal aperture that would never know human breath. Maitland noted the even structure of the teeth, adherent to a well-formed jaw. Despite his instinctive repulsion, he was surprisingly observant.

It appeared to him that the skull was unusually small and delicate, remarkably well preserved despite a yellow tinge hinting of age. But Christopher Maitland was most impressed by one undeniable peculiarity. The skull was *different,* indeed.

This skull did not grin!

Through some peculiar formation or malformation of cheekbone in juxtaposition of jaws, the death's-head did not simulate a smile. The classic mockery of mirth attributed to all skulls was absent here.

The skull had a sober, serious look about it.

Maitland blinked and uttered a self-conscious cough. What was he doing, entertaining these idiotic fancies about a skull? It was ordinary enough. What was old Marco's game in bringing him such a silly object with so much solemn preamble?

Yes, what *was* Marco's game?

The little fat man held the skull up before the firelight, turning it from time to time with an impressive display of pride. His smirk of self-satisfaction contrasted oddly with the sobriety set indelibly upon the skull's bony visage.

Maitland's puzzlement found expression at last. "What are you so smug about?" he demanded. "You bring me the skull of a woman or an adolescent youth—"

Marco's chuckle cut across his remark. "Exactly what the phrenologists said!" he wheezed.

"Damn the phrenologists, man! Tell me about this skull, if there's anything to tell."

Marco ignored him. He turned the skull over in his fat hands, with a gloating expression which repelled Maitland.

"It may be small, but it's a beauty, isn't it?" the little man mused. "So delicately formed, and look—there's almost the illusion of a patina upon the surface."

"I'm not a paleontologist," Maitland snapped. "Nor a graverobber, either. You'd think we were Burke and Hare! Be reasonable, Marco—why should I want an ordinary skull?"

"Please, Mr. Maitland! What do you take me for? Do you think I would presume to insult your intelligence by bringing you an ordinary skull? Do you imagine I would ask a thousand pounds for the skull of a nobody?"

Maitland stepped back.

"A thousand pounds?" he shouted. "A thousand pounds for *that?*"

"And cheap at the price," Marco assured him. "You'll pay it gladly when you know the story."

"I wouldn't pay such a price for the skull of Napoleon," Maitland assured him. "Or Shakespeare, for that matter."

"You'll find that the owner of this skull tickles your fancy a bit more," Marco assured him.

"Enough of this. Let's have it, man!"

Marco faced him, one pudgy forefinger tapping the osseous brow of the death's-head.

"You see before you," he murmured, "the skull of Donatien Alphonse François, the Marquis de Sade."

2

Giles de Retz was a monster. Torquemada's inquisitors exercised the diabolic ingenuity of the fiends they professed to exorcise. But it remained for the Marquis de Sade to epitomize the living lust for pain. His name symbolizes cruelty incarnate — the savagery men call "sadism."

Maitland knew de Sade's weird history, and mentally reviewed it.

The Count, or Marquis, de Sade was born in 1740, of distinguished Provençal lineage. He was a handsome youth when he joined his cavalry regiment in the Seven Years' War — a pale, delicate, blue-eyed man, whose foppish diffidence cloaked an evil perversity.

At the age of twenty-three he was imprisoned for a year as the result of a barbaric crime. Indeed, twenty-seven years of his subsequent life he spent in incarceration for his deeds — deeds which even today are only hinted at. His flagellations, his administration of *outré* drugs and his tortures of women have served to make his name infamous.

But de Sade was no common libertine with a primitive urge toward the infliction of suffering. He was, rather, the "philosopher of pain" — a keen scholar, a man of exquisite taste and breeding. He was wonderfully well-read, a disciplined thinker, a remarkable psychologist — and a sadist.

How the mighty Marquis would have squirmed had he envisioned the petty perversions which today bear his name! The tormenting of animals by ignorant peasants, the beating of children by hysteric attendants in institutions, the infliction of senseless cruelties by maniacs upon others or by others upon maniacs — all these matters are classified as "sadistic" today. And yet none of them are manifestations of de Sade's unnatural philosophy.

De Sade's concept of cruelty had in it nothing of concealment or deceit. He practiced his beliefs openly and wrote explicitly of such matters during his years in prison. For he was the Apostle of Pain, and his gospel was made known to all men in JUSTINE, JULIETTE, ALINE ET VALCOUR, the curious LA PHILOSOPHIE DANS LE BOUDOIR and the utterly abominable LES 120 JOURNÉES. And de Sade practiced what he preached. He was a lover of many women

—a jealous lover, willing to share the embraces of his mistresses with but one rival. That rival was Death, and it is said that all women who knew de Sade's caresses came to prefer those of his rival, in the end.

Perhaps the tortures of the French Revolution were indirectly inspired by the philosophy of the Marquis—a philosophy that gained circulation throughout France following the publication of his notorious tomes.

When the guillotine arose in the public squares of the cities, de Sade emerged from his long series of imprisonments and walked abroad among men maddened at the sight of blood and suffering.

He was a gray, gentle little ghost—short, bald, mild-mannered and soft-spoken. He raised his voice only to save his aristocratic relatives from the knife. His public life was exemplary during these latter years.

But men still whispered of his private life. His interest in sorcery was rumored. It is said that to de Sade the shedding of blood was a sacrifice. And sacrifices made to certain beings bring black boons. The screams of pain-maddened women are as prayer to the creatures of the Pit. . . .

The Marquis was cunning. Years of confinement for his "offenses against society" had made him wary. He moved quite cautiously and took full advantage of the troubled times to conduct quiet and unostentatious burial services whenever he terminated an amour.

Caution did not suffice, in the end. An ill-chosen diatribe directed against Napoleon served as an excuse for the authorities. There were no civil charges; no farcical trial was perpetrated.

De Sade was simply shut up in Charenton as a common lunatic. The men who knew his crimes were too shocked to publicize them—and yet there was a satanic grandeur about the Marquis which somehow precluded destroying him outright. One does not think of assassinating Satan. But Satan chained—

Satan, chained, languished. A sick, half-blind old man who tore the petals from roses in a last gesture of demoniac destructiveness, the Marquis spent his declining days forgotten by all men. They preferred to forget, preferred to think him mad.

In 1814, he died. His books were banned, his memory desecrated, his deeds denied. But his name lived on—lives on as an eternal symbol of innate evil. . . .

Such was de Sade, as Christopher Maitland knew him. And as a collector of *curiosa*, the thought of possessing the veritable skull of the fabulous Marquis intrigued him.

He glanced up from revery, glanced at the unsmiling skull and the grinning Marco.

"A thousand pounds, you said?"

"Exactly," Marco nodded. "A most reasonable price, under the circumstances."

"Under what circumstances?" Maitland objected. "You bring me a skull. But what proofs can you furnish me as to its authenticity? How did you come by this rather unusual *memento mori*?"

"Come, come, Mr. Maitland—please! You know me better than to question my source of supply. That is what I choose to call a trade secret, eh?"

"Very well. But I can't just take your word, Marco. To the best of my recollection, de Sade was buried when he died at Charenton, in 1814."

Marco's oozing grin expanded.

"Well, I can set you right about *that* point," he conceded. "Do you happen to have a copy of Ellis's STUDIES about? In the section entitled *Love and Pain* there is an item which may interest you."

Maitland secured the volume, and Marco riffled through the pages.

"Here!" he exclaimed triumphantly. "According to Ellis, the skull of the Marquis de Sade was exhumed and examined by a phrenologist. Phrenology was a popular pseudoscience in those days, eh? Chap wanted to see if the cranial formation indicated the Marquis was truly insane.

"It says he found the skull to be small and well-formed, like a woman's. Exactly your remark, as you may recall!

"But the real point is this. The skull wasn't reinterred.

"It fell into the hands of a Dr. Londe, but around 1850 it was stolen by another physician, who took it to England. That is all Ellis knows of the matter. The rest I could tell—but it's better not to speak. Here is the skull of the Marquis de Sade, Mr. Maitland.

"Will you meet my offer?"

"A thousand pounds," Maitland sighed. "It's too much for a shoddy skull and a flimsy story."

"Well—let us say eight hundred, perhaps. A quick deal and no hard feelings?"

Maitland stared at Marco. Marco stared at Maitland. The skull stared at them both.

"Five hundred, then," Marco ventured. "Right now."

"You must be faking," Maitland said. "Otherwise you wouldn't be so anxious for a sale."

Marco's smile oozed off again. "On the contrary, sir. If I were trying to do you, I certainly wouldn't budge on my price. But I want to dispose of this skull quickly."

"Why?"

For the first time during the interview, fat little Marco hesitated. He twisted the skull between his hands and set it down on the table. It seemed to Maitland as if he avoided looking at it as he answered.

"I don't exactly know. It's just that I don't fancy owning such an item, really. Works on my imagination. Rot, isn't it?"

"Works on your imagination?"

"I get ideas that I'm being followed. Of course it's all nonsense, but—"

"You get ideas that you're followed by the police, no doubt," Maitland accused. "Because you stole the skull. Didn't you, Marco?"

Marco averted his gaze. "No," he mumbled. "It isn't that. But I don't like skulls—not my idea of ornaments, I assure you. Squeamish I am, a bit.

"Besides, you live in this big house here. You're safe. I live in Wapping now. Down on my luck at the moment and all that. I sell you the skull. You tuck it away here in your collection, look at it when you please—and the rest of the time it's out of sight, not bothering you. I'll be free of it knocking around in my humble diggings. Matter of fact, when I sell it, I'll vacate the premises and move to decent lodgings. That's why I want to be rid of it, really. For five hundred, cash in hand."

Maitland hesitated. "I must think it over," he declared. "Give me your address. Should I decide to purchase it, I'll be down tomorrow with the money. Fair enough?"

"Very well." Marco sighed. He produced a greasy stub of pencil and tore a bit of paper from the discarded wrappings on the floor.

"Here's the address," he said.

Maitland pocketed the slip as Marco commenced to enclose the skull in tinfoil once more. He worked quickly, as though eager to obscure the shining teeth and the yawning emptiness of the eye sockets. He twisted the butcher's paper over the tinfoil, grasped his overcoat in one hand, and balanced the round bundle in the other.

"I'll be expecting you tomorrow," he said. "And by the way—be careful when you open the door. I've a police dog now, a savage brute. He'll tear you to pieces—or anyone else who tries to take the skull of the Marquis de Sade."

3

It seemed to Maitland that they had bound him too tightly. He knew that the masked men were about to whip him, but he could not understand why they had fastened his wrists with chains of steel.

Only when they held the metal scourges over the fire did he comprehend the reason—only when they raised the white-hot rods high above their heads did he realize why he was held so securely.

For at the fiery kiss of the lash Maitland did not flinch—he convulsed. His body, seared by the hideous blow, described an arc. Bound by thongs, his hands would tear themselves free under the stimulus of the unbearable torment. But the steel chains held, and Maitland gritted his teeth as the two black-robed men flogged him with living fire.

The outlines of the dungeon blurred, and Maitland's pain blurred too. He sank down into a darkness broken only by the consciousness of rhythm—

the rhythm of the savage, sizzling steel flails that descended upon his naked back.

When awareness returned, Maitland knew that the flogging was over. The silent, black-robed men in masks were bending over him, unfastening the shackles. They lifted him tenderly and led him gently across the dungeon floor to the great steel casket.

Casket? This was no casket. Caskets do not stand open and upended. Caskets do not bear upon their lids the raised, molded features of a woman's face.

Caskets are not spiked, inside.

Recognition was simultaneous with horror.

This was the Iron Maiden!

The masked men were strong. They dragged him forward, thrust him into the depths of the great metal matrix of torment. They fastened wrists and ankles with clamps. Maitland knew what was coming.

They would close the lid upon him. Then, by turning a crank, they would move the lid down—move it down as spikes drove in at his body. For the interior of the Iron Maiden was studded with cruel barbs, sharpened and lengthened with the cunning of the damned.

The longest spikes would pierce him first as the lid descended. These spikes were set so as to enter his wrists and ankles. He would hang there, crucified, as the lid continued its inexorable descent. Shorter spikes would next enter his thighs, shoulders and arms. Then, as he struggled, impaled in agony, the lid would press closer until the smallest spikes came close enough to penetrate his eyes, his throat, and—mercifully—his heart and brain.

Maitland screamed, but the sound served only to shatter his eardrums as they closed the lid. The rusty metal grated, and then came the harsher grating of the machinery. They were turning the crank, bringing the banks of spikes closer to his cringing body. . . .

Maitland waited, tensed in the darkness, for the first sharp kiss of the Iron Maiden.

Then, and then only, he realized that he was not *alone* here in the blackness.

There were no spikes set in the lid! Instead, a figure was pressed against the opposite iron surface. As the lid descended, it merely brought the figure closer to Maitland's body.

The figure did not move, or even breathe. It rested against the lid, and as the lid came forward Maitland felt the pressure of cold and alien flesh against his own. The arms and legs met his in unresponsive embrace, but still the lid pressed down, squeezing the lifeless form closer and closer. It was dark, but now Maitland could see the face that loomed scarcely an inch from his eyes. The face was white, phosphorescent. The face was — *not a face!*

And then, as the body gripped his body in blackness, as the head touched his head, as Maitland's lips pressed against the place where lips *should* be, he knew the ultimate horror.

The face that was *not* a face was the skull of the Marquis de Sade!

And the weight of charnel corruption stifled Maitland, and he went down into darkness again with the obscene memory pursuing him to oblivion.

Even oblivion has an end, and once more Maitland woke. The masked men had released and were reviving him. He lay on a pallet and glanced toward the open doors of the Iron Maiden. He was oddly grateful to see that the interior was empty. No figure rested against the inside of the lid. Perhaps there had been no figure.

The torture played strange tricks on a man's mind. But it was needed now. He could tell that the solicitude of the masked ones was not assumed. They had subjected him to this ordeal for strange reasons, and he had come through unscathed.

They anointed his back, lifted him to his feet, led him from the dungeon. In the great corridor beyond, Maitland saw a mirror. They guided him up to it.

Had the torture changed him? For a moment Maitland feared to gaze into the glass.

But they held him before the mirror, and Maitland stared at his reflection — stared at his quivering body, on which was set the grim, unsmiling death's-head of the Marquis de Sade!

4

Maitland told no one of his dream, but he lost no time in discussing Marco's visit and offer.

His confidant was an old friend and fellow collector, Sir Fitzhugh Kissroy. Seated in Sir Fitzhugh's comfortable study the following afternoon, he quickly unburdened himself of all pertinent details.

Genial, red-bearded Kissroy heard him out in silence.

"Naturally, I want that skull," Maitland concluded. "But I can't understand why Marco is so anxious to dispose of it at once. And I'm considerably worried about its authenticity. So I was wondering — you're quite an expert, Fitzhugh. Would you be willing to visit Marco with me and examine the skull?"

Sir Fitzhugh chuckled and shook his head.

"There's no need to examine it," he declared. "I'm quite sure the skull, as you describe it, is that of the Marquis de Sade. It's genuine enough."

Maitland gaped at him.

"How can you be so positive?" he asked.

Sir Fitzhugh beamed. "Because, my dear fellow—that skull was stolen from me!"

"What?"

"Quite so. About ten days ago, a prowler got into the library through the French windows facing the garden. None of the servants were aroused, and he made off with the skull in the night."

Maitland rose. "Incredible," he murmured. "But of course you'll come with me, now. We'll identify your property, confront old Marco with the facts, and recover the skull at once."

"Nothing of the sort," Sir Fitzhugh replied. "I'm just as glad the skull was stolen. And I advise you to leave it alone.

"I didn't report the theft to the police, and I have no intention of doing so. Because that skull is—unlucky."

"Unlucky?" Maitland peered at his host. "You, with your collection of cursed Egyptian mummies, tell me that? You've never taken any stock in such superstitious rubbish."

"Exactly. Therefore, when I tell you that I sincerely believe that skull is dangerous, you must have faith in my words."

Maitland pondered. He wondered if Sir Fitzhugh had experienced the same dreams that tormented his own sleep upon seeing the skull. Was there an associative aura about the relic? If so, it only added to the peculiar fascination exerted by the unsmiling skull of the Marquis de Sade.

"I don't understand you at all," he declared. "I should think you couldn't wait to lay hands on that skull."

"Perhaps I'm not the only one who can't wait," Sir Fitzhugh muttered.

"What are you getting at?"

"You know de Sade's history. You know the power of morbid fascination such evil geniuses exert upon the imagination of men. You feel that fascination yourself; that's why you want the skull.

"But you're a normal man, Maitland. You want to *buy* the skull and keep it in your collection of *curiosa.* An abnormal man might not think of buying. He might think of stealing it—or even killing the owner to possess it. Particularly if he wanted to do more than merely own it; if, for example, he wanted to *worship* it."

Sir Fitzhugh's voice sank to a whisper as he continued, "I'm not trying to frighten you, my friend. But I know the history of that skull. During the last hundred years it has passed through the hands of many men. Some of them were collectors, and sane. Others were perverted members of secret cults —worshippers of pain, devotees of Black Magic. Men have died to gain that grisly relic, and other men have been—sacrificed to it.

"It came to me quite by chance, six months ago. A man like your friend

Marco offered it to me. Not for a thousand pounds, or five hundred. He gave it to me as a gift, because he was afraid of it.

"Of course I laughed at his notions, just as you are probably laughing at mine now. But during the six months that the skull has remained in my hands, I've suffered.

"I've had queer dreams. Just staring at the unnatural, unsmiling grimace is enough to provoke nightmares. Didn't you sense an emanation from the thing? They said de Sade wasn't mad—and I believe them. He was far worse—he was *possessed*. There's something *unhuman* about that skull. Something that attracts others, living men whose skulls hide a bestial quality that is also unhuman or inhuman.

"And I've had more than my dreams to deal with. Phone calls came, and mysterious letters. Some of the servants have reported lurkers on the grounds at dusk."

"Probably ordinary thieves, like Marco, after a valuable object," Maitland commented.

"No," Sir Fitzhugh sighed. "Those unknown seekers did more than attempt to steal the skull. *They came into my house at night and adored it!*

"Oh, I'm quite positive about the matter, I assure you! I keep the skull in a glass case in the library. Often, when I came to see it in the mornings, I found that it had been moved during the night.

"Yes, moved. Sometimes the case was smashed and the skull placed on the table. Once it was on the floor.

"Of course I checked up on the servants. Their alibis were perfect. It was the work of outsiders—outsiders who probably feared to possess the skull completely, yet needed access to it from time to time in order to practice some abominable and perverted rite.

"They came into my house, I tell you, and worshipped that filthy skull! And when it was stolen, I was glad—very glad.

"All I can say to you is, keep away from the whole business! Don't see this man Marco, and don't have anything to do with that accursed graveyard relic!"

Maitland nodded. "Very well," he said. "I am grateful to you for your warning."

He left Sir Fitzhugh shortly thereafter.

Half an hour later, he was climbing the stairs to Marco's dingy attic room.

5

He climbed the stairs to Marco's room; climbed the creaking steps in the shabby Soho tenement and listened to the curiously muffled thumping of his own heartbeat.

But not for long. A sudden howl resounded from the landing above, and Maitland scrambled up the last few stairs in frantic haste.

The door of Marco's room was locked, but the sounds that issued from within stirred Maitland to desperate measures.

Sir Fitzhugh's warnings had prompted him to carry his service revolver on this errand; now he drew it and shattered the lock with a shot.

Maitland flung the door back against the wall as the howling reached the ultimate frenzied crescendo. He started into the room, then checked himself.

Something hurtled toward him from the floor beyond; something launched itself at his throat.

Maitland raised his revolver blindly and fired.

For a moment sound and vision blurred. When he recovered, he was half-kneeling on the floor before the threshold. A great shaggy form rested at his feet. Maitland recognized the carcass of a gigantic police dog.

Suddenly he remembered Marco's reference to the beast. So that explained it! The dog had howled and attacked. But—why?

Maitland rose and entered the sordid bedroom. Smoke still curled upward from the shots. He gazed again at the prone animal, noting the gleaming yellow fangs grimacing even in death. Then he stared around at the shoddy furniture, the disordered bureau, the rumpled bed—

The rumpled bed on which Mr. Marco lay, his throat torn in a red rosary of death.

Maitland stared at the body of the little fat man and shuddered.

Then he saw the skull. It rested on the pillow near Marco's head, a grisly bedfellow that seemed to peer curiously at the corpse in ghastly camaraderie. Blood had spattered the hollow cheekbones, but even beneath this sanguinary stain Maitland could see the peculiar solemnity of the death's-head.

For the first time he fully sensed the aura of evil which clung to the skull of de Sade. It was palpable in this ravaged room, palpable as the presence of death itself. The skull seemed to glow with actual charnel phosphorescence.

Maitland knew now that his friend had spoken the truth. There *was* a dreadful magnetism inherent in this bony horror, a veritable Elixir of Death that worked and preyed upon the minds of men—and beasts.

It must have been that way. The dog, maddened by the urge to kill, had finally attacked Marco as he slept and destroyed him. Then it had sought to attack Maitland when he entered. And through it all the skull watched, watched and gloated just as de Sade would gloat had his pale blue eyes flickered in the shadowed sockets.

Somewhere within the cranium, perhaps, the shriveled remnants of his cruel brain were still attuned to terror. The magnetic force it focused had a compelling enchantment even in the face of what Maitland knew.

That is why Maitland, driven by a compulsion he could not wholly explain or seek to justify, stooped down and lifted the skull. He held it for a long moment in the classic pose of Hamlet.

Then he left the room, forever, carrying the death's-head in his arms.

Fear rode Maitland's shoulders as he hurried through the twilit streets. Fear whispered strangely in his ear, warning him to hurry, lest the body of Marco be discovered and the police pursue him. Fear prompted him to enter his own house by a side door and go directly to his rooms so that none would see the skull he concealed beneath his coat.

Fear was Maitland's companion all that evening. He sat there, staring at the skull on the table, and shivered with repulsion.

Sir Fitzhugh was right, he knew it. There *was* a damnable influence issuing from the skull and the black brain within. It had caused Maitland to disregard the sensible warnings of his friend; it had caused Maitland to steal the skull itself from a dead man; it had caused him now to conceal himself in this lonely room.

He should call the authorities; he knew that. Better still, he should dispose of the skull. Give it away, throw it away, rid the earth of it forever. There was something puzzling about the cursed thing—something he didn't quite understand.

For, knowing these truths, he still desired to possess the skull of the Marquis de Sade. There was an evil enchantment here; the dormant baseness in every man's soul was aroused and responded to the loathsome lust which poured from the death's-head in waves.

He stared at the skull, shivered—yet knew he would not give it up; could not. Nor had he the strength to destroy it. Perhaps possession would lead him to madness in the end. The skull would incite others to unspeakable excesses.

Maitland pondered and brooded, seeking a solution in the impassive object that confronted him with the stolidity of death.

It grew late. Maitland drank wine and paced the floor. He was weary. Perhaps in the morning he could think matters through and reach a logical, sane, conclusion.

Yes, he was upset. Sir Fitzhugh's outlandish hints had disturbed him; the gruesome events of the late afternoon preyed on his nerves.

No sense in giving way to foolish fancies about the skull of the mad Marquis . . . better to rest.

Maitland flung himself on the bed. He reached out for the switch and extinguished the light. The moon's rays slithered through the window and sought out the skull on the table, bathing it in eerie luminescence. Maitland stared once more at the jaws that should grin and did not.

Then he closed his eyes and willed himself to sleep. In the morning he'd call Sir Fitzhugh, make a clean breast of things, and give the skull over to the authorities.

Its evil career—real or imaginary—would come to an end. So be it.

Maitland sank into slumber. Before he dozed off he tried to focus his attention on something . . . something puzzling . . . an impression he'd received upon gazing at the body of the police dog in Marco's room. The way its fangs gleamed.

Yes. That was it. There had been no blood on the muzzle of the police dog. Strange. For the police dog had bitten Marco's throat. No blood—how could that be?

Well, that problem was best left for morning too. . . .

It seemed to Maitland that as he slept, he dreamed. In his dream he opened his eyes and blinked in the bright moonlight. He stared at the table-top and saw that the skull was no longer resting on its surface.

That was curious, too. No one had come into the room, or he would have been aroused.

If he had not been sure that he was dreaming, Maitland would have started up in terror when he saw the stream of moonlight on the floor—the stream of moonlight through which the skull was rolling.

It turned over and over again, its bony visage impassive as ever, and each revolution brought it closer to the bed.

Maitland's sleeping ears could almost hear the thump as the skull landed on the bare floor at the foot of the bed. Then began the grotesque progress so typical of night fantasies. The skull climbed the side of the bed!

Its teeth gripped the dangling corner of a bedsheet, and the death's-head literally whirled the sheet out and up, swinging it in an arc which landed the skull on the bed at Maitland's feet.

The illusion was so vivid he could feel the thud of its impact against the mattress. Tactile sensation continued, and Maitland felt the skull rolling along up the covers. It came up to his waist, then approached his chest.

Maitland saw the bony features in the moonlight, scarcely six inches away from his neck. He felt a cold weight resting on his throat. The skull was moving now.

Then he realized the grip of utter nightmare and struggled to awake before the dream continued.

A scream rose in his throat—but never issued from it. For Maitland's throat was seized by champing teeth—teeth that bit into his neck with all the power of a moving human jawbone.

The skull tore at Maitland's jugular in cruel haste. There was a gasp, a gurgle and then no sound at all.

After a time, the skull righted itself on Maitland's chest. Maitland's chest no longer heaved with breathing, and the skull rested there with a curious simulation of satisfied repose.

The moonlight shone on the death's-head to reveal one very curious circumstance. It was a trivial thing, yet somehow fitting under the circumstances.

Reposing on the chest of the man it had killed, the skull of the Marquis de Sade was no longer impassive. Instead, its bony features bore a definite, unmistakably *sadistic* grin.

THE BOGEY MAN WILL GET YOU

THE FIRST TIME Nancy met Philip Ames he didn't even notice her. Of course you really couldn't blame him. After all, she was only fifteen—just a kid. But that was last year, and this time it was different.

Nancy's folks went back to Beaver Lake for the summer in June, and she could hardly wait to find out if Philip Ames still had his cottage down the road.

Hedy Schuster said he was up, all right. She said Mr. Ames lived at the cottage all year. Everybody knows how cold it gets at the lake in winter—practically out of this world. But Hedy Schuster knew, because she talked to Mr. Prentiss down at the store and he said so. That Prentiss was like an old woman. He had his nose in everybody's business.

The first chance she got, Nancy took a walk up the road past Philip Ames's cottage. The door was closed and there were curtains on the windows, so she didn't see anything. But then, Mr. Ames wasn't around much in the daytime. Practically a hermit. Hedy Schuster said it was because he was writing his Ph.D. thesis for the university. He only shined around at night.

"But after all, that's the best time, isn't it?" Hedy Schuster said. It was just like her to make such a snotty remark to Nancy, knowing how it would burn her up.

Not that Nancy ever tried to hide the way she felt about Philip Ames. Why should she? After all, she was sixteen, she had a mind of her own. And Philip Ames was really something.

Nancy always liked tall men, and Philip Ames was positively statuesque. He had such luscious black hair and dark eyes and his skin was so white. That came from not getting any sun at the lake. She wondered how he would look in bathing trunks and if he would spend much time with her folks again

61

this year. He was very friendly with them the last season. He seemed to like Ralph—but then, everybody liked her Dad. And Laura was glad to have company.

Of course, if her mother even suspected how Nancy felt about the man she would be positively furious. But she needn't know, yet. Not unless that Hedy Schuster gave it away, and she'd better not or Nancy would kill her.

Hedy knew some boys around the other side of the lake who had a roadster, and she wanted Nancy to double-date some night, but the first few evenings Nancy stayed at the cottage. Of course she was hoping Philip Ames would come over, and she dressed very carefully; no bobbysocks or kid stuff, only her best slacks and one of those luscious sweaters Laura bought for her at Saks. Those sweaters really did something for her, and it was about time Mr. Philip Ames found it out.

But he didn't come over and he didn't come over, and it was almost a week now and Nancy was going stark raving goony because Hedy kept telling her what she was missing not coming along.

And then, Philip Ames came over. He was even better than she'd remembered—she'd forgotten all about that deep voice of his. A real man's voice, and he didn't laugh all the time like those repulsive young icks Hedy was so excited about. He really was reserved; you could tell he was deep. He was glad to see Ralph and Laura, but he didn't smile.

Then Laura said, "You remember our Nancy, don't you, Phil?" and he looked at her and nodded and then he just looked.

Honestly, it just sent shivers through her. You'd think she was a mere infant, standing there and trying to keep from blushing. But he didn't seem to notice that. He noticed other things, though, because when they all went out on the porch and sat down, he sat next to her and asked her all sorts of questions.

It wasn't that he was trying to be polite. Nancy could tell the difference. For the first time he was looking at her as a woman; she knew it. And she would never forget it, never. Some day they would both remember this moment together. Some day—

Ralph and Laura kept interrupting Philip with questions about his thesis. He said it was coming along and he hoped to finish it this summer. Then Ralph insisted on telling him about his old construction job, and Nancy knew he was just enduring it all. He wasn't really interested a bit.

Philip asked her why she didn't have much of a tan, and she said she wasn't going out much these days.

"I don't know what's gotten into her," Laura butted in. "She just mopes around the cottage all day, reading. I wish she'd get some fresh air."

"Oh, Mother!" Nancy said. You'd think Laura was talking about a ten-year-old child or something.

"I don't get out very much myself these days," Philip said, rescuing her. "We serious students have to stick together. What say we go for a hike tomorrow evening? Like to see what's going on at the pavilion across the lake, Nancy?"

Would she? Imagine showing up with Philip when Hedy Schuster and her crowd was around. Why it would be—

"No objection, I hope?" Philip was asking Ralph and Laura now and it was OK, of course.

"All right, young lady. See you about eight, then."

That was all that mattered. Of course Ralph had to kid her later about her new boyfriend, and the next afternoon Laura made her promise on her bended knees that she'd be back before eleven. "After all, we don't really know very much about Mr. Ames. He seems like a very fine young man, but—"

"Please, Mother! I hope you don't tell me about the bees and flowers."

Laura looked just a little bit shocked, but she didn't say any more, and Nancy went back to work on her hair.

She scarcely took time out for supper because the upsweep was so difficult. Her hair wasn't really long enough for an upsweep yet, but it added years to her appearance and it was worth it. After all, Philip was older. Twenty-seven? Twenty-eight? Certainly not thirty. Maybe she could ask him tonight. Or in a couple of nights. Because there would be other nights. The whole summer was ahead of them. Their summer.

At quarter to eight, Nancy was out on the porch, waiting. It would be just childish to pull that old gag about not being ready yet. Philip didn't deserve such treatment. So she was all ready when he came up the path.

"Good evening, my dear."

Yes. He said it. "My dear." Nancy was glad he couldn't see her face plainly in the shadows. The sun was just setting.

She started down the path to join him. "I'm all ready," she said.

Philip sort of backed away and looked down.

"I—I'm sorry," he mumbled. "Came around to tell you I couldn't make it tonight. Something came up all of a sudden—"

"Oh!"

"I hope you understand—"

Why did he keep backing away from her? What was the matter?

"Well, I'll have to be running along now. Some other time, perhaps."

Nancy just stood there with her mouth open. It was a brush-off, all right. Who did he think he was, anyway? Was he crazy?

She wanted to say something but couldn't seem to think. It made her so mad she almost cried. The tears came into her eyes and she saw Philip sort of swimming away from her. The moon was just rising over the lake now, cutting the darkness. Philip was disappearing down the path.

All at once he was gone, and then she noticed this thing flying low, along the trees. It squeaked at her and came for her head.

It came straight from where Philip had been standing, and when it got close she could smell it, all rubbery, and see its little red glaring eyes.

It was a black bat.

Nancy didn't scream. She didn't make a sound, just ran straight into the house and up to the bedroom. She didn't begin to cry until she had her mouth biting into the pillow.

Laura was really swell about the whole thing. She didn't say a word. She pretended she never even noticed. Nancy would have died if she did.

Besides, what was there to say?

The brush-off wasn't so bad. Nancy got over that. But when she was lying there in bed, in the middle of the night, she got the other idea. And you wouldn't even dare whisper about things like that.

But it had to be that way. He couldn't have just stood her up on the spur of the moment. He wanted to be with her.

Oh, she was being silly. Frightened of a bat. Just because Philip Ames lived up there all year and nobody saw him in the daytime and he broke a date when the moon came up and all at once this bat—

Maybe somebody would know something. That old woman of a Mr. Prentiss down at the store. Of course you couldn't come right out and ask him that.

Then Nancy thought of a way. The next morning she went down to the store and gave Mr. Prentiss the works.

"We're going to have Mr. Ames over for dinner this week and Mother wanted to find out if there's something special he might like—you know, some kind of canned stuff—"

Mr. Prentiss said it, then. She knew he would.

"He don't trade here at all. Never seen him in my place."

Yes. Philip Ames lived here all the year round, but he never came out in the daytime. Never. And he never bought any food. Never. And it was a lie about having him over for dinner because come to think of it, Nancy had never seen him eat anything.

That proved it.

But—she had to be sure. Weren't there other tests?

In the afternoon Nancy made a date with Hedy Schuster to visit the boys across the lake. She was glad, because when she got home after dark, Ralph said he'd met Philip. Philip was coming over tonight for a while.

So Nancy was able to tell him she already had a date and wouldn't be there because she just simply could not break it.

Yes, she was glad. She couldn't face him tonight, after what happened and after—what she thought.

And also, that meant tonight would be a good chance to do what she planned. If Philip was out, she could go to the cottage.

It wasn't easy. Hedy was just ready to blow her top when Nancy broke the date. But she didn't ask any questions, and it was only about nine when Nancy sneaked back past the cottage.

Philip was in there, all right. Nancy went up the path then to his place. It was dark, and there were clouds over the moon. She almost fell flat on her face before she got to the door.

It was locked anyway. But the window was open. Nancy took off the screen and crawled inside.

The cottage was just a cottage. She had a pencil flashlight and held it down low while she looked around. But there was nothing to see. Nothing!

Of course, the bed hadn't been slept in. At least, it was made pretty well for a man. And he didn't have any dishes or stuff. Not even a camp stove in the place. There were suits in the closet and a drawer full of clothes.

It gave Nancy a funny feeling to open his bureau and feel the shirts and socks and stuff, all lying there in stacks. Most of it was brand-new.

There was no mirror above the bureau. There was no mirror in the bathroom, or anywhere else. Of course there wouldn't be, if—

But she had to be sure.

Nancy finally went over to the worktable. There was a typewriter on it, and a big stack of manuscript on one side. Maybe he was writing a thesis, after all.

She ruffled through the pile of papers, looking for the title page. It was there.

SOME NOTES UPON THE EMPIRICAL APPROACH
TO DEMONOLOGY IN THE MODERN WORLD.

Somehow, that shocked her more than anything else. It seemed to all tie in. Demonology. In the modern world, today. He was writing about demons, and—things.

Nancy knew now that she'd have to do something, tell somebody.

Yes. That was it. Tonight, after Philip left, she'd tell Laura. Tell her that Philip didn't eat and there were no mirrors and he was so pale and nobody saw him in the daytime and a bat flew out of the sunset.

Tell her that Philip was . . . a vampire.

Nancy never knew how she managed to get through that night after she told Laura. Laura was afraid she would go into hysterics, until she managed to deadpan. If Laura wanted to take it that way, let her. Some people are just too superior for their own good.

But Nancy wouldn't stop now. She couldn't. If her own mother acted that way, how could you expect anyone else to — ?

There was only one thing left to do and that was see it through. At least Laura wouldn't say anything — she positively wouldn't dare.

So the next night, when she heard that Philip might drop in again, Nancy excused herself just in time. She waited outside until she saw Philip come up the path. It was cloudy again, but that suited her. Then she headed straight for the cottage down the path.

After she finished there, Nancy came back to their place. Philip was still talking with Laura and Ralph. She could hear him through the window.

"You're afraid of the dark, aren't you?

"Oh, but you are. I know all about you, do you understand? You were afraid of the dark when you were a child. Not because of robbers . . . or thieves . . . or murderers. Children don't think of such things. You were afraid of the dark because of . . . the Bogey Man!

"That's the term your parents used. Bogey Man. One of those smart, sophisticated, grown-up terms, designed to hide the terror behind it. But the terror exists.

"Because, when you were a child, you knew what the Bogey Man looked like. You would see him in your dreams — that black, grinning face with the wicked red eyes. You heard his buzzing voice mumbling to you in sleep, when you had nightmares. And you'd wake up, screaming for your mother.

"Admit it. You did scream, didn't you? And now that you're grown up, you laugh about it. Now you're ashamed of your fear.

"But — you're still afraid. You may have learned to sneer at witchcraft and demonology. You read slick, scientific explanations, dismissing the basic phobias with a psychiatric phrase. Mythology, folklore, primitive ignorance — that's what tales of witches and wizards are, aren't they? There is no Satan, no Hell. Right?

"Yet somehow, you can't keep away from such thoughts. You will buy books about the supernatural and patronize horror movies, and visit spiritualists, and listen to ghost stories, and talk about your dreams, and speculate on the Faust legend. Even though you parrot the arguments you've learned — you can't keep away from the mysteries. And ever so often, you'll find yourself in the darkness with that deep fear; the fear which all bravado and pretending cannot drive from your soul.

"Because you know it's true. There are such things, such forces, such Evil. And . . . the Bogey Man will get you if you don't watch out!"

Philip laughed. "Now — in the face of all that — is it so difficult for you to understand why your daughter might think I'm a vampire?"

They all laughed. But Nancy didn't laugh. She crouched under the window and bit her lip.

Laura had opened her trap, after all. And — to him! Probably blabbed everything; about the food and the bat and all the rest. Now they were having a good time over it.

"Damn them!" she muttered.

Philip had keen ears. She heard him get up and come to the window. There was no use in trying to hide. Nancy walked around to the porch and opened the door.

"Why, hello, my dear."

"Nancy—back so soon?"

They were all grinning at her at once. She couldn't look at them. Philip had a big smile on his face, and for the first time she noticed his teeth. His big, white teeth; the points hidden under his full red lips. That was all she could see—Philip's teeth, gleaming at her.

Nancy made the sign of the cross and ran sobbing into her room.

The next day they had it out.

Laura told her she was acting like a child. She had just embarrassed them to death.

"But why did you have to tell him about it?" Nancy wanted to know.

"Because he asked us."

"Asked you?"

"Yes. Somebody told him you were making inquiries about him at the store."

So that was it. That was why he came up with his long line about the Bogey Man. Oh, he was clever, all right. Making them think she was just pulling some kid stuff. Making them laugh at her.

It was no use talking to Laura at all, after that. She was just waiting to fly off the handle about the whole thing.

"Let's skip it," Nancy said, and went out.

She sat under the trees for a long time that afternoon, just trying to think things out.

After all, she could have made a mistake. There were lots of bats flying around at sunset. A man doesn't have to keep house for himself—he can always eat in restaurants. Maybe he did work all day on his thesis. You don't have to be a vampire to write about demonology. Many people have gleaming white teeth. And nobody had been bitten in the throat, or killed, or stuff like that. . . .

But something was wrong. She felt it. Nancy knew what Laura thought . . . that she was just burned up because Philip had brushed her off on the date. That she had been reading too much silly stuff in books. That she invented the whole thing just to make Philip notice her.

Well—it was true. She did want him to notice her. He was the most attractive man she'd ever met. If only it wasn't true. It couldn't be true. But Philip had no mirrors. . . .

She went on like that for hours. It was getting dark before she pulled herself together. Laura and Ralph would be going ahead with supper by now.

Nancy got up and started along the path near the lake. She had the jitters, all right; the shadows kept jumping around so, and she walked fast.

All at once something moved out of the shadows up ahead. She nearly jumped out of her skin.

"Did I startle you?"

He was standing there.

"Sorry, I didn't mean to frighten you, my dear."

Just standing there, smiling at her.

"But say, I've been up at the house looking for you."

"For—me?"

"Yes. I wanted to talk to you. Let's take a walk, shall we?"

"Oh, I'm sorry. I have a date—"

"Too bad. I was hoping we might get together. You aren't angry with me about the other night, are you?"

"Not at all." Nancy couldn't figure out what the score was. Philip sounded like an ordinary drip, now. Well, she could handle that one.

They kept walking along the path. It was getting darker now, and she wondered if the clouds would lift. Not that she was really frightened, but—

Philip was rubbing his eye.

"What's the matter?"

"Got a speck in my eye, or something. Have you got a mirror in your purse, my dear?"

"A—mirror?"

"Yes. If you please."

Nancy's hands trembled so she nearly dropped the purse. But she got the mirror out and gave it to him.

He looked straight into it and rubbed his eye.

Nancy leaned over his shoulder and saw his reflection. He had a reflection.

She didn't know what she was doing, what she was saying. The words just blurted out. "You—you looked into the mirror!"

Philip smiled and handed the mirror back to her.

"Of course I did. And I found that sprig of hemlock on my doorknob last night, too. The one you put there when you sneaked off before coming into the cottage to make the sign of the cross at me."

"Why—I—"

"Oh, don't look so startled, Nancy! I know all about your ideas. You thought I was a vampire, didn't you?"

She couldn't say a word. She felt as if she would sink right into the ground.

But Philip grinned.

"Just because I work all day and eat in restaurants and walk at night, you wondered about me. My thesis had you puzzled too, didn't it?

"But you're wrong, you know. Vampires wear long black cloaks and during the day they sleep in coffins or grave-earth. You didn't find any cloaks or coffins when you searched my cottage."

"But I—"

"I'm not angry with you, my dear. I just wanted you to get things straight. I wanted you to know that I can touch hemlock and look in mirrors and all the rest."

Nancy looked away. The clouds were lifting from the moon. Like the weight was lifting from her heart.

"I see," she whispered. "I guess you think I'm an awful dope, Philip."

"Not at all." He took her hand. A vampire's hand is cold, but his touch was warm. "I think you're a very lovely girl. You have beautiful hair, Nancy. Did you know that? Look—the moon is rising. Gleaming on your hair. I can see you, now. Nancy—you aren't afraid of me any more?"

"No, Philip. I never was afraid. Not really. I—I guess Laura was right. It was my subconscious."

"Subconscious? Scientific, aren't we?"

"You know. I must have thought up all this vampire stuff just to make you notice me. And besides, vampires are supposed to be tall, dark and handsome—like you—"

Philip held her very close, then.

"You're a very clever little girl, Nancy. Very clever. It's a pity you had to stir up such a fuss over nothing."

"But I didn't mean it, really. And it's all over now. Only Laura and Ralph know."

Philip didn't kiss her yet. He shook his head. "I'm afraid it isn't that simple after all. Like throwing a stone into a pool. Ripples."

"Ripples?"

"Laura and Ralph will talk to people. Make a joke out of it. Laura has, already—she said something to Prentiss. Pretty soon people will start whispering. Wondering. A stranger is always a suspect, Nancy. A reputation is a very flimsy thing. It's no use, my dear. I shall have to clear out of here."

Nancy couldn't believe her ears.

"What do you care?" she whispered. "Let them talk. We'll just laugh at them."

"I'll laugh at them," said Philip. "You won't."

He held her very close and she couldn't see his face. He mumbled against her shoulder.

"Too bad you were such a meddling little fool, Nancy. But I can't let you get away now. It would spoil everything. You've guessed too much."

Nancy pulled away, but he held her. He was very strong.

"Philip! Let me go!"

He kept pulling her closer — closer — there was no escape.

The moonlight was full on his face now, and for the first time Nancy noticed the change.

"Philip — it's true, then! You are a vampire!"

"Oh no, my dear," he whispered. "I'm not a vampire, I'm . . . just a werewolf!"

Frozen Fear

Walter Krass used to cut his fingernails over the kitchen sink.

Ruby would give him hell if she found any nail parings lying around. Ruby was like that. She enjoyed giving him hell in one form or another.

Krass was used to that, after four years of marriage.

But one afternoon he came home early from the office and found that Ruby had gone out. While rummaging around in a bureau drawer, looking for a tobacco pouch, Walter Krass happened to find some old nail parings.

They were imbedded in the body of a little wax doll—a tiny mannikin with a mop of brown hair and a curiously familiar face.

Walter Krass recognized his hair in the doll, and the features had been molded to resemble his own.

Then he knew that Ruby was trying to kill him.

He looked at the little wax figure for a long moment, then dropped it into the drawer again and covered it with a pile of Ruby's handkerchiefs.

Krass padded out of the bedroom and sat down in the parlor. His pudgy little body slumped in the easy chair, and he ran stubby fingers through his sandy brown cowlick.

He felt shocked, but not surprised. Ruby had Cajun blood, and in her hatred of him she would resort to Cajun superstitions. He knew she hated him, of course.

But this attempt on his life was another matter.

It could mean only one thing. Somehow, Ruby had found out about Cynthia.

Yes. She knew. And her reaction was typical. Ruby would never think of a separation, or a divorce. She'd rather kill him.

Krass shrugged. He wasn't worried about wax images, or herb poisons,

71

or any of the childish Cajun methods she might employ. He could destroy dolls and avoid eating unusually flavored foods.

But he couldn't destroy her intention — her purpose. And sooner or later she would abandon her silly beliefs and resort to direct action. A knife, or a bullet. Yes, Ruby would do just that.

Unless —

Unless he acted first.

Suppose he just quietly turned his assets into cash and left town with Cynthia some night?

It was a tempting notion, but of course it wouldn't work. Ruby would find him. She'd put them on his trail; ruin him, ruin Cynthia. She'd make trouble for him as long as she lived.

As long as she lived —

Walter Krass snapped his fingers. They made a curious echoing sound in the room. Like a death rattle.

Ruby's death rattle, for instance. . . .

Ruby was out shopping again the night Walter Krass brought the deep-freeze unit home.

He hauled it over on the trailer and sneaked it down to the cellar. It was hooked up and working by the time she arrived.

Ruby was all set to fix supper, but he suggested she come down to the cellar with him.

"I have a surprise for you," he announced.

Ruby loved surprises.

She lost no time following him down the cellar stairs. For once, she fairly bubbled with high spirits, and it pleased Krass to see her in such good humor.

"Oh Walter, I'm so excited! What can it be?"

Krass gestured and pointed around the cellar. "Take a look, Ruby. Notice anything different?"

Then she saw it.

"Walter! Not really? A deep-freeze unit — just what I've always wanted!"

"Like it?"

"Oh, it's a wonderful surprise, darling!"

Krass stepped back as she bent over the unit. Then he cleared his throat.

"But that's not the real surprise," he said.

"Isn't it?"

"No. I have another surprise for you, Ruby."

"Another one? What is it?"

"This," said Krass.

He gave her the real surprise, then. A poker, in the back of the head.

* * *

It took Krass a long time to do what he had to do—even though the cleaver was sharp. He had a pile of old newspapers and some butcher's paper. It was necessary to make six separate bundles before he could fit Ruby's remains into the freezing compartment of the small unit.

Krass was glad when he finished and put the packages in the deep-freeze. He turned the lock handle and sighed. He had never realized that chopping up a woman's body would be such hard work.

Well, live and learn. . . .

Krass turned and surveyed the cellar. Everything was in order. A bit of mopping had done the trick as far as any stains were concerned. The poker was back in place, the cleaver was tucked away in the corner once more, and the papers disposed of down the drain.

The deep-freeze hummed away, squatting and purring in the gloom like some monstrous beast that has just dined well.

Walter Krass hummed a bit himself as he went upstairs. He was sweating, but merely from exertion—not from fright. Strange. He'd expected fright, shock, revulsion. Instead, there was just a sense of relief. Relief at the thought of escaping Ruby forever; escaping her animal vitality, her overwhelming energy, her frenzied possessiveness which used to assume the proportions of a positive aura.

Well, it was over now. And why should he be afraid? After all, he had a plan, and a good one.

Now it was time to put that plan into action.

Krass went straight to the telephone and called Cynthia.

She answered immediately; she had been waiting for the call.

Their conversation was short but sweet. Krass hung up the receiver knowing that all was well. They were rolling, now.

Early in the morning, Cynthia would be taking the train for Reno. She had papers, photographs, all the necessary items; even some of Ruby's clothes that Krass smuggled out for her. Cynthia had practiced Ruby's mannerisms for hours, just as she concentrated on imitating her handwriting.

It was set. Cynthia, traveling under the name of Mrs. Ruby Krass, would arrive in Reno, establish residence, and obtain a divorce. Exit, Ruby.

And at this end—

All Krass had to do was wait. Wait for the summer to end. Wait for house-heating time. Then, a nice little fire in the furnace, stoked by six packages from the deep-freeze unit.

Exit, Ruby.

That was that. Sell the house, clear out, join Cynthia on the Coast. Everything was neatly wrapped up—just as neatly as those packages downstairs in the deep-freeze.

Krass took a drink on that.

It was too early to go to bed, so he had another. Then a third. After all, it had been a strain. He could admit that to himself, now. He deserved a little relaxation. Another drink, for instance—

That fourth drink brought relaxation. Krass leaned his head back in the armchair. His eyes closed. His mouth opened. Everything was quiet . . . very quiet . . .

Except for the bumping.

The sound seemed to come from the stairs—the cellar stairs. The noise didn't resemble footsteps at all; just a bumping. Something was flopping and thudding, and then it was rolling, rolling closer and closer.

Ruby's head rolled into the room.

Just her head.

It stopped about a yard away from where Krass was slouching in his chair. He could have stretched out his leg and touched the upturned face with his foot, if he wanted to.

He didn't want to.

The face glared at him, and then the lips parted. Lips don't part when the head is severed—but then, severed heads don't roll, either.

But here it was. And the lips were parted.

Krass heard her whispering.

"Can you hear me, Walter? You think I'm dead, don't you? You think you killed me and locked me away, forever. Well, you're wrong, Walter. You couldn't kill me. You couldn't lock me away.

"Oh, you killed my body all right, and locked that away. But you couldn't kill my hate. You can't lock my hatred away. It will seek you out, Walter—seek you out and destroy you!"

She was talking nonsense, melodramatic nonsense. Yes, the head of the dead woman was talking nonsense, all right. But Krass listened, anyway.

He listened as Ruby's voice told him everything. All about his plans with Cynthia. All about her trip, and the divorce, and selling the house, and going away. She knew everything, it seemed.

"You meant to keep my body in the deep-freeze until fall, until you could build a fire in the furnace and burn it. That was a clever idea of yours, Walter.

"But it won't work. Because I'm not staying in that deep-freeze. My hatred won't let me. We Cajuns know how to hate, Walter. And we know how to kill—even from beyond the grave!

"You don't dare run away from this house and leave my body here. And you don't dare to build a fire until fall comes. It would arouse suspicion.

"So you're trapped here, Walter. Trapped, do you hear?"

Walter Krass didn't hear. The words were lost in the sound of his own gasping. It was the gasping that caused him to awake.

The minute he opened his eyes he knew it was a dream. There was nobody there with him—no head staring up.

But he had to be sure, quite sure.

That was why he went back down into the cellar. He cursed himself for a drunken, overimaginative fool the minute he switched on the light down there. Naturally, everything was all right.

The deep-freeze hummed its merry little song over in the corner. The lock was still set.

Just out of curiosity, Krass turned the lock handle and slid the door back.

A wave of cold air hit his face as he bent and examined the packages. Nothing was missing, of course. All six of the bundles were still there.

Except that the big package . . . the round package . . . the one Krass had put on the bottom . . . was now on top!

Krass got out of the cellar, fast, but not until he made sure that the deep-freeze was securely locked once more.

By the time he got upstairs again he knew it was just a mistake. It had to be. It was just a nightmare—the voice of his own conscience.

The next morning Krass felt all right again. He phoned Cynthia's apartment. No answer. That was good—it meant she had really left for Reno. Things would work out now, if only he kept his nerve.

He put down the telephone and went out to the kitchen to make breakfast.

It was then that he saw it, lying on the floor near the cellar steps.

It wasn't much to look at. Just a little strip of butcher's paper—a little bloody strip of butcher's paper that might have come off a bundle of meat!

Krass was a brave man. He didn't gasp, or faint, or hide under the bed.

He marched down the steps into the cellar and opened the deep freeze unit. He didn't have to unlock it—it was unlocked.

There were only five packages in the unit now.

One of the bundles was missing!

Krass turned away, hanging onto the edge of the deep-freeze for support. He locked it and walked over to the corner to pick up the cleaver.

Then, cleaver in hand, he began to search the cellar.

He didn't even dare admit to himself just what he was looking for. It had been a long, thin package—and he could imagine something crawling around in the cellar shadows like a big white snake. But he couldn't find it.

After a while, Krass went upstairs. He still carried the cleaver, just in case. But it wasn't upstairs. It wasn't anywhere. It was hiding. Yes, hiding.

Sooner or later, he'd fall asleep. Then it would come out. It would slither across the floor, wind around his neck and strangle him.

Yes—it was no dream. Ruby's body was still alive down there; alive and filled with hate.

She was right. Krass couldn't go away, because they'd break in sooner or later and find her there. He couldn't light a fire, either, in midsummer.

So he would have to stay here. That's what she wanted. He would stay here and fall asleep, and then she'd—

No. It mustn't be that way.

Better to take the risk and run away. If he was clever, perhaps they wouldn't find him. Ruby's absence was accounted for by Cynthia, posing as her in Reno.

Maybe if he spread the story of the "divorce" around and said he was leaving to follow Ruby and persuade her to return—that might do the trick. Then he could meet Cynthia there and they'd hide out together. They could go to Mexico, anywhere.

Yes. That was the way. The only way. And he'd better not wait any longer.

"Trapped, do you hear me?"

Well, he wouldn't stay trapped. He'd get out, now.

Krass went upstairs and started packing his suitcase. There was no time for a careful selection—he took what clothes and articles he really needed and let the rest go. He'd travel light and travel fast.

The case held everything he needed, except money. That was in the wall-safe in the dining room he'd converted into a "library."

He lugged his suitcase downstairs to the hall, set it down, and went into the library to get the case. There was about eight hundred dollars in small bills, plus his bonds, insurance policies, and bankbook. He'd stop at the bank on his way to the office. Better think up a good sob story for the bunch down there.

It seemed to him, as he turned the corner, that a shadow scuttled across the floor. But shadows don't scuttle. And shadows don't make a thumping noise. . . .

Walter Krass stared down at his suitcase. It wasn't locked and closed any more. It was open. Open—and unpacked!

His clothing lay littered all over the hall floor.

And from the cellar stairs came the sound of thumping . . . a faint, receding thumping. . . .

Yes. Something was crawling back into the cellar. He couldn't let it get away this time. It could open the windows, it could follow him. But he wouldn't permit it to escape!

Krass ran upstairs to the bedroom. He'd left the cleaver on the bed. This time he'd make a thorough search. First of all, he'd take the rest of the packages out of the deep-freeze and chop them to bits. Then he'd find the missing bundle and give it the same treatment.

Chop everything into little bits. That was the way!

Panting heavily, he ran down the stairs and made for the cellar steps. He shifted the cleaver to his left hand as he clicked on the cellar lightswitch. Now he could see everything down there. Nothing would escape him. Nothing would escape the cleaver.

The deep-freeze unit hummed. The droning seemed to blur into a mocking frenzy of sound as Krass slid the lid open and peered down into the cold depths.

It was empty.

The packages were gone. All the packages were gone!

Krass straightened up. He gripped the handle of the cleaver and whirled around to face the cellar walls.

"I'm not afraid," he shouted. "I know you're down here! But I have the cleaver. Before I leave, I'll find you—and chop you into bits!"

A sharp click put a period to his words.

It was the click of the wall-switch at the head of the stairs. The lights had been turned out!

"Ruby!" he shrieked. "Ruby—you've turned out the lights. But I'll find you! I can still hear you, Ruby!"

It was true. He could hear.

The rustling was all around him. A soft, brittle sound, like the unwrapping of paper from a parcel. From several parcels.

There was a slithering, too, and a thumping.

Krass edged back until he stood against the wall. He whirled the cleaver around in darkness. He began to swing it in a wide arc across the floor at his feet.

But the thudding and bumping went on. It came closer, and closer.

Suddenly Krass began to chop at the floor with his cleaver. He rasped out great racking gouts of laughter as he hacked away at the air.

Something was slithering around behind him. He felt the coldness all over him now . . . the touch of icy fingers, the kiss of frigid lips, the clammy caress of a frozen hand. And then the icy band was tight around his neck.

The scream was cut off. The cleaver clattered to the floor. Krass felt the coldness constricting his windpipe, felt himself falling back into a greater coldness. He fell into the coldness but he didn't know, because everything was freezing, freezing. . . .

It was weeks later when Cynthia was exposed as an impostor in Reno, and almost a month had passed before they actually broke into the Krass residence.

Even after entering the house, it took fifteen minutes of preliminary searching before Lieutenant Lee of the Homicide Squad went down into the cellar.

Another fifteen minutes were spent in frantic conjecture and incredulous surmise.

It was then, and only then, that Lee put through his phone call.

"Hello . . . this Burke? Lee, Homicide. Yes . . . we're at the house now. Found a body in the cellar — locked in a deep-freeze unit.

"No . . . it was a man. Walter Krass.

"His wife? Yeah . . . we found her, all right. Chopped into pieces, lying all around the deep-freeze. All but her right arm.

"Missing? No, it isn't missing. It's on top of the deep freeze. I said, it's on top of the deep-freeze, holding the lock shut.

"I don't know how to tell you this . . . but it almost looks like that arm pushed Walter Krass into the deep-freeze and then — locked him in!"

THE TUNNEL OF LOVE

THE ENTRANCE TO THE TUNNEL had been painted to resemble a woman's mouth, with Cupid's-bow lips bordering it in vivid red. Marco stared into the yawning darkness beyond. A woman's mouth—how often had he dreamed of it, this past winter?

Now he stood before the entrance, stood before the mouth, waiting to be engulfed.

Marco was all alone in the amusement park; none of the other concessionaires had come to inspect their property and put it in working order for the new season. He was all alone, standing before the mouth; the scarlet mouth that beckoned him to come, be swallowed, be devoured.

It would be so easy to run away, clear out and never come back. Maybe when the summer season opened he could sell the concession. He'd tried all winter long, but there'd been no takers, even at a ridiculously low price. Yes, he could sell out and go away, far away. Away from the tunnel, away from the red mouth with its black throat gaping for some human morsels.

But that was nonsense, dream stuff, nightmare. The Tunnel of Love was a good stand, a money maker. A four-months' take was enough to support him for an entire year. And he needed the money, needed it more than ever since he'd married Dolores.

Perhaps he shouldn't have married her, in view of his troubles, but in a way that's just why he had to marry her. He wanted something to cling to, something to shut out the fears that came to him at night. She loved him, and she would never suspect; there was no need for her to suspect if he kept his own head. Everything was going to be all right once the season started. Now all he needed to do was check up on his equipment.

The ticket booth was in good shape; he'd opened it and found no damage through leaking or frost. A good coat of paint would help, and he'd put a new stool inside for Dolores. She'd sell the tickets next season and cut down on his overhead. All he need bother about would be running the boats through; shoving them off and docking them for the benefit of the giggling couples who eagerly tasted the delights of the Tunnel of Love.

Marco had checked the six gondolas stored in the shed behind the boards fronting his concession. All were sound. The treadmill motor was oiled and ready. The water intake and outlet were unrusted. He had dragged one of the flat-bottomed gondolas out and it lay ready for launching once he flooded the channel and started the treadmill operation.

Now he hesitated before the tunnel entrance. This was it. He had to make up his mind, once and for all. Would he . . .

Turning his back deliberately on the jaws of the monster (he had to stop thinking like that, he *had* to!) Marco stepped over and opened the water. It ran down into the channel, a thin brown trickle, a muddy jet, a gushing frothy stream. The tunnel swallowed it. Now the treadmill was obscured; the water rushed into the tunnel full force. It rose as it flowed until the normal depth of three feet was attained. Marco watched it pour into the mouth. The mouth was thirsty. Thirsty for water, thirsty for . . .

Marco closed his eyes. If only he could get rid of that crazy notion about mouths! Funny thing, the exit of the tunnel didn't bother him at all. The exit was just as big, just as black. The water would rush through the entrance, complete the circuit of the tunnel, and emerge on the other side from the exit. It would sweep over the dry treadmill, clean out the dirt and the debris, the accumulation of past months. It would sweep it out clean, bring everything from the tunnel, it was coming now, yes, he could hear it now; he wanted to run, he couldn't look!

But Marco had to look. He had to know. He had to find out what floated on that bubbling, gurgling stream; had to see what bobbed and twisted in the torrent that emerged from the tunnel exit.

The water trickled, eddied, churned, swept out in a raging and majestic tide. Marco knelt in the gutter and stared down at the flow. It would be a hemorrhage, it would be blood, he knew that; but how could it be? Marco stared and saw that it wasn't blood. Nothing emerged from the tunnel but dirty water—dirty water carrying caravels of leaves, a fleet of twigs, a flotilla of old gum-wrappers and cigarette butts. The surface of the water was rainbow-veined with oil and grease. It eddied and mingled once again with the steady flow from the faucets leading back into the tunnel. The level rose to the markings on the side of the treadle-pit.

So the tunnel was empty. Marco sighed gratefully. It had all been a nightmare; his fears were groundless. Now all he needed to do was launch the single gondola and go through the tunnel for an inspection of the lights on his exhibits.

Yes, all he had to do was sail into the waiting mouth, the hungry mouth, the grinning jaws of death—

Marco shrugged, shook his head. No use stalling, he had to go through with it. He'd turn the lights on; he could use the handswitches en route to stop the treadle if needs be. Then he could inspect the cutoff and see if everything was barricaded off. There was nothing to worry about, but he had to be quite *sure*.

He slid the heavy gondola off its truck and into the channel. Holding it with a boat hook, he stooped again and switched on the motor. It chugged. The treadle groaned under the water, and he knew it was moving. The deep, flat-bottomed gondola rested on the moving treadle-struts. Marco let the boat hook fall and stepped into the forward seat of the boat. It began to move forward, move toward the red lips, the black mouth. The entrance of the tunnel loomed.

Marco leaped from the boat with a spastic, convulsive tremor agitating his limbs. Frantically, he switched off the motor and halted the gondola at the lip of the tunnel. He stood there, all panting and perspiration, for a long moment.

Thank God, he'd thought of it in time! He'd almost gone into the tunnel without remembering to turn on the lights. That he could never do, he knew; the lights were necessary. How could he have forgotten? *Why* had he forgotten? Did the tunnel want him to forget? Did it want him to go into the blackness all alone, so that it could . . .

Marco shook his head. Such thoughts were childish. Quite deliberately, he walked into the ticket booth and plugged in the cord controlling the tunnel light circuit. He started the treadle going and jumped into the moving boat, barking his left shin. He was still rubbing the sore spot as the boat glided into darkness.

Quite suddenly Marco was in the tunnel, and he wasn't afraid any more. There was nothing to be afraid of, nothing at all. The boat bumped along slowly, the water gurgled, the treadle groaned. Little blue lights cast a friendly glow at intervals of forty feet—little blue lights behind the glass walls of the small papier-mâché exhibit booths set in the tunnel sides. Here was Romeo and Juliet, here was Antony and Cleopatra, here was Napoleon and Josephine, here was the cutout. . . .

Marco stopped the boat—halted the treadle, rather, by reaching out and pulling the handswitch set near the water's edge in the left wall of the tunnel.

Here was the cutout. . . .

Formerly the tunnel had contained an extra loop; a hundred and twenty feet more of winding channel through which boats had doubled back on an auxiliary treadle. Since November this channel had been cut out, boarded up, sealed up tightly and cemented at the cracks by Marco's frantic fingers.

He had worked until after midnight to do the job, but it was well done. Marco stared at the wall. It had held. Nothing leaked into the cutout, nothing leaked out of it. The air of the tunnel was fetid, but that was merely a natural musty odor soon to be dispelled — just as Marco's fears were dispelled now by the sight of the smooth walled surface.

There was nothing to worry about, nothing at all. Marco started the treadle. The boat swept on. Now he could lean back in his double seat and actually enjoy the ride. The Tunnel of Love would operate again. The bobby-soxers and the college kids, the sailors and the hicks would have their romance, their smooching, their dime's worth of darkness. Yes, Marco would sell darkness for a dime. He lived on darkness. He and Dolores would be together; just like Romeo and Juliet, Antony and Cleopatra, Marco and — but *that* was over.

Marco was actually grinning when the boat glided out into the light of day again.

Dolores saw the grin and thought it was meant for her. She waved from the side of the channel.

"Hello, darling!"

Marco gaped at the tall blonde in the flowered print dress. She waved at him, and as the boat drew up opposite the disembarking point she stooped, stopped the motor, and held out her arms to the man in the gondola. His grin disappeared as he rose.

"What are you doing here?"

"Just thought I'd surprise you. I guessed where you'd be going." Her arms pressed his back.

"Oh." He kissed her without giving or receiving any sensation.

"You aren't mad, are you, darling? After all, I'm your wife — and I'm going to be working here with you, aren't I? I mean, I'd like to see this old tunnel you've been so mysterious about."

Lord, she was a stupid female! Maybe that's why he loved her; because she was stupid, and uncalculating, and loyal. Because she wasn't dark and intense and knowing and hysterical like . . .

"What on earth were you doing?" she asked.

The question threw him off balance. "Why, just going through the tunnel."

"All alone?" Dolores giggled. "What's the sense of taking a boat ride through the Tunnel of Love by yourself? Couldn't you find some girl to keep you company?"

If you only knew, thought Marco, but he didn't say it. He didn't care. "Just inspecting the place," he said. "Seems to be in good shape. Shall we go now?"

"Go?" Dolores pouted. "I want to see, too."

"There's nothing to see."

"Come on, darling—take me through the tunnel, just once. After all, I won't be getting a chance after the season opens."

"But . . ."

She teased his hair with her fingers. "Look, I drove all the way down here just to see. What're you acting so mysterious about? You hiding a body in the tunnel, or something?"

Good Lord, not that, Marco thought. He couldn't allow her to become suspicious.

Not Dolores, of all people.

"You really want to go through?" he murmured. He knew she did, and he knew he had to take her, now. He had to show her that there was nothing to be afraid of, there was nothing in the tunnel at all.

And why couldn't he do just that? There *was* nothing to fear, nothing at all. So—"Come along," said Marco.

He helped her into the boat, holding the gondola steady in the swirling water as he started the treadle. Then he jumped into the seat beside her and cast off. The boat bumped against the sides of the channel and swayed as he sat down. She gasped.

"Be careful or we'll tip!" she squealed.

"Not a chance. This outfit's safe. Besides, the water's only three feet deep at most. You can't get hurt here."

Oh, can't you? Marco wiped his forehead and grimaced as the gondola edged toward the gulping black hole of the Tunnel of Love. He buried his face against her cheek and closed his eyes against the engulfing darkness.

"Gee, honey, isn't it romantic?" Dolores whispered. "I bet you used to envy the fellows who took their girls through here, didn't you? Or did you get girls and go through yourself?"

Marco wished she'd shut up. This kind of talk he didn't like to hear.

"Did you ever take that girl you used to have in the ticket booth in here with you?" Dolores teased. "What was her name—Belle?"

"No," said Marco.

"What did you say happened to her at the end of the season, darling?"

"She ran out on me." Marco kept his head down, his eyes closed. They were in the tunnel now and he could smell the mustiness of it. It smelled like old perfume—stale, cheap perfume. He knew that smell. He pressed his face against Dolores's cheek. She wore scent, but the other smell still came through.

"I never liked her," Dolores was saying. "What kind of a girl was she, Marco? I mean, did you ever . . ."

"No—no!"

"Well, don't snap at me like that! I've never seen you act like this before, Marco."

"Marco." The name echoed through the tunnel. It bounced off the ceiling,

off the walls, off the cutout. It echoed and reechoed, and then it was taken up from far away in a different voice; a softer voice, gurgling through water. *Marco, Marco, Marco,* over and over again until he couldn't stand it.

"Shut up!" yelled Marco.

"Why . . ."

"Not you, Dolores. Her."

"Her? Are you nuts or something? There's nobody but the two of us here in the dark, and . . ."

In the dark? How could that be? The lights were on, he'd left them on. What was she talking about?

Marco opened his eyes. They *were* in the dark. The lights were out. Perhaps a fuse had blown. Perhaps a short circuit.

There was no time to think of possibilities. All Marco knew was the certainty; they were gliding down the dark throat of the tunnel in the dark, nearing the center, nearing the cutout. And the echo, the damned drowned echo, whispered, *"Marco."*

He had to shut it out, he had to talk over it, talk against it. And all at once he was talking, fast and shrill.

"She did it, Dolores, I know she did it. Belle. She's here now, in the tunnel. All winter long I felt her, saw her, heard her in my dreams. Calling to me. Calling to me to come back. She said I'd never be rid of her, you'd never have me, nobody and nothing could take me away from her. And I was a fool—I came back, I let you come with me. Now we're here and she's here. Can't you feel it?"

"Darling." She clung to him in the dark. "You're not well, are you? Because there's nobody here. You understand that, don't you? Belle ran away, remember, you told me yourself. She's not here."

"Oh yes she is!" Marco panted. "She's here, she's been here all along, ever since last season. She died in this tunnel."

Dolores wasn't clinging to him any more. She drew away. The boat rocked and bumped the channel sides. He couldn't see anything in the perfumed blackness, and he had to get her arms around him again. So he talked faster.

"She died here. The night we took a ride together after I closed the concession. The night I told her I was going to marry you, that it was all over between her and me. She jumped out of the boat and tried to take me with her. I guess I fought her.

"Belle was hysterical, you must understand that. She kept saying it over and over again, that I couldn't leave her, that she'd never give me up, never. I tried to pull her back into the boat and she choked me and then she—drowned."

"You killed her!"

"I didn't. It was an accident, suicide, really. I didn't mean to hold her so tight but she was fighting me—it was just suicide. I knew it looked like murder, I knew what would happen if anyone found out. So I buried her, walled her up behind the cutout. And now she's coming back, she won't let me go, what shall I do, Dolores, what can I do?"

"You . . ."

Dolores screamed.

Marco tried to put his arms around her. She moved away, shrieking. The echo shattered the darkness. He lunged at her. The boat rocked and tipped. There was a splash.

"Come back, you fool!" Marco stood up, groping in darkness. Somewhere Dolores was wailing and gurgling. The gondola was empty now. The blackness was spinning round and round, sucking Marco down into it. He felt a bump, knew the boat had stopped. He jumped out into the water. The treadles were slippery with slime. Cold waves lapped about his waist. He tried to find Dolores in the darkness, in the water. No wailing now, no gurgles.

"Dolores!"

No answer. No sound at all. The bumping and the lapping ceased.

"Dolores!"

She hadn't run away. There was nowhere to run to, and he would have heard the splashing. Then she was . . .

His hands found flesh. Wet flesh, floating flesh. She had fallen against the side of the boat, bumped her head. But only a few seconds had passed. Nobody drowns in a few seconds. She had passed out, poor kid.

He dragged her into the boat. Now it moved away, moved through the darkness as he propped her on the seat beside him and put his arm around the clammy, soggy wetness of her dress. Her head lolled on his shoulder as he chafed her wrists.

"There, now. It's all right. Don't you see, darling, it's all right now? I'm not afraid any more. Belle isn't here. There's nothing to worry about. Everything will be all right."

The more he said it, the more he knew it was true. What had he done, frightening the girl half to death? Marco cursed the slowness of the treadles as the boat bumped its way out of the tunnel. The mechanism wasn't working properly. But there was no time to bother about that. He had to bring Dolores around.

He kissed her hair. He kissed her ear. She was still cold. "Come on, honey," he whispered. "Brace up. This is the Tunnel of Love, remember?"

The boat bumped out into the daylight. Marco stared ahead. They were safe now. Safe from the tunnel, safe from Belle. He and Dolores . . .

Dolores.

Marco peered at the prow of the bumping gondola as it creaked over the treadles. He peered at the obstruction floating in its path; floating face upward in the water as if tied to the boat with a red string running from its gashed forehead.

Dolores!

She had fallen in the water when she jumped out of the gondola, fallen and struck her head the way Belle had struck her head. It was Dolores's body that bumped against the front of the boat and retarded its progress. She was dead.

But if that was Dolores out there in the water, then what . . .

Marco turned his head, ever so slowly. For the first time he glanced down at the seat beside him, at what lay cradled in his arms.

For the first time Marco saw what he had been kissing . . .

. . . the boat glided back into the Tunnel of Love.

THE UNSPEAKABLE BETROTHAL

"Not far thence is the secret garden in which grow like strange flowers the kinds of sleep, so different one from the other . . . the sleep induced by datura, by the multiple extracts of ether, the sleep of belladonna, of opium, of valerian; flowers whose petals remain shut until the day when the predestined visitor shall come and, touching them, bid them open, and for long hours inhale the aroma of their peculiar dreams into a marvelling and bewildered being."

Proust: REMEMBRANCE OF THINGS PAST

AVIS KNEW SHE WASN'T REALLY as sick as Doctor Clegg had said. She was merely bored with living. The death impulse perhaps; then again, it might have been nothing more than her distaste for clever young men who persisted in addressing her as *"O rara Avis."*

She felt better now, though. The fever had settled until it was no more than one of the white blankets which covered her—something she could toss aside with a gesture, if it weren't so pleasant just to burrow into it, to snuggle deeply within its confining warmth.

Avis smiled as she realized the truth; monotony was the one thing that didn't bore her. The sterility of excitement was the really jading routine, after all. This quiet, uneventful feeling of restfulness seemed rich and fertile by comparison. Rich and fertile—creative—womb.

The words linked. Back to the womb. Dark room, warm bed, lying doubled up in the restful, nourishing lethargy of fever. . . .

It wasn't the womb, exactly; she hadn't gone back that far, she knew. But it did remind her of the days when she was a little girl. Just a little girl with big round eyes, mirroring the curiosity that lay behind them. Just a little girl, living all alone in a huge old house, like a fairy princess in an enchanted castle.

Of course her aunt and uncle had lived here too, and it wasn't a really truly castle, and nobody else knew that she was a princess. Except Marvin Mason, that is.

Marvin had lived next door and sometimes he'd come over and play with her. They would come up to her room and look out of the high window — the little round window that bordered on the sky.

Marvin knew that she was a sure enough princess, and he knew that her room was an ivory tower. The window was an enchanted window, and when they stood on a chair and peeked out they could see the world behind the sky.

Sometimes she wasn't quite sure if Marvin Mason honest and truly saw the world beyond the window; maybe he just said he did because he was fond of her.

But he listened very quietly while she told him stories about that world. Sometimes she told him stories she had read in books, and other times she made them up out of her very own head. It was only later that the dreams came, and she told him *those* stories, too.

That is, she always started to, but somehow the words would go wrong. She didn't always know the words for what she saw in those dreams. They were very special dreams; they came only on those nights when Aunt May left the window open, and there was no moon. She would lie in the bed, all curled up in a little ball, and wait for the wind to come through the high, round window. It came quietly, and she would feel it on her forehead and neck, like fingers stroking. Cool, soft fingers, stroking her face; soothing fingers that made her uncurl and stretch out so that the shadows could cover her body.

Even then she slept in the big bed, and the shadows would pour down from the window in a path. She wasn't asleep when the shadows came, so she knew they were real. They came on the breeze, from the window, and covered her up. Maybe it was the shadows that were cool and not the wind; maybe the shadows stroked her hair until she fell asleep.

But she would sleep then, and the dreams always came. They followed the same path as the wind and the shadows; they poured down from the sky, through the window. There were voices she heard but could not understand; colors she saw but could not name; shapes she glimpsed but which never seemed to resemble any figures she found in picture books.

Sometimes the same voices and colors and shapes came again and again, until she learned to recognize them, in a way. There was the deep, buzzing voice that seemed to come from right inside her own head, although she knew it really issued from the black, shiny pyramid thing that had the arms with eyes in it. It didn't look slimy or nasty, and there was nothing to be afraid of—Avis could never understand why Marvin Mason made her shut up when she started telling about those dreams.

But he was only a little boy, and he got scared and ran home to his Mommy. Avis didn't have any Mommy, only Aunt May; but she would never tell Aunt May such things. Besides, why should she? The dreams didn't frighten her, and they were so very real and interesting. Sometimes, on gray, rainy days when there was nothing to do but play with dolls or cut out pictures to paste in her album, she wished that night would hurry up and come; then she could dream and make everything real again.

She got so she liked to stay in bed, and would pretend to have a cold so she didn't have to go to school. Avis would look up at the window and wait for the dreams to come—but they never came in the daytime; only at night.

Often she wondered what it was like *up there.*

The dreams must come from the sky; she knew that. The voices and shapes *lived* way up, somewhere beyond the window. Aunt May said that dreams came from tummy aches, but she knew that wasn't so.

Aunt May was always worried about tummy aches, and she scolded Avis for not going outside to play; she said she was getting pale and puny.

But Avis felt fine, and she had her secret to think of. Now she scarcely ever saw Marvin Mason any more, and she didn't bother to read. It wasn't much fun to pretend she was a princess, either. Because the dreams were ever so much more real, and she could talk to the voices and ask them to take her with them when they went away.

She got so she could almost understand what they were saying. The shiny thing that just hung through the window now—the one that looked like it had so much more to it she couldn't see—it made music inside her head that she recognized. Not a real tune; more like words in a rhyme. In her dreams she asked it to take her away. She would crawl up on its back and let it fly with her up over the stars. That was funny, asking it to fly; but she knew that the part beyond the window had wings. Wings as big as the world.

She begged and pleaded, but the voices made her understand that they couldn't take little girls back with them. That is, not entirely. Because it was too cold and too far, and something would change her.

She said she didn't care how she changed; she wanted to go. She would let them do anything they wanted if only they would take her. It would be nice to be able to talk to them all the time and feel that cool softness; to dream forever.

One night they came to her and there were more things than she had ever seen before. They hung through the window and in the air all over the room—they were so funny, some of them; you could see through them and sometimes one was partly inside another. She knew she giggled in her sleep, but she couldn't help it. Then she was quiet and listening to them.

They told her it was all right. They would carry her away. Only she mustn't tell anyone and she mustn't be frightened; they would come for her soon. They couldn't take her as she was, and she must be willing to change.

Avis said yes, and they all hummed a sort of music together and went away.

The next morning Avis was really and truly sick and didn't want to get up. She could hardly breathe, she was so warm — and when Aunt May brought in a tray she wouldn't eat a bite.

That night she didn't dream. Her head ached, and she tossed all night long. But there was a moon out, so the dreams couldn't get through anyway. She knew they would come back when the moon was gone again, so she waited. Besides, she hurt so that she really didn't care. She had to feel better before she was ready to go anywhere.

The next day Doctor Clegg came to see her. Doctor Clegg was a good friend of Aunt May's and he was always visiting her because he was her guardian.

Doctor Clegg held her hand and asked her what seemed to be the matter with his young lady today?

Avis was too smart to say anything, and besides there was a shiny thing in her mouth. Doctor Clegg took it out and looked at it and shook his head. After a while he went away and then Aunt May and Uncle Roscoe came in. They made her swallow some medicine that tasted just awful.

By that time it was getting dark and there was a storm coming outside. Avis wasn't able to talk much, and when they shut the round window she couldn't ask them to please leave it open tonight because there was no moon and they were coming for her.

But everything kept going round and round, and when Aunt May walked past the bed she seemed to flatten out like a shadow, or one of the things, only she made a loud noise which was really the thunder outside and now she was sleeping really and truly even though she heard the thunder but the thunder wasn't real nothing was real except the things, that was it nothing was real any more but the things.

And they came through the window; it wasn't closed after all because she opened it and she was crawling out high up there where she had never crawled before but it was easy without a body and soon she would have a new body they wanted the old one because they carried it but she didn't care because she didn't need it and now they would carry her *ulnagr Yuggoth Farnomi ilyaa* . . .

That was when Aunt May and Uncle Roscoe found her and pulled her down from the window. They said later she had screamed at the top of her voice, or else she would have gone over without anyone noticing.

After that Doctor Clegg took her away to the hospital where there were no high windows and they came in to see her all night long. The dreams stopped.

When at last she was well enough to go back home, she found that the window was gone, too.

Aunt May and Uncle Roscoe had boarded it up, because she was a somnambulist. She didn't know what a somnambulist was, but guessed it had something to do with her being sick and the dreams not coming any more.

For the dreams stopped, then. There was no way of making them come back, and she really didn't want them any more. It was fun to play outside with Marvin Mason now, and she went back to school when the new semester began.

Now, without the window to look at, she just slept at night. Aunt May and Uncle Roscoe were glad, and Doctor Clegg said she was turning out to be a mighty fine little specimen.

Avis could remember it all now as though it were yesterday or today. Or tomorrow.

How she grew up. How Marvin Mason fell in love with her. How she went to college and they became engaged. How she felt the night Aunt May and Uncle Roscoe were killed in the crash at Leedsville. That was a bad time.

An even worse time was when Marvin had gone away. He was in Service now, overseas. She had stayed on all alone in the house, for it was her house now.

Reba came in days to do the housework, and Doctor Clegg dropped around, even after she turned twenty-one and officially inherited her estate.

He didn't seem to approve of her present mode of living. He asked her several times why she didn't shut up the house and move into a small apartment downtown. He was concerned because she showed no desire to keep up the friendships she had made in college; Avis was curiously reminded of the solicitude he had exhibited during her childhood.

But Avis was no longer a child. She proved that by removing what had always seemed to her a symbol of adult domination; she had the high round window in her room unboarded once more.

It was a silly gesture. She knew it at the time, but somehow it held a curious significance for her. For one thing it reestablished a linkage with her childhood, and more and more childhood came to epitomize happiness for her.

With Marvin Mason gone, and Aunt May and Uncle Roscoe dead, there was little enough to fill the present. Avis would sit up in her bedroom and pore over the scrapbooks she had so assiduously pasted up as a girl. She had kept her dolls and the old fairy tale books; she spent drowsy afternoons examining them.

It was almost possible to lose one's time sense in such pastimes. Here surroundings were unchanged. Of course, Avis was larger now and the bed wasn't quite as massive nor the window as high.

But both were there, waiting for the little girl that she became when, at nightfall, she curled up into a ball and snuggled under the sheets — snuggled and stared up at the high, round window that bordered the sky.

Avis wanted to dream again.

At first, she *couldn't.*

After all, she was a grown woman, engaged to be married; she wasn't a character out of PETER IBBETSON. And those dreams of her childhood had been silly.

But they were *nice.* Yes, even when she had been ill and nearly fallen out of the window that time, it had been pleasant to dream. Of course those voices and shapes were nothing but Freudian fantasies — everyone knew that.

Or did they?

Suppose it were all real? Suppose dreams are not just subconscious manifestations, caused by indigestion and gas pressure?

What if dreams are really a product of electronic impulse — or planetary radiations — attuned to the wavelength of the sleeping mind? Thought is an electrical impulse. Life itself is an electrical impulse. Perhaps a dreamer is like a spiritualist medium; placed in a receptive state during sleep. Instead of ghosts, the creatures of another world or another dimension can come through, if the sleeper is granted the rare gift of acting as a *filter.* What if the dreams feed on the dreamer for substance, just as spirits attain ectoplasmic being by draining the medium of energy?

Avis thought and thought about it, and when she had evolved this theory, everything seemed to fit. Not that she would ever tell anyone about her attitude. Doctor Clegg would only laugh at her, or still worse, shake his head. Marvin Mason didn't approve either. Nobody wanted her to dream. They still treated her like a little girl.

Very well, she would be a little girl; a little girl who could do as she pleased, now. She would dream.

It was shortly after reaching this decision that the dreams began again; almost as though they had been waiting until she would fully accept them in terms of their own reality.

Yes, they came back, slowly, a bit at a time. Avis found that it helped to concentrate on the past during the day; to strive to remember her childhood. To this end she spent more and more time in her room, leaving Reba to tend to housework downstairs. As for fresh air, she always could look out of her window. It was high and small, but she would climb on a stool and gaze up at the sky through the round aperture; watching the clouds that veiled the blue beyond, and waiting for night to come.

Then she would sleep in the big bed and wait for the wind. The wind soothed and the darkness slithered, and soon she could hear the buzzing, blurring voices. At first only the voices came back, and they were faint and far away. Gradually, they increased in intensity and once more she was able to discriminate to recognize individual intonations.

Timidly, hesitantly, the figures reemerged. Each night they grew stronger. Avis Long (little girl with big round eyes in big bed below round window) welcomed their presence.

She wasn't alone any more. No need to see her friends, or talk to that silly old Doctor Clegg. No need to waste much time gossiping with Reba, or fussing over meals. No need to dress or venture out. There was the window by day and the dreams by night.

Then all at once she was curiously weak, and this illness came. But it was all false, somehow; this physical change.

Her mind was untouched. She knew that. No matter how often Doctor Clegg pursed his lips and hinted about calling in a "specialist," she wasn't afraid. Of course Avis knew he really wanted her to see a psychiatrist. The doddering fool was filled with glib patter about "retreat from reality" and "escape mechanisms."

But he didn't understand about the dreams. She wouldn't tell him, either. He'd never know the richness, the fullness, the sense of completion that came from experiencing contact with other worlds.

Avis knew *that* now. The voices and shapes that came in the window were from other worlds. As a naive child she had invited them by her very unsophistication. Now, striving consciously to return to the childlike attitude, she again admitted them.

They were from other worlds; worlds of wonder and splendor. Now they could meet only on the plane of dreams, but someday; someday soon, she would bridge the gap.

They whispered about her body. Something about the trip, making the "change." It couldn't be explained in *their* words. But she trusted them, and after all, a physical change was of slight importance contrasted with the opportunity.

Soon she would be well again, strong again. Strong enough to say "yes." And then they would come for her when the moon was right. Until then, she could strengthen the determination, and the dream.

Avis Long lay in the great bed and basked in the blackness; the blackness that poured palpably through the open window. The shapes filtered down, wriggling through the warps, feeding upon the night; growing, pulsing, encompassing all.

They reassured her about the body but she didn't care and she told them she didn't care because the body was unimportant and yes, she would gladly consider it an exchange if only she could go and she knew she belonged.

Not beyond the rim of the stars but between it and amongst substance dwells that which is blackness in blackness for Yuggoth is only a symbol, no that is wrong there are no symbols for all is reality and only perception is limited *ch'yar ul'nyar shaggornyth . . .*

It is hard for us to make you understand but I do understand *you can not fight it* I will not fight it *they will try to stop you* nothing shall stop me for I belong *yes you belong* will it be soon *yes it will be soon* very soon *yes very soon . . .*

Marvin Mason was unprepared for this sort of reception. Of course, Avis hadn't written, and she wasn't at the station to meet him—but the possibility of her being seriously ill had never occurred to him.

He had come out to the house at once, and it was a shock when Doctor Clegg met him at the door.

The old man's face was grim, and the tenor of his opening remarks still grimmer.

They faced each other in the library downstairs; Mason self-consciously diffident in khaki, the older man a bit too professionally brusque.

"Just what is it, Doctor?" Mason asked.

"I don't know. Slight, recurrent fever. Listlessness. I've checked everything. No TB, no trace of low-grade infection. Her trouble isn't—organic."

"You mean something's wrong with her mind?"

Doctor Clegg slumped into an armchair and lowered his head.

"Mason, I could say many things to you; about the psychosomatic theory of medicine, about the benefits of psychiatry, about—but never mind. It would be sheer hypocrisy.

"I've talked to Avis; rather, I've tried to talk to her. She won't say much, but what she does say disturbs me. Her actions disturb me even more.

"You can guess what I'm driving at, I think, when I tell you that she is leading the life of an eight-year-old girl. The life she *did* lead at that age."

Mason scowled. "Don't tell me she sits in her room again and looks out of that window?"

Dr. Clegg nodded.

"But I thought it was boarded up long ago, because she's a somnambulist and—"

"She had it unboarded, several months ago. And she is not, never was, a somnambulist."

"What do you mean?"

"Avis Long never walked in her sleep. I remember the night she was found on that window's edge; not ledge, for there is no ledge. She was perched on the edge of the open window, already halfway out; a little tyke hanging through a high window.

"But there was no chair beneath her, no ladder. No way for her to climb up. She was simply *there*."

Dr. Clegg looked away before continuing.

"Don't ask me what it means. I can't explain, and I wouldn't want to. I'd have to talk about the things she talks about—the dreams, and the presences that come to her; the presences that want her to go *away*.

"Mason, it's up to you. I can't honestly move to have her committed on the basis of material evidence. Confinement means nothing to *them*; you can't build a wall to keep out dreams.

"But you can love her. You can save her. You can make her well, make her take an interest in reality. Oh, I know it sounds mawkish and stupid, just as the other sounds wild and fantastic.

"Yet, it's true. It's happening right now, to her. She's asleep up in her room at this very moment. She's hearing the voices—I know that much. Let her hear your voice."

Mason walked out of the room and started up the stairs.

"But what do you mean, you can't marry me?"

Mason stared at the huddled figure in the swirl of bedclothes. He tried to avoid the direct stare of Avis Long's curiously childlike eyes; just as he avoided gazing up at the black, ominous aperture of the round window.

"I can't, that's all," Avis answered. Even her voice seemed to hold a childlike quality. The high, piercing tones might well have emanated from the throat of a little girl; a tired little girl, half-asleep and a bit petulant about being abruptly awakened.

"But our plans—your letters—"

"I'm sorry, dear. I can't talk about it. You know I haven't been well. Doctor Clegg is downstairs, he must have told you."

"But you're getting better," Mason pleaded. "You'll be up and around again in a few days."

Avid shook her head. A smile—the secret smile of a naughty child—clung to the corners of her mouth.

"You can't understand, Marvin. You never *could* understand. That's because you belong here." A gesture indicated the room. "I belong somewhere else." Her finger stabbed, unconsciously, toward the window.

Marvin looked at the window now. He couldn't help it. The round black hole that led to nothingness. Or—something. The sky outside was dark, moonless. A cold wind curled about the bed.

"Let me close the window for you, dear," he said, striving to keep his voice even and gentle.

"No."

"But you're ill—you'll catch cold."

"That isn't why you want to close it." Even in accusation, the voice was curiously piping. Avis sat bolt upright and confronted him.

"You're jealous, Marvin. Jealous of me. Jealous of *them*. You would never let me dream. You would never let me go. And I want to go. They're coming for me.

"I know why Doctor Clegg sent you up here. He wants you to persuade me to go away. He'd like to shut me up, just as he wants to shut the window.

He wants to keep me here because he's afraid. You'll all afraid of what lies — out there.

"Well, it's no use. You can't stop me. You can't stop *them!*"

"Take it easy, darling — "

"Never mind. Do you think I care what they do to me, if only I can go? I'm not afraid. I know I can't go as I am now. I know they must alter me.

"There are certain parts they want for reasons of their own. You'd be frightened if I told you. But I'm not afraid. You say I'm sick and insane, don't deny it. Yet I'm healthy enough, sane enough to face them and their world. It's you who are too morbid to endure it all."

Avis Long was wailing now; a thin, high-pitched wail of a little girl in a tantrum.

"You and I are leaving this house tomorrow," Mason said. "We're going away. We'll be married and live happily ever after — in good old storybook style. The trouble with you, young lady, is that you've never had to grow up. All this nonsense about goblins and other worlds — "

Avis screamed.

Mason ignored her.

"Right now I'm going to shut that window," he declared.

Avis continued to scream. The shrill ululation echoed on a sustained note as Mason reached and closed the round pane of glass over the black aperture. The wind resisted his efforts, but he shut the window and secured the latch.

Then her fingers were digging into his throat from the rear, and her scream was pouring down his ear.

"I'll kill you!" she wailed. It was the wail of an enraged child.

But there was nothing of the child, or the invalid, in the strength behind her clawing fingers. He fought her off, panting.

Then, suddenly, Doctor Clegg was in the room. A hypodermic needle flashed and gleamed in an arc of plunging silver.

They carried her back to the bed, tucked her in. The blankets nestled about the weary face of a child in sleep.

The window was closed tightly now.

Everything was in order as the two men turned out the light and tiptoed from the room.

Neither of them said a word until they stood downstairs once again.

Facing the fireplace, Mason sighed.

"Somehow I'll get her out of here tomorrow," he promised. "Perhaps it was too abrupt — my coming back tonight and waking her. I wasn't very tactful.

"But something about her; something about that room, frightened me."

Doctor Clegg lit his pipe. "I know," he said. "That's why I couldn't pretend to you that I completely understand. There's more to it than mere hallucination."

"I'm going to sit up here tonight," Mason continued. "Just in case something might happen."

"She'll sleep," Doctor Clegg assured him. "No need to worry."

"I'll feel better if I stay. I'm beginning to get a theory about all this
talk—other worlds, and changes in her body before a trip. It ties in with the
window, somehow. And it sounds like a fantasy on suicide."

"The death impulse? Perhaps. I should have thought of that possibility.
Dreams foreshadowing death—on second thought, Mason, I may stay with
you. We can make ourselves comfortable here before the fire, I suppose."

Silence settled.

It must have been well after midnight before either of them moved from
their place before the fire.

Then a sharp splinter of sound crashed from above. Before the tinkling
echo died away, both men were on their feet and moving toward the stairway.

There was no further noise from above, and neither of them exchanged a
single word. Only the thud of their running footsteps on the stairs broke the
silence. And as they paused outside Avis Long's room, the silence seemed
to deepen in intensity. It was a silence palpable, complete, accomplished.

Doctor Clegg's hand darted to the doorknob, wrenched it ineffectually.

"Locked!" he muttered. "She must have gotten up and locked it."

Mason scowled.

"The window—do you think she could have—?"

Doctor Clegg refused to meet his glance. Instead he turned and put his
massive shoulder to the door panel. A bulge of muscle ridged his neck.

Then the panel splintered and gave way. Mason reached around and
opened the door from inside.

They entered the darkened room, Dr. Clegg in the lead, fumbling for the
lightswitch. The harsh, electric glare flooded the scene.

It was a tribute to the power of suggestion that both men glanced, not at
the patient in the bed, but at the round window high up on the wall.

Cold night air streamed through a jagged aperture, where the glass had
been shattered, as though by the blow of a gigantic fist.

Fragments of glass littered the floor beneath, but there was no trace of
any missile. And obviously, the glass had been broken from the outer side of
the pane.

"The wind," Mason murmured, weakly, but he could not look at Dr.
Clegg as he spoke. For there was no wind, only the cold, soft breeze that
billowed ever so gently from the nighted sky above. Only the cold, soft
breeze, rustling the curtains and prompting a sarabande of shadows on the
wall; shadows that danced in silence over the great bed in the corner.

The breeze and the silence and the shadows enveloped them as they
stared now at the bed.

Avis Long's head was turned toward them on the pillow. They could see her face quite plainly, and Doctor Clegg realized on the basis of experience what Mason knew instinctively — Avis Long's eyes were closed in death.

But that is not what made Mason gasp and shudder — nor did the sight of death alone cause Doctor Clegg to scream aloud.

There was nothing whatsoever to frighten the beholder of the placid countenance turned toward them in death. They did not scream at the sight of Avis Long's face.

Lying on the pillow of the huge bed, Avis Long's face bore a look of perfect peace.

But Avis Long's body was . . . gone.

TELL YOUR FORTUNE

THE SCALES aren't here any more. Look, Buster, I don't want any trouble. I run a nice quiet little place here, no rough stuff. I'm telling you—the scales aren't here. You must be the twentieth guy this week who come in looking for those scales. But they're gone. Damned good thing, too, if you ask me.

No, I'm not the bouncer. I'm the manager. So help me, I am. If you're looking for Big Pete Mosko, he's gone. Tarelli's gone, too, and the girl.

Didn't you read about it in the papers? I thought everybody knew it by now, but like I said, guys keep coming in. The heat was on here for a month before I bought the place and made the fix. Now I run it strictly on the percentages; I level with the customers. Not like Mosko, with his crooked wheels and the phony cubes. Look the house over. No wires, no gimmicks. You want to make a fast buck at the table, you get your chance. But the sucker stuff is out. And I wouldn't be caught dead with those scales in here, after what has happened.

No, I don't think you're nosy. I'll take that drink, sure. Might as well tell you about it. Like I say, it was in the papers—but only part of it. Screwiest thing you ever heard of. Matter of fact, a guy needs a drink or two if he wants to finish the story.

If you come in here in the old days, then you probably remember Big Pete Mosko all right. Six feet four, three hundred pounds, built like a brick backhouse, with that Polack haircut and the bashed-in nose. Don't like to give anyone the finger, but it looks like Pete Mosko had to be that big to hold all the meanness in him. Kind of a guy they'd have to bury with a corkscrew, too. But a very smart apple.

He come here about three years ago when this pitch was nothing but a combination tavern and bowling alley. A Mom and Pop setup, strictly for

Saturday nights and a beer license. He made this deal with the county boys and tore out the bowling alley. Put in this layout downstairs here and hired a couple of sticks to run tables. Crap games only, at first. A fast operation.

But Mosko was a smart apple, like I say. The suckers come downstairs here and dropped their bundles one-two-three. Mosko, he stayed upstairs in the bar and made like your genial host. Used to sit there in a big chair with a ten-dollar smile plastered all over his ugly mush. Offering everybody drinks on the house when they come up from the cleaners. Let everybody kid him about how fat he was and how ugly he was and how dumb he was. Mosko dumb? Let me tell you, he knew what he was doing.

Way he worked it, he didn't even need to keep a bouncer on the job. Never any strong-arm stuff, even though business got good and some of the Country Club gang used to come out here and drop maybe a G or so at a time on Saturdays. Mosko saw to that. He was the buffer. A guy got a rimming on Mosko's tables, but he never got sore at Mosko. Mosko stayed upstairs and kidded him along.

Show you how smart he was, Mosko played up his fatness. Played it up so he could be ribbed. Did it on purpose — wearing those big baggy suits to make him look even heavier — and putting that free lunch in front of himself when he sat in his chair at the end of the bar. Mosko wasn't really what you call a big eater, but he kept nibbling away at the food all evening, whenever somebody was around to look. Suffered something awful from indigestion, and he used to complain in private, but he put on a good show for the marks.

That's why he got a scale put in the tavern, to begin with. All a part of Mosko's smart act. He used to weigh himself in front of the suckers. Made little bets — fin or a sawbuck — on what he weighed. Lost them on purpose, too, just to make the marks feel good.

But that was an ordinary scale, understand. And Mosko was running an ordinary place, too — until Tarelli came.

Seems like Mosko wasn't happy just to trim suckers on the dice tables. If his appetite for food wasn't so good, he made up for it in his appetite for a fast buck. Anyhow, when he had the bowling alley ripped out downstairs, the carpenters built him a couple of little rooms, way in back. Rooms to live in.

Of course Mosko himself lived upstairs, over the tavern. These rooms weren't for him. They were for any of Mosko's private pals.

He had a lot of private pals. Old buddies from Division Street in Chi. Fraternity brothers from Joliet. Any lamster was a pal of Mosko's when the heat was on — if he had the moola to pay for hiding out in one of those private rooms downstairs. Mosko picked up a nice hunk of pocket money hiding hot items — and I guess he had visitors from all over the country staying a week or a month in his place. Never asked about it; you didn't ask Mosko about such things if you wanted to keep being a good insurance risk.

Anyhow, it was on account of those rooms that Tarelli come here. He was out of Havana—illegal entry, of course—but he wasn't a Cuban. Eyetie, maybe, from the looks of him. Little dark customer with gray hair and big brown eyes, always grinning and mumbling to himself. Funny to see a squirt like him standing next to a big tub of lard like Mosko.

I saw him the day he arrived. I was working for Big Pete Mosko, then, bouncing and keeping the customers quiet. Mosko never talked about his little private deals handling hot characters in the back room, and I clammed up whenever I was with him—it was strictly business between us. But even though I kept my mouth shut, I kept my eyes open, and I saw plenty.

Like I say, I saw Tarelli arrive. He got off the five-spot bus right in front of the tavern, just at twilight. I was out front switching on the neon when he ambled up, tapped me on the shoulder, and said, "Pardon. Can you inform me if this is the establishment of Signor Mosko?"

I gave him a checkup, a fastie. Funny little guy, about the size of a watch charm, wearing a set of checkered threads. He carried a big black suitcase, holding it stiff-armed in a way that made it easy to tell he had a full load. He wasn't wearing a hat, and his gray hair was plastered down on his head with some kind of perfume or tonic on it which smelled like DDT and was probably just as deadly.

"Inside, Buster," I told him.

"Pardon?"

"Mosko's inside. Wait, I'll take you." I steered him toward the door.

"Thank you." He gave me the big grin—full thirty-two-tooth salute— and lugged the keister inside after me, mumbling to himself.

What he could possibly want with Mosko I didn't know, but I wasn't being paid to figure it out. I just led him up to Big Pete behind the bar and pointed. Then I went outside again.

Of course, I couldn't help hearing some stuff through the screen door. Mosko had a voice that could kill horseflies at five hundred feet. He talked and Tarelli mumbled. Something like this:

"Finally made it, huh? Rico fly you in?"

"Mumble-mumble-mumble."

"All set. Where's the cash?"

"Mumble-mumble "

"Okay. Stay as long as you want. Rico tells me you can do a few jobs for me, too."

"Mumble-mumble-mumble."

"Brought your own equipment, eh? That's fine. We'll see how good you are, then. Come on, I'll show you where you'll bunk. But remember, Tarelli —you stay out of sight when customers are here. Don't want you to show your profile to any strangers. Just stick downstairs and do what you're told and we'll get along fine."

That told me all I needed to know, except what Tarelli was going to do for

Big Pete Mosko while he hid out from the fuzz in the basement back rooms. But I found out the rest soon enough.

Couple of days later, I'm downstairs stashing liquor in the storage room and I come back through the crap table layout. First thing I see is a couple of roulette wheels, some big new tables, and little Tarelli.

Tarelli is sitting on an orange crate, right in the middle of the wheels and furniture, and he's having himself a ball. Got a mess of tools laying around, and a heap more in his big black suitcase. He's wiring the undersides of the tables and using instruments on the wheels, squatting on this crate and grinning like a gnome in Santy Claus's workshop. I hear him mumbling to himself, and I figure it's only sociable I should stop by and maybe case the job a little.

He pays me no attention at all, just keeps right on with his wiring, soldering connections and putting some small batteries under the wheels. Even though he grins and mumbles, I can tell when I watch his hands that Tarelli knows what he is doing. The little foreign character is a first-class mechanic.

I watch him slip some weights under the rims of the three roulette wheels and it's easy to see that he's bored holes through them for an electric magnet below the Zero and Double-Zero, and then—*wham!*

Something smacks me in the back of the neck and I hear Big Pete Mosko yelling, "Whaddya think you're doing here? Get out before I break your lousy neck!"

I took the hint and ducked, but I learned something, again. Big Pete Mosko was putting in three crooked roulette wheels, and business was picking up.

Sure enough, less than a week later the tables were installed and ready for action. I kept out of the basement as much as possible, because I could see Mosko didn't want anybody around or asking questions. I made it my business to steer shy of Tarelli, too. There was no sense asking for trouble.

Must have been all of ten days before I saw him again. This was just after the wheels were operating. Mosko brought in two more sharpies to run them, and he was taking them into town one afternoon, leaving me and the day bartender on duty. I went downstairs to clean up, and I swear I wasn't getting my nose dirty. It was Tarelli who started it.

He heard me walking around, and he come out from his room. "Pardon," he said. "Pardon, signor."

"Sure," I said. "What's the pitch?"

"Ees no pitch. Ees only that I weesh to explain that I am sorry I make trouble between you and Signor Mosko."

"You mean when he caught me watching you? That's all right, Tarelli. He loses his cool—I'm used to it. Guess I shouldn't have butted into his business."

"Ees dirty business. Dirty."

I stared at him. He was grinning and nodding, but he wasn't kidding.

"Feelthy!" He grinned harder. "I hate of myself that I do thees for Signor Mosko. For cheating people. Ees feelthy! That I, Antonio Tarelli, would come to such an end—"

"Take it easy, Buster. We all gotta live."

"You call thees living?" He shrugged at me, at the tables, at the cellar, at the whole damned world. "I come to thees country to make a new life. Rico, he tells me I can do good here. Signor Mosko, I pay him the monies, he weel arrange. Ees no good. I am—how you say?—hung up. I must do as Signor Mosko tells. He discovers I am craftsman, he makes me do thees dirty work."

"Why don't you blow out of here, then? I mean, it's none of my business, but why don't you just scram right this afternoon? Even if Mosko plays it below the belt and hollers copper, you can split into town and take a room. Nobody would find you. Lotsa guys in this country on illegal entry; they make out. Like I say, Tarelli, I'm not trying to steer you. But if you don't like crooked dealing, better cut out fast. How about it?"

Tarelli cocked his head up at me and grinned again. Then he squeezed my arm.

"You know sometheeng? I like you. You are honest man."

That was a laugh. But who was I to argue with a dumb foreigner? I just grinned back.

"Look," he mumbled. "Come, I show you why I not leave here right away now."

He took me down to his little room—an ordinary little room, with a rickety old bed, a straight chair, a secondhand dresser, and a dirty rug on the floor. "Come een," he said, and I stepped inside.

I wish somebody had cut my legs off, instead.

Tarelli went to the closet and dragged out his big black suitcase. He opened it up and pulled something out—a little picture, in a frame.

"Look," he said, and I looked.

I wish somebody had torn my eyes out, instead.

"Rosa," he mumbled. "Ees my daughter. Eighteen years. You like?"

I liked, and I said so.

I wish somebody had cut my tongue off, instead.

But I walked into his little room and looked at the girl with the black hair and the black eyes, and I told him she was beautiful and I sat there staring at her and he grinned and he spilled it all out to me. Everything.

I can remember almost every word, just as I can remember almost everything that happened from that afternoon on until the end.

Yeah, I learned a lot. Too much.

Let me boil it down, though. About Tarelli—he wasn't a lamster, in the old country. He was a Professor. Sounds screwy, but the way he pitched it, I knew he was leveling with me. He was a Professor in some big college over there, university, I don't know what they call it. Had to blow during the war, got as far as Cuba, got mixed up in some mess down there, and then met Big Pete Mosko's pal, Rico. Rico got him into this country, which is what he wanted, and now he was looking for a way to latch onto a bundle.

"I am what you call financial embarrass," he said. "Rico, for bringing me here take all I have save up."

This I could understand. Any pal of Big Pete Mosko would be apt to be like that. A grabber.

"So now I work. Mosko employs the physicist, the most eminent of metaphysicians, to — rig, they say it? — games of chance. Ha! But I weel do anytheeng to earn money, to have Rosa here."

The deal was all set, I gathered. All Tarelli needed to do was scrape together a G-note and Rico would fetch Rosa on the plane. Easy as *goniffing* candy from a brat.

"So you're saving your pennies, huh?" I said, taking another look at Rosa's picture. "What's Mosko paying you for this machine job?"

"Twenty dollar."

Twenty dollars for a piece of work Mosko would have to pay easy two–three grand for if he got it done by any professional. Twenty dollars for three crooked wheels that would pay off maybe a grand or more a week clear profit. Big-hearted guy, Mister Mosko. And at that rate, Tarelli would have his Rosa over here just in time to collect her old-age pension.

I took another look at Rosa's picture and decided it wasn't fair to make poor old Tarelli wait that long. Matter of fact, I didn't want to wait that long, either.

It wouldn't do much good to tell Tarelli that Mosko was playing him for a sucker. The thing to do was figure an angle, and fast.

I put Rosa's picture away. "We'll work something out," I said. "We got to."

"Thank you," said Tarelli.

Which was a funny thing for him to say, because I was talking to the picture.

I didn't have much time to talk to pictures the next couple weeks. Because Mosko had his roulette wheels operating and the take was good. I kept busy quieting the squawkers, hustling out the phonies, and handling the guys who were sauced up. The two hotshots he hired to handle the wheels kept rolling.

Mosko was busy, too — just sitting in his office and counting the take. Must have been about two–three weeks after the wheels went in that I happened to pass his little private back office when Tarelli went in and gave him a pitch.

I couldn't help but hear what they were saying, because both of them were yelling pretty loud.

"But you promise," Tarelli was saying. "Rosa, she ees all alone. Ees not good for young girl to be alone. She must come here."

"That's your worry. Blow now. I got things to do."

"Theengs to do like counteeng monies? Monies you make from the crooked wheels I feex?"

"Never mind. Get outta here before I lose my temper."

"Ees worth plenty, thees job I do for you. Get Rosa for me. I pay you back. I work long, hard. Anytheeng you say."

"Blow."

"You must do sometheeng. You must!" Tarelli was almost bawling, now. "How you like, I tell somebody about crooked wheels?"

"Listen. One peep outta you and I tell somebody," said Big Pete Mosko. "I tell somebody about a guy who sneaked into this country without a passport. Get me?"

"You would not do thees!"

"Wait and see."

Everything was quiet for a minute. Way I figured it, things would stay quiet. Mosko had Tarelli, but good. If the little guy didn't watch his step, Mosko could turn him over to the Feds. There was nothing anybody could do about it. Except—

"One theeng more—" Tarelli said.

"Blow."

"No. Leesten. Suppose I construct for you something very special?"

"How special?"

"Sometheeng—how can I tell you?—no one ever has before."

"Gambling device?"

"Perhaps."

"Cost money to make?"

"A few pennies."

"New, huh?"

"Special."

"All right, go ahead. We'll see."

"Then you weel send for Rosa?"

"We'll see."

Mosko let it go at that, and I didn't butt in. I was willing to see, too. And in another couple of weeks, I saw.

I was there the morning Tarelli took the wraps off his big secret. It was on a Sunday, and Mosko and the four sharpies who worked his wheels for him were downstairs, divvying up the take from the big Saturday night play.

Me and Al, the bartender, were sitting around in the tavern upstairs all alone, chopping the heads off a couple glasses of beer. There weren't any customers—never were on Sunday—so Al looked kind of surprised when he saw this little truck drive up and stop outside.

"We got company," he said.

"Company? Why, it's Tarelli," I told him.

Sure enough, little Tarelli hopped out of the truck and made some motions to the big lug who was driving it. The lug went around back and then he and Tarelli lifted down a big weighing machine. Before I knew what was happening, they dragged it into the tavern and set it up right in the corner.

"Hey," says Al. "Whatsa big idea?"

"Ees no idea. Ees scales. For weighing," Tarelli said, turning on his grin.

"Who ordered scales around here?"

Al came around the bar and we walked up to the weighing machine.

"I order," Tarelli told him. "I promise Mistair Mosko to find sometheeng wonderful."

"Don't see anything wonderful about a penny scale machine," I said, giving it a fast case.

And there wasn't anything wonderful to see. It was just a regular weighing machine with a round clock face glass front, and a pointer that spun up to four hundred pounds, depending on who stood on it and dropped a penny in the slot. It was made by the Universal Scale Company of Waterville, Indiana, and the decal on the back said, "This machine property of Acme Coin Machine Distributors."

I noticed all this stuff kind of quick, without paying too much attention— but later, I memorized it. Checked up on it, too, when the time came, and it was all true. Just an ordinary weighing machine, made at the factory and rented out to Mosko for ten bucks a month plus 30 percent of the take in pennies.

Oh, one other thing. Besides the big glass front over the dial showing the weight, there was another little hunk of glass and a spinner knob you turned when you dropped your penny. This knob turned about twenty slides up, for fortunetelling. You know, the regular questions you always find on scales. Like, *"Will I marry rich?"* Then when you dropped your penny, out comes a card with a gag answer on it, like, *"No, you won't marry rich. You'll marry Eddie."* Corny stuff. And on top of the machine it said, *"Tell your fortune—1¢. Honest weight, no springs."*

Al and I looked at the scales and the guy driving the truck went away from there. Tarelli kept grinning up at us and at last he said, "How you like?"

"Phooey!" said Al. "Whatsa matter with you, Tarelli? You oughtta know bettern'n to louse up the joint with a penny machine. We got customers come in here to drop a big wad at the tables; you think they gonna fish out pennies to get their weight told?"

"Yeah," I said. "Does Mosko know you ordered this?"

"No," Tarelli answered. "But he find out fast."

"And he'll get sore faster," I told him.

"No he don't. You see."

"I'm gonna hate to see, Tarelli. When Big Pete sees this phony fortune-telling gimmick he'll go through the roof. He thought you were coming through with something big."

"Right. Thees ees of the most wonderful. Wait until I feex."

Tarelli waved at me and went downstairs. Al and I got back to our beers. Every once in a while Al would look over at the big, ugly white scales in the corner and shake his head. Neither of us said anything, though.

In a little while Tarelli come upstairs again. This time he was lugging his suitcase and a big canvas tarp. He set his suitcase down right next to the scales and then he got out a hammer and nailed up the tarp, right across the corner. It hid the scales and it hid Tarelli and his suitcase.

"Hey, now what you up to?" Al yelled.

"No questions. I feex. You cannot see."

"Lissen, you sawed-off little jerk—who you giving orders to around here?" Al hollered.

He got up, but I held his arm. "Take it easy," I said. "Give the little guy a chance. He's doing this for Mosko, remember? Maybe he's got some angle. Look what he did for the wheels."

"All right. But what's the big idea of the tarpaulin?"

"Secret," Tarelli called out. "Nobody must know. Three weeks I work to do. Ees miracle. You see."

We didn't see anything. We didn't even hear much of anything; some banging and clanking around, but not much. I guessed Tarelli was working on the weighing machine with special tools from his suitcase, but I couldn't figure the angle. All I know is he worked on and on, and Al and I kept drinking beers and waiting for Big Pete Mosko to come upstairs and bust up the act.

But Mosko must of been plenty busy counting the take. He didn't show. And the fidgeting went on behind the curtain until Al and I were going screwy trying to figure things out.

"I got it!" Al says, at last. "Sure, I got it. Plain as daylight. Tarelli fixed the wheels downstairs for the big-time marks, diden' he? Well, this is for the little sucker—Mr. Bates, who comes in upstairs for a drink. We work the old routine on him, see? Plant a steerer at the bar, get him into an argument about what he weighs, work him into a bet. Five, ten, twenty bucks. I hold the dough, get it? Then we take him over to the scales. Mr. Bates knows what he weighs, because before the showdown the steerer goes away to wash his hands, and I say to Mr. Bates, 'Quick, hop on the scales before he gets back. Then we'll know what you weigh for sure.' So the chump weighs himself and let's say he weighs 165. The steerer comes back and this time Mr. Bates offers to double or triple the bet. He can't lose, see? So the steerer falls for it and we have Mr. Bates for fifty or a hundred bucks. Then we weigh him official. And of course the scales says 170 or 175 — whatever I want. Because I got my foot down on the pedal that fixes the scales. Get it? A natural!"

Somehow it didn't seem like such a natural to me. In the first place, no Mr. Bates was going to be dumb enough not to see through the routine with the crooked scales, and he'd raise a holy stink about being cleaned. Secondly, Tarelli had promised Mosko something really wonderful. And for some funny reason I had faith in Tarelli. I knew he was working to get Rosa over here — and he'd do anything for her. After seeing her picture, I could understand that. No, I expected Tarelli to come through. A big scientist, physicist or whatever kind of Professor he was in the old country, would do better than fix a weighing machine.

So I waited to see what would happen when Tarelli finished and took the tarp down.

Finally he did, and I saw — exactly nothing. Tarelli ripped down the canvas, carried his bag back downstairs, and left the scales standing there, exactly like before. I know, because Al and I rushed up to look at the machine.

Only two things were changed, and you had to look pretty hard to realize that much. First of all, the little selector knob you could spin to choose your fortunetelling question just didn't spin any more. And second, the small glass-covered opening above it which gave the questions was now blank. Instead of printed questions like, *"Will I marry rich?"* there was now a sort of black disk behind the glass. It kind of moved when you got up close to it, as though it was a mirror, only black.

I know that sounds screwy and it was screwy; but that's the only way I can describe it. It was a little black disk that sort of caught your reflection when you stood on the scales, only of course you can't get a reflection off something dull and black.

But it was as if the scales were *looking at you.*

I hopped up and fished around for a penny. Closer I stood, the more I felt like something or somebody inside the scales was giving me a cold, fishy stare. Yes, and there was, come to think of it, a soft humming noise when I stood on the platform. Deep down humming from inside.

Al went around back and said, "Little jerk opened up the machinery here, all right. Soldered the back on tight again, though. Wonder what he was up to? Coin company's sure gonna squawk when they see this."

I found my penny and got ready to drop it in. I could see my reflection in the big glass dial where the weight pointer was. I had a kind of funny grin, but I guess that came from looking at the black disk below and listening to the humming and wondering about the wonderful thing Tarelli had done.

I held my penny over the slot, and —

Big Pete Mosko come running up the stairs. Tarelli was right behind him, and right behind Tarelli were the four sharpies.

"What's the pitch?" Mosko yelled. "Get off that machine and throw it out of here."

I got off the machine, fast. If I hadn't, Mosko would of knocked me off.

"Wait," Tarelli chattered. "Wait—you see—ees what I promise you. Wonderful."

"Scales!" Mosko grabbed Tarelli by the collar and shook him until his hair flopped all over his face. "What do I need with scales?"

"But they tell fortunes—"

"Tell fortunes?" Mosko began to shake Tarelli until it looked like his hair would be torn right out of his head. "What do I need with phony fortunes?"

"Ees—ees not phony fortunes like you say. That ees the wonderful. The fortunes, they are true!"

"True?"

Mosko was still yelling, but the shaking stopped. He put Tarelli down and stared at him, hard.

Tarelli managed another one of his grins. "Yes, true. You get on machine. You put een penny. Fortune card comes out. Ees really true fortune. Tell your future."

"Malarkey!"

One of the sharpies, character named Don, started to laugh. He was a lanky blond guy with buck teeth, and he looked like a horse. In a minute we were all laughing. All but Tarelli.

"Take it easy, Tarelli," said Don, grinning and sticking out his big yellow teeth. He walked over to the little old man and stood looking down at him. It was funny to see the two of them together; Tarelli in his old overalls, and this sharpie Don in a handsome set of threads that matched the color of his convertible parked outside in the driveway. It was funny, and then it wasn't so funny, because the grin on Don's face was mean, and I knew he was just working up to something nasty.

"Look, Tarelli," Don said, still grinning. "Maybe you're a big scientist back in the University of Boloney or wherever you come from. But for my money, over here, you're just a schmoe, see? And I never heard that any scientist could invent a machine that really reads a person's future." Don reached down and patted Tarelli on the shoulder. "Now you know Mister Mosko here is a busy man," he said. "So if you got anything else to say, spit it out. Then I won't waste any more time before I kick you out in the road."

"Huh!" Mosko grunted. "I got no time for screwballs at all, Don. Telling what's gonna happen to you by science—"

"Ees not science." Tarelli talked real soft and looked at the floor.

"Not science?"

"No. I do anytheeng to get Rosa here, remember, I tell you that? I do what science cannot do. I make pact. Make vow. Make bargain."

"What kind of a bargain? With who?"

"I not say. My business, eh? But eet work. So I can build what I need for machine. Ees not science work here. Ees magic."

"What the —"

Mosko was yelling again, but Tarelli's soft voice cut him right off. "Magic," he repeated. "Black magic. I don' care who you are, what you are. You get on scales. Scales read your soul, your past, see you like you really are. Drop penny, scales tell your fortune. Read your future. Here, try eet — you see."

Then Don cut loose with his horselaugh. Only this time he laughed alone. And when he shut up, Tarelli turned to Mosko again.

"Understan' what I tell you? Thees scale read the future. Tell anybody's fortune. Ees worth much money to have here. You can make beeg business from thees. Now you get Rosa for me?"

"Sure," said Mosko. "I'll get Rosa. If it works. Hey, Tarelli, whyn-cha get on the machine and see if it tells your fortune about Rosa? Maybe it'll say she's coming. Ha!"

Mosko was ribbing him, but Tarelli didn't know it. He turned kind of pale and stepped back.

"Oh no, Meestair Mosko. Not me! I not get on thees machine for any-theeng. Ees black magic. I do it only for Rosa — but I fear."

"Well, what we all wasting time standing around for?" Don snickered. "Tarelli's chicken. Afraid he'll get on the scales and nothing will happen, so we boot him out. Well, I'm not scared. Here, gimme that."

He snatched the penny out of my hand, hopped on the scales, and slid the penny down. I could hear the faint humming, and then when the penny disappeared I could hear the humming a little louder. The black disk on the scales got cloudy for a second. The pointer on the big dial behind the glass swung over to 182. Don stood on the scales, 182 pounds of what the well-dressed man will wear, including his nasty grin.

"So?" he shrugged. "Nothing happens."

There was a click, and a little white card slid out of the slot below the black disk. Don picked it up and read it. He shook his head and passed the card to Mosko and the others. Eventually it got to me.

It was a plain white card with plain lettering on it — but it wasn't regular printing, more like a mimeograph in black ink that was still damp. I read it twice.

WHEN THE BLACK CAT CROSSES
YOUR PATH YOU DIE

That's all it said. The old superstition. Kid stuff.

"Kid stuff!" Don sneered. "Tell you what. This faker musta gummed up the machinery in this scale and put a lot of phony new fortunetelling cards of his own. He's crazy."

Tarelli shook his head. "Please," he said. "You no like me. Well, I no like you, much. But even so, I geev you the warning—watch out for black cats. Scales say black cat going to breeng you death. Watch out."

Don shrugged. "You handle this deal, Mosko," he said. "I got no more time to waste. Heavy date this afternoon."

Mosko nodded at him. "Just make sure you don't get loaded. I need you at the tables tonight."

"I'll be here," Don said, from the doorway. "Unless some mangy alley cat sneaks up and conks me over the head with a club."

For a little while nobody said anything. Tarelli tried to smile at me, but it didn't go over. He tugged at Mosko's sleeve but Mosko ignored him. He stared at Don. We all stared at Don.

We watched him climb into his convertible and back out of the driveway. We watched him give it the gun and he hit the road. We watched him race by toward town. We watched the black cat come out of nowhere and scoot across the highway, watched Don yank the wheel to swerve out of its path, watched the car zoom off to one side toward the ditch, watched it crash into the culvert, then turn a somersault and go rolling over and over and over into the gully.

There was running and yelling and swearing and tugging and hauling, and finally we found all that was left of 182 pounds and a brand-new suit under the weight of that wrecked convertible. We never saw Don's grin again, and we never saw the cat again, either.

But Tarelli pointed at the fortunetelling card and smiled. And that afternoon, Big Pete Mosko phoned Rico to bring Rosa to America.

She arrived on Saturday night. Rico brought her from the plane; big Rico with his waxed mustache and plastered-down hair, with his phony diamond ring and his phony polo coat that told everybody what he was, just as if he had a post office reader pinned to his back.

But I didn't pay any attention to Rico. I was looking at Rosa. There was nothing phony about her black hair, her white skin, her red mouth. There was nothing phony about the way she threw herself into Tarelli's arms, kissing the little man and crying for joy.

It was quite a reunion downstairs in the back room, and even though she paid no attention when she was introduced to me, I felt pretty good about it all. It did something to me just to watch her smiling and laughing, a few minutes later, while she talked to her old man. Al, the bartender, and the sharpies stood around and grinned at each other, too, and I guess they felt the same way I did.

But Big Pete Mosko felt different. He looked at Rosa, too, and he did his share of grinning. But he wasn't grinning at her—he was grinning at something inside himself. Something came alive in Mosko, and I could see it—something that wanted to grab and paw and rip and tear at Rosa.

"It's gonna be nice having you here," he told her. "We gotta get acquainted."

"I must thank you for making this possible," she said, in her soft little voice—the kid spoke good English, grammar and everything, and you could tell she had class. "My father and I are very, very grateful. I don't know how we are going to repay you."

"We'll talk about that later," said Big Pete Mosko, licking his lips and letting his hands curl and uncurl into fists. "But right now you gotta excuse me. Looks like a heavy night for business."

Tarelli and Rosa disappeared into his room, to have supper off a tray Al brought down. Mosko went out to the big downstairs pitch to case the tables for the night's play. Rico hung around for a while, kidding with the wheel operators. I caught him mumbling in the corner and dragged him upstairs for a drink.

That's where Mosko found us a couple minutes later. Rico gave him the office.

"How's about the dough?" he said.

"Sure, sure, just a minute." Mosko hauled out a roll and peeled off a slice for Rico. I saw it—five Cs. And it gave me a bad time to watch Rico take the money because I knew Mosko wouldn't hand out five hundred bucks without getting plenty in return.

And I knew what he wanted in return. Rosa.

"Hey, what's the big idea of this?" Rico asked, pointing over at the scales in the corner.

I didn't say anything, and I wondered if Mosko would spill. All week long the weighing machine had stood there with a sign on it, OUT OF ORDER. Mosko had it lettered the day after Don got killed, and he made sure nobody got their fortune told. Nobody talked about the scales, and I kept wondering if Mosko was going to yank the machine out of the place or use it, or what he had in the back of his head.

But Mosko must of figured Rico was one of the family, seeing as how he flew in illegal immigrants and all, because he told Rico the whole story. There wasn't many around the bar yet that early—our Saturday night players generally got in about ten or so—and Mosko yapped without worrying about listeners.

"So help me, it'sa truth," he told Rico. "Machine'll tell just what's gonna happen to your future. For a stinkin' penny."

Rico laughed.

"Don't give me that con," he said. "Business with Don and the cat was just a whatchacallit—coincidence."

"Yeah? Well, you couldn't get me on those scales for a million bucks, brother," Mosko told him.

"Maybe so. But I'm not scared of any machine in the world," Rico snorted. "Here, watch me."

And he walked over to the scales and dropped a penny. The pointer went up. 177. The black disk gleamed. I heard the humming and the click, and out came the white card. Rico looked at him and grinned. I didn't crack a smile. I was thinking of Don.

But Rico chuckled and handed the card around for all of us to see. It said:

YOU WILL WIN WITH RED

"Good enough," he said, waving the card under Mosko's nose. "Now if I was a sucker, I'd go downstairs and bet this five hundred smackers on one of your crooked wheels, red to win. If I was a superstitious jerk, that is."

Mosko shrugged. "Suit yourself," he said. "Look, customers. I gotta get busy." He walked away.

I got busy myself, then. The marks started to arrive and it looked like a big Saturday night. I didn't get downstairs until after midnight and that was the first time I noticed that Rico must of kidded himself into believing the card after all.

Because he was playing the wheel. And playing it big. A new guy, name of Spencer, had come in to replace Don, and he was handling the house end on this particular setup. A big crowd was standing around the rig, watching Rico place his bets. Rico had a stack of chips a foot high and he was playing them fast.

And winning.

I must of watched him for about fifteen minutes, and during that time he raked in over three Gs, cold. Played odds, played numbers. Played red, and played black, too. Won almost every spin.

Mosko was watching, too. I saw him signal Spencer the time Rico put down a full G in blue chips on black to win. I saw Spencer wink at Mosko. But I saw the wheel stop on black.

Mosko was ready to bust, but what could he do? A crowd of marks was watching, it had to look legit. Three more spins and Rico had about six or seven Gs in chips in front of him. Then Mosko stepped in and took the table away from Spencer.

"See you in my office," he mumbled, and Spencer nodded. He stared at Rico but Rico only smiled and said, "Excuse me, I'm cashing in." Mosko looked at me and said, "Tail him."

Then he shook his head. "Don't get it," he said. He was working the wire now, finding everything in order.

Out of the corner of my eye I saw Rico over at the cashier's window, counting currency and stuffing it into his pocket. Spencer had disappeared. Rico began walking upstairs, his legs scissoring fast. I followed, hefting the brass knucks in my pocket.

Rico went outside. I went outside. He heard my feet behind him of the gravel and turned around.

"Hey," I said. "What's your hurry?"

Rico just laughed. Then he winked. That wink was the last thing I saw before everything exploded.

I went down on the gravel, and I didn't get up for about a minute. Then I was just in time to see the car pull away with Rico waving at me, still laughing. The guy who had sapped me was now at the wheel of the car. I recognized Spencer.

"It's a frame, is it?" Big Pete Mosko had come up from downstairs and was standing behind me, spitting out pieces of his cigar. "If I'da known what those dirty rats would pull on me—he was working with Spencer to trim me—"

"You did know," I reminded him.

"Did I?"

"Sure. Remember what the fortunetelling card said? Told Rico, *you will win with red*, didn't it?"

"But Rico was winning with both colors," Mosko yelled. "It was that dog Spencer who let him win."

"That's what the card said," I told him. "What you and I forget is that 'Red' is Spencer's nickname."

We went back inside because there was nothing else to do—no way of catching Rico or Spencer without rough stuff and Mosko couldn't afford that. Mosko went back to the tables and took the suckers for a couple hours straight, but it didn't make him any happier.

He was still in a lousy temper the next morning when he cut up the week's take. It was probably the worst time in the world to talk to him about anything—and that's, of course, where Tarelli made his mistake.

I was sitting downstairs when Tarelli came in with Rosa and said, "Please, Meestair Mosko."

"Whatcha want?" Mosko would have yelled it if Rosa hadn't been there, looking cool and sweet in a black dress that curved in and out and in again.

"I want to know if Rosa and I, we can go now?"

"Go?"

"Yes. Away from here. Into town, to stay. For Rosa to get job, go to school nights maybe."

"You ain't goin' no place, Tarelli."

"But you have what you weesh, no? I feex machines. I make for you the marvelous scale of fortune, breeng you luck—"

"Luck?" Rosa or no Rosa, Mosko began to yell. He stood up and shoved his purple face right against Tarelli's button nose. "Luck, huh? You and your lousy machine—in one week it kills my best wheel man, and lets another one frame me with Rico for over seven grand! That's the kind of luck you bring me with your magic! You're gonna stick here, Tarelli, like I say, unless you want Uncle Sam on your tail, but fast!"

"Please, Meestair Mosko—you let Rosa go alone, huh?"

"Not on your life!" He grinned, then. "I wouldn't let a nice girl like Rosa go up into town with nobody to protect her. Don't you worry about Rosa, Tarelli. I got plans for her. Lotsa plans."

Mosko turned back to the table and his money. "Now, blow and lemme alone," he said.

They left. I went along, too, because I didn't like to leave Rosa out of my sight now.

"What is this all about, Father?" Rosa asked the question softly as we all three of us sat in Tarelli's little room.

Tarelli looked at me and shrugged.

"Tell her," I said. "You must."

So Tarelli explained about being here illegally and about the phony roulette wheels.

"But the machine—the scales of fortune, what do you mean by this?"

Again Tarelli looked at me. I didn't say anything. He sighed and stared down at the floor. But at last, he told her.

A lot of it I didn't understand. About photoelectric cells and mirrors and a tripping lever he was supposed to have invented. About books with funny names and drawing circles in rooster blood and something called evocations or invocations or whatever they call it. And about a bargain with Sathanas, whoever that is. That must of been the magic part.

I guessed it was, because of the way Rosa acted when she heard it. She turned pale and began to stare and breathe funny, and she stood up and shook Tarelli's shoulders.

"No—you did not do this thing! You couldn't! It is evil, and you know the price—"

"Necromancy, that ees all I can turn to to get you here," Tarelli said. "I do anytheeng for you, Rosa. No cost too much."

"It is evil," Rosa said. "It must not be permitted. I will destroy it."

"But Mosko, he owns the machine now. You cannot—"

"He said himself it brought bad luck. And he will never know. I will replace it with another scale, an ordinary one from the same place you got this. But your secret, the fortunetelling mechanism, must go."

"Rosa," I said, "you can't. He's a dangerous customer. Look, why don't you and your old man scram out of here today? I'll handle Mosko, somehow. He'll be sore, sure, but I'll cool him off. You can hide out in town, and I'll join you later. Please, Rosa, listen to me. I'll do anything for you, that's why I want you to go. Leave Mosko to me."

She smiled, then, and stared up into my eyes. She stood very close and I could smell her hair. Almost she touched me. And then she shook her head. "You are a good man," she said. "It is a brave thing you propose. But I cannot go. Not yet. Not while the machine of evil still exists. It will bring harm into the world, for my father did a wicked thing when he trafficked with darkness to bring it into being. He did it for me, so I am in a way responsible. And I must destroy it."

"But how? When?"

"Tonight," Rosa said. "Tomorrow we will order a new scale brought in. But we must remove the old one tonight."

"Tarelli," I said. "Could you put the regular parts back in this machine if you take out the new stuff?"

"Yes."

"Then that's what we'll do. Too dangerous to try a switch. Just stick the old fortunetelling gimmick back in, maybe we can get by for a while without Mosko noticing. He won't be letting anybody near it now for a while, after what happened."

"Good," said Tarelli. "We find a time."

"Tonight," Rosa repeated. "There must be no more cursed fortunes told."

But she was wrong.

She was wrong about a lot of things. Like Mosko not having any use for the fortunetelling scales, for instance. He lied when he told Tarelli the machine was useless.

I found that out later the same afternoon, when Mosko cornered me upstairs in the bar. He'd been drinking a little and trying to get over his burn about the stolen money.

"I'll get it back," he said. "Got a gold mine here. Bigges' gold mine inna country. Only nobody know it yet but you and me." He laughed, and the bottles rattled behind the bar. "If that dumb guy only could figure it, he'd go crazy."

"Something worked up for the fortunetelling," I needled.

"Sure. Look, now. I get rich customers in here, plenty of 'em. Lay lotsa dough onna line downstairs. Gamblers, plungers, superstitious. You see 'em come in. Rattling lucky charms and rabbit foots and four leaf clovers. Playin' numbers like seven and thirteen on hunches. What you think? Wouldn't they pay plenty for a chance to know what's gonna happen to them tomorrow or next year? Why it's a natural, that's what—I can charge plenty to give 'em a fortune from the scales. Tell you what, I'm gonna have a whole new setup just for this deal. Tomorrow we build a new special room, way in back. I got

a pitch figured out, how to work it. We'll set the scales up tomorrow, lock
the door of the new room, and then we really operate."

I listened and nodded, thinking about how there wasn't going to be any
tomorrow. Just tonight.

I did my part. I kept pouring the drinks into Mosko, and after supper he
had me drive him into town. There wasn't any play on the wheels on Monday,
and Mosko usually hit town on his night off to relax. His idea of relaxation
was a little poker game with the boys from the City Hall—and tonight I was
hot to join him.

We played until almost one, and I kept him interested as long as I could,
knowing that Rosa and Tarelli would be working on the machine back at the
tavern. But it couldn't last forever, and then we were driving back and Big
Pete Mosko was mumbling next to me in the dark.

"Only the beginning, boy," he said. "Gonna make a million off that
scales. Talk about fortunes—I got one when I got hold of Tarelli! A million
smackers and the girl. Hey, watch it!"

I almost drove the car off the road when he mentioned the girl. I wish I
had, now.

"Tarelli's a brainy apple," Mosko mumbled. "Dumb, but brainy—you
know what I mean. I betcha he's got some other cute tricks up his sleeve,
too. Whatcha think? You believe that stuff about magic, or is it just a machine?"

"I don't know," I told him. "I don't know nothing about science, or magic,
either. All I know is, it works. And it gives me the creeps just to think about
it—the scales sort of look at you, size you up, and then give you a payoff.
And it always comes true." I began to pitch, then. "Mosko, that thing's
dangerous. It can make you a lot of trouble. You saw what it did to Don, and
what happened to you when Rico had his fortune told. Why don't you get rid
of it before something else happens? Why don't you let Tarelli and Rosa go
and forget about it?"

"You going soft inna head?" Mosko grabbed my shoulder and I almost
went off the road again. "Leave go of a million bucks and a machine that tells
the truth about the future? Not me, buddy! And I want Tarelli, too. But most
of all I want Rosa. And I'm gonna get her. Soon. Maybe—tonight."

What I wanted to do to Big Pete Mosko would have pinned a murder rap
on me for sure. I had to have time to think, to figure out some other angle.
So I kept driving, kept driving until we pulled up outside the dark entrance
to the tavern.

Everything was quiet, and I couldn't see any light, so I figured whatever
Rosa and Tarelli had done was finished. We got out and Mosko unlocked the
front door. We walked in.

Then everything happened at once.

I heard the clicking noise from the corner. Mosko heard it, too. He yelled and grabbed at something in the dark. I heard a crash, heard Tarelli curse in Italian. Mosko stepped back.

"No, you don't!" he hollered. He had a gun, the gun had a bullet, the bullet had a target.

That's all.

Mosko shot, there was a scream and a thud, and then I got the lights on and I could see.

I could see Tarelli standing there next to the scales. I could see the tools scattered around and I could see the queer-looking hunk of flashing mirrors that must have been Tarelli's secret machinery. I could see the old back of the scales, already screwed into place again.

But I didn't look at these things, and neither did Mosko and neither did Tarelli.

We looked at Rosa, lying on the floor.

Rosa looked back, but she didn't see us, because she had a bullet between her eyes.

"Dead!" Tarelli screamed. "You murdered her!"

Mosko blinked, but he didn't move.

"How was I to know?" he said. "Thought somebody was busting into the place. What's the big idea, anyhow?"

"Ees no idea. You murder her."

Mosko had his angle figured, now. He sneered down at Tarelli. "You're a fine one to talk, you lousy little crook! I caught you in the act, didn't I — tryin' to steal the works, that's what you was doing. Now get busy and put that machinery back into the scales before I blow your brains out."

Tarelli looked at Mosko, then at Rosa. All at once he shrugged and picked the little box of mirrors and flashing disks from the floor. It was small, but from the way he hefted it I could tell it was heavy. When he held it, it hummed and the mirrors began to slide every which way, and it hurt my eyes to look at it.

Tarelli lifted the box full of science, the box full of magic, whatever it was; the box of secrets, the box of the future. Then he smiled at Mosko and opened his arms.

The box smashed to the floor.

There was a crash, and smoke, and a bright light. Then the noise and smoke and light went away, and there was nothing but old Tarelli standing in a little pile of twisted wires and broken glass and tubes.

Mosko raised his gun. Tarelli stared straight into the muzzle and grinned.

"You murder me, too, now, eh? Go 'head, Meestair Mosko. Rosa dead, the fortunetelling machine dead, too, and I do not weesh to stay alive either. Part of me dies with Rosa, and the rest — the rest was machine."

"Machine?" I whispered under my breath, but he heard me.

"Yes. Part of me went to make machine. What you call the soul."

Mosko tightened his finger on the trigger. "Never mind that, you crummy little rat! You can't scare me with none of that phony talk about magic."

"I don't scare you. You are too stupid to un'rstand. But before I die I tell you one theeng more. I tell your fortune. And your fortune is—death. You die, too, Meestair Mosko. You die, too!"

Like a flash Tarelli stooped and grabbed the wrench from the tools at his feet. He lifted it and swung—and then Mosko let him have it. Three slugs in a row.

Tarelli toppled over next to Rosa. I stepped forward. I didn't know what I'd of done next—jumped Mosko, tried to kill him with his own gun. I was in a daze.

Mosko turned around and barked. "Quit staring," he said. "Help me clean up this mess and get rid of them, fast. Or do you wanna get tied in as an accessory for murder?"

That word, *murder*—it stopped me cold. Mosko was right. I'd be in on the deal if they found the bodies. Rosa was dead, Tarelli was dead, the scales and their secret was gone.

So I helped Mosko.

I helped him clean up, and I helped him load the bodies into the car. He didn't ask me to go along with him on the trip, and that was good.

Because it gave me a chance, after he'd gone, to go to the phone and ring up the Sheriff. It gave me a chance to tell the Sheriff and the two deputies the whole story when they came out to the tavern early in the morning. It gave me a chance to see Big Pete Mosko's face when he walked in and found us waiting for him there.

They collared him and accused him and he denied everything. He must of hid the bodies in a good safe place, to pull a front act like that, but he never cracked. He denied everything. My story, the murders, the works.

"Look at him," he told the Sheriff, pointing at me. "He's shakin' like a leaf. Outta his head. Everybody knows he's punchy. Why the guy's off his rocker—spilling a yarn like that! Magic scales that tell your fortune! Ever hear of such a thing? Why that alone ought to show you the guy's slug-nutty."

Funny thing is, I could see him getting to them. The Sheriff and his buddies began to give me a look out of the corner of their eyes.

"First of all," said Mosko, "there never was no such person as Tarelli, and he never had a daughter. Look around—see if you can find anything that looks like we had a fight in here, let alone a double murder. All you'll see is the scales here. The rest this guy made up out of his cracked head."

"About those scales—" the Sheriff began.

Mosko walked over and put his hand on the side of the big glass dial on top of the scales, bold as you please. "Yeah, what about the scales?" he asked. "Look 'em over. Just ordinary scales. See for yourself. Drop a penny, out comes a fortune. Regular stuff. Wait, I'll show you."

We all looked at Mosko as he climbed up the scales and fumbled in his pocket for a penny. I saw the deputies edge closer to me, just waiting for the payoff.

And I gulped. Because I knew the magic was gone. Tarelli had put the regular works back into the scales and it was just an ordinary weighing machine, now. *Honest weight, no springs.* Mosko would dial a fortune and one of the regular printed cards would come out.

We'd hidden the bodies, cleaned up Tarelli's room, removed his clothes, the tools, everything. No evidence left, and nobody would talk except me. And who would believe me, with my crazy guff about a magic scales that told the real future? They'd lock me up in the nuthouse, fast, when Mosko got off the scales with his fortune told for a penny.

I heard the click when the penny dropped. The dial behind the glass went up to 297 pounds. Big fat Mosko turned and grinned at all of us. "You see?" he said.

Then it happened. Maybe he was clumsy, maybe there was oil on the platform, maybe there was a ghost and it pushed him. I don't know. All I know is that Mosko slipped, leaned forward to catch himself, and rammed his head against the glass top.

He gurgled once and went down, with a two-foot razor of glass ripping across his throat. As he fell he tried to smile, and one pudgy hand fumbled at the side of the scales, grabbing out the printed slip that told Big Pete Mosko's fortune.

We had to pry that slip out of his hands—pry it out and read the dead man's future.

Maybe it was just an ordinary scale now, but it told Mosko's fortune, for sure. You figure it out. All I know is what I read, all I know is what Tarelli's scale told Mosko about what was going to happen, and what did happen.

The big white scale stood grinning down on the dead man, and for a minute the cracked and splintered glass sort of fell into a pattern and I had the craziest feeling that I could see Tarelli's face. He was grinning, the scale was grinning, but we didn't grin.

We just pried the little printed slip out of Big Pete Mosko's hand and read his future written there. It was just a single sentence, but it said all there was to be said . . .

YOU ARE GOING ON A LONG JOURNEY

THE HEAD MAN

1

HIS NAME WAS OTTO KRANTZ, and he was the greatest actor in Berlin. And was not Berlin the capital of the entire reasonable world?

He appeared before the public every day in the same drama, in the same role. Now, in 1937, it appeared as though the show might run forever, but no one seemed bored by his performance. And Otto Krantz did his best to keep it this way. He was never satisfied, but continued to rehearse and seek improvements in his part.

Take the matter of costume, for example. Krantz always appeared in evening clothes, but of a very simple cut. This sober garb was a surprising contrast, for many of the minor players wore gaudy uniforms or sought attention by wearing outlandish rags. But Krantz, after much study, realized his modest attire brought him more popular approval than the extravagant outfits of the others.

Again, the other actors were given to impassioned gestures as gaudy as their clothing. They shouted at the audience, they ranted, raved, wept, scowled, went into hysterics.

The spectators were never impressed. They much preferred the business-like approach of Otto Krantz, who said little but acted with the finesse of a master. He never played to the gallery. While on stage, he went through the "business" as if the audience didn't exist. For this reason, Krantz remained the most popular actor in Berlin, playing over and over again the selfsame role in the selfsame Comedy.

The Comedy was entitled *The Third Reich.*

The stage was the platform of the public executioner.

Otto Krantz filled the role of Official Headsman.

Each performance boasted a new supporting cast and a growing audience to cheer the Comedy on.

It was always the same. Every morning Krantz made his grand entrance in the bleak courtyard, instructed the new players in a stage whisper, and graciously conducted them to the center of the platform. With becoming modesty, the great actor allowed each a moment alone in the spotlight in which to receive the tribute of the spectators.

After this, the show proceeded swiftly. Capable assistants did the placing and the binding—but it was Otto Krantz who tested the straps, bowed politely to the military escort, and then raised the bright, shining blade of the headsman's axe from its place in a block of ice.

Then came the glorious moment of climax; the moment that never failed to move both the minor players and the crowd. And when it was over, Otto Krantz lifted the head from the basket and held it up to his applauding audience with an honest smile of workmanlike pride.

This happened not once, but as often as ten or a dozen times in a single morning. Yet Krantz never faltered, never grew tired, never missed a line or a cue.

A sneering Prussian of the old school, the sniveling young son of a lower-class family, a withered *hausfrau* or a rosy-cheeked beauty—all received the same efficient courtesy at the hands of the executioner; hands that grew stained and red with the drops that fell as each head was lifted from the basket.

At the end of the performance, Otto Krantz bowed, retired, and washed his hands like a common laborer. Democratic, was the Official Headsman.

Outside of his public appearances, Krantz led a quiet life. A glass of *schnapps* when work was through, perhaps a little beer to wash down dinner at some humble *bierstube*; a stroll through the street to hear the news, and then home to the big upstairs room near SS District Headquarters. In the evening there might be a Party meeting to attend, or a summons notifying him of tomorrow's labors.

It was a simple existence, for Otto Krantz did not share the hysteria of the times. He served the Reich with no thought of personal pleasure or profit. Let others raise the rabble and bluster in public meetings. In his time, Krantz had cut short a good many of these speakers—cut them short by a neck. These days might bring honors to a wiser head—but many wiser heads fell into his basket.

Krantz was content. A year ago he had been a humble butcher. Since leaving the slaughterhouse for a public post, he had seen enough of the world and its ways, and had met many people. Officially, in the past year, he had met several thousand. Each acquaintance was of painfully short duration, but it was enough.

He had gazed into the faces of the best families of Germany. He had held those faces in his hands—those proud, proud faces that would never smile again. And he knew that the blue-bloods stained his axe with gore as red as that of the lowest thief.

So Krantz was content. Until, gradually, the faces came *too fast*. It was impossible to ignore them any longer. He felt himself becoming interested in them because they passed in such an endless variety before his eyes. For each face masked a secret, each skull held a story. Young, old, pure, debauched, innocent, guilty, foolish, wise, shamed, defiant, cringing, bold—ten a day, twenty a day, they mounted the platform and bent their necks to the yoke of Death.

Who were these people he conducted into eternity? He, a simple butcher, was shaping the destiny of Germany. Shaping it with the axe.

What was the nature of that Destiny?

These faces knew.

Krantz tried to find out. He began to peer more closely at each prisoner in turn. Without realizing it, he gazed deeper into dead eyes, felt the shapes of skulls, traced the texture of hair and skin.

One day after work he entered a bookstall and bought texts on phrenology and physiography. That had been two months ago and now he had gone farther in his speculations.

Now, when work was through, he went home quickly and threw himself down on the bed. With eyes closed he waited for the faces of the day to pass in review.

They came—pallid, noble faces molded in sadness or rage; three thousand death masks, and the end not yet! And with them came a message.

"You, Otto Krantz, are our Master! You are the most powerful man in the Reich. Not Hitler, not Goebbels, not Himmler or the others. You, Otto Krantz, hold the real power of life and death!"

At first, Krantz was afraid of such thoughts. But every day came a dozen new reminders, a dozen new faces to review in darkness, to remember, to relish.

To relish? But of course, it was a pleasure now. To be quiet. To dress in black. To wear a mask. To hide the secret thoughts and then come home to revel alone with three thousand memories!

For weeks now his memories had seemed to center around one particular moment—the moment when he held up the head and gazed into the face. Lately he had been forced to hold himself sternly in check as he did so, lest he betray his excitement. This was the supreme thrill, to hold the heads. If there was only some way to recapture that thrill, that sensation of power, at will! If only he could—

Steal the heads.

No. That was madness. If he were discovered, he would die. And for what? The foolish face of a gaping old wastrel?

Not that. Not a gray old head with a cruel, stupid face. It was not worth the risk. But there were other heads — strange heads of debauchees, golden heads of beautiful ladies that hung before him in dreams. These were worth possessing, worth the risk. To sit in his room and behold forever such symbols of his secret glory — there was a dream!

He must find a way, Krantz decided. It would be necessary to visit the condemned cells nightly, when the lists of execution were given out. Then he could inspect the crop and make his choices. He might make an arrangement with old Fritz, the scavenger who did the burials of all the unclaimed bodies. For a few marks Fritz would do anything. Then Otto Krantz could go home with a burlap bag slung over his shoulder. Nobody would be the wiser.

Krantz thought it all out carefully. He had to be careful, make sure no one suspected, for if they knew they would not understand. They might think he was crazy and shut him away. Then he wouldn't have his axe any more. He wouldn't be able to polish the heavy, gleaming blade every morning before work started. And he couldn't see the heads every day. That must not be permitted to happen.

So he was very careful the next few times he went to work. Nobody who noticed the tall, broad-shouldered man with the close-cropped mustache and bald head would suspect that behind his stern, impassive countenance there lurked a dream.

Even his victims didn't realize it when he stared at their faces each morning. Perhaps the black mask he wore helped to disguise the hideous intensity of his searching stare. It also concealed his disappointment.

For none of these traitors had the face that would satisfy him. None seemed to hold the symbol of power he desired. There was nothing but a succession of commonplace countenances. Krantz was disappointed, but he didn't give up.

He went to Gestapo headquarters one evening late in the week. He passed up the broad stairs and received the salute of the sentinel Troopers with the dignity befitting an official of the Reich. He had no trouble in the outer offices.

The man at the desk chuckled when he heard Krantz make his request.

"You want to see the list for tomorrow? Here, it's ready. Only seven of the swine, for high treason. You can probably do the job with one hand."

Otto Krantz didn't laugh. He spoke again, smoothly. "If you please, I should like to see the prisoners."

"*See* them?"

"Yes."

The man at the desk shrugged. "That is very irregular. I'm afraid you'd have to ask Inspector Grunert for permission."

"But can't you—?"

"One must obey orders, you know. Let me announce you." The desk official buzzed the intercom, spoke briefly and then raised his head. "You may go right in," he said, nodding toward the door behind him.

Krantz forced a rigid smile. He had to go through with this, carry it off. If only he could get permission, it would be easy to make further plans.

As he entered Inspector Grunert's office, the rigid smile became suffused with incredulous delight. For there, sitting on the bench before the Inspector's desk, were the two prisoners he wanted—the answers to his prayers, his dreams.

Otto Krantz stared at them closely, noting with growing pleasure each detail of their faces.

The man was old, for only the old have long white hair. The man was young, for only the young have smooth, delicately pointed features unwrinkled by the years. The man was ageless, for only the ageless have great green glowing eyes that burn upwards from unthinkable recesses of the brain behind.

Then he looked at the other prisoner, the woman.

The woman was a wanton, for only wantons have wildly burnished locks that flow like flame above their brows. The woman was a saint, for only a saint has the white, ecstatic purity of a face transfigured by suffering. The woman was a child, for only a child has eyes that beam in beauty.

"*She is the woman I want,*" droned the voice within Otto Krantz.

He couldn't tear his eyes from them. The long white hair, the long red hair. The slim necks. The greenish glow of their eyes. Father and daughter? Father and daughter of Mystery. Creatures of another world, a world of dreams.

And tomorrow they would become *his* dreams. His to possess. Symbols of his power, the power of the headsman's axe. These were the two he wanted. . . .

"Ah, Krantz, here you are." Smiling, Grunert rose and extended a fleshy palm. "Just in time to meet two future clients." The fat Inspector bowed sardonically in the direction of the prisoners. "Allow me to present Joachim Fulger and his daughter, Eva."

They did not stir. Neither man nor girl looked at Otto Krantz. Their eyes rejected the presence of the Headsman, the Inspector, and the room itself.

Grunert chuckled. "Cool heads, eh?"

"*Wonderful heads,*" purred the voice inside Otto Krantz, but his lips remained closed.

"Yes," continued the Inspector. "One runs across all types in line of duty. Queer fish. Take these two specimens, for example."

"*I'm going to,*" whispered the inner voice.

Grunert could not hear it as he went on. "What do you suppose these two have been doing?" he inquired. "You'll never guess, so I'll tell you. They just signed the confession, in case you don't believe me."

"What?" asked Otto Krantz, knowing it was expected of him.

"Practicing sorcery against the Reich—can you imagine such a thing in this day and age? Sticking pins in images of our *Fuehrer!*"

Grunert scowled reflectively. "Their block leader got wind of it last month. Sounded fantastic, but he checked them just as a matter of routine. Everyone in the neighborhood seemed to know they were queer ones— selling love philtres, telling fortunes, and all that.

"But when the block leader dropped in to pay them a visit—all very pleasant, not in an official capacity or anything—this swine of a magician and his unnatural offspring put an ice pick into his throat!"

The two prisoners did not stir. Inspector Grunert nodded at Krantz and tapped his head significantly. "You see how it is," he shrugged. "They could get the camp or a firing squad. But I decided the sorcery charge was the one to press. Make it high treason, I said. Herr Goebbels is always looking for a story—and here is a good example to set before those who work secretly against the *Fuehrer.*"

He rose and confronted the silent, unblinking pair. "Cool as cucumbers, aren't they? But they cursed enough when we had them brought in, I can tell you! A few days here and they signed the confessions without a murmur.

"Crazy fanatics! Trying to kill men by sticking pins in photographs and dolls. Why, it's barbaric!"

A laugh crawled up out of Joachim Fulger's white throat. The voice that followed it was curiously disturbing.

"Do you hear, Eva, my child? *We* are barbaric, says this barbarian in his murderer's uniform! He sits here in his torture chamber and explains our barbarism to the brutal savage whose axe will shear our heads from our necks tomorrow morning."

Again, the laughter.

Otto Krantz watched it well out of the white throat. The axe would bite there—so—

The girl's voice came now. "We are sorcerers, too, by his standards. But our magic is cleaner than the spells of these madmen with their chanting slogans, their howling worship of ancient gods. Our crime is that we have fought evil with evil, and apparently we have lost.

"But the day will come. Those who take the sword must perish by the sword; those that take whips shall die beneath them, and those who wield the axe will lie beneath it."

The words moved Krantz until he remembered she was possessed; a witch, a lunatic. But she was beautiful. That long white throat—he'd strike it there—

"Let them rave," Grunert chuckled. "But you wanted to see me about something, Krantz?"

"It does not matter. Some other time," muttered the Headsman.

"Very well." Grunert faced the prisoners. "You will meet Krantz again tomorrow morning. Perhaps then he can match your sharp tongues with something sharper. Eh, Otto?"

"Yes," Krantz whispered. He couldn't tear his eyes from them. The long white hair, the long red hair. The slim necks. The greenish glow of their eyes. Creatures from another world, a world of dreams. And tomorrow they would become his dreams. His to possess. Symbols of the power of the axe. These were the heads he wanted. . . .

Abruptly, Otto Krantz turned and stumbled out of the room. He had remembered a duty to perform. A most important duty. He had to get back to his room and begin.

It wasn't until he busied himself at the vital task that Krantz permitted himself to feel the thrill of anticipation again. But then it could no longer be held back, and Otto Krantz grinned in glee as he sat in the darkness of his room and delicately sharpened the headsman's axe.

2

"You want I should let you have the heads from those two bodies and bury the corpses secretly? *Nein!*"

Fritz the scavenger shook his head in bewildered but emphatic denial.

"But nobody has registered to claim the bodies. No one will know if you quicklime them with the heads or not," Krantz wheedled.

"I cannot do this thing," Fritz grumbled.

Otto Krantz smiled.

"Fifty marks in it for you," he whispered.

Fritz blinked. But still he shook his head.

"I can get you extra butter rations," Krantz murmured. "I will talk to the District Leader tomorrow."

Fritz sighed. "I would do it for you without pay," he said. "But I cannot. You see, the Fulgers are not going to be beheaded after all."

"What?" Krantz reacted with a shocked grimace. "But the Inspector himself told me — "

Fritz shrugged. "I have just come from Headquarters. It was decided to drop the sorcery charge as foolish. The murder charge was upheld. They will die early in the morning, before a firing squad. Shot, not beheaded."

Then and only then did Otto Krantz realize how much the possession of those two heads meant to him.

He had come away from his room in the middle of the night, carrying his axe in its velvet case. He had scurried through the streets, his official evening dress gaining him free passage from any SS troopers encountered on the way. He had hurried here to the little room beneath the cell blocks where Fritz the scavenger dwelt. And all the while he had been hugging the thought of what was to come, gloating over the attainment of his goal.

Now the opportunity had slipped away.

With it, something slipped in Otto Krantz's brain. He could feel it, the usurpation of his consciousness by that single pulsing urge. He couldn't define the sensation. He knew only one thing—he must get those heads.

They hung before him in midair, those mocking twin faces. One with long white curls, one with red. They were laughing at his confusion, his dismay, his defeat.

His defeat? Never.

Krantz thought fast, spoke rapidly.

"It is still true that no one has claimed the bodies?"

"Yes, that is so."

"Then after the Fulgers are shot, you will still take them to the lime vats?"

"I suppose."

"Who has signed the papers for execution?"

"No one, of course. You remember. Inspector Grunert always does that when he arrives, first thing in the morning."

Krantz rubbed his hands. "So no orders have actually been issued yet. No firing squad is appointed, no time has been set?"

"That is true."

"Very well, then. Fritz, I offer a hundred marks to you for the heads."

"But there will be no heads, I tell you—they'll be shot."

Krantz smiled. "No they won't! I'm taking the Fulgers out to the yard right now. I'll get the job over with before the official ceremony begins at dawn."

"But the orders—"

"Who will know? I'll tell Grunert I picked up the order along with the rest at his office and took the liberty of assigning a squad to do the job, just to save him the trouble. He'll sign the order afterwards and forget about it. He'll never bother to ask who did the shooting, and since the bodies are unclaimed, you can cart them away."

"The risk, they'll see you do it—"

"No one will see. I shall bring them here myself."

"Here, to my room?"

"I'll tidy it up again for you, my fastidious friend."

"No, I won't permit it. We'll be caught!"

"*Fritz.*"

Krantz's voice was very soft when he uttered the name. But his face was hard. His hands, his butcher's hands, were harder as they closed about the throat of the old scavenger.

Fritz fell back, choking. "Yes—yes—but hurry. It's nearly dawn now."

Krantz hurried.

He picked up the necessary papers in the Inspector's office. He raced down the silent, night-lined halls to the cell blocks, located a blinking guard, and bawled orders to the surprised fellow in convincing tones.

"Where's the escort?" the guard protested.

"Upstairs, waiting," snapped Krantz.

"You're going to take them up alone?"

"You saw the orders. Get the Fulgers for me. At once, *dummkopf!*"

Befuddled, the guard led him to the cell.

"*Raus!*"

The Fulgers were waiting. Yes, they were waiting, and their green eyes gleamed in the murky dawn.

There was no trouble. They preceded Krantz up the stairs without a word. The Headsman followed, slamming the outer door in the guard's face.

"This way," said Otto Krantz. He indicated a door.

Fulger and his daughter obeyed. The outer halls were deserted and Krantz, with a pounding heart, knew that they would reach Fritz's quarters without being seen.

They did.

Fritz had everything in readiness. He'd hauled out an extra block of ice, and the axe was imbedded deeply therein, to keep the edge sharp. He had set up the official block as well. The basket and sawdust were waiting. It was all done in the proper regulation manner, just as it would be outside. He handed Otto Krantz the Headsman's mask.

Krantz donned it.

Joachim and Eva Fulger stood against the wall of the little room under the cell blocks and stared. The old man turned to Krantz.

"But the court decreed that we be shot," he murmured. "Why the axe? And why here, inside? Where are the guards, where are the officials—"

The bony fingers of Otto Krantz raked across his mouth.

"Silence!"

Eva's expression did not change. She merely opened her mouth a trifle and screamed.

Krantz stopped that. Her curls helped. Twisted expertly about her throat, they muffled further outcry.

Fritz had the old man kneeling now. He kicked the block into place.

Krantz drew the axe from the ice.

There was a deathly silence in the little room.

A deathly silence. . . .

"I warn you," murmured Joachim Fulger. "As ye sow, so shall ye reap."

Krantz had a sharp retort for that.

The axe—

3

The nightmare was over. Cleaning the room, hiding the bodies until they were ready for the lime, getting the burlap sack—Fritz tended to all that.

Otto Krantz appeared in the courtyard promptly at dawn, ready for his official duties. Grunert was there, and some others. The seven victims were led out. Krantz labored.

It was all a red blur. He plodded through his task mechanically now, as he had in the slaughterhouse long ago. The significance was gone from the moment. Sheep bleated, sheep died.

He could hardly wait to get home. . . .

Grunert casually inquired about the Fulgers, after the executions were over. Krantz mentioned taking the liberty of arranging for the firing squad on his own authority, then quite indifferently presented the order for signing. Grunert shrugged, signed without reading, and sent it along with the rest for the official files.

It was over, then.

Fritz had his hundred marks in a wallet.

And Otto Krantz—he had his sack. He hugged it to his breast as he sped through the streets toward home. No need to stop for food or drink today. There was a substitute for food and drink in the sack—for here were dreams come true.

Krantz ran the last few blocks, his feet moving in rhythm with his pulsing heart.

When he locked himself in the room, he was almost afraid to look, for a moment.

Suppose they had *changed*?

But they had not changed.

White-haired Joachim and auburn-tressed Eva stared up at him with glowing green eyes. Their faces were set in grimaces of undying hate.

And Krantz stared, stared as Perseus stared into the countenance of Medusa.

He gazed at their Gorgonic grinning and laughed aloud. Someone seeing him right now might think him mad, he reflected. But he was not mad. Not he, Otto Krantz, Official Headsman of the Third Reich. No madman could have been as clever, as cunning, as crafty as he.

These two had been mad. Mad, with their babbling of sorcery and witch-craft. They had not even had the sense to be afraid of death. They had mocked him, ridiculed him, called him a crude barbarian.

Well, perhaps he was a barbarian. A headhunter, maybe. Like those Indians in South America—Jivaros, weren't they? That's what he was, a headhunter!

Krantz laughed.

They had mocked him, so now he mocked them. He talked to the heads for a long time. He flung their words in their teeth. "Those that live by the axe shall perish beneath it," they had said. And, "as ye sow, so shall ye reap."

Krantz told them what he thought of that. He told them a great deal. After a while he no longer realized that he was talking to the dead. The heads seemed to nod and shake in answer to his words. The grins expanded sardonically.

They were laughing at him again!

Krantz grew angry. He shouted at the heads. He shouted so loudly that at first he didn't hear the knocking on his door.

Then, when it rose to thunderous crescendo, he turned.

With a start, he realized it was already dusk. Where had the day gone to? The knocking persisted.

Krantz got out the burlap bag, filled it, and shoved it under his bed. Then he answered the door, straightening his collar and striving to control the trembling of his lips.

"*Lieber Gott*, let me in!"

It was Fritz, the scavenger. He stood quivering in the doorway until Otto Krantz dragged him across the threshold by the scruff of the neck.

"What is it?"

"The Fulgers—their bodies have been claimed by a relative. A cousin, I think. He comes tonight to take them for burial."

"No, he can't do that!"

"But he is, he has received permission. And we shall be found out, and it will mean the axe for us."

Krantz managed to control his voice. He thought fast, frantically. Desperation blossomed into inspiration.

"Where are the bodies now?" he whispered.

"I have them out at the lime pits, behind the walls—near the old quarry."

"And this cousin of the Fulgers will not come for them until late tonight?"

"That is right. He has received permission to bring a hearse and two coffins."

Otto Krantz smiled. "Good. We shall be all right, then. This cousin of the Fulgers will not examine the bodies too closely, I think. He will not even bother to search for bullet wounds."

"But they are headless—"

"Exactly." A smile crept over Krantz's face. Even in the twilight Fritz could see that smile, and he shuddered.

"What is it you will do?"

"Do you remember the last words of Joachim Fulger?" Krantz whispered.

"Yes. As ye sow, so shall ye reap. That's from the Bible isn't it?"

"Exactly." Krantz grinned. "The old fool meant it as a warning. Instead, it will be our salvation."

"But I don't see—"

"Never mind. Go at once to the shop down the street. Purchase five yards of strong catgut and a surgical needle. I will meet you at the lime pits tonight at eight. I'll bring the sack with me. Now do you understand?"

Fritz understood. He was still shuddering as Krantz pushed him out into the hall toward the stairs.

4

It was a grisly ordeal. They worked in darkness, lest a light betray their presence to SS troopers on guard in the pits beyond.

They crouched in the little shed in utter blackness and groped their way about the business in silence. Fortunately, there was no trouble in locating the bodies. Fritz had carefully set them aside for immediate interment.

The rest was up to Krantz. He was no surgeon, but his fingers held a skill born of utter desperation. If he bungled the task, his life was forfeit, and he knew it. He strung the catgut and sewed.

The needle rose and fell, rose and fell, rose and fell in darkness as Otto Krantz pursued his fancywork.

And then it was done—done amidst the shuddering whimpers that rose from Fritz's frantic throat.

But Krantz held his nerve to the last. It was he who added the final touch—binding the high collars about the two white throats and carefully patting the prison shirts into place beneath. His sense of touch served him well in this last gesture of precaution. At last he sighed, signifying that the task was complete.

Fritz wanted to bolt for it then. Krantz whispered that he must wait, must hide by the wall across the way from the shed, until they saw the cousin actually come and take the bodies away. Then and only then would he be certain of their safety.

So they waited, waited until midnight in the darkness. What phantasms it held for Fritz, Otto Krantz could not say. But as he stared into the night he saw the grinning faces of Joachim and Eva Fulger hanging bodiless in midair, their eyes alive with undying mockery.

Krantz pressed his eyelids together, but the faces remained, their leering mouths twisted as though in an effort to speak from beyond the barrier of death.

What were they trying to tell him?

Krantz didn't know. He didn't want to know. The hands which had wielded the surgical needle so expertly now hung limply at his sides as he waited.

Then the hearse came. The cousin, escorted by a guard, went into the little shed. Two mortician's assistants brought the coffins. Krantz held his breath as they disappeared inside the shed.

They were not inside long. Soon they reappeared, carrying the closed coffins. They did not speak, there was no sign of agitation. The coffins were placed inside the hearse and the car drove away.

It was then that Krantz broke and ran, sobbing, from the scene.

He was safe. Everything was over, and he was safe. The heads were back on their bodies.

He got to his room somehow. Perhaps he might snatch a few hours of sleep before dawn. Then he must get up and return to duty as though nothing had happened. But now, to sleep—

But Otto Krantz did not sleep.

The heads were back on their bodies, yet they would not go away. They were waiting for Krantz in his room. He saw them hanging in the shadows, even when he turned on the lights.

They hung there—the head of the old man with the long white hair, and the head of the girl with her flaming curls—and they laughed at Krantz. They laughed at him.

Krantz bared his teeth.

Let them laugh! He was Otto Krantz, Headsman of the Reich. Krantz, the executioner, whom all men feared.

He had outsmarted them after all. Now they would be buried away in a grave and no one would ever know that Krantz had murdered them.

Krantz told them this in whispers, and they nodded to each other, sharing secrets. But Krantz did not mind. He was no longer afraid.

He almost welcomed the coming of dawn in this changed mood. He donned his immaculate evening dress carefully. He brushed his stiff collar into place before the bureau. The heads laughed at him over his shoulder in the mirror, but he didn't care about that now.

He swaggered through the street on his way to Headquarters, cradling the axe in its case against his brawny chest. A passing guard drew stiffly to attention as Krantz marched by.

Krantz laughed. There—wasn't that proof of his importance, his cleverness? Let the heads understand that he was a man of position, of power.

Otto Krantz knew he had nothing to fear. He would go about his duties today without question. He squared his shoulders and marched up the steps, into the outer office. He wasn't worried. He knew no one else could see the heads but himself.

He smiled at the man behind the desk. That was the way—brazen it out!

"I'd like to see Inspector Grunert, please. About today's orders. Is he here yet?"

"The Inspector left word for you to go right in."

There. The Inspector was waiting for him! That's the kind of a man Otto Krantz was. Inspectors waited for his arrival.

He smiled derisively at the heads.

Then he strutted into Inspector Grunert's office.

The Inspector *was* waiting.

Krantz realized that just as soon as the two Gestapo men stepped from behind the door and pinned his arms close to his sides. They took the axe, they held him tightly, he could not struggle, he could only gape, he could only pant, he could only listen to what Grunert was saying.

"Otto Krantz, I arrest you in the name of the Third Reich, for the murder of Joachim and Eva Fulger."

But what was he talking about? The Fulgers were in their graves by now, buried.

No—they weren't.

The Inspector was pulling the sheet from the table over in the corner.

And Otto Krantz stared. He saw the heads again, and this time everyone could see them. They were grinning up at him now from over the tops of the sheets.

Somehow he dragged his captors forward with him. He bent over the bodies. He wanted to know how, know why they had been discovered.

They looked all right. The heads had been sewed on tightly. Perfectly. The high collars were still in place. Nothing was wrong with his work, nothing looked suspicious. Why, the collars hadn't even been pulled back to disclose any of the sewing!

Then what was wrong?

Krantz gazed at the still bodies, trying to read the secret. He didn't hear any of Inspector Grunert's mumblings about madmen, about murder. He was trying to remember what had happened.

"As ye sow," the old man had warned. "As ye sow—"

Then Otto Krantz's gaze traveled up again to the heads of the dead wizard and his daughter. He screamed, once.

"Too bad you didn't have any light to work with in that shed," Inspector Grunert purred.

Otto Krantz didn't hear him.

He was staring madly at the grinning heads of the old man and the girl—the heads he had sewed back on in the darkness and inadvertently *switched.*

THE SHADOW FROM THE STEEPLE

WILLIAM HURLEY WAS BORN an Irishman and grew up to be a taxicab driver—therefore it would be redundant, in the face of both of these facts, to say that he was garrulous.

The minute he picked up his passenger in downtown Providence that warm summer evening, he began talking. The passenger, a tall thin man in his early thirties, entered the cab and sat back, clutching a briefcase. He gave an address on Benefit Street and Hurley started out, shifting both taxi and tongue into high gear.

Hurley began what was to be a one-sided conversation by commenting on the afternoon performance of the New York Giants. Unperturbed by his passenger's silence, he made a few remarks about the weather—recent, current, and expected. Since he received no reply, the driver then proceeded to discuss a local phenomenon; namely the reported escape, that morning, of two black panthers or leopards from the traveling menagerie of Langer Brothers Circus, currently appearing in the city. In response to a direct inquiry as to whether he had seen the beasts roaming at large, Hurley's customer shook his head.

The driver then made several uncomplimentary remarks about the local police force and their inability to capture the beasts. It was his considered opinion that a given platoon of law enforcement officers would be unable to catch a cold if immured in an icebox for a year. This witticism failed to amuse his passenger, and before Hurley could continue his monologue they had arrived at the Benefit Street address. Eighty-five cents changed hands, passenger and briefcase left the cab, and Hurley drove away.

He could not know it at the time, but he thus became the last man who could or would testify to seeing his passenger alive.

The rest is conjecture, and perhaps that is for the best. Certainly it is easy enough to draw certain conclusions as to what happened that night in the old house on Benefit Street, but the weight of those conclusions is hard to bear.

One minor mystery is easy enough to clear up—the peculiar silence and aloofness of Hurley's passenger. That passenger, Edmund Fiske, of Chicago, Illinois, was meditating upon the fulfillment of fifteen years of questing; the cab trip represented the last stage of this long journey, and he was reviewing the circumstances as he rode.

Edmund Fiske's quest had begun, on August 8th, 1935, with the death of his close friend, Robert Harrison Blake, of Milwaukee.

Like Fiske himself at the time, Blake had been a precocious adolescent interested in fantasy-writing, and as such became a member of the "Lovecraft circle"—a group of writers maintaining correspondence with one another and with the late Howard Phillips Lovecraft, of Providence.

It was through correspondence that Fiske and Blake had become acquainted; they visited back and forth between Milwaukee and Chicago, and their mutual preoccupation with the weird and the fantastic in literature and art served to form the foundation for the close friendship which existed at the time of Blake's unexpected and inexplicable demise.

Most of the facts—and certain of the conjectures—in connection with Blake's death have been embodied in Lovecraft's story, *The Haunter of the Dark*, which was published more than a year after the younger writer's passing.

Lovecraft had an excellent opportunity to observe matters, for it was on his suggestion that young Blake had journeyed to Providence early in 1935, and had been provided with living-quarters on College Street by Lovecraft himself. So it was both as friend and neighbor that the elder fantasy writer had acted in narrating the singular story of Robert Harrison Blake's last months.

In his story, he tells of Blake's efforts to begin a novel dealing with a survival of New England witch-cults, but modestly omits his own part in assisting his friend to secure material. Apparently Blake began work on his project and then became enmeshed in a horror greater than any envisioned by his imagination.

For Blake was drawn to investigate the crumbling black pile on Federal Hill—the deserted ruin of a church that had once housed the worshippers of an esoteric cult. Early in spring he paid a visit to the shunned structure and there made certain discoveries which (in Lovecraft's opinion) made his death inevitable.

Briefly, Blake entered the boarded-up Free Will Church and stumbled across the skeleton of a reporter from the *Providence Telegram*, one Edwin M. Lillibridge, who had apparently attempted a similar investigation in

1893. The fact that his death was not explained seemed alarming enough, but more disturbing still was the realization that no one had been bold enough to enter the church since that date and discover the body.

Blake found the reporter's notebook in his clothing, and its contents afforded a partial revelation.

A certain Professor Bowen, of Providence, had traveled widely in Egypt, and in 1843, in the course of archeological investigations of the crypt of Nephren-Ka, had made an unusual find.

Nephren-Ka is the "forgotten pharaoh," whose name has been cursed by the priests and obliterated from official dynastic records. The name was familiar to the young writer at the time, due largely to the work of another Milwaukee writer who had dealt with the semi-legendary ruler in his tale, *Fane of the Black Pharaoh*. But the discovery Bowen made in the crypt was totally unexpected.

The reporter's notebook said little of the actual nature of that discovery, but it recorded subsequent events in a precise, chronological fashion. Immediately upon unearthing his mysterious find in Egypt, Professor Bower abandoned his research and returned to Providence, where he purchased the Free Will Church in 1844 and made it the headquarters of what was called the "Starry Wisdom" sect.

Members of this religious cult, evidently recruited by Bowen, professed to worship an entity they called the "Haunter of the Dark." By gazing into a crystal they summoned the actual presence of this entity and did homage with blood sacrifice.

Such, at least, was the fantastic story circulated in Providence at the time—and the church became a place to be avoided. Local superstition fanned agitation, and agitation precipitated direct action. In May of 1877 the sect was forcibly broken up by the authorities, due to public pressure, and several hundred of its members abruptly left the city.

The church itself was immediately closed, and apparently individual curiosity could not overcome the widespread fear which resulted in leaving the structure undisturbed and unexplored until the reporter, Lillibridge, made his ill-fated private investigation in 1893.

Such was the gist of the story unfolded in the pages of his notebook. Blake read it, but was nevertheless undeterred in his further scrutiny of the environs. Eventually he came upon the mysterious object Bowen had found in the Egyptian crypt—the object upon which the "Starry Wisdom" worship had been founded—the asymmetrical metal box with its curiously hinged lid, a lid that had not been closed for countless years. Blake thus gazed at the interior, gazed upon the four-inch red-black crystal polyhedron hanging suspended by seven supports. He not only gazed *at* but also *into* the polyhedron; just as the cult-worshippers had purportedly gazed, and with the same results. He was assailed by a curious psychic disturbance; he seemed to "see visions of other lands and the gulfs beyond the stars," as superstitious accounts had told.

And then Blake made his greatest mistake. He closed the box.

Closing the box—again, according to the superstitions annotated by Lillibridge—was the act that summoned the alien entity itself, the "Haunter of the Dark." It was a creature of darkness and could not survive light. And in that boarded-up blackness of the ruined church, the thing emerged by night.

Blake fled the church in terror, but the damage was done. In mid-July, a thunderstorm put out the lights in Providence for an hour, and the Italian colony living near the deserted church heard bumping and thumping from inside the shadow-shrouded structure.

Crowds with candles stood outside in the rain and played candles upon the building, shielding themselves against the possible emergence of the feared entity by a barrier of light.

Apparently the story had remained alive throughout the neighborhood. Once the storm abated, local newspapers grew interested, and on the 17th of July two reporters entered the old church, together with a policeman. Nothing definite was found, although there were curious and inexplicable smears and stains on the stairs and the pews.

Less than a month later—at 2:35 A.M. on the morning of August 8th, to be exact—Robert Harrison Blake met his death during an electrical storm while seated before the window of his room on College Street.

During the gathering storm, before his death occurred, Blake scribbled frantically in his diary, gradually revealing his innermost obsessions and delusions concerning the "Haunter of the Dark." It was Blake's conviction that by gazing into the curious crystal in its box he had somehow established a linkage with the nonterrestial entity. He further believed that closing the box had summoned the creature to dwell in the darkness of the church steeple, and that in some way his own fate was now irrevocably linked to that of the monstrosity.

All this is revealed in the last messages he set down while watching the progress of the storm from his window.

Meanwhile, at the church itself, on Federal Hill, a crowd of agitated spectators gathered to play lights upon the structure. That they heard alarming sounds from inside the boarded-up building is undeniable; at least two competent witnesses have testified to the fact. One, Father Merluzzo of the Spirito Santo Church, was on hand to quiet his congregation. The other, Patrolman (now Sergeant) William J. Monahan, of Central Station, was attempting to preserve order in the face of growing panic. Monahan himself saw the blinding "blur" that seemed to issue, smokelike, from the steeple of the ancient edifice as the final lightning-flash came.

Flash, meteor, fireball—call it what you will—erupted over the city in a blinding blaze; perhaps at the very moment that Robert Harrison Blake, across town, was writing, "Is it not an avatar of Nyarlathotep, who in antique and shadowy Khem even took the form of man?"

A few moments later he was dead. The coroner's physician rendered a verdict attributing his demise to "electrical shock" although the window he faced was unbroken. Another physician, known to Lovecraft, quarreled privately with that verdict and subsequently entered the affair the next day. Without legal authority, he entered the church and climbed to the windowless steeple where he discovered the strange asymmetrical—was it golden?—box and the curious stone within. Apparently his first gesture was to make sure of raising the lid and bringing the stone into the light. His next recorded gesture was to charter a boat, take box and curiously-angled stone aboard, and drop them into the deepest channel of Narragansett Bay.

There ended the admittedly fictionalized account of Blake's death as recorded by H.P. Lovecraft. And there began Edmund Fiske's fifteen-year quest.

Fiske, of course, had known some of the events outlined in the story. When Blake had left for Providence in the spring, Fiske had tentatively promised to join him the following autumn. At first, the two friends had exchanged letters regularly, but by early summer Blake ceased correspondence altogether.

At the time, Fiske was unaware of Blake's exploration of the ruined church. He could not account for Blake's silence, and wrote Lovecraft for a possible explanation.

Lovecraft could supply little information. Young Blake, he said, had visited with him frequently during the early weeks of his stay; had consulted with him about his writing, and had accompanied him on several nocturnal strolls through the city.

But during the summer, Blake's neighborliness ceased. It was not in Lovecraft's reclusive nature to impose himself upon others, and he did not seek to invade Blake's privacy for several weeks.

When he did so—and learned from the almost hysterical adolescent of his experiences in the forbidding, forbidden church on Federal Hill—Lovecraft offered words of warning and advice. But it was already too late. Within ten days of his visit came the shocking end.

Fiske learned of that end from Lovecraft on the following day. It was his task to break the news to Blake's parents. For a time he was tempted to visit Providence immediately, but lack of funds and the pressure of his own domestic affairs forestalled him. The body of his young friend duly arrived and Fiske attended the brief ceremony of cremation.

Then Lovecraft began his own investigation—an investigation which ultimately resulted in the publication of his story. And there the matter might have rested.

But Fiske was not satisfied.

His best friend had died under circumstances which even the most skeptical must admit were mysterious. The local authorities summarily wrote off the matter with a fatuous and inadequate explanation.

Fiske determined to ascertain the truth.

Bear in mind one salient fact—all three of these men; Lovecraft, Blake and Fiske—were professional writers and students of the supernatural or the supranormal. All three of them had extraordinary access to a bulk of written material dealing with ancient legend and superstition. Ironically enough, the use to which they put their knowledge was limited to excursions into so-called "fantasy fiction" but none of them, in the light of their own experience, could wholly join their reading audience in scoffing at the myths of which they wrote.

For, as Fiske wrote to Lovecraft, "the term, myth, as we know, is merely a polite euphemism. Blake's death was not a myth, but a hideous reality. I implore you to investigate fully. See this matter through to the end, for if Blake's diary holds even a distorted truth, there is no telling what may be loosed upon the world."

Lovecraft pledged cooperation, discovered the fate of the metal box and its contents, and endeavored to arrange a meeting with Doctor Ambrose Dexter, of Benefit Street. Doctor Dexter, it appeared, had left town immediately following his dramatic theft and disposal of the "Shining Trapezehedron," as Lovecraft called it.

Lovecraft then apparently interviewed Father Merluzzo and Patrolman Monahan, plunged into the files of the *Bulletin*, and endeavored to reconstruct the story of the Starry Wisdom sect and the entity they worshipped.

Of course he learned a good deal more than he dared to put into his magazine story. His letters to Edmund Fiske in the late fall and early spring of 1936 contain guarded hints and references to "menaces from Outside." But he seemed anxious to reassure Fiske that if there had been any menace, even in the realistic rather than the supernatural sense, the danger was now averted because Doctor Dexter had disposed of the Shining Trapezehedron which acted as a summoning talisman. Such was the gist of his report, and the matter rested there for a time.

Fiske made tentative arrangements, early in 1937, to visit Lovecraft at his home, with the private intention of doing some further research on his own into the cause of Blake's death. But once again, circumstances intervened. For in March of that year, Lovecraft died. His unexpected passing plunged Fiske into a period of mental despondency from which he was slow to recover; accordingly, it was not until almost a year later that Edmund Fiske paid his first visit to Providence, and to the scene of the tragic episodes which brought Blake's life to a close.

For somehow, always, a black undercurrent of suspicion existed. The coroner's physician had been glib, Lovecraft had been tactful, the press and general public had accepted matters completely — yet Blake was dead, and there had been an entity abroad in the night.

Fiske felt that if he could visit the accursed church himself, talk to Doctor Dexter and find out what had drawn him into the affair, interrogate the reporters, and pursue any relevant leads or clues he might eventually hope to uncover the truth and at least clear his dead friend's name of the ugly shadow of mental unbalance.

Accordingly, Fiske's first step after arriving in Providence and registering at a hotel was to set out for Federal Hill and the ruined church.

The search was doomed to immediate, irremediable disappointment. For the church was no more. It had been razed the previous fall and the property taken over by the city authorities. The black and baleful spire no longer cast its spell over the Hill.

Fiske immediately took pains to see Father Merluzzo, at Spirito Santo, a few squares away. He learned from a courteous housekeeper that Father Merluzzo had died in 1936, within a year of young Blake.

Discouraged but persistent, Fiske next attempted to reach Doctor Dexter, but the old house on Benefit Street was boarded up. A call to the Physicians' Service Bureau produced only the cryptic information that Ambrose Dexter, M.D., had left the city for an indeterminate stay.

Nor did a visit with the city editor of the *Bulletin* yield any better result. Fiske was permitted to go into the newspaper's morgue and read the aggravatingly short and matter-of-fact story on Blake's death, but the two reporters who covered the assignment and subsequently visited the Federal Hill church had left the paper for berths in other cities.

There were, of course, other leads to follow, and during the ensuing week Fiske ran them all to the ground. A copy of WHO's WHO added nothing significant to his mental picture of Doctor Ambrose Dexter. The physician was Providence-born, a lifelong resident, 40 years of age, unmarried, a general practitioner, member of several medical societies — but there was no indication of any unusual "hobbies" or "other interests" which might provide a clue as to his participation in the affair.

Sergeant William J. Monahan of Central Station was sought out, and for the first time Fiske actually managed to speak to someone who admitted an actual connection with the events leading to Blake's death. Monahan was polite, but cautiously noncommittal.

Despite Fiske's complete unburdening, the police officer remained discreetly reticent.

"There's really nothing I can tell you," he said. "It's true, like Mister Lovecraft said, that I was at the church that night, for there was a rough crowd out and there's no telling what some of them ones in the neighborhood will do when riled up. Like the story said, the old church had a bad name, and I guess Sheeley could have given you many's the story."

"Sheeley?" interjected Fiske.

"Bert Sheeley—it was his beat, you know, not mine. He was ill of pneumonia at the time and I substituted for two weeks. Then, when he died—"

Fiske shook his head. Another possible source of information gone. Blake dead, Lovecraft dead, Father Merluzzo dead, and now Sheeley. Reporters scattered, and Doctor Dexter mysteriously missing. He sighed and persevered.

"That last night, when you saw the blur," he asked, "can you add anything by way of details? Were there any noises? Did anyone in the crowd say anything? Try to remember—whatever you can add may be of great help to me."

Monahan shook his head. "There were noises aplenty," he said. "But what with the thunder and all. I couldn't rightly make out if anything came from inside the church, like the story has it. And as for the crowd, with the women wailing and the men muttering, all mixed up with thunderclaps and wind, it was as much as I could do to hear myself yelling to keep in place let alone make out what was being said."

"And the blur?" Fiske persisted.

"It was a blur, and that's all. Smoke, or a cloud, or just a shadow before the lightning struck again. But I'll not be saying I saw any devils, or monsters, or whatchamacallits as Mister Lovecraft would write about in those wild tales of his."

Sergeant Monahan shrugged self-righteously and picked up the desk phone to answer a call. The interview was obviously at an end.

And so, for the nonce, was Fiske's quest. He didn't abandon hope, however. For a day he sat by his own hotel phone and called up every "Dexter" listed in the book in an effort to locate a relative of the missing Doctor; but to no avail. Another day was spent in a small boat on Narragansett Bay, as Fiske assiduously and painstakingly familiarized himself with the location of the "deepest channel" alluded to in Lovecraft's story.

But at the end of a futile week in Providence, Fiske had to confess himself beaten. He returned to Chicago, his work, and his normal pursuits. Gradually the affair dropped out of the foreground of his consciousness, but he by no means forgot it completely or gave up the notion of eventually unraveling the mystery—if mystery there was.

In 1941, during a three-day furlough from Basic Training, Pvt. First Class Edmund Fiske passed through Providence on his way to New York City and again attempted to locate Doctor Ambrose Dexter, without success.

During 1942 and 1943, Sgt. Edmund Fiske wrote, from his stations overseas, to Doctor Ambrose Dexter, c/o General Delivery, Providence, R.I. His letters were never acknowledged, if indeed they were received.

In 1945, in a USO library lounge in Honolulu, Fiske read a report in—of all things—a journal on astrophysics which mentioned a recent gathering at Princeton University, at which the guest speaker, Doctor Ambrose Dexter, had delivered an address on *"Practical Applications in Military Technology."*

Fiske did not return to the States until the end of 1946. Domestic affairs, naturally, were the subject of his paramount consideration during the following year. It wasn't until 1948 that he accidentally came upon Doctor Dexter's name again—this time in a listing of "investigators in the field of nuclear physics" in a national weekly newsmagazine. He wrote the editors for further information, but received no reply. And another letter, dispatched to Providence, remained unanswered.

But in 1949, late in autumn, Dexter's name again came to his attention through the news columns; this time in relation to a discussion of work on the secret H-bomb.

Whatever he guessed, whatever he feared, whatever he wildly imagined, Fiske was impelled to action. It was then that he wrote to a certain Ogden Purvis, a private investigator in the city of Providence, and commissioned him to locate Doctor Ambrose Dexter. All that he required was that he be placed in communication with Dexter, and he paid a substantial retainer fee. Purvis took the case.

The private detective sent several reports to Fiske in Chicago and they were, at first, disheartening. The Dexter residence was still untenanted. Dexter himself, according to the information elicited from governmental sources, was on a special mission. The private investigator seemed to assume from this that he was a person above reproach, engaged in confidential defense work.

Fiske's own reaction was panic.

He raised his offer of a fee and insisted that Ogden Purvis continue his efforts to find the elusive Doctor.

Winter of 1950 came, and with it, another report. The private investigator had tracked down every lead Fiske suggested, and one of them led, eventually, to Tom Jonas.

Tom Jonas was the owner of the small boat which had been chartered by Doctor Dexter one evening in the late summer of 1935—the small boat which had been rowed to the "deepest channel of Narragansett Bay."

Tom Jonas had rested his oars as Dexter threw overboard the dully-gleaming, asymmetrical metal box with the hinged lid open to disclose the Shining Trapezehedron.

The old fisherman had spoken freely to the private detective; his words were reported in detail to Fiske via confidential report.

"Mighty peculiar" was Jonas's own reaction to the incident. Dexter had offered him "twenty smackers to take the boat out in the middle o' midnight and heave this funny-lookin' contraption overboard. Said there was no harm in it; said it was just an old keepsake he wanted to git rid of. But all the way out he kep' starin' at the sort of jewel-thing set in some iron bands inside the box, and mumblin' in some foreign language, I guess. No, 'tweren't French or German or Wop talk either. Polish, mebbe. I don't remember any words, either. But he acted sort-of drunk. Not that I'd say anything against Doctor Dexter, understand; comes of a fine old family, even if he ain't been around these parts since, to my knowing. But I figgered he was a bit under the influence, you might say. Else why would he pay me twenty smackers to do a crazy stunt like that?"

There was more to the verbatim transcript of the old fisherman's monologue, but it did not explain anything.

"He sure seemed glad to get rid of it, as I recollect. On the way back he told me to keep mum about it, but I can't see no harm in telling at this late date; I wouldn't hold anythin' back from the law."

Evidently the private investigator had made use of a rather unethical stratagem—posing as an actual detective in order to get Jonas to talk.

This did not bother Fiske, in Chicago. It was enough to get his grasp on something tangible at last; enough to make him send Purvis another payment, with instructions to keep up the search for Ambrose Dexter. Several months passed in waiting.

Then, in late spring, came the news Fiske had waited for. Doctor Dexter was back; he had returned to his house on Benefit Street. The boards had been removed, furniture vans appeared to discharge their contents, and a manservant appeared to answer the door, and to take telephone messages.

Doctor Dexter was not at home to the investigator, or to anyone. He was, it appeared, recuperating from a severe illness contracted while in government service. He took a card from Purvis and promised to deliver a message, but repeated calls brought no indication of a reply.

Nor did Purvis, who conscientiously "cased" the house and neighborhood, ever succeed in laying eyes upon the Doctor himself or in finding anyone who claimed to have seen the convalescent physician on the street.

Groceries were delivered regularly; mail appeared in the box; lights glowed in the Benefit Street house nightly until all hours.

As a matter of fact, this was the only concrete statement Purvis could make regarding any possible irregularity in Doctor Dexter's mode of life—he seemed to keep electricity burning twenty-four hours a day.

Fiske promptly dispatched another letter to Doctor Dexter, and then another. Still no acknowledgment or reply was forthcoming. And after several more unenlightening reports from Purvis, Fiske made up his mind. He would go to Providence and see Dexter, somehow, come what may.

He might be completely wrong in his suspicions; he might be completely wrong in his assumption that Doctor Dexter could clear the name of his dead friend; he might be completely wrong in even surmising any connection between the two—but for fifteen years he had brooded and wondered, and it was time to put an end to his own inner conflict.

Accordingly, late that summer, Fiske wired Purvis of his intentions and instructed him to meet him at the hotel upon his arrival.

Thus it was that Edmund Fiske came to Providence for the last time; on the day that the Giants lost, on the day that the Langer Brothers lost their two black panthers, on the day that cabdriver William Hurley was in a garrulous mood.

Purvis was not at the hotel to meet him, but such was Fiske's own frenzy of impatience that he decided to act without him and drove, as we have seen, to Benefit Street in the early evening.

As the cab departed, Fiske stared up at the paneled doorway; stared at the lights blazing from the upper windows of the Georgian structure. A brass nameplate gleamed on the door itself, and the light from the windows played upon the legend, *Ambrose Dexter, M.D.*

Slight as it was, this seemed a reassuring touch to Edmund Fiske. The Doctor was not concealing his presence in the house from the world, however much he might conceal his actual person. Surely the blazing lights and the appearance of the nameplate augured well.

Fiske shrugged, rang the bell.

The door opened quickly. A small, dark-skinned man with a slight stoop appeared and made a question of the word, "Yes?"

"Doctor Dexter, please."

"The Doctor is not in to callers. He is ill."

"Would you take a message, please?"

"Certainly." The dark-skinned servant smiled.

"Tell him that Edmund Fiske of Chicago wishes to see him at his convenience for a few moments. I have come all the way from the Middle West for this purpose, and what I have to speak to him about would take only a moment or two of his time."

"Wait, please."

The door closed. Fiske stood in the gathering darkness and transferred his briefcase from one hand to the other.

Abruptly, the door opened again. The servant peered out at him.

"Mr. Fiske — are you the gentleman who wrote the letters?"

"Letters — oh, yes, I am. I did not know the Doctor ever received them."

The servant nodded. "I could not say. But Doctor Dexter said that if you were the man who had written him, you were to come right in."

Fiske permitted himself an audible sigh of relief as he stepped over the threshold. It had taken him fifteen years to come this far, and now —

"Just go upstairs, if you please. You will find Doctor Dexter waiting in the study, right at the head of the hall."

Edmund Fiske climbed the stairs, turned at the top to a doorway, and entered a room in which the light was an almost palpable presence, so intense was its glare.

And there, rising from a chair beside the fireplace, was Doctor Ambrose Dexter.

Fiske found himself facing a tall, thin, immaculately dressed man who may have been fifty but who scarcely looked thirty-five; a man whose wholly natural grace and elegance of movement concealed the sole incongruity of his aspect—a very deep suntan.

"So you are Edmund Fiske."

The voice was soft, well-modulated, and unmistakably "New England"—and the accompanying handclasp warm and firm. Doctor Dexter's smile was natural and friendly. White teeth gleamed against the brown background of his features.

"Won't you sit down?" invited the Doctor. He indicated a chair and bowed slightly. Fiske couldn't help but stare; there was certainly no indication of any present or recent illness in his host's demeanor or behavior. As Doctor Dexter resumed his own seat near the fire and Fiske moved around the chair to join him, he noted the bookshelves on either side of the room. The size and shape of several volumes immediately engaged his rapt attention—so much so that he hesitated before taking a seat, and instead inspected the titles of the tomes.

For the first time in his life, Edmund Fiske found himself confronting the half-legendary DE VERMIS MYSTERIIS, the LIBER IVONIS, and the almost mythical Latin version of the NECRONOMICON. Without seeking his host's permission, he lifted the bulk of the latter volume from the shelf and riffled through the yellowed pages of the Spanish translation of 1622.

Then he turned to Doctor Dexter, and all traces of his carefully-contrived composure dropped away. "Then it must have been you who found these books in the church," he said. "In the rear vestry room beside the apse. Lovecraft mentioned them in his story, and I've always wondered what became of them."

Doctor Dexter nodded gravely. "Yes, I took them. I did not think it wise for such books to fall into the hands of authorities. You know what they contain, and what might happen if such knowledge were wrongfully employed."

Fiske reluctantly replaced the great book on the shelf and took a chair facing the Doctor before the fire. He held his briefcase on his lap and fumbled uneasily with the clasp.

"Don't be uneasy," said Doctor Dexter, with a kindly smile. "Let us proceed without fencing. You are here to discover what part I played in the affair of your friend's death."

"Yes, there are some questions I wanted to ask."

"Please." The Doctor raised a slim brown hand. "I am not in the best of health and can give you only a few minutes. Allow me to anticipate your queries and tell you what little I know."

"As you wish." Fiske stared at the bronzed man, wondering what lay behind the perfection of his poise.

"I met your friend Robert Harrison Blake only once," said Doctor Dexter. "It was on an evening during the latter part of July, 1935. He called upon me here, as a patient."

Fiske leaned forward eagerly. "I never knew that!" he exclaimed.

"There was no reason for anyone to know it," the Doctor answered. "He was merely a patient. He claimed to be suffering from insomnia. I examined him, prescribed a sedative, and acting on the merest surmise, asked if he had recently been subjected to any unusual strain or trauma. It was then that he told me the story of his visit to the church on Federal Hill and of what he had found there. I must say that I had the acumen not to dismiss his tale as the product of a hysterical imagination. As a member of one of the older families here, I was already acquainted with the legends surrounding the Starry Wisdom sect and the so-called Haunter of the Dark.

"Young Blake confessed to me certain of his fears concerning the Shining Trapezehedron—intimating that it was a focal point of primal evil. He further admitted his own dread of being somehow linked to the monstrosity in the church.

"Naturally, I was not prepared to accept this last premise as a rational one. I attempted to reassure the young man, advised him to leave Providence and forget it. And at the time I acted in all good faith. And then, in August, came news of Blake's death."

"So you went to the church," Fiske said.

"Wouldn't you have done the same thing?" parried Doctor Dexter. "If Blake had come to you with his story, told you of what he feared, wouldn't his death have moved you to action? I assure you, I did what I thought best. Rather than provoke a scandal, rather than expose the general public to needless fears, rather than permit the possibility of danger to exist, I went to the church. I took the books. I took the Shining Trapezehedron from under the noses of the authorities. And I chartered a boat and dumped the accursed thing in Narragansett Bay, where it could no longer possibly harm mankind. The lid was up when I dropped it—for as you know, only darkness can summon the Haunter, and now the stone is eternally exposed to light.

"But that is all I can tell you. I regret that my work in recent years has prevented me from seeing or communicating with you before this. I appreciate your interest in the affair and trust my remarks will help to clarify, in a small way, your bewilderment. As to young Blake, in my capacity as examining physician, I will gladly give you a written testimony to my belief in his sanity at the time of his death. I'll have it drawn up tomorrow and send it to your hotel if you give me the address. Fair enough?"

The Doctor rose, signifying that the interview was over. Fiske remained seated, shifting his briefcase.

"Now if you will excuse me," the physician murmured.

"In a moment. There are still one or two brief questions I'd appreciate your answering."

"Certainly." If Doctor Dexter was irritated, he gave no sign.

"Did you by any chance see Lovecraft before or during his last illness?"

"No. I was not his physician. In fact, I never met the man, though of course I knew of him and his work."

"What caused you to leave Providence so abruptly after the Blake affair?"

"My interests in physics superseded my interest in medicine. As you may or may not know, during the past decade or more, I have been working on problems relative to atomic energy and nuclear fission. In fact, starting tomorrow, I am leaving Providence once more to deliver a course of lectures before the faculties of eastern universities and certain governmental groups."

"That is very interesting to me, Doctor," said Fiske. "By the way, did you ever meet Einstein?"

"As a matter of fact, I did, some years ago. I worked with him on—but no matter. I must beg you to excuse me, now. At another time, perhaps, we can discuss such things."

His impatience was unmistakable now. Fiske rose, lifting his briefcase in one hand and reaching out to extinguish a table lamp with the other.

Doctor Dexter crossed swiftly and lighted the lamp again.

"Why are you afraid of the dark, Doctor?" asked Fiske, softly.

"I am not af—"

For the first time the physician seemed on the verge of losing his composure. "What makes you think that?" he whispered.

"It's the Shining Trapezehedron, isn't it?" Fiske continued. "When you threw it in the bay you acted too hastily. You didn't remember at the time that even if you left the lid open, the stone would be surrounded by darkness there at the bottom of the channel. Perhaps the Haunter didn't want you to remember. You looked into the stone just as Blake did, and established the same psychic linkage. And when you threw the thing away, you gave it into perpetual darkness, where the Haunter's power would feed and grow.

"That's why you left Providence—because you were afraid the Haunter would come to you, just as it came to Blake. And because you knew that now the thing would remain abroad forever."

Doctor Dexter moved toward the door. "I must definitely ask that you leave now," he said. "If you're implying that I keep the lights on because I'm afraid of the Haunter coming after me, the way it did Blake, then you're mistaken."

Fiske smiled wryly. "That's not it at all," he answered. "I know you don't fear that. Because it's too late. The Haunter must have come to you long before this—perhaps within a day or so after you gave it power by consigning the Trapezehedron to the darkness of the Bay. It came to you, but unlike the case of Blake, it did not kill you. It used you. That's why you fear the dark. You fear it as the Haunter itself fears being discovered. I believe that in the darkness you look *different*. More like the old shape. Because when the Haunter came to you, it did not kill but instead, *merged*. *You* are the Haunter of the Dark!"

"Mr. Fiske, really—"

"There is no Doctor Dexter. There hasn't been any such person for many years, now. There's only the outer shell, possessed by an entity older than the world, an entity that is moving quickly and cunningly to bring destruction to all mankind. It was you who turned 'scientist' and insinuated yourself into the proper circles, hinting and prompting and assisting foolish men into their sudden 'discovery' of nuclear fission. When the first atomic bomb fell, how you must have laughed! And now you've given them the secret of the hydrogen bomb, and you're going on to teach them more, show them new ways to bring about their own destruction.

"It took me years of brooding to discover the clues, the keys to the so-called wild myths that Lovecraft wrote about. For he wrote in parable and allegory, but he wrote the truth. He has set it down in black and white time and again, the prophecy of your coming to Earth—Blake knew it at the last when he identified the Haunter by its rightful name."

"And that is?" snapped the Doctor.

"Nyarlathotep!"

The brown face creased into a grimace of laughter. "I'm afraid you're a victim of the same fantasy-projections as poor Blake and your friend Lovecraft. Everyone knows that Nyarlathotep is pure invention—part of the Lovecraft mythos."

"I thought so, until I found the clue in his poem. That's when it all fitted in; the Haunter of the Dark, your fleeing, and your sudden interest in scientific research. Lovecraft's words took on a new meaning:

"And at last from inner Egypt came
The strange dark one to whome the fellahs bowed"

Fiske chanted the lines, staring at the dark face of the physician.

"Nonsense—if you must know, this dermatological disturbance of mine is the result of exposure to radiation at Los Alamos."

Fiske did not heed, he was continuing Lovecraft's poem.

" —That wild beasts followed him and licked his hands.
Soon from the sea a noxious birth began;
Forgotten lands with weedy spires of gold.
The ground was cleft and mad auroras rolled

Down on the quaking cities of man.
Then crushing what he chanced to mould in play
The idiot Chaos blew Earth's dust away."

Doctor Dexter shook his head. "Ridiculous on the face of it," he as-
serted. "Surely, even in your—er—upset condition, you can understand
that, man! The poem has no literal meaning. Do wild beasts lick my hands?
Is something rising from the sea? Are there earthquakes and auroras? Nonsense! You're suffering from a bad case of what we call 'atomic jitters'—I
can see it now. You're preoccupied, as so many laymen are today, with the
foolish obsession that somehow our work in nuclear fission will result in the
destruction of the Earth. All this rationalization is a product of your imagin-
ings."

Fiske held his briefcase tightly. "I told you it was a parable, this prophecy
of Lovecraft's. God knows what he *knew* or *feared*; whatever it was, it was
enough to make him cloak his meaning. And even then, perhaps, *they* got to
him because he knew too much."

"*They?*"

"They from the Outside . . . the ones you serve. You are their Messenger, Nyarlathotep. You came, in linkage with the Shining Trapezehedron,
out of inner Egypt, as the poem says. And the 'fellahs'—the common
workers of Providence who became converted to the Starry Wisdom sect,
bowed before the 'strange dark one' they worshipped as the Haunter.

"The Trapezehedron was thrown into the Bay, and soon from the sea
came this noxious birth—your birth, or incarnation in the body of Doctor
Dexter. And you taught men new methods of destruction; destruction with
atomic bombs in which the 'ground was cleft and mad auroras rolled down on
the quaking cities of man.' Oh, Lovecraft knew what he was writing, and
Blake recognized you too. And they both died. I suppose you'll try to kill me
now, so you can go on. You'll lecture, and stand at the elbows of the laboratory men urging them on and giving them new suggestions to result in
greater destruction. And finally you'll blow Earth's dust away."

"Please." Doctor Dexter held out both hands. "Control yourself—let me
get you something! Can't you realize this whole thing is absurd?"

Fiske moved toward him, hands fumbling at the clasp of the briefcase.
The flap opened, and Fiske reached inside, then withdrew his hand. He held
a revolver now, and he pointed it quite steadily at Doctor Dexter's breast.

"Of course it's absurd," Fiske muttered. "No one ever believed in the
Starry Wisdom sect except a few fanatics and some ignorant foreigners. No
one ever took Blake's stories or Lovecraft's, or mine for that matter, as
anything but a rather morbid form of amusement. By the same token, no one
will ever believe there is anything wrong with you, or with so-called scientific investigation of atomic energy, or the other horrors you plan to loose on
the world to bring about its doom. And that's why I'm going to kill you now!"

"Put down that gun!"

Fiske began suddenly to tremble; his whole body shook in a spectacular spasm. Dexter noted it and moved forward. The younger man's eyes were bulging, and the physician inched toward him.

"Stand back!" Fiske warned. The words were distorted by the convulsive shuddering of his jaws. "That's all I needed to know. Since you arc in a human body, you can be destroyed by ordinary weapons. And so I do destroy you—Nyarlathotep!"

His finger moved.

So did Doctor Dexter's. His hand went swiftly behind him, to the wall master-lightswitch. A click and the room was plunged into utter darkness.

Not utter darkness—for there was a glow.

The face and hands of Doctor Ambrose Dexter glowed with a phosphorescent fire in the dark. There are presumably forms of radium poisoning which can cause such an effect, and no doubt Doctor Dexter would have so explained the phenomenon to Edmund Fiske, had he the opportunity.

But there was no opportunity. Edmund Fiske heard the click, saw the fantastic flaming features, and pitched forward to the floor.

Doctor Dexter quietly switched on the lights, went over to the younger man's side and knelt for a long moment. He sought a pulse in vain.

Edmund Fiske was dead.

The Doctor sighed, rose, and left the room. In the hall downstairs he summoned his servant.

"There has been a regrettable accident," he said. "That young visitor of mine—a hysteric—suffered a heart attack. You had better call the police, immediately. And then continue with the packing. We must leave tomorrow, for the lecture tour."

"But the police may detain you."

Doctor Dexter shook his head. "I think not. It's a clearcut case. In any event, I can easily explain. When they arrive, notify me. I shall be in the garden."

The Doctor proceeded down the hall to the rear exit and emerged upon the moonlit splendor of the garden behind the house on Benefit Street.

The radiant vista was walled off from the world, utterly deserted. The dark man stood in moonlight and its glow mingled with his own aura.

At this moment two silken shadows leaped over the wall. They crouched in the coolness of the garden, then slithered forward toward Doctor Dexter. They made panting sounds.

In the moonlight, he recognized the shapes of two black panthers.

Immobile, he waited as they advanced, padding purposefully toward him, eyes aglow, jaws slavering and agape.

Doctor Dexter turned away. His face was turned in mockery to the moon as the beasts fawned before him and licked his hands.

2

THE MAN WHO COLLECTED POE

Durıng the whole of a dull, dark and soundless day in the autumn of the year, when the clouds hung oppressively low in the heavens, I had been passing alone, by automobile, through a singularly dreary tract of country; and at length found myself, as the shades of the evening drew on, within view of my destination.

I looked upon the scene before me — upon the mere house and the simple landscape features of the domain, upon the bleak walls, upon the vacant eyelike windows, upon a few rank sedges, and upon a few white trunks of decayed trees — with a feeling of utter confusion commingled with dismay. For it seemed to me as though I had visited this scene once before, or read of it, perhaps, in some frequently rescanned tale. And yet assuredly it could not be, for only three days had passed since I had made the acquaintance of Launcelot Canning and received an invitation to visit him at his Maryland residence.

The circumstances under which I met Canning were simple; I happened to attend a bibliophilic meeting in Washington and was introduced to him by a mutual friend. Casual conversation gave place to absorbed and interested discussion when he discovered my preoccupation with works of fantasy. Upon learning that I was traveling upon a vacation with no set itinerary, Canning urged me to become his guest for a day and to examine, at my leisure, his unusual display of *memorabilia*.

"I feel, from our conversation, that we have much in common," he told me. "For you see, sir, in my love of fantasy I bow to no man. It is a taste I have perhaps inherited from my father and from his father before him, together with their considerable acquisitions in the genre. No doubt you would be gratified with what I am prepared to show you, for in all due modesty I beg to style myself the world's leading collector of the works of Edgar Allan Poe."

I confess that his invitation as such did not enthrall me, for I hold no brief for the literary hero-worshipper or the scholarly collector as a type. I own to a more than passing interest in the tales of Poe, but my interest does not extend to the point of ferreting out the exact date upon which Mr. Poe first decided to raise a mustache, nor would I be unduly intrigued by the opportunity to examine several hairs preserved from that hirsute appendage.

So it was rather the person and personality of Launcelot Canning himself which caused me to accept his proffered hospitality. For the man who proposed to become my host might have himself stepped from the pages of a Poe tale. His speech, as I have endeavored to indicate, was characterized by a courtly *rodomontade* so often exemplified in Poe's heroes—and beyond certainty, his appearance bore out the resemblance.

Launcelot Canning had the cadaverousness of complexion, the large, liquid, luminous eyes, the thin, curved lips, the delicately modeled nose, finely molded chin, and dark, weblike hair of a typical Poe protagonist.

It was this phenomenon which prompted my acceptance and led me to journey to his Maryland estate which, as I now perceived, in itself manifested a Poe-etic quality of its own, intrinsic in the images of the gray sedge, the ghastly tree stems, and the vacant and eyelike windows of the mansion of gloom. All that was lacking was a tarn and a moat—and as I prepared to enter the dwelling I half-expected to encounter therein the carved ceilings, the somber tapestries, the ebon floors and the phantasmagoric armorial trophies so vividly described by the author of TALES OF THE GROTESQUE AND ARABESQUE.

Nor, upon entering Launcelot Canning's home, was I too greatly disappointed in my expectations. True to both the atmospheric quality of the decrepit mansion and to my own fanciful presentiments, the door was opened in response to my knock by a valet who conducted me, in silence, through dark and intricate passages to the study of his master.

The room in which I found myself was very large and lofty. The windows were long, narrow and pointed, and at so vast a distance from the black oaken floor as to be altogether inaccessible from within. Feeble gleams of encrimsoned light made their way through the trellised panes and served to render sufficiently distinct the more prominent objects around; the eye, however, struggled in vain to reach the remoter angles of the chamber or the recesses of the vaulted and fretted ceiling. Dark draperies hung upon the walls. The general furniture was profuse, comfortless, antique and tattered. Many books and musical instruments lay scattered about, but they failed to give any vitality to the scene.

Instead, they rendered more distinct that peculiar quality of quasi-recollection; it was as though I found myself once again, after a protracted absence, in a familiar setting. I had read, I had imagined, I had dreamed, or I had actually beheld this setting before.

Upon my entrance, Launcelot Canning arose from a sofa on which he had been lying at full length and greeted me with a vivacious warmth which had much in it, I at first thought, of an overdone cordiality.

Yet his tone, as he spoke of the object of my visit, of his earnest desire to see me, of the solace he expected me to afford him in a mutual discussion of our interests, soon alleviated my initial misapprehension.

Launcelot Canning welcomed me with the rapt enthusiasm of the born collector—and I came to realize that he was indeed just that. For the Poe collection he shortly proposed to unveil before me was actually his birthright.

The nucleus of the present accumulation, he disclosed, had begun with his grandfather, Christopher Canning, a respected merchant of Baltimore. Almost eighty years ago he had been one of the leading patrons of the arts in his community and as such was partially instrumental in arranging for the removal of Poe's body to the southeastern corner of the Presbyterian Cemetery at Fayette and Green Streets, where a suitable monument might be erected. This event occurred in the year 1875, and it was a few years prior to that time that Canning laid the foundation of the Poe collection.

"Thanks to his zeal," his grandson informed me, "I am today the fortunate possessor of a copy of virtually every existing specimen of Poe's published works. If you will step over here,"—and he led me to a remote corner of the vaulted study, past the dark draperies, to a bookshelf which rose remotely to the shadowy ceiling—"I shall be pleased to corroborate that claim. Here is a copy of AL AARAAF, TAMERLANE AND OTHER POEMS in the 1829 edition, and here is the still earlier TAMERLANE AND OTHER POEMS of 1827. The Boston edition, which, as you doubtless know, is valued today at $15,000. I can assure you that Grandfather Canning parted with no such sum in order to gain possession of this rarity."

He displayed the volumes with an air of commingled pride and cupidity which is ofttimes characteristic of the collector and is by no means to be confused with either literary snobbery or ordinary greed. Realizing this, I remained patient as he exhibited further treasures—copies of the *Philadelphia Saturday Courier* containing early tales, bound volumes of *The Messenger* during the period of Poe's editorship, *Graham's Magazine*, editions of the *New York Sun* and the *New York Mirror* boasting, respectively, of *The Balloon Hoax* and *The Raven*, and files of *The Gentleman's Magazine*. Ascending a short library ladder, he handed down to me the Lea and Blanchard edition of TALES OF THE GROTESQUE AND ARABESQUE, the CONCHOLOGIST'S FIRST BOOK, the Putnam EUREKA, and, finally, the little paper booklet, published in 1843 and sold for 12½¢, entitled THE PROSE ROMANCES OF EDGAR A. POE—an insignificant trifle containing two tales which is valued by present-day collectors at $50,000.

Canning informed me of this last fact and, indeed, kept up a running commentary upon each item he presented. There was no doubt but that he was a Poe scholar as well as a Poe collector, and his words informed tattered specimens of the *Broadway Journal* and *Godey's Lady's Book* with a singular fascination not necessarily inherent in the flimsy sheets or their contents.

"I owe a great debt to Grandfather Canning's obsession," he observed, descending the ladder and joining me before the bookshelves. "It is not altogether a breach of confidence to admit that his interest in Poe did reach the point of an obsession, and perhaps eventually of an absolute mania. The knowledge, alas, is public property, I fear.

"In the early Seventies he built this house, and I am quite sure that you have been observant enough to note that it in itself is almost a replica of a typical Poesque mansion. This was his study, and it was here that he was wont to pore over the books, the letters and the numerous mementos of Poe's life.

"What prompted a retired merchant to devote himself so fanatically to the pursuit of a hobby, I cannot say. Let it suffice that he virtually withdrew from the world and from all other normal interests. He conducted a voluminous and lengthy correspondence with aging men and women who had known Poe in their lifetimes—made pilgrimages to Fordham, sent his agents to West Point, to England and Scotland, to virtually every locale in which Poe had set foot during his lifetime. He acquired letters and souvenirs as gifts, he bought them and—I fear—stole them, if no other means of acquisition proved feasible."

Launcelot Canning smiled and nodded. "Does all this sound strange to you? I confess that once I too found it almost incredible, a fragment of romance. Now, after years spent amidst these surroundings, I have lost my own objectivity."

"Yes, it is strange," I replied. "But are you quite sure that there was not some obscure personal reason for your grandfather's interest? Had he met Poe as a boy, or been closely associated with one of his friends? Was there, perhaps, a distant, undisclosed relationship?"

At the mention of the last word, Canning started visibly, and a tremor of agitation overspread his countenance.

"Ah!" he exclaimed. "There you voice my own inmost conviction. A relationship—assuredly there must have been—I am morally, instinctively certain that Grandfather Canning felt or knew himself to be linked to Edgar Poe by ties of blood. Nothing else could account for his strong initial interest, his continuing defense of Poe in the literary controversies of the day, his final melancholy lapse into a world of delusion and illusion.

"Yet he never voiced a statement or put an allegation upon paper — and I have searched the collection of letters in vain for the slightest clue.

"It is curious that you so promptly divine a suspicion held not only by myself but by my father. He was only a child at the time of my Grandfather Canning's death, but the attendant circumstances left a profound impression upon his sensitive nature. Although he was immediately removed from this house to the home of his mother's people in Baltimore, he lost no time in returning upon assuming his inheritance in early manhood.

"Fortunately being in possession of a considerable income, he was able to devote his entire lifetime to further research. The name of Arthur Canning is still well known in the world of literary criticism, but for some reason he preferred to pursue his scholarly examination of Poe's career in privacy. I believe this preference was dictated by an inner sensibility; that he was endeavoring to unearth some information which would prove his father's, his, and for that matter, my own, kinship to Edgar Poe."

"You say your father was also a collector?" I prompted.

"A statement I am prepared to substantiate," replied my host, as he led me to yet another corner of the shadow-shrouded study. "But first, if you would accept a glass of wine?"

He filled, not glasses, but veritable beakers from a large carafe, and we toasted one another in silent appreciation. It is perhaps unnecessary for me to observe that the wine was a fine old Amontillado.

"Now, then," said Launcelot Canning. "My father's special province in Poe research consisted of the accumulation and study of letters."

Opening a series of large trays or drawers beneath the bookshelves, he drew out file after file of glassined folios, and for the space of the next half hour I examined Edgar Poe's correspondence — letters to Henry Herring, to Doctor Snodgrass, Sarah Shelton, James P. Moss, Elizabeth Poe; missives to Mrs. Rockwood, Helen Whitman, Anne Lynch, John Pendleton Kennedy; notes to Mrs. Richmond, to John Allan, to Annie, to his brother, Henry — a profusion of documents, a veritable epistolatory cornucopia.

During the course of my perusal my host took occasion to refill our beakers with wine, and the heady draught began to take effect — for we had not eaten, and I own I gave no thought to food, so absorbed was I in the yellowed pages illumining Poe's past.

Here was wit, erudition, literary criticism; here were the muddled, maudlin outpourings of a mind gone in drink and despair; here was the draft of a projected story, the fragments of a poem; here was a pitiful cry for deliverance and a paean to living beauty; here was dignified response to a dunning letter and an auctorial *pronunciamento* to an admirer; here was love, hate, pride, anger, celestial serenity, abject penitence, authority, wonder, resolution, indecision, joy, and soul-sickening melancholia.

Here was the gifted elocutionist, the stammering drunkard, the adoring husband, the frantic lover, the proud editor, the indigent pauper, the grandiose dreamer, the shabby realist, the scientific inquirer, the gullible metaphysician, the dependent stepson, the free and untrammeled spirit, the hack, the poet, the enigma that was Edgar Allan Poe.

Again the beakers were filled and emptied. I drank deeply with my lips, and with my eyes more deeply still.

For the first time the true enthusiasm of Launcelot Canning was communicated to my own sensibilities—I divined the eternal fascination found in a consideration of Poe the writer and Poe the man; he who wrote Tragedy, lived Tragedy, was Tragedy; he who penned Mystery, lived and died in Mystery, and who today looms on the literary scene as Mystery incarnate.

And Mystery Poe remained, despite Arthur Canning's careful study of the letters. "My father learned nothing," my host confided, "even though he assembled, as you see here, a collection to delight the heart of a Mabbott or a Quinn. So his search ranged farther. By this time I was old enough to share both his interest and his inquiries. Come," and he led me to an ornate chest which rested beneath the windows against the west wall of the study.

Kneeling, he unlocked the repository, and then drew forth, in rapid and marvelous succession, a series of objects, each of which boasted of intimate connection with Poe's life.

There were souvenirs of his youth and his schooling abroad; a book he had used during his sojourn at West Point; mementos of his days as a theatrical critic in the form of playbills; a pen used during his editorial period; a fan once owned by his girl-wife, Virginia; a brooch of Mrs. Clemm's—a profusion of objects including such diverse articles as a cravat and, curiously enough, Poe's battered and tarnished flute.

Again we drank, and I own the wine was potent. Canning's countenance remained cadaverously wan but, moreover, there was a species of mad hilarity in his eyes—an evident restrained hysteria in his whole demeanor. At length, from the scattered heap of *curiosa*, I happened to draw forth and examine a little box of no remarkable character, whereupon I was constrained to inquire its history and what part it had played in the life of Poe.

"In the *life* of Poe?" A visible tremor convulsed the features of my host, then rapidly passed in transformation to a grimace, a rictus of amusement. "This little box—and you will note how, by some fateful design or contrived coincidence it bears a resemblance to the box he himself conceived of and described in his tale, *Berenice*—this little box is concerned with his death rather than his life. It is, in fact, the selfsame box my grandfather Christopher Canning clutched to his bosom when they found him down there."

Again the tremor, again the grimace. "But stay, I have not yet told you of the details. Perhaps you would be interested in seeing the spot where Christopher Canning was stricken; I have already told you of his madness, but I did no more than hint at the character of his delusions. You have been patient with me, and more than patient. Your understanding shall be rewarded, for I perceive you can be fully entrusted with the facts."

What further revelations Canning was prepared to make I could not say, but his manner was such as to inspire a vague disquiet and trepidation in my breast.

Upon perceiving my unease he laughed shortly and laid a hand upon my shoulder. "Come, this should interest you as an aficionado of fantasy," he said. "But first, another drink to speed our journey."

He poured, we drank, and then he led the way from that vaulted chamber, down the silent halls, down the staircase, and into the lowest recesses of the building until we reached what resembled a dungeon, its floor and the interior of a long archway carefully sheathed in copper. We paused before a door of massive iron. Again I felt in the aspect of this scene an element evocative of recognition or recollection.

Canning's intoxication was such that he misinterpreted, or chose to misinterpret, my reaction.

"You need not be afraid," he assured me. "Nothing has happened down here since that day, almost seventy years ago, when his servants discovered him stretched out before this door, the little box clutched to his bosom; collapsed, and in a state of delirium from which he never emerged. For six months he lingered, a hopeless maniac — raving as wildly from the very moment of his discovery as at the moment he died — babbling his visions of the giant horse, the fissured house collapsing into the tarn, the black cat, the pit, the pendulum, the raven on the pallid bust, the beating heart, the pearly teeth, and the nearly liquid mass of loathsome — of detestable putridity from which a voice emanated.

"Nor was that all he babbled," Canning confided, and here his voice sank to a whisper that reverberated through the copper-sheathed hall and against the iron door. "He hinted other things far worse than fantasy — of a ghastly reality surpassing the phantasms of Poe.

"For the first time my father and the servants learned the purpose of the room he had built beyond this iron door, and learned too what Christopher Canning had done to establish his title as the world's foremost collector of Poe.

"For he babbled again of Poe's death, thirty years earlier, in 1849 — of the burial in the Presbyterian Cemetery and of the removal of the coffin in 1875 to the corner where the monument was raised. As I told you, and as was known then, my grandfather had played a public part in instigating that removal. But now we learned of the private part — learned that there was a monument and a grave, but no coffin in the earth beneath Poe's alleged resting place. The coffin now rested in the secret room at the end of this passage. That is why the room, the house itself, had been built.

"I tell you, he had stolen the body of Edgar Allan Poe—and as he shrieked aloud in his final madness, did not this indeed make him the greatest collector of Poe?

"His ultimate intent was never divined, but my father made one significant discovery—the little box clutched to Christopher Canning's bosom contained a portion of the crumbled bones, the veritable dust that was all that remained of Poe's corpse."

My host shuddered and turned away. He led me back along that hall of horror, up the stairs, into the study. Silently, he filled our beakers, and I drank as hastily, as deeply, as desperately as he.

"What could my father do? To own the truth was to create a public scandal. He chose instead to keep silence, to devote his own life to study in retirement.

"Naturally, the shock affected him profoundly; to my knowledge he never entered the room beyond the iron door and, indeed, I did not know of the room or its contents until the hour of his death—and it was not until some years later that I myself found the key amongst his effects.

"But find the key I did, and the story was immediately and completely corroborated. Today I am the greatest collector of Poe—for he lies in the keep below, my eternal trophy!"

This time I poured the wine. As I did so, I noted for the first time the imminence of a storm—the impetuous fury of its gusts shaking the casements and the echoes of its thunder rolling and rumbling down the time-corroded corridors of the old house.

The wild, overstrained vivacity with which my host hearkened, or apparently hearkened, to these sounds did nothing to reassure me—for his recent revelation led me to suspect his sanity.

That the body of Edgar Allan Poe had been stolen; that this mansion had been built to house it; that it was indeed enshrined in a crypt below; that grandsire, son and grandson had dwelt here alone, apart, enslaved to a sepulchral secret—was beyond sane belief or tolerance.

And yet, surrounded now by the night and the storm, in a setting torn from Poe's own frenzied fancies, I could not be sure. Here the past was still alive, the very spirit of Poe's tales breathed forth its corruption upon the scene.

As thunder boomed, Launcelot Canning took up Poe's flute, and, whether in defiance of the storm without or as a mocking accompaniment, he played; blowing upon it with drunken persistence, with eerie atonality, with nerve-shattering shrillness. To the shrieking of that infernal instrument the thunder added a braying counterpoint.

Uneasy, uncertain and unnerved, I retreated into the shadows of the bookshelves at the farther end of the room and idly scanned the titles of a row of ancient tomes. Here was the CHIROMANCY of Robert Flud; the DIREC-

TORIUM INQUISITORIUM, a rare and curious book in quarto Gothic that was the manual of a forgotten church; and betwixt and between the volumes of pseudo-scientific inquiry, theological speculation and sundry incunabula I found titles that arrested and appalled me. DE VERMIS MYSTERIIS and the LIBER EIBON, treatises on demonology, on witchcraft, on sorcery, moldered in crumbling bindings. The books were old, the books were tattered and torn, but the books were not dusty. They had been read—

"Read them?" It was as though Canning divined my inmost thoughts. He had put aside his flute and now approached me, tittering as though in continued drunken defiance of the storm. Odd echoes and boomings now sounded through the long halls of the house, and curious grating sounds threatened to drown out his words and his laughter.

"Read them?" said Canning. "I study them. Yes, I have gone beyond Grandfather, and Father, too. It was I who procured the books that held the key, and it was I who found the key. A key more difficult to discover, and more important, than the key to the vaults below. I often wonder if Poe himself had access to these selfsame tomes, knew the selfsame secrets. The secrets of the grave and what lies beyond, and what can be summoned forth if one but holds the key."

He stumbled away and returned with wine. "Drink," he said. "Drink to the night and the storm."

I brushed the proffered glass aside. "Enough," I said. "I must be on my way."

Was it fancy, or did I find fear frozen on his features? Canning clutched my arm and cried, "No, stay with me! This is no night on which to be alone; I swear I cannot abide the thought of being alone. You must not, cannot leave me here alone; I can bear to be alone no more!"

His incoherent babble mingled with the thunder and the echoes; I drew back and confronted him. "Control yourself," I counseled. "Confess that this is a hoax, an elaborate imposture arranged to please your fancy."

"Hoax? Imposture? Stay, and I shall prove to you beyond all doubt—" And so saying, Launcelot Canning stooped and opened a small drawer set in the wall beneath and beside the bookshelves. "This should repay you for your interest in my story, and in Poe," he murmured. "Know that you are the first other than myself to glimpse these treasures."

He handed me a sheaf of manuscripts on plain white paper—documents written in ink curiously similar to that I had noted while perusing Poe's letters. Pages were clipped together in groups, and for a moment I scanned titles alone.

"*The Worm of Midnight, by Edgar Poe*," I read, aloud. "*The Crypt*," I breathed. And here, "*The Further Adventures of Arthur Gordon Pym*." In my agitation I came close to dropping the precious pages. "Are these what they appear to be—the unpublished tales of Poe?"

My host bowed. "Unpublished, undiscovered, unknown, save to me—and to you."

"But this cannot be," I protested. "Surely there would have been a mention of them somewhere, in Poe's own letters or those of his contemporaries. There would have been a clue, an indication—somewhere, someplace, somehow."

Thunder mingled with my words, and thunder echoed in Canning's shouted reply.

"You dare to presume an imposture? Then compare!" He stooped again and brought out a glassined folio of letters. "Here—is this not the veritable script of Edgar Poe? Look at the calligraphy of the letters, then at the manuscripts. Can you say they are not penned by the selfsame hand?"

I looked at the handwriting, wondered at the possibility of a monomaniac's forgery. Could Launcelot Canning, a victim of mental disorder, thus painstakingly simulate Poe's hand?

"Read, then!" Canning screamed through the thunder. "Read, and dare to say that these tales were written by any other than Edgar Poe, whose genius defies the corruption of Time and the Conqueror Worm!"

I read but a line or two, holding the topmost manuscript close to eyes that strained beneath wavering candlelight; but even in the flickering illumination I noted that which told me the only, the incontestable truth. For the paper, the curiously *unyellowed* paper, bore a visible watermark; the name of a firm of modern stationers and the date—1949.

Putting the sheaf aside, I endeavored to compose myself as I moved away from Launcelot Canning. For now I knew the truth; knew that, one hundred years after Poe's death, a semblance of his spirit still lived in the distorted and disordered soul of Canning. Incarnation, reincarnation, call it what you will; Canning was, in his own irrational mind, Edgar Allan Poe.

Stifled and dull echoes of thunder from a remote portion of the mansion now commingled with the soundless seething of my own inner turmoil, as I turned and rashly addressed my host.

"Confess!" I cried. "Is it not true that you have written these tales, fancying yourself the embodiment of Poe? Is it not true that you suffer from a singular delusion born of solitude and everlasting brooding upon the past; that you have reached a stage characterized by the conviction that Poe still lives on in your own person?"

A strong shudder came over him, and a sickly smile quivered about his lips as he replied. "Fool! I say to you that I have spoken the truth. Can you doubt the evidence of your senses? This house is real, the Poe collection exists, and the stories exist—exist, I swear, as truly as the body in the crypt below!"

I took up the little box from the table and removed the lid. "Not so," I answered. "You said your grandfather was found with this box clutched to his breast, before the door of the vault, and that it contained Poe's dust. Yet you cannot escape the fact that the box is empty." I faced him furiously. "Admit it, the story is a fabrication, a romance. Poe's body does not lie beneath this house, nor are these his unpublished works, written during his lifetime and concealed."

"True enough." Canning's smile was ghastly beyond belief. "The dust is gone because I took it and used it—because in the works of wizardry I found the formulae, the arcana whereby I could raise the flesh, recreate the body from the essential salts of the grave. Poe does not *lie* beneath this house—he *lives!* And the tales are *his posthumous works!*"

Accented by thunder, his words crashed against my consciousness.

"That was the be-all and end-all of my planning, of my studies, of my work, of my life! To raise, by sorcery, the veritable spirit of Edgar Poe from the grave—reclothed and animate in flesh—and set him to dwell and dream and do his work again in the private chambers I built in the vaults below— and this I have done! To steal a corpse is but a ghoulish prank; mine is the achievement of true genius!"

The distinct, hollow, metallic and clangorous, yet apparently muffled, reverberation accompanying his words caused him to turn in his seat and face the door of the study, so that I could not see the workings of his countenance—nor could he read my reaction to his ravings.

His words came but faintly to my ears through the thunder that now shook the house in a relentless grip; the wind rattling the casements and flickering the candle flame from the great silver candelabra sent a soaring sighing in anguished accompaniment to his speech.

"I would show him to you, but I dare not; for he hates me as he hates life. I have locked him in the vault, alone, for the resurrected have no need of food nor drink. And he sits there, pen moving over paper, endlessly moving, endlessly pouring out the evil essence of all he guessed and hinted at in life and which he learned in death.

"Do you not see the tragic pity of my plight? I sought to raise his spirit from the dead, to give the world anew of his genius—and yet these tales, these works, are filled and fraught with a terror not to be endured. They cannot be shown to the world, he cannot be shown to the world; in bringing back the dead I have brought back the fruits of death!"

Echoes sounded anew as I moved toward the door—moved, I confess, to flee this accursed house and its accursed owner.

Canning clutched my hand, my arm, my shoulder. "You cannot go!" he shouted above the storm. "I spoke of his escaping, but did you not guess? Did you not hear it through the thunder—the grating of the door?"

I pushed him aside and he blundered backward, upsetting the candela-bra, so that flames licked now across the carpeting.

"Wait!" he cried. "Have you not heard his footstep on the stair? MAD-MAN, I TELL YOU THAT HE NOW STANDS WITHOUT THE DOOR!"

A rush of wind, a roar of flame, a shroud of smoke rose all about us. Throwing open the huge antique panels to which Canning pointed, I staggered into the hall.

I speak of wind, of flame, of smoke—enough to obscure all vision. I speak of Canning's screams, and of thunder loud enough to drown all sound. I speak of terror born of loathing and of desperation enough to shatter all sanity.

Despite these things, I can never erase from my consciousness that which I beheld as I fled past the doorway and down the hall.

There without the doors there *did* stand a lofty and enshrouded figure; a figure all too familiar, with pallid features, high, domed forehead, mustache set above a mouth. My glimpse lasted but an instant, an instant during which the man—the corpse, the apparition, the hallucination, call it what you will—moved forward into the chamber and clasped Canning to its breast in an unbreakable embrace. Together, the two figures tottered toward the flames, which now rose to blot out vision forevermore.

From that chamber, and from that mansion, I fled aghast. The storm was still abroad in all its wrath, and now fire came to claim the house of Canning for its own.

Suddenly there shot along the path before me a wild light, and I turned to see whence a gleam so unusual could have issued—but it was only the flames, rising in supernatural splendor to consume the mansion, and the secrets, of the man who collected Poe.

LUCY COMES TO STAY

"YOU CAN'T GO ON this way."

Lucy kept her voice down low, because she knew the nurse had her room just down the hall from mine, and I wasn't supposed to see any visitors.

"But George is doing everything he can—poor dear, I hate to think of what all those doctors and specialists are costing him, and the sanatorium bill, too. And now that nurse, that Miss Higgins, staying here every day."

"It won't do any good. You know it won't." Lucy didn't sound like she was arguing with me. She knew. That's because Lucy is smarter than I am. Lucy wouldn't have started the drinking and gotten into such a mess in the first place. So it was about time I listened to what she said.

"Look, Vi," she murmured. "I hate to tell you this. You aren't well, you know. But you're going to find out one of these days anyway, and you might as well hear it from me."

"What is it, Lucy?"

"About George, and the doctors. They don't think you're going to get well." She paused. "They don't want you to."

"Oh, Lucy!"

"Listen to me, you little fool. Why do you suppose they sent you to that sanatorium in the first place? They said it was to take the cure. So you took it. All right, you're cured, then. But you'll notice that you still have the doctor coming every day, and George makes you stay here in your room, and that Miss Higgins who's supposed to be a special nurse—you know what she is, don't you? She's a guard."

I couldn't say anything. I just sat there and blinked. I wanted to cry, but I couldn't, because deep down inside I knew Lucy was right.

"Just try to get out of here," Lucy said. "You'll see how fast she locks the

165

door on you. All that talk about special diets and rest doesn't fool me. Look at yourself—you're as well as I am! You ought to be getting out, seeing people, visiting your friends."

"But I have no friends," I reminded her. "Not after that party, not after what I did—"

"That's a lie." Lucy nodded. "That's what George wants you to think. Why, you have hundreds of friends, Vi. They still love you. They tried to see you at the hospital and George wouldn't let them in. They sent flowers to the sanatorium and George told the nurses to burn them."

"He did? He told the nurses to burn the flowers?"

"Of course. Look, Vi, it's about time you faced the truth. George wants them to think you're sick. George wants you to think you're sick. Why? Because then he can put you away for good. Not in a private sanatorium, but in the—"

"No!" I began to shake. I couldn't stop shaking. It was ghastly. But it proved something. They told me at the sanatorium, the doctors told me, that if I took the cure I wouldn't get the shakes any more. Or the dreams, or any of the other things. Yet here it was—I was shaking again.

"Shall I tell you some more?" Lucy whispered. "Shall I tell you what they're putting in your food? Shall I tell you about George and Miss Higgins?"

"But she's older than he is, and besides he'd never—"

Lucy laughed.

"Stop it!" I yelled.

"All right. But don't yell, you little fool. Do you want Miss Higgins to come in?"

"She thinks I'm taking a nap. She gave me a sedative."

"Lucky I dumped it out." Lucy frowned. "Vi, I've got to get you away from here. And there isn't much time."

She was right. There wasn't much time. Seconds, hours, days, weeks—how long had it been since I'd had a drink?

"We'll sneak off," Lucy said. "We could take a room together where they wouldn't find us. I'll nurse you until you're well."

"But rooms cost money."

"You have that fifty dollars George gave you for a party dress."

"Why, Lucy," I said. "How did you know that?"

"You told me ages ago, dear. Poor thing, you don't remember things very well, do you? All the more reason for trusting me."

I nodded. I could trust Lucy. Even though she was responsible, in a way, for me starting to drink. She just had thought it would cheer me up when George brought all his high-class friends to the house and we went out to impress his clients. Lucy had tried to help. I could trust her. I must trust her—

"We can leave as soon as Miss Higgins goes tonight," Lucy was saying. "We'll wait until George is asleep, eh? Why not get dressed now, and I'll come back for you."

I got dressed. It isn't easy to dress when you have the shakes, but I did it. I even put on some makeup and trimmed my hair a little with the big scissors. Then I looked at myself in the mirror and said out loud, "Why, you can't tell, can you?"

"Of course not," said Lucy. "You look radiant. Positively radiant."

I stood there smiling, and the sun was going down, just shining through the window on the scissors in a way that hurt my eyes, and all at once I was so sleepy.

"George will be here soon, and Miss Higgins will leave," Lucy said. "I'd better go now. Why don't you rest until I come for you?"

"Yes," I said. "You'll be very careful, won't you?"

"Very careful," Lucy whispered as she tiptoed out quietly.

I lay down on the bed and then I was sleeping, really sleeping for the first time in weeks, sleeping so the scissors wouldn't hurt my eyes, the way George hurt me inside when he wanted to shut me up in the asylum so he and Miss Higgins could make love on my bed and laugh at me the way they all laughed except Lucy and she would take care of me she knew what to do now I could trust her when George came and I must sleep and sleep and nobody can blame you for what you think in your sleep or do in your sleep. . . .

It was all right until I had the dreams, and even then I didn't really worry about them because a dream is only a dream, and when I was drunk I had a lot of dreams.

When I woke up I had the shakes again, but it was Lucy shaking me, standing there in the dark shaking me, I looked around and saw that the door to my room was open, but Lucy didn't bother to whisper.

She stood there with the scissors in her hand and called to me.

"Come on, let's hurry."

"What are you doing with the scissors?" I asked.

"Cutting the telephone wires, silly! I got into the kitchen after Miss Higgins left and dumped some of that sedative into George's coffee. Remember, I told you the plan."

I couldn't remember now, but I knew it was all right. Lucy and I went out through the hall, past George's room, and he never stirred. Then we went downstairs and out the front door and the streetlights hurt my eyes. Lucy made me hurry right along, though.

We took a bus around the corner. This was the difficult part, getting away. Once we were out of the neighborhood there'd be no worry. The wires were cut.

The lady at the rooming house on the South Side didn't know about the wires being cut. She didn't know about me, either, because Lucy got the room.

Lucy marched in bold as brass and laid my fifty dollars down on the desk. The rent was $12.50 a week in advance, and Lucy didn't even ask to see the room. I guess that's why the landlady wasn't worried about baggage.

We got upstairs and locked the door, and then I had the shakes again.

Lucy said, "Vi—cut it out!"

"But I can't help it. What'll I do now, Lucy? Oh, what'll I do? Why did I ever—"

"Shut up!" Lucy opened my purse and pulled something out. I had been wondering why my purse felt so heavy, but I never dreamed about the secret.

She held the secret up. It glittered under the light, like the scissors, only this was a nice glittering. A golden glittering.

"A whole pint!" I gasped. "Where did you get it?"

"From the cupboard downstairs, naturally. You knew George still keeps the stuff around. I slipped it into your purse, just in case.'"

I had the shakes, but I got that bottle open in ten seconds. One of my fingernails broke, and then the stuff was burning and warming and softening—

"Pig!" said Lucy.

"You know I had to have it," I whispered. "That's why you brought it."

"I don't like to see you drink," Lucy answered. "I never drink and I don't like to see you hang one on, either."

"Please, Lucy. Just this once."

"Why can't you take a shot and then leave it alone? That's all I ask."

"Just this once, Lucy, I have to."

"I won't sit here and watch you make a spectacle of yourself. You know what always happens—another mess."

I took another gulp. The bottle was half empty.

"I did all I could for you, Vi. But if you don't stop now, I'm going."

That made me pause. "You couldn't do that to me. I need you, Lucy. Until I'm straightened out, anyway."

Lucy laughed, the way I didn't like. "Straightened out! That's a hot one! Talking about straightening out with a bottle in your hand. It's no use, Vi. Here I do everything I can for you, stop at nothing to get you away, and you're off on another."

"Please. You know I can't help it."

"Oh, yes, you can help it, Vi. But you don't want to. You've always had to make a choice, you know. George or the bottle. Me or the bottle. And the bottle always wins. I think deep down inside you hate George. You hate me."

"You're my best friend."

"Nuts!" Lucy talked vulgar sometimes, when she got really mad. And she was mad now. It made me so nervous I had another drink.

"Oh, I'm good enough for you when you're in trouble, or have nobody else around to talk to. I'm good enough to lie for you, pull you out of your messes. But I've never been good enough for your friends, for George. And I can't even win over a bottle of rotgut whiskey. It's no use, Vi. What I've done for you today you'll never know. And it isn't enough. Keep your lousy whiskey. I'm going."

I know I started to cry. I tried to get up, but the room was turning round and round. Then Lucy was walking out the door and I dropped the bottle and the light kept shining the way it did on the scissors and I closed my eyes and dropped after the bottle to the floor. . . .

When I woke up they were all pestering me, the landlady and the doctor and Miss Higgins and the man who said he was a policeman.

I wondered if Lucy had gone to them and betrayed me, but when I asked the doctor said no, they just discovered me through a routine checkup on hotels and rooming houses after they found George's body in his bed with my scissors in his throat.

All at once I knew what Lucy had done, and why she ran out on me that way. She knew they'd find me and call it murder.

So I told them about her and how it must have happened. I even figured out how Lucy managed to get my fingerprints on the scissors.

But Miss Higgins said she'd never seen Lucy in my house, and the landlady told a lie and said I had registered for the room alone, and the man from the police just laughed when I kept begging him to find Lucy and make her tell the truth.

Only the doctor seemed to understand, and when we were alone together in the little room he asked me all about her and what she looked like, and I told him.

Then he brought over a mirror and held it up and asked me if I could see her. And sure enough —

She was standing right behind me, laughing. I could see her in the mirror and I told the doctor so, and he said yes, he thought he understood now.

So it was all right after all. Even when I got the shakes just then and dropped the mirror, so that the little jagged pieces hurt my eyes to look at, it was all right.

Lucy was back with me now, and she wouldn't ever go away any more. She'd stay with me forever. I knew that. I knew it, because even though the light hurt my eyes, Lucy began to laugh.

After a minute, I began to laugh, too. And then the two of us were laughing together, we couldn't stop even when the doctor went away. We just stood there against the bars, Lucy and I, laughing like crazy.

THE THINKING CAP

1

He opened the cupboard door.

An empty gin bottle tilted forward and crashed to the floor. He ignored it and groped inside the cupboard, his fingers scrabbling air. As he did so, he began to talk to himself. A nasty habit, but one he seemed to have acquired.

"But when she got there, the cupboard was bare, and so the poor dog had none. Poor dog. That's me, all right. Poor, poor dog." He paused. "Eureka!"

At the very back of the cupboard his hand encountered and closed around a can. He pulled it out and inspected the label. "Not Eureka after all. Beans. That's better. And so the poor dog had beans."

He put the can of beans on the table and switched on the little electric grill that rested on the washstand. He bent down, found a small pan—it wasn't really too dirty—and set it on the glowing grid.

"Can opener," he muttered. "Can't open her without a can opener. Canopius. Canopy. Canopy soup." He stood there for a moment and all the words rushed through his head, rushed in riot, uncontrolled. "Soup. Super. Superman has found a can. Can he open? Open sesame. Sesame seed. Sesame seed something. Sesame seed a can of beans. Baked beans. Human beans. Norman Bean—that's the name Edgar Rice Burroughs used at first. When he was still poor, and trying to get a break, and eating beans. Like me. Nobody likes me. Nobody loves me. I don't even have a can opener."

Suddenly he stopped, and his voice sank to a whisper. He didn't know who he'd been talking to *before*, but now he was really talking to *himself*. And he whispered, very softly, "Look now, you've got to stop this. You've got to get hold of yourself. You don't want to go crazy, do you? Or do you?"

He abandoned the search for the can opener and stepped over to the mirror. It didn't take him long. The whole room was only ten by fourteen, plus the closet. Grill, cupboard, washbowl, bed, two chairs, end table with the cheap portable radio, and of course the card table with the portable typewriter resting on it. That was the inventory, the inventory of the room's contents.

Now he stood in front of the mirror above the washbowl and took inventory of himself.

The long, thin face was even longer and thinner today. The cheeks seemed to be slightly sunken—where had he seen that particular conformation before?

The eyes were bright blue but slightly glazed, and this phenomenon, too, was familiar.

His brown hair was plastered back on his forehead, and it lay dully and without luster. Somehow, he recognized a similarity here, also.

His skin was pale. Waxy pale. He knew that pallor. It was somehow tied in with the sunken cheeks and the glazed eyes and the dully plastered hair, because it was associated with the look of a—

"Corpse!" he whispered. "You look like a corpse. You're dead. Dead, or dying. Got to do something. Got to."

Yes, he had to do something, but what? Drinking hadn't helped. And he couldn't drink any more, anyway, because the last of the money was gone. He couldn't get out of this dingy little furnished room, either—not until the end of the month. Then he'd be thrown out.

And worst of all, he couldn't write.

That was the crux of the problem. He couldn't write. The portable typewriter rested on the card table. It rested. But he didn't rest. He couldn't rest. He couldn't rest because he couldn't write, and then he drank because he couldn't rest, and when he drank he couldn't write, either. Not writing led to drinking which led to not writing which led to—looking like a corpse. Becoming a corpse. If he didn't go mad first.

"Save me," he whispered to himself in the mirror. "Save me!" But the face staring back was impassive. The face knew all there was to know about him.

Barnaby Codd, aged thirty. Occupation, writer. Status, single. Future, dubious. Or all too certain.

And the face knew the facts behind the facts. Knew about the seven years of work, the stories rejected, the stories sold, the brave beginnings and the bitter end. It knew about Peggy and the broken engagement—about the furnished apartment with its five rooms when the writing came easily. It knew about the cases of bonded whiskey when the stuff was selling to the better markets, and it knew about the empty bottle of the cheapest gin (going crazy, how can there be an *empty* bottle of cheapest anything?) when he hit the slump. When the slump hit him, which was now, now, now. When he couldn't rest, couldn't keep from drinking, couldn't start the writing. When he got into this horrible habit of talking to himself and his brain ran away with the words and the thoughts and left nothing but a morass of maudlin self-pity.

Barnaby Codd stared at himself in the mirror and himself stared back with the impassivity of death. He was calm now. Calm as if in a coma. Coma, comma, Lake Como, Lake Perry Como, comme çi, comme ça, come wind, come rain, come hell or high water, come Dunder and Blitzen and Prancer and Rudolph the Rednosed Can Opener. Damn it to hell, where was the can opener, where was the magic key that opened the silver portals that led to the regal banquet of beans for His Majesty's pleasure?

It was very funny. No reason for him to cry. And yet he was crying, suddenly. The mirror was blurring, the room was beginning to spin, and there was a ringing in his ears.

"Telephone!" Mrs. Bixby, calling him. "Telephone, Mister Codd!"

Barnaby Codd rubbed his eyes, groped his way down the hall, answered the phone. "Hello . . . yes . . . yes . . . why, sure . . . yes, that would be fine . . . glad to . . . thanks."

He hung up. This was it, this was the reprieve, this was the last-minute call from the governor as they strapped him into the chair.

He was going to a party. A cocktail party, with a buffet supper. There'd be food, food, food—lots of food. And there'd be drink, drink, drink—lots of drink. And people. People like Hank Olcott, who'd invited him. People who still thought of him as a creative talent, who would introduce him, with a certain flourish of pride: "This is my friend, Barnaby Codd, the writer."

Yes, he still had a clean suit. And he could shave the hollow cheeks. He would go, and he would glow, and he could talk to others instead of to himself, and he could eat something better than beans and drink something better than cheap gin.

So Barnaby Codd washed and shaved and dressed and combed his hair. He turned off the electric grill. He picked up his hat and started for the door. Then he paused, turned back.

He went over to the washstand, grabbed up the can of baked beans and hurled it into the wastebasket.

2

Hank Olcott led him across the room and introduced him with a certain flourish. "This is my friend, Barnaby Codd, the writer." He did it once, he did it twice, he did it half a dozen times.

Codd kept feeling better and better. All that food, all that liquor, all these people milling around. A chance to talk, to notice and be noticed. Everything was becoming quite *real* once more, and Codd felt very much alive.

There must be at least forty people in the apartment, he estimated; they kept arriving and departing — the elegant, the effete, the eccentric and the egocentric. Where Olcott picked them up he didn't know. He had some odd friends, Codd mused. He himself was a good example.

As time passed, the character of the crowd changed. Some strangers had appeared; apparently the word was going around. It was the old story. Olcott told his friends he was holding a party, and they told *their* friends, and *they* told their friends, acquaintances, even their enemies.

Hank Olcott wasn't introducing him to very many people now. He didn't know very many people in this crowd. Codd speculated about making his departure. He felt very good, quite self-assured. Better quit now while he was ahead. Another drink might be one too many. Another introduction might be boring. But —

Then he saw the crimson poppy.

It swayed on its long green stem, its scarlet petals unfurled. It stood in slender splendor near the far windows, and Codd felt irresistibly drawn to its aura. He bent his head as if to inhale the perfume of its presence.

"My name is Barnaby Codd," he whispered.

"I'm Cleo Fane," said the crimson poppy.

Codd stared at the sheathing green gown, at the flowing red hair. This was no poppy, but a far more exotic flower. Face of Grecian marble, eyes cut from Chinese jade — Codd checked himself abruptly. He was letting go again, he realized; all this business of flowers, sculpture, purple prose. She was the most beautiful woman he'd ever seen — wasn't that enough?

And she was staring up at him with something very much like admiration in her slanted oval eyes.

"Do you belong here?" she was asking.

"Belong here?"

"Do you know these people?"

"Why — yes. That is, I know Olcott, our host. Great patron of the arts — dilettante, really. That's how I got in. I'm a writer."

She nodded. "I know."

A warm glow came over Codd. He smiled. "What do you do?" he asked.

"I don't belong here."

"Then let's leave, shall we?"

She put her arm on his. "Very well."

And that's all there was to it. In one minute he'd met the most beautiful woman he'd ever seen and walked away with her.

Olcott was standing at the portable bar, surrounded by an assortment of longhairs and crewcuts, and Codd made no effort to bid him goodbye.

Instead he walked out, floated out, flew out into the night with the ravishing redhead. Ravishing—

"Won't you be my guest for a few moments?" she was asking. "I have a place. It isn't far."

Codd had difficulty in comprehending her invitation. It was just too good to be true. This was the way it happened in stories; the way it happened in some of the stories he used to write.

Elation combined with alcohol within him to produce a strange alchemy. He knew he was drunk, he knew he couldn't walk very well, he knew that he had only a blurred awareness of the street, of movement, of entering a tall building and being ushered into a large room. A dim lamp glowed in the corner. Codd smelt a perfume that might have been incense, might have been the woman who stood close beside him, sat close beside him now on the long, low divan.

And then she turned to him, and it was like the surge of the sea, the warm tide flowing over him and bearing him up on its crest, and all at once he could talk, and the formless phrases and wild words made a certain sense.

". . . don't know how long I've been looking for someone like you . . . not someone *like* you, but *you*, though I never knew it . . . never thought anyone like you existed . . . never believed in Fate . . . or that Fate was a woman with red hair and green eyes and lips shaped as strange gateways to dreams . . ."

"What do you write?" She sat up suddenly, and her voice was almost crisp.

"Why—I—I— " Codd fumbled for reality. "What do I write? That's an odd question. I write many things. Poetry, and short stories, and there are two novels, half of a third—but that was over a year ago, when I stopped." He gulped, then took the plunge. "I'll be honest. I *was* a writer. But I can hardly claim to be one now. For a year I've been in a slump. Something happened to me, I don't know how to explain it. I can't write any more."

Cleo nodded in private affirmation. "That's why I wanted to meet you. I knew you needed help."

"What do you mean?"

For answer, Cleo rose. She disappeared somewhere in the dimness of the room. Codd sat there, wondering and waiting. He felt quite drunk now. Things were happening too quickly, and he had no way of evaluating the reality of events. On one level, it seemed like years since he'd been crying in front of the washstand mirror. On another, no time had elapsed at all.

Then Cleo was back. She was holding something in her hand, but the hand was below the level of the divan and Codd couldn't see anything from where he sat.

"This writing problem," she said. "Would you say you had established some sort of mental block?"

Codd sat up stiffly. "Say, what is this—are you a lady psychiatrist?"

Cleo laughed, a soft laugh of darkness and musk. "No. But I understand something about creation and its problems." Her voice became a persuasive purr. "I want to help you, you know."

"I know. And I'm trying to answer honestly. I just can't seem to function as a writer any more. I can't seem to grasp ideas properly, coherently. Everything flies apart into words, phrases, sentences. There's nothing consistent or coherent—I can't seem to concentrate." Codd's voice sank to a whisper. "Sometimes, lately, I wonder if I'm losing my mind."

"Losing your mind." Cleo smiled a smile of her own. "Odd that you should use that particular phrase."

"Why is it odd?"

"Have you ever stopped to think of what it means, what image it conveys? If you *lose* your mind, that indicates it has been mislaid—that it's *somewhere else*. Where is your mind now, Mr. Barnaby Codd?"

"Lost in flames," Codd whispered, as intoxication flooded over him again. "Lost in the flames of your hair and your eyes and your lips and—"

"Not now." She pushed him away. "This is important. To you. To me. And to someone else."

"Someone else?"

"Of course. I'm only what you might call an emissary. An agent. I couldn't invent something like this."

The hand came up from below the divan's level now. It came up in all its shining silver slimness, holding the odd-looking object.

"What in the world—or out of the world—is that?" Codd breathed.

"What does it look like?"

"Well, I'd say it was some kind of headdress, or helmet."

"You're correct. It is meant to be worn on the head."

"And those antennae, with the coiled tubing between them—make me think of television, and space pilots, and all that kid stuff."

"Let me assure you there is nothing childish about this invention. As you will soon learn, to your profit."

"I still don't understand."

"You will. I was directed to go out and find a subject for the experiment. A creative artist—painter, sculptor, musician, writer. Someone possessing a sensitive imagination, but unchanneled, undisciplined. To be blunt, an unsuccessful creative artist. A successful artist, in any field, wouldn't want or need to wear the helmet. You will."

"You mean somebody invented this and wants me to put it on my head?"

"Exactly."

"Now, wait a minute." Codd was suddenly quite sober. "This doesn't make sense. I may be going crazy, but I'm not *that* crazy. A beautiful woman comes to me and asks me to wear a Buck Rogers helmet invented by some mysterious screwball, and I'm supposed to go along with the gag."

"This is serious. You cannot begin to imagine just how serious. However, I am beginning to see I made a mistake. Yours is not the temperament I had judged it to be. I think you had better leave now."

Cleo stood up, moved away. And every inch of retreat was agony to Codd, every movement of withdrawal was poignant with pain. He couldn't lose her, he'd do anything, anything—

"Wait! Perhaps if you'd explain to me what this is all about, what the helmet is supposed to do, I'd understand."

"No. You are not the man I want."

"Please!" He was frankly begging her now. "I'll do anything you ask, anything."

She smiled and came closer. "That's better. Much, much better."

She held out the helmet. "Here, put it on."

"Now?"

"Exactly."

He held it in his hand. The metal was cool but oddly light and malleable. In the dim light he could not discern the nature of the coiled tubing or the antennae to which it was attached.

"What—what am I supposed to do when I wear it?"

"You'll understand everything. Just put it on." Her smile was mocking, now. "What's the matter? Afraid I'm going to harm you?"

It was the proper challenge for the moment. Barnaby Codd lifted the helmet. He placed it on his head firmly—Napoleon grasping the coronet from the Pope and crowning himself emperor. The helmet fitted snugly over his skull. At the point where the two antennae were based, something began to bore into his brain.

He stared ahead for a moment, looking at Cleo. Her face was rapt, her eyes closed. He had the oddest sensation that her eyes were in the antennae, that the antennae were in his brain, that his brain was in another world. He stared at her hair, and the flames leapt up, and Barnaby Codd drowned in their fire.

Then he didn't feel the helmet, didn't see her any more. He was in another world. . . .

3

The sky was green.

The moons were green too—and there were three of them. The trees and grass and rocks were green. In the distance the green lake rippled, and Codd could see the curious emerald reflection coursing across it.

He gazed up at the source of the reflection and perceived the green girl riding the green dog. The dog was something like a poodle, with enormously exaggerated ears. But then, everything about the dog was enormously exaggerated—it must have been five feet high and fifteen feet long.

The dog wore one of the curious helmets too, and it bounded in twenty-foot leaps across the greensward.

Riding on the dog's back was a green girl. A helmet rested on her green curls, and her green eyes glittered lividly. Yes, she had green curls—but she was Cleo!

Codd stared. That was all he could do—simply stare. He wanted to move toward her, wanted to cry out, but he couldn't. He willed his feet to move. Nothing happened.

Then he glanced down and saw the answer. He had no feet. He had no feet, no legs, no torso, no arms, nothing. He was wearing the helmet, but he had no head. He could see, but he had no eyes.

There was nothing to do but watch and wait—watch and wait as the green girl bounded past on the green dog. Then the rocket roared across the green sky, and Codd blinked. *Codd* blinked; his eyes didn't, for he had none.

The rocket was not green. It was silver, and an orange jet blasted behind it. If the rocket was not green, that meant it was not of this world. It came from somewhere else. It swooped across the horizon, disappeared. Then, abruptly, it reappeared over the lake. It was lower now, ready to make a landing.

Codd wanted to be close to it when it landed.

Abruptly, he *was* closer. He watched the landing, watched the men emerge.

Cleo and the dog had disappeared. There were only the men, now: the Earthmen of the future on a strange green planet. He found that he could *will* himself to move closer or away; they could not see him, although he could see them. He found that he could hear them, too, faintly or plainly, as he desired. The sensation was similar to that of watching a motion picture and photographing it simultaneously, choosing the camera angles he wished.

And during the next hour, he saw the picture unreel. The planet was explored by the rocket ship's crew. The captain and the three leading crewmen enacted a private drama of their own. The crew was going mad. It was the color that did it—the effort of adjusting to a world where everything was green. They mutinied. They tried to steal the ship. The captain alone did not crack. He fought them off. They succumbed, one by one, to the green lure of the lake, to the call of the green jungle, to the green death of the swamp. It was, in a way, an absorbing psychological study—the unpredictable effect of subjecting a normal mind and a normal pair of eyes to a single, unvarying, constant color.

The last crew member died in a crazy attempt to paint the rocket ship green. He succeeded—and failed, for the captain shot him.

And now the captain was alone. Alone, and sane, for he wouldn't yield to his environment. He was stronger than the planet, stronger than the mysterious force of chlorophyll or radiation or combination of both that made everything on its surface conform to its greenness.

His will did not break, his mind did not give way. He prepared to return to Earth alone. It was only when he reached the end of his ordeal and found the safety of his cabin that he stared in the mirror—and saw that he had turned green.

The film ended there. Or rather, the green came up. Codd felt himself falling away from it, falling into greenness, falling into blackness, falling into redness. . . .

Her hair, covering his face. And her voice whispering, "Wake up, now. Wake up. I've taken it off."

He was awake, and she *had* taken off the helmet. He sat there, dazed, and she handed him a drink. Outside the windows a false dawn paled, then was blotted out in final darkness.

"What happened?" he whispered.

"You tell me," she suggested. *"You* wore the helmet."

Barnaby Codd told her. She nodded from time to time, nodded thoughtfully.

"But I don't understand it at all," he concluded. "You were in the dream, and there was a dog, and a spaceship, and everything was green, yet it made a story."

"That's the whole point," said Cleo. "The experiment was successful, because it made a story. Do you think you could write that story, now, and sell it?"

Codd stood up. "Why—yes, I guess so. I've never tried anything in science fiction or fantasy before, but the market is there. And this psychological angle, about the effects of color, would work in."

"Then why don't you do it?" the woman suggested.

"Because I've got to know what happened, first. I've got to understand this thing. Where did the story come from?"

"From your own mind, of course," Cleo told him. "The helmet merely organized the various subconscious images in a coherent form. I don't pretend to know the mechanism—but the helmet integrates thought patterns. Some of the elements you observed are simple enough to figure out."

"Such as?"

"Well, myself, for example. I belonged in the prelude to the story because I was 'on your mind,' you might say. And the dog—" She hesitated.

"Go on," he prompted.

"The dog was probably a symbol of yourself. You *have* felt like a dog lately, even told yourself that you were a 'dog,' haven't you?"

Codd smiled. "Tell me more."

"The rocket ship? Well, you spoke of the helmet as if it was a science fiction gadget. Pure association there."

Codd nodded. "And the color green?"

Cleo sighed. "I must admit to a little cheating, there. I had to do something that would help me check. So while you wore the helmet and stared off into nothingness—"

"Is that what I did all that time?" Codd interrupted.

"Yes. You just sat in a trance, eyes open, until it was over. And while you stared, I held this in front of your eyes."

The girl extended her hand and Codd stared at the jewel blazing up at him. An emerald, of course.

"Then it's all a matter of suggestion, of self-hypnosis?"

"Perhaps. But the helmet is the agent. You wear it, and your thoughts weave a pattern. It will help you to create. You speak of losing your mind. The helmet permits you to find it again."

"But how does it work?"

"I cannot answer that. And you must not question me too closely. This much, and this much only, need you know. I am empowered to offer you the loan of the helmet for an indefinite period, for experimental purposes.

"You can wear it whenever you want, write whatever you want as a result of your experiences while wearing it. I believe you are going to find this a most profitable undertaking."

"And what do you—and your mysterious inventor friend—get for this privilege?"

"Merely the opportunity to test the helmet and observe its effects. The record of effects will be found in the stories you write."

"But where's the catch?"

"There is no catch. Perhaps, some day, we will want you to go on record as to the way in which the helmet performs. We may patent and market it on a wide scale. We may find other uses for it. I cannot say at present."

Codd paced the floor. "I don't know. It sounds crazy."

"Can you sell the story?"

"Certainly."

"Then remember this—you'll write other stories. Tonight your mind was at singularly low ebb; you were confused, half-drunk. What do you suppose you'll be capable of once you're clearly confident, once you begin to organize your talent and utilize all your creativity with the helmet's aid? Why, you'll be able to turn out bestsellers! You'll be rich, famous, perhaps immortal. Wouldn't you like that?"

Wouldn't he? An abrupt vision of the frowsy furnished room came unbidden to his brain. Codd nodded. Of course he wanted to be rich and famous. And what had he to lose, what had he to fear?

"Suppose I accept," he said. "Are there any restrictions?"

"None. Of course, you will keep this secret. You'll have to, at first—you know as well as I do what people would say if you came to them with such a fantastic explanation."

"Agreed," said Codd.

"You may not take the helmet off while a dream is in progress. And you are further instructed not to tamper with the helmet in any way. If you have any notion of running off to some scientific testing laboratory and discover the 'secret' of its mechanism, I can assure you that the attempt will end in disaster. You'll end up with a damaged, useless instrument — and know nothing. Because today's science does not operate in a frame of reference sufficient to make this phenomenon intelligible to mankind." She smiled. "But I become ponderous. All I mean to do is use that old phrase — what is it again? — 'Never look a gift horse in the mouth.' "

She extended the helmet. Codd grasped it, moved toward the door.

"And when do I see you again?" he asked.

"Soon. Quite soon." Cleo Fane smiled. "I'll see you in my dreams."

4

Barnaby Codd wrote *The Green Planet* as a novelette, in three sittings. He sold it, first trip out, for three hundred dollars. It was printed, and successfully received, four months later, and the editor asked for more. The editor had illustrated it with a cover showing four or five colors instead of just green, but nobody seemed upset about that. Codd wasn't upset either, because by the time the story appeared he was already out of the science fiction field.

He was out of the furnished room, too, and established in a pleasant apartment once more. The actual mechanics of locating a new place and furnishing it proved tiresome — but then, for several weeks after writing the story, everything was tiring to Codd. He felt oddly drained and depleted of energy.

Yet he had energy enough to make an effort to locate Cleo Fane. He tried the phone book, of course, and to no avail. Then he consulted the city directory and drew a blank. So he went to Hank Olcott.

"Cleo Fane?" Hank considered for a moment. "No, can't say that I recognize the name." He tapped a cigarette and leaned back. "Should I?"

"Well, she was at your party," Codd persisted. "Surely you remember her — tall redhead in a green dress."

Hank shook his head slowly. "Sorry. I don't recall seeing her. Of course, there were so many strangers barging in and out all night long. I can ask some of the gang."

"I wish you would," Codd urged. "I must find her."

Hank Olcott chuckled. "I thought you told me you went out together. Don't you know where she lives?"

Codd tried to explain. He didn't know, he'd had too much to drink, he'd tried to retrace his steps and couldn't find the building on the sidestreet.

Olcott listened patiently, promised to make inquiries, and did so. But he learned nothing.

Nor did Codd, in the days that followed. He sat at home, waiting for a call that never came. He might have had a few drinks to pass the time, but he found he no longer wanted to drink. He might have turned to the typewriter and done some work, but he found that he couldn't work. In that respect his status was unchanged—he was still in a writer's slump. The novelette had been an accident, after all.

But it wasn't an accident. It was merely the result of wearing the helmet. The helmet gave him the story. Why not use it now? Besides, what had she told him at the last?

"I'll see you in my dreams."

Codd took the helmet out of its place of concealment, at the bottom of his suitcase. He cradled it, examining it curiously. The light, malleable metal was silver, and its surface held the tarnish of age. The peculiar antennae and tubular filament between defied his analysis. This apparatus had not been sewed or riveted or soldered on—it seemed to be an inherent part of the whole. How the helmet was made or what process had been used in its contrivance it was beyond his power to determine. It was all a mystery.

And so was its power, and so was the woman, and so was her power over him—mystery.

Codd sighed. He switched off the lamp, sat in darkness. The helmet gave off a faint phosphorescent glow. He raised it to his face, then placed it on his head. The phosphorescent glow flooded the room, flooded his brain and being.

Codd was back on the green planet now. He stood against the hillside and stared down. Cleo came bounding past, on the back of a gigantic wolf. The wolf looked up at him and howled. Cleo waved once—at least he thought she waved. Then she disappeared.

And now, oddly, the planet disappeared. Codd was somewhere else—in a modern city. He was watching another story unfold.

This was the story of David Harris, the man on the ragged edge of sanity. Codd knew the man, knew his thoughts, because he found he could get *inside* the man and read his mind. Not that alone; to a certain extent he could *be* the man if he so desired.

He watched Harris, discharged from the asylum, roaming through the city and seeking companionship, seeking a friend to save him from loneliness. For loneliness was the source of his aberration; being alone would drive him mad once more. He followed Harris through the drabness of his days, the empty impersonality of his contacts in a strange city. He suffered all the defeats which Harris met in his efforts to establish even a small acquaintanceship with his fellow men. He fought, as Harris fought, the terrifying hatreds that welled up in him, hatreds directed against all living things. He tried to conquer the delusion that all men were his enemies.

And he followed Harris to the tavern the night he met the girl. The girl was Cleo, of course — but this time she was a blonde, and he discovered she was a waitress out of a job and down on her luck. She was lonely too. Then Harris took her to his room, and they spent the night, and Harris made the discovery of communication, of freedom from loneliness and fear. It seemed to Harris that this was too much to bear, that his mind would burst with the realization of his love, that his love was a torment worse than loneliness, that by losing himself in love he lost his identity, which was that of a man to whom all men were enemies.

As Harris, he slept, and awoke in the morning to find the girl gone. Then he followed Harris through the streets, followed him in his search for the girl who had become to him the symbol of salvation. He must find her now or go mad forever. And he searched and he searched, and his panic grew, and he knew that he was on the borderline, on the ragged edge, and he couldn't endure it without her. And he tried to think back to last night and couldn't, and the hatred came welling up in him again, and he went back to his room, and then he sensed her presence there.

The mere thought of her presence was enough to save him; he realized now, for the first time, how close he had come to the brink last night when he'd met her. It had only been a matter of hours, or perhaps even minutes, before he would have cracked, if he hadn't found her. No wonder he'd blacked out there at the last as they made love.

But now her presence was strong, she was with him, somehow, and he knew she would be with him always. He'd done something — he couldn't remember what it was, just now — to ensure that. He'd done something to save himself by keeping her with him forever.

Harris couldn't remember. Not until he decided to go out, and went to the closet and opened the door, and found her propped stiffly in the corner with his knife in her throat. . . .

Then Harris went mad, phosphorescently mad, and Codd got out of him quickly, got out of the phosphorescence and ripped off the helmet.

He sat there panting in the dark for a long moment before he was able to stand up, switch on the light, and walk over to the typewriter.

That night he wrote *The Ragged Edge* in one sitting.

5

During the next three months Barnaby Codd wrote nine short stories and two novelettes. Both of the novelettes and the last six stories sold to the slicks, and Codd acquired a bright, brisk agent named Freeman who negotiated a motion picture sale for one of the novelettes and sold TV rights to three of the stories. He kept urging Codd to tackle a novel now, and talked about "deals" and "percentages" and "building up a name while things are hot."

Things were hot, all right. Too hot. Codd had new furniture and a new car. He had a bank balance of over seven thousand dollars. He was in a position to satisfy his gregarious instincts and aggrandize his ego. There was no need to wait for a phone call from the Hank Olcotts of this world — he could give his own parties whenever he chose.

He tried it, once. The party was not a success. Oh, Hank came and the rest of the crowd came, and they seemed to have a good time. They complimented him and joined with Freeman in marveling over his sudden, unprecedented success. But Codd didn't enjoy himself. He kept waiting for a scarlet poppy to blossom in the corner — and, of course, it didn't.

Then he tried to drink, and found he hadn't the taste for it any longer. Nor the energy. The party tired him. He was glad when they all went away, finally, and he could turn out the lights and put on the helmet.

Because when he put on the helmet, she came. She always came, and always in the same way. He'd find himself back on the green planet under the three green moons. An instant of waiting, and then she'd bound across the landscape on an animal. Each time the animal was different — a lion, tiger, stallion, boar. Each time the action was the same — the creature bounded, she waved, then disappeared. And he'd be off in a dream plot. The plots inevitably were a product of some previous reality; twisted, inverted, expanded and projected. *The Ragged Edge* had been the result of his own search for Cleo. Other plots had been remotely based on subsequent daily incidents in his life.

Tonight, his dream concerned a party — a charity ball. Cleo was there (odd, she seemed to turn up in disguise as a character, regularly), and this time she was a brunette. A reigning movie queen, internationally famous, a symbol of scandal and sophistication.

There was a raffle, and she danced with the holders of the winning tickets. Codd knew the winners — he *became* the winners, each in turn. And he followed their lives.

He was Homer Johnson, meek little bespectacled Homer Johnson, the bookkeeper with the nagging wife. And as a result of his moment of glory, his dance with a dream, he found the courage to leave his wife, tell off his boss, and go on to his romantically cherished ambition of life in the merchant marine. The dance made him a hero.

He was young Derek; Derek, the fortunate. Blond, handsome rich man's son, with an assured future and a girl who worshipped him. But he danced with a dream and thereafter the girl meant nothing to him, and no woman was good enough. He went down, down, to an inevitable end. The dance destroyed him.

He was Geoffrey Farr, a once-great name on the legitimate stage and now an extra voice, a bit character actor in soap operas. He'd wangled his invitation, taken his last five dollars to buy a raffle ticket because he couldn't

afford to be shamed in front of the "public." And he'd won a dance, too—
won it in his rented tuxedo, danced with splitting seams, danced with a
tearing pain in his chest—because he was old, too old for the constant
strain of "keeping up appearances" and too old for the excitement.

The star had been nice to him when they danced, and some *Life* photographer had remembered his name and taken a shot on the off-chance that
this was a good "human interest angle" to play up. And the ballroom buzzed.

Before the night was over, Geoffrey Farr had been "rediscovered" by two
agents, a producer casting a Broadway show and the star's personal direc-
tor. There would be contracts in the morning, and Geoffrey Farr would be
back on top again.

Before the night was over, Geoffrey Farr died of a heart attack, brought
on by the strain and the excitement. He had danced with a dream, and the
dream was death.

Codd died, took off the helmet, and began to set down the complete
outline of THE DANCERS. It was going to be quite a novel—some of the
touches were pure corn, he realized, but the kind of corn that sells. The
kind that logically lends itself to rental library circulation, to mass motion
picture audience appeal. "A" corn. He had the angle now. A sort of combination of GRAND HOTEL and LETTER TO THREE WIVES.

He could write it in a month, he knew that.

And he did.

Freeman was enthusiastic when he saw the finished manuscript. "This is
it!" he kept crowing. "I knew you'd do it, Barnaby. You've been getting
farther and farther away from all that morbid fantasy stuff. Now you've got
the commercial angle. I'm going to get busy on this tomorrow. Don't worry
about a thing. I'd suggest you go home and take a good long rest. You look
tired, man. This job must have knocked you out."

Codd drove home. The new car handled perfectly, but driving was an
effort. Everything had been an effort during the past month. He hadn't worn
the helmet while writing, but the effects were there. Aside from work, he
moved in a daze. Action and reaction were oddly altered. Of course, that
often happened when he was working on a story—the story became more
real than the external world. But even the story hadn't seemed real.

The dreams were real.

That was the way he'd felt. The dreams were real. The rest was ephem-
eral, unimportant. Only the dream world existed. Cleo had been the bait to
get him to wear the helmet. The stories and the success were the bait that
kept him wearing the helmet. Somebody or something wanted him to do
that, and it was real.

Codd went up to the apartment. He realized that he was in a bad state
and realized—sensibly enough—that he was letting his mind run away.
Freeman was right; he was just tired from overwork.

Well, he didn't have to work that hard any more. Somehow he knew he had a winner; Freeman confirmed it. He'd sell the novel, get a decent motion picture sale, and take things easy. After all, he was a writer in his own right—he didn't have to depend on the helmet. The whole thing was beginning to prey on his mind—guilty secrets, and all that sort of rot. From now on it might be a good idea to forget about everything that had gone before.

Cleo, whoever she was, had disappeared. Nobody knew about the helmet. Nobody had come to blackmail him or accuse him or threaten him. Why not call the whole thing off and start all over, start fresh, as his own man?

His own man. . . .

Barnaby Codd stood in front of the mirror and took inventory of himself.

The Brooks Brothers suit was immaculate. The Sulka tie had a certain subdued resplendence. But the long, lean face was thin, the cheeks were sunken, the brown hair was lusterless, the skin was waxy pale, and the glazed eyes held the glitter of horrified recognition.

Nothing had changed. He was still a walking corpse.

And if he could still walk, it was time for the headshrinker.

6

It was very comfortable on the leather couch.

Sometimes it's nice to be a corpse, to be laid out in state with hands folded peacefully over the chest, eyes open and unseeing, ready for eternal rest.

When you accept death, nothing else matters any more, and it's easier to talk. So much, much easier.

Barnaby Codd told Doctor Fine all about this feeling. It was not difficult to talk to the quiet little psychoanalyst. Olcott had recommended him, seemed to think it was a good idea. And it was a good idea, so far.

Fine was willing to dispense with all the preliminaries, to take Codd's word for it that he understood his problem. And with that encouragement, Codd talked.

He'd been talking now for almost an hour. He told the whole story—about the writing, and meeting Cleo Fane, and the curious aftermath to that evening. He told about the helmet and the dreams. He held nothing back.

Doctor Fine listened attentively, patiently. Codd felt a growing conviction that he could be helped here, that Doctor Fine knew the answers.

He concluded on a hopeful note. "What do you think? What does it all mean to you, Doctor?"

Codd sat up and fished for a cigarette. Little Doctor Fine sat back and smiled. "It doesn't matter, really, what it means to me. The important question is—what does it mean to you? How would you explain it?"

"I—I can't explain it."

"Then make a guess."

"Are you serious?"

"Naturally. Are you? Then make a guess."

"Well." Codd lit the cigarette and sought significant symbolism in a spiral of smoke. "One theory would be that when I went to the party, I was already cracking up. Alcohol worked upon me autosuggestively." He paused.

"Go on. This is interesting."

"I remember that Olcott never saw this woman. His friends don't seem to know her. So perhaps there was no woman. Perhaps I imagined the whole thing—manufactured a stimulus, an excuse to continue writing. You might say that I hypnotized myself."

The Doctor nodded. "It's theoretically possible," he conceded.

"Except for one thing." Codd stood up, walked over to the coatrack, fished in the pocket of his overcoat. "She gave me the helmet. Here it is."

He extended the curious metallic headpiece, and Doctor Fine inspected it carefully.

"You couldn't make it yourself," he mused. "I don't suppose—"

"I don't suppose, either," Codd answered. "Supposition won't help me. And I suspect that no laboratory on earth could accurately analyze the component structure of a magic helmet. She warned me against trying to find out—I'm wondering now whether or not it might be a good idea to at least make the attempt. At least it could help convince me of my own sanity."

Doctor Fine gazed at the antennae, at the coils, at the odd patina of the silver. "If you'll permit me, I'd be glad to have it examined for you," he said. "But before you resign yourself to believing in the power of the helmet, why not think this thing through a little farther?"

Codd finished his cigarette, crushed it out. "All right. Let's take the other tack. Cleo Fane exists. I did see her. She did give me this helmet, for her own mysterious purposes. And the helmet—"

"Ignore the helmet," Doctor Fine suggested. "Suppose the helmet was, and is, just a costume piece. What then?"

"But I had the dreams," Codd objected. "I had the first dream there in her apartment. And when I woke up, she was still there, with the emerald. She seemed to be in the dream and to know all about it—"

"Think!" insisted Doctor Fine. "What could that mean?"

"It could mean—it could mean that I didn't hypnotize myself—that I did dream—but that *she* hypnotized me. Darkness and quiet and fatigue and alcohol and suggestion. She made me believe that I'd dream when I put the helmet on. And then she used the emerald as a focal point. No wonder she knew my dream—she was planting it in my mind, telling me what I was dreaming all the time!"

Doctor Fine purred like a plump little cat. The canary had gone down nicely, it seemed. But—

"Wait!" exclaimed Codd. "That wouldn't work, either. Because I dreamed again. And again. Whenever I wore the helmet, I had a dream. She wasn't present to suggest anything, not once. And so—"

"Did you ever hear of post-hypnotic suggestion?" asked the Doctor.

"I get it! She did it all at the one sitting—told me that from that time on, whenever I wore the helmet, I'd dream. Perhaps planted the whole series in my subconscious. From that time on the helmet itself was the focal agent for hypnosis. And it's still working!"

From the sound of the deep purr, the Doctor had found another canary.

"Two more questions, Doctor. It's clearer to me now, and I feel better once I realize there are other explanations than crazy, supernatural ones. But two questions have to be answered. The first is—"

"Why should anyone attempt such a thing?" Doctor Fine was creeping up on his third canary, and he couldn't wait. "Because, unfortunately, you are not alone in the need for analytical therapy, my friend. The world is full of disorganized personalities. Your Cleo Fane, with her calculated air of mystery, her fabricated helmet and fabricated story, may well be acting compulsively and dramatizing her own private fantasies of power. She was 'looking for a creative artist,' she told you. An instrument of masculinity, perhaps, a surrogate for—"

Then followed five minutes of abstruse terminology, all of which added up, reassuringly, to the fact that Cleo Fane was nuttier than a fruitcake. It was good therapy for Barnaby Codd—to be told that *she* was the crazy one, not he.

But there was still a second question. He asked it now.

"How can I get rid of the dreams?" he pleaded. "How do I escape from this post-hypnotic suggestion business?"

Doctor Fine smiled. "You're already more than half-free now," he said. "Just analyzing matters this way is a great step forward. You'll see. The final step is simple. It merely lies in reevaluating the helmet."

"Yes?"

"Realizing, objectively and subjectively, completely, that it's all a trick. That the helmet in itself has no magical power over your mind. The next time you wear it, you'll not wait for the dream to end. You'll take it off, of your own volition, right in the middle of the so-called dream sequence. And that will be that. Simple." He smiled. "Then, if you still want to, we'll have the gadget examined and come up with answers. Chances are, it was manufactured somewhere in New Jersey. We can attend to all that later this week."

"But, wait a minute—I can't take the helmet off in the middle of a dream! She warned me, she wouldn't let me, I'm not able to command my actions when I wear it—"

Doctor Fine listened to him, and from the expression on his face it was plain he was hearing the chirps of the fourth canary. He smiled cheerfully.

"Of course you can take the helmet off," he said. "It's all a matter of suggestion. Of counter-hypnosis, if you wish. Now if you'll just stretch out on the couch once more, I think I can promise you that next time you'll be able to remove the helmet." He hummed. "It's all a matter of suggestion."

It was.

7

Codd didn't feel like a corpse any more. Corpses don't have six months of solid booking with psychoanalysts. They don't have the hopeful feeling that their problems are all on their way to being solved, that they are about to be helped, to get rid of their delusions, and can walk unaided on their own feet, on a path of their own choosing.

Codd had these feelings strongly now. It was all so simple. The Doctor would cure him of his block against writing, would enable him to summon new strength and resolution instead of depending on suggestion and a weird belief in "magic."

Back at the apartment he looked at himself in the mirror once again, and that was the clincher. He was smiling, self-possessed, and there was some color in his cheeks. He was Barnaby Codd—not the old Codd, but the new Codd. The successful Codd. The Codd who had just written a novel which might well be a bestseller. The Codd who was going to have all the things he'd ever dreamed of having. The Codd who could—and it wasn't at all unthinkable now—write masterpieces.

The phone rang. He groped for it in the gathering dusk.

"Codd? This is Freeman. Got news for you. It looks like we've hit the jackpot." Codd listened, nodded at the mouthpiece. The book had sold. Freeman named the publisher, named the advance. One of the big book clubs was reading the carbon of the manuscript. The second carbon had been requested by the New York office of a major movie studio. Codd must appear at Freeman's office tomorrow morning and go through the pleasant motions of signing contracts.

Codd made the usual elated answers and hung up. He floated over to a chair in the dusk of the parlor.

This was it. This was real living. And only the beginning. From now on he'd enjoy it as a whole man, as his own master. He would break this foolish fixation, this morbid dependency on a crazy girl and her crazy story. His conscious mind was already free. And once he removed the helmet during a dream, his subconscious resolution would be made, thanks to Doctor Fine and the powers of suggestion. The powers of suggestion—fight fire with fire. Science was wonderful—what a romantic, melodramatic fool he had been. Now was the time to end it.

Yes, now was the time to end it. Get it over with. He couldn't wait, shouldn't wait. Perhaps that was Doctor Fine's hypnotic command, too.

That he should don the helmet at once and go through with the traumatic incident.

At any rate, the urge was strong. The urge was overpowering, irresistible. Codd got the helmet from his coat. He felt the coolness against his palms. He felt the coolness against his skull as he sat back on the sofa and adjusted the helmet. It fitted snugly.

And that was all.

It just rested on his head. Nothing happened. Doctor Fine was right — perhaps he'd done a better job than he'd dared hope to do. Already the power of the helmet was gone. Codd didn't believe in it. He was his own man. He wasn't in the power of the helmet, in the power of Cleo Fane. He wasn't her man. He wasn't her man. He wasn't —

Codd fell asleep naturally. His head slipped down, and he dozed. The phosphorescence was coming now, and the familiar sense of seeing without being, of moving without body.

He waited for the three moons to appear. Strange, now that he had visited Doctor Fine, how he could analyze what was happening. That green planet had become not only familiar to him but natural, accepted. It had truly seemed more real to him than actual surroundings in his waking state. And the inevitable prelude to his visions — Cleo riding across the green landscape on a strange beast — that was accepted and expected too. He expected it now, but he wouldn't accept it this time. Only a dream.

Oddly enough, this time there was no green planet and no glimpse of Cleo riding an animal. He was somewhere else. He was many places else, at many times. He was in her mind, or she was in his.

A glimpse of her face, looming out of the sky, blotting out the horizon with the blinding redness of her hair. And her voice whispering.

"You tried to disobey. You weren't content with my gifts, so you tried to disobey. Didn't I give you enough? You wanted the ability to create, you wanted the rewards of creation. I gave them to you freely. Was that, then, not enough?"

It was a question, but he did not answer. She knew the answer. She knew everything. Her voice held an ageless grief. "It was not enough. It's never been enough for any of them. They want to *know*, also. They want to pry and meddle. It is their nature, because they are only men. You are only a man. You do not understand the gods.

"And like a man, you believe yourself greater than the gods, stronger than their spells. So you tried to disobey. You wanted to know."

Her face faded away, and now was the time to take off the helmet. Or could he wait another minute?

He waited, tense even in sleep, and the voice came again. "Very well. You shall know. Not because you desire it, but because I *permit* it. For the first thing you must know is that this is *my* dream — not yours. I make the dream, the dreams of men who have the helmets.

"Yes, there are many helmets. Did you think you were the only one I have sought through the centuries? Did you believe yourself the sole favorite of the gods, the sole creator whose creations come through the dreams I grant?

"That is the secret—and some there are who have been content with it and have not sought to disobey. They have learned their lesson, guarded their helmets as a sacred secret. They created masterpieces."

Codd's mind was a kaleidoscope now, a montage of fugitive, fleeting fragments. He saw—and to his startled horror recognized—the faces and features of a dozen titans. Great composers, famous artists, renowned writers, immortal sculptors. In an instant they embraced the red-haired essence of womankind, wore their helmets, created, lived, died. He comprehended everything, and the melange melted, merged, went back into Time for thousands of years.

How long had it been going on, and why, and who was Cleo Fane or that which called itself Cleo Fane?

"I grant you all answers," came the thought-voice. "Behold, if you dare."

Then he was on the island and he knew it for Aeae, and knew her for what she was—the eternal sorceress of all legend, the immortal, the undying, the symbol of creation and destruction known to blind Homer. Red-haired Circe, whose delight it was to ensnare the souls of men. And men were unworthy of that embrace, they sinned against the gods and became beasts. Swine and stallions, lions and wolves; she took from them the creative power they despised and left them only the animal. They became animals.

So had Homer sung the story   and ceased. But the story did not end. It could never end, for the gods are immortal. And when Aeae sank into the sea, Circe sought refuge. Not on Earth—for what is Time or Space to an immortal?—but far, far beyond.

Now Codd was back on the green planet once more, the far green planet with the three moons. This was Circe's new island, her island in space. Here men did not visit her, so she went among men from time to time.

"Always I seek ecstasy," the voice echoed. "Always I seek the thrill which comes only in participating in the act of creation. And it is my eternal curse that I cannot create of myself. I can only transform. I must go to men, to half-beasts who possess but do not appreciate this power, in order to awaken them. And when they reject their power, deny me a share of their souls' surrender, I avenge myself. I transform them into the animals they deserve to be. For they reject the gift of the gods, the helmet—"

Codd comprehended and, with a thrill of recognition, comprehended that he comprehended. This dream was different; a part of him was aloof, analytical. He wasn't in her power, wasn't in the helmet's power. He had the armor of Science, the weapons of Doctor Fine. He was invulnerable. He could listen, accept or reject at will. This was a new plot, perhaps. If he liked it he'd use it when he awoke; if not, he'd throw it away. Just as now, at any time he chose, he'd rip off the helmet and leave the crazy woman with her garbled dreams.

She was a woman, all right, and insane. And she'd given him hours of free fantasy while he was under hypnosis—all her mad delusions had been impressed on his brain. That's where the plots had come from, and no wonder he'd felt depressed while he was writing them! And now, ultimately, came the final product of her suggestions, the central core of her fixation. She was a sorceress—Circe, no less. And a streamlined, modern Circe who lived on a planet of her own, far out in space. Three moons, indeed! And all men were beasts, and she was greater than men, and she lured artists to their doom—

He saw her with the animals around her, now, and they wore helmets too. And they fawned on her and licked her naked feet, and she chose a mount and bounded off across the weird landscape that was no landscape but merely a reflection of the twisted convolutions of her own disordered brain.

She was pleading with him now, and shouting at him, and threatening him. He must not try to find out about the helmet, he must not resist the dreams, he must not seek any vengeance.

"I'll give you dreams to weave wonders," she whispered. "You shall be famous, your name will live for all time. And all I ask is that I share. That I share the ecstatic moments of creation with your soul."

Codd pitied her then; pitied her as she must have been when she sat beside him in the darkness and poured out her madness to his sleeping mind.

"But if you disobey, you know your punishment," the voice threatened. "And you cannot escape. You cannot escape, ever. It will go on, forever and ever, as long as the three moons wheel. So choose, choose! Would you be one with the gods, or a base and craven dog, a howling cur in the wilderness of a faraway world? Yours is the power of choice—mine the power to punish or reward. So choose, choose!"

There was pity in Codd's mind, but there was also a growing revulsion. He couldn't stand the morbidity much longer. He must remove himself from this source of aberration, return to sanity as a whole man. And he could do it. He heard her voice, saw the green world—and at the same time realized that he sat in his own apartment, wearing the absurd helmet. Doctor Fine had told him what to do. The Doctor was Fine, everything was fine, everything would be all right once he removed the helmet, removed the crazy notion from his head. Beast, was he? Dog, eh? He was a man, his own man.

And he could prove it. He could feel, and he could act. Act as he acted now. Barnaby Codd lifted his hands to his head. He felt the helmet—it was real. And he could take it off.

She was screaming now, screaming and laughing. Probably she had done so at the last, when she broke down completely in her delirium and cast her final "spell." In her way, the poor woman had actually been "possessed"— she thought of herself as a sorceress, and so she had been.

But spells must be broken. Dreams must end.

He reached up and took off the helmet.

The screaming stopped. It stopped inside his head, stopped outside his head.

The helmet was off. He was free.

This was reality.

He was crouching now, panting, but he knew he had broken the spell. This was real. It was over, irrevocably over.

Barnaby Codd opened his eyes. Then *she* came over and patted his head, mounted his back. He lifted up his shaggy head and howled to the three moons. . . .

CONSTANT READER

ONCE UPON A TIME they were called strait jackets.

When you put one on, you were "in restraint" according to the polite psychiatric jargon of the day. I know, because I've read all about it in books. Yes, real books, the old-fashioned kind that were printed on paper and bound together between leather or board covers. They're still available in some libraries, Earthside, and I've read a lot of them. As a matter of fact, I own quite a collection myself. It's a peculiar hobby, but I enjoy it much more than telolearning or going to the sensorals.

Of course, I admit I'm a little bit maladjusted, according to those same psychiatric texts I mentioned. That's the only possible explanation of why I enjoy reading, and why I pick up so many odd items of useless information.

This business about strait jackets and restraint, for example. All I ever got out of it was a peculiar feeling whenever we hit grav, on a Rec. Flight.

I got it again, now, as Penner yelled, "Act alert, Dale—put down that toy and strap up!"

I dropped my book and went over to the Sighter Post. Already I could feel the preliminary pull despite the neutralizer's efforts. I strapped up and hung there in my cocoon, hung there in my strait jacket.

There I was, nicely in restraint, in our own little private asylum—Scout #3890-R, two months out of Home Port 19/1, and now approaching 68/5 planet for Reconnaissance.

Before looking out of the Sighter, I took another glance at my fellow inmates. Penner, Acting Chief, Temp., was strapped in at Mechontrol; all I could see of him was the broad back, the bullet head bent in monomaniac concentration. Swanson, Astrog., 2nd Class, hung at his side, cake-knife nose in profile over the Obsetape. Little Morse, Tech., was stationed at my left and old Levy, Eng., hung to my right. All present and accounted for—Penner, Swanson, Morse, Levy and myself. George Dale, Constant Reader and erstwhile Service Observer, hanging in his strait jacket after two months in a floating madhouse.

Two months of anything is a long time. Two months of Rec. Flight is an eternity. Being cooped up with four other men in a single compartment for that length of time is no picnic, and our strait jackets seemed singularly appropriate.

Not that any of us were actually psycho; all of us had a long record of similar missions, and we managed to survive. But the sheer monotony had worn us down.

I suppose that's why Service gave us the extra seven pounds per man—Lux. Allotment, it was called. But the so-called luxuries turn out to be necessities after all. Swanson usually put his poundage into solid food; candy, and the like. Chocolate capsules kept him sane. Morse and Levy went in for games—cards, dice, superchess and the necessary boards. Penner, amazingly enough, did sketching on pads of old-fashioned paper. And I had this habit of my own—I always managed to bring three or four books within the weight limit.

I still think my choice was the best; candy-munching, free-hand sketching and the delights of dicing and superchessmanship palled quickly enough on my four companions. But the books kept me interested. I had a peculiar background—learned to read as a child rather than as an adult—and I guess that's why I derived such queer satisfaction from my hobby.

Naturally, the others laughed at me. Naturally, we got on each other's nerves, quarreled and fretted and flared up. But now, resting quietly in our strait jackets as we entered grav, a measure of sanity returned. With it came anticipation and expectation.

We were approaching 68/5 planet.

New worlds to conquer? Not exactly. It was a new world, and therein lay the expectation. But we weren't out to conquer, we on Rec. Flight merely observed and recorded. Or, rather, our instruments recorded.

At the moment we slid in on Mechontrol, about five hundred miles above the surface. 68/5 was small, cloud-wreathed; it had atmosphere apparently, as did its companions. Now we were moving closer and we peered through the Sighters at a dull, flat surface that seemed to be rushing toward us at accelerating speed.

"Pretty old," little Morse grunted. "No mountains, and no water, either—dried up, I guess."

"No life." This from old Levy. "That's a relief." Levy was what the books would have called a misanthrope. Although his mis wasn't confined to anthropes. He seemed to have a congenital aversion to everything that vasn't strictly mechanical—why he didn't stick to robotics, I'll never know.

We came down faster. Fifty miles, forty, thirty. I saw Swanson making arrangements to drop the roboship. Penner gave the signal as he righted us above the surface. The roboship glided away, guided by Swanson at the Obsetape. It drifted down, down, down. We followed slowly, dropping below the cloud barrier and following it closely.

"Hit!" snapped Swanson. "Right on the button." We waited while the roboship did its job. It was our star reporter, our roving photographer, our official meteorologist, our staff geologist, our expert in anthropology and mineralogic, our trusted guide and—most important, on many occasions— our stalking-horse.

If there was life present on a planet, the landing of the roboship generally brought it forth. If there was death on a planet, the roboship found it for us. And always, it recorded. It was, in a way, a complete expedition encapsulated, a nonhuman functional without the human capability of error or terror.

Now it went into action, cruising over the surface, directed by Swanson's delicate manipulation of the Obsetape unit controls. We waited patiently, then impatiently. An hour passed, two hours.

"Bring it in!" Penner ordered. Swanson moved his fingers and the roboship returned.

Penner snapped on the Temporary Balance. "Everybody unstrap," he said. "Let's take a look!"

We went down the ramp to the lower deck and Swanson opened the roboship. The photos were ready, the tapes were spooled. We were busy with findings for another hour. At the end of that time we had all the preliminary data necessary on 68/5 planet.

Oxygen content high. Gravity similar to Earthside—as seemed constant in this particular sector and system. No detectable life forms. But life had existed here, once, and life of a high order. The photos proved that. City ruins galore.

And the planet was old. No doubt about that. Morse had been right; mountains were worn away to dust, and the dust did not support vegetable life. Strange that the oxygen content was so high. I'd have supposed that carbonization—

"Let's snap out," Penner said. "We don't need Temporary Balance or straps according to the gravity reading. Might as well go in for a landing right away. The day-cycle here is 20.1 hours—computer gives us a good 5 hours to go, right now. So we can all take a look around."

We filed back upstairs and Swanson brought us in.

It was only a dead planet, a desert of dust without trees or grass or water; a flat, slate-colored surface where everything was the same, same, same. But it was solid, you could put your feet down on it, you could walk across the sand for miles and feel the air flow against your face.

And there were ruins to explore. That might be interesting. At least, it was a change.

I could feel the tension and excitement mount; it was as palpable as the momentary shock and shudder of landing. We crowded around the lock, struggling out of our suits and putting on the light plastikoids, buckling on the gear and weapons as prescribed by regulation. Morse handed us our equipment and we zipped and strapped and adjusted in a frenzy of impatience. Even Penner was eager, but he remembered to grab his sketchpad before the lock was opened.

Normally, I suppose he would have insisted on maintaining a watch on board, but in the absence of life it didn't really matter. And after two months, everybody wanted out.

The lock opened. The ladder went down. We inhaled, deeply, turned our faces to the warmth of the distant orange sun.

"Single file — keep together!" Penner cautioned.

It's the last day of school, and dismissal is sounded, and the boys rush out onto the playground. So the teacher warns, "Single file — keep together!" and what happens?

Just what happened now. In a moment we were racing across the soft sand, grinning and tossing handfuls of the fine grains high into the clean, dry air. We ran across the brand-new world on our brand-new legs.

We moved in the direction we couldn't help thinking of as west — because the orange sun hung there and we turned to the sun as naturally as flowers recently transplanted from a hothouse.

We moved buoyantly and joyfully and freely, for this was vacation and picnic and release from the asylum all in one. The smiles on the faces of my companions bespoke euphoria. It was all good: the gritty, sliding sand under our feet, the pumping of legs in long strides, the grinding ball-and-socket action of the hips, the swinging of the arms, the rise and fall of the chest, the lungs greedily gasping in and squandering recklessly, the eyes seeing far, far away. Yes, it was good to be here, good to be alive, good to be free.

Once again we measured minutes in terms of movements, rather than abstract units of time-passage we must endure. Once again we consciously heightened our awareness of existence, rather than dulled it to make life bearable.

It seemed to me that I'd never felt so completely alive, but I was wrong. I was wrong, because I didn't notice the blackout.

None of us were aware of it: even now, I can't begin to comprehend it. I don't know what happened. It was just that — blackout.

Before it happened, we marched toward the sun — Penner, Swanson and Morse a little in the lead, Levy and I a pace or two behind, all of us trudging up a slight incline in the sand.

And then, without any seeming transition at all, we were marching in darkness—Penner, Swanson, Morse, Levy and I in a solid group, trudging down into a valley.

"What happened?"

"Eclipse?"

"Where's the sun?"

"Where are we?"

"How long we been walking? I feel like I passed out."

We halted and exchanged comments.

"Something wrong here. We're going back. Get out the beamers." Penner issued orders swiftly.

We broke out the beamers, adjusted the slow-strobes, put pathways of light before us. There was nothing to see but slaty sand. Only Swanson's bearings with the scope guided us in retracing our steps. We moved swiftly through the pall of a purple night. A mist shrouded the stars; a mist mantled our memories.

That's when we compared notes, realized for the first time that the phenomenon had occurred to all of us simultaneously. Gas, shock, temporary dislocation—we argued about the cause for hours, and all the while we marched on the alert, up hummocks and down into little valleys between the dunes.

And we were tired. Unused muscles strained, hearts pumped, feet blistered, and still we marched. I was hungry and thirsty and tired; more than that, I was puzzled and a little bit afraid. I didn't understand just what had happened—how could we, all of us, go on walking that way while we were out on our feet? How could we lose almost four hours? And what did it mean?

At the moment we were in no danger of being lost, and it was more and more obvious that this planet contained no life, hostile or otherwise. But why the blackout? It puzzled me, puzzled all of us.

Swanson took the lead. His beaklike profile loomed on a rise in my beamer's path. He turned and yelled, "I can see the ship now!"

We toiled up the slope and joined him. Yes, the ship was there, snug and safe and secure, and the adventure was over.

Or—was it?

"Look down there!" Levy swiveled his beamer to the left. "We must have missed it on the way out."

Five rays played, pooled, pointed in a single beam. Five rays found, focused and flooded upon the objects rising from the sand. And then we were all running together toward the ruins.

Just before we reached them, Penner yelled, "Stop!"

"What's wrong?" I said.

"Nothing—maybe. Then again, you never know. That blackout bothers me." Penner put his hand on my shoulder. "Look, Dale, I want you and Morse to go back to the ship and wait. The three of us will take a trip through the ruins. But I want at least two men on ship at all times, in case there's any trouble. Go ahead, now—we won't move until we see you're on board. Flash us a signal to let us know everything's all right when you get there."

Morse and I trudged off.

"Just my luck," little Morse grumbled under his breath and waved his beamer in disgust. "Run around for hours in the sand and then when we finally hit something it's back to the ship. Huh!"

"He's right, though," I answered. "Got to be careful. And besides, we can eat and take our shoes off."

"But I want to see those ruins. Besides, I promised my girl some souvenirs—"

"Tomorrow we'll probably get our turn," I reminded him. He shrugged and plodded on. We reached the ship, boarded, and took a quick look around. All clear.

Morse went over to the panel and pushed the blinker. Then we sat down next to the Sighter and stared out. All we could see at this distance was a purple blur, through which three beams moved and wavered.

I opened foodcaps and we swallowed, still straining to see. The lights moved separately at first, then coalesced into a single unit.

"Must have found something," Morse speculated. "Wonder what?"

"We'll find out soon enough," I predicted.

But they didn't come back, and they didn't come back—we sat for hours, waiting.

Finally the beams moved our way. We were waiting as Penner, Swanson and Levy boarded. An excited babble wavered into words and the words became sentences.

"Never saw anything like them—"

"Smaller than dwarfs; couldn't be, but I'd swear they were human."

"Gets me is the way they disappeared, just like somebody had scooped them all up at once."

"Wasn't their city, I'm sure of that. First of all, it was ages old, and secondly it wasn't built to their size-scale at all—"

"Think we just imagined the whole thing? That blackout was peculiar enough, and then, seeing them this way—"

I raised my voice. "What's all this about? What did you find?"

The answer was more babbling in unison, until Penner signaled for silence.

"See what you make of this, Dale," he said. He pulled out his sketchpad and went to work, swiftly. As he worked, he talked. Story and sketches emerged almost simultaneously.

He passed the first drawing to me.

"Ruins," he said. "Ruins of a city. All we really saw were the rooftops, but they're enough to give you some idea of the probable size of the place. You'll note everything was solid stone. Plenty of broad, flat surfaces. Here's a sketch of me standing between two rooftops. Probably a street in between, at one time. What do you make of it?"

I studied his sketch; it was crude, but graphically explicit. "They must have been humanoid," I said. "If we accept functionalism in architectural representation—"

"Never mind the book words," Penner interrupted. "Look at the width of that street. Would you say that the inhabitants were large or small?"

"Large, of course." I looked at the sketch again. "Must have been much taller than we are, perhaps seven or eight feet if they worked according to our proportions. Of course, that's just a rough guess."

"Good enough. And we geigered the stones a bit. Levy, here, places them at fourteen thousand years."

"The very least," Levy broke in. "Possibly older than that."

Penner was sketching again. He passed the second drawing over to me. "Here's what we found wandering around in the ruins," he told me. "I've shown two of them standing next to me, but there must have been hundreds."

I looked. There stood Penner, and—at his feet—two tiny manlike beings.

"You actually saw these things?"

"Of course. We all did, there's no doubt about it. One minute we were climbing around among the stones, and then they appeared. Just like that, out of nowhere, you might say. And not one or two, but hundreds of them." He turned. "Isn't that right, Swanson?"

"Correct."

I gazed at the sketch again. Penner had an eye for detail. I was particularly impressed with the way the creatures were dressed.

"These look like ancient Earth-garments," I said. "They're wearing little armored breastplates, and helmets. And they carry spears."

"That's exactly how they looked," Levy corroborated. "Some of them had those—what were they called?—bows and arrows."

Penner eyed me. "You've got a theory, Dale?"

"No, but I'm getting one. These little things never built the city. They don't live in the ruins, now. They couldn't possibly wear Earth-garments like these. They appeared suddenly, you say, and disappeared just as suddenly."

"Sounds silly, the way you sum it up," Penner admitted.

"Yes. Unless you accept one overall theory."

"And that is?"

"That they don't exist! They never existed at all, except in your imagination."

"But we all saw them. Saw them, and heard them!"

"We all went through a blackout together, a few hours ago," I reminded him. "And I'm beginning to think that ties in, somehow. Suppose 68/5 isn't uninhabited. Suppose it does contain life."

"That's out of the question!" Swanson interrupted. "The roboship tapes are infallible. Any signs of existence would have been detected and recorded. You know that."

"Yet suppose there were no signs," I answered. "Suppose we're dealing with an intangible intelligence —"

"Absurd!" This from Penner.

"No more absurd than the story you've told me. Suppose the intelligence can control our minds. It blacked us out and planted hypnotic suggestion. A little while later you saw little men —"

"No. It doesn't add up," Levy insisted. "There's a flaw." He pointed at the second sketch. "How would your intelligence know about Earth-garments such as these? I'm sure none of us were aware of such things. You're the bookworm around here —"

"Bookworm!" I paused. "Wait a minute. You say these creatures talked to you?"

"That's right," Penner answered.

"Do you remember any of the words?"

"I think so. They had little shrill voices and they were shouting to each other. Sounded something like *Hekinah degul* and *Langro dehul san*."

"One of them pointed at you and said *Hurgo* over and over," Swanson reminded him.

"*Hurgo*," I repeated. "Wait a minute." I walked over to my shelf and pulled down one of my books. "Look at this," I said. "No pictures in this edition, of course, but read this page."

Penner read slowly as the others crowded around. He raised his head, scowled. "Sounds like our creatures," he said. "What is this?"

I turned to the frontispiece and read: "Gulliver's Travels, by Jonathan Swift. Published, 1727."

"No!" said Penner.

I shrugged. "It's all in the book," I told him. "Descriptions, words, phrases. Some intelligent force out there tried to read our minds and — I think — failed. So it read the book, instead, and reproduced a part of it."

"But what possible force could exist? And how could it read the book? And why did it reproduce the —" Penner halted, groping for the word which I supplied.

"Lilliputians."

"All right, why did it reproduce Lilliputians?"

I didn't know the answers. I couldn't even guess. All I had was a feeling, which I expressed in one short sentence. "Let's get out of here."

Penner shook his head. "We can't. You know that. We've stumbled across something without precedent, and it's our job to investigate it fully. Who knows what we might learn? I say we get some rest and go back tomorrow."

There was a mumble of agreement. I had nothing more to say, so I kept quiet. Swanson and Morse and Levy sought their bunks. I started across to mine, when Penner tapped me on the shoulder.

"By the way, Dale, would you mind letting me have that book of yours? I want to read up on those creatures — might come in handy tomorrow."

I gave him the book and he went forward. Then I lay down and prepared to sleep. Before closing my eyes I took a last look out of the nearest Sighter. The planet was dark and dead. There was nothing out there — nothing but sand and ruins and loneliness. And something that made up Lilliputians, something that read in order to learn, and learned in order to plan, and planned in order to act —

I didn't get much sleep that night.

The sun was lemon-colored the next morning when Swanson roused us.

"Come on," he said. "Penner says we're going out again. Two of us will stay on ship, but we'll take turns. Morse, you and Dale can get ready."

"Orders?" I asked.

"No. I don't think so. It's just that it's really your turn to see the ruins."

I faced him. "I don't want to see the ruins. And my advice is that we all stay on ship and blast off, right now."

"What's the trouble?" Penner loomed up behind Swanson.

"He doesn't want to go out," Swanson said. "Thinks we ought to leave." He smiled at Penner, and said, "Coward."

Penner grinned at me and his grin said, "Psycho."

I didn't let my face talk for me. This was serious. "Look, now," I began. "I've been awake most of the night, thinking. And I've got a hunch."

"Let's hear it." Penner was courteous enough, but over his shoulder he said, "Meanwhile, why don't you men get into your suits?"

"This intelligence we talked about last night — we all agreed it must exist. But it can't be measured or located."

"That's what we're going to try to do this morning," Penner said.

"I advise against it."

"Go on."

"Let's think about intelligence for a moment. Ever try to define it? Pretty difficult thing to do. We all know there are hundreds of worlds that don't contain intelligence but do contain life. New worlds and old worlds alike have a complete existence and cycle independent of conscious intelligence."

"What's this, a book lecture?" asked Morse.

"No, just my own ideas. And one of my ideas is that what we call intelligence is a random element, arising spontaneously under certain conditions just as life itself does. It isn't necessary for the existence of a world — it's extraneous, it's a parasite, an alien growth. Usually it uses brain cells as a host. But suppose it could evolve to the point where it isn't limited to brain cells?"

"All right, then what?" Penner snapped.

"Suppose, when life dies on a planet, intelligence finds a means of survival? Suppose it adapts itself to something other than the tissue of the cortex? Suppose the highest point of evolution is reached—in which the planet itself, as host, becomes the seat of intelligence?"

"Mean to say that 68/5 can think?"

"It's worth considering. Remember, when intelligence enters brain cells it identifies itself with its host, and tries in every way to help its host survive. Suppose it enters, finally, into the planet—when life dies out— and tries to help the planet survive?"

"Thinking planets! Now I've heard everything!" This from Swanson. "Dale, you read too many books."

"Perhaps. But consider what's happened. We can't locate any life form here. Nevertheless, we black out. And something creates, out of reading and imagination, a duplicate of GULLIVER'S TRAVELS. Think in terms of a combined number of intelligences, fused into a single unit housed in the body of this world itself. Think of its potential power, and then think of its motives. We're outsiders, we may be hostile, we must be controlled or destroyed. And that's what the planet is trying to do. It can't read our minds, but it can read my books. And its combined force is enough to materialize imaginative concepts in an effort to destroy us. First came little Lilliputians with bows and arrows and tiny spears. The intelligence realized these wouldn't be effective, so it may try something else. Something like—"

Penner cut me off with a gesture. "All right, Dale. You don't have to come with us if you don't want to." It was like a slap in the face. I stared around the circle. The men had their suits on. Nobody looked at me.

Then, surprisingly enough, Levy spoke up. "Maybe he's right," he said. "Somebody else has to stay behind, too. Think I'll keep Dale company here."

I smiled at him. He came over, unfastening his suit. The others didn't say anything. They filed over to the stairs.

"We'll watch you through the Sighters," Levy said. Penner nodded, disappeared with the others.

Minutes later we caught sight of them toiling up the sunbaked slope of the ridge leading toward the ruins. In the clear light now the ruins were partially visible. Even though only rooftops were clear of sand, they looked gigantic and imposing. An ancient race had dwelt here. And now a new race had come. That was the way life went. Or death—

"What are you worrying about?" Levy asked. "Stop squirming."

"I don't like it," I said. "Something's going to happen. You believed me too or you wouldn't have stayed."

"Penner's a fool," Levy said. "You know, I used to read a few books myself, once upon a time."

"Once upon a time!" I stood up. "I forgot!"

"Where are you going?"

"I'm looking for my other two books," I said. "I should have thought of that."

"Thought of what?" Levy talked to me, but he was watching the others, outside, through the Sighter.

"If it can read one book, it can read the others," I told him. "Better get rid of them right away, play it safe."

"What are the other two books?" Levy asked the question, but I never answered him. Because his voice changed, cracked, and he said, *"Dale, come here, hurry!"*

I stared through the Sighter. I adjusted the control and it was like a close-up. I could see Penner and Swanson and Morse as if they were standing beside me. They had just reached the top of the ridge, and the ruined stones of the cyclopean city rose before them. *Cyclopean.*

The word came, the concept came, and then the reality. The first giant towered up from behind the rocks. He was thirty feet tall and his single eye was a burning beacon.

They saw him and turned to flee. Penner tugged at his waist, trying to draw his tube and fire. But there wasn't time now, for the giants were all around them—the bearded, one-eyed monsters out of myth.

The giants laughed, and their laughter shook the earth, and they scooped up great rocks from the ruins and hurled them at the men, crushing them. And then they lumbered over to the crushed forms and began to feast, their talons rending and tearing the bodies as I now tore the pages from the book I was holding.

"Cyclops," Levy whispered. "*THE ODYSSEY*, isn't it?" The torn fragments of the second book fell from my fingers as I turned away.

Levy was already working at the panels. "Only two of us," he said. "But we can make it. Takeoff's automatic once we blast. I'm pretty sure we can make it, aren't you, Dale?"

"Yes," I said, but I didn't really care.

The floor was beginning to vibrate. In just a minute, now, we'd blast.

"Come on, Dale, strap up! I'll handle the board. You know what to do."

I knew what to do.

Levy's face twitched. "What's the matter now? Is it the third book? Are you going to get rid of the third book?"

"No need to. The third one's harmless," I said. "Here, I'll show you."

"What is the third book?" he asked.

I stepped over to the Sighter for the last time and he followed me. I adjusted for close-up very carefully.

"Look," I said.

We stared out across the barren plain, the plain which no longer held life because it had *become* life for this planet.

The Cyclops had disappeared, and what was left of Penner, and Swanson and Morse lay undisturbed in the dreaming ruins under an orange sun.

Somewhere, somehow, the reader turned a page—

"The third book," I whispered. "Watch."

It scampered out from behind one of the stones, moving swiftly on tiny legs. The Sighter brought it so close that I could see the very hairs of its whiskers, note the design of its checkered waistcoat, read the numerals on the watch it took out of the waistcoat pocket. Before I turned away, I almost fancied I could read its lips.

That wasn't necessary, of course, because I knew what it was saying.

"Oh dear! Oh dear! I shall be too late!" it murmured.

Mincing daintily on thin legs, the White Rabbit scampered among the bodies as we blasted off.

THE PIN

Somehow, somewhere, someone would find out.

It was inevitable.

In this case the *someone* was named Barton Stone. The *somewhere* was an old loft over a condemned office building on Bleecker Street.

And the *somehow* . . .

Barton Stone came there early one Monday morning as the sun shone yellow and cold over the huddled rooftops. He noted the mass of the surrounding buildings, rearranged them into a more pleasing series of linear units, gauged his perspective, evaluated the tones and shadings of sunlight and shadow with his artist's eye. There was a picture here, he told himself, if only he could find it.

Unfortunately he wasn't looking for a picture. He had plenty of subjects in mind. Right now he was looking for a place in which to paint. He wanted a studio, wanted it quickly. And it must be cheap. Running water and north light were luxuries beyond his present consideration. As for other aesthetic elements, such as cleanliness — Stone shrugged as he mounted the stairs, his long fingers trailing dust from the rickety railing.

There was dust everywhere, for this was the domain of dust, of darkness and desertion. He stumbled upward into the silence.

The first two floors of the building were entirely empty, just as Freed had told him. And the stairs to the loft were at the end of the hall on the second floor.

"You'll have it all to yourself," the rental agent had promised. "But remember to stay in the loft. Nobody'd ever bother looking up there. Damned inspectors come around — they keep telling us to raze the building. But the floor's safe enough. All you got to do is keep out of sight — why, you could

207

hide out there for years without being caught. It's no palace, but take a look and see what you think. For twenty bucks a month you can't go wrong."

Stone nodded now as he walked down the debris-littered hall toward the loft stairs. He couldn't go wrong. He sensed, suddenly and with utter certainty, that this was the place he'd been searching for during all of these frustrating futile weeks. He moved up the stairs with inevitable—

Then he heard the sound.

Call it a thud; call it a thump; call it a muffled crash. The important thing was that it sounded from above, from the deserted loft.

Stone paused on the second step from the top. There was someone in the loft. *For twenty bucks a month you can't go wrong*—but *you could hide out there for years without being caught.*

Barton Stone was not a brave man. He was only a poor artist, looking for a cheap loft or attic to use as a studio. But his need was great, great enough to impel him upward, carry him to the top of the loft stairs and down the short corridor leading to the entry.

He moved quietly now, although there was thunder in his chest. He tiptoed delicately toward the final door, noted the overhead transom, noted, too, the small crate in the corner against the wall.

There was silence beyond the door and silence in the hall now as he carefully lifted the crate and placed it so that he could mount the flat top and peer over the open transom.

No sense in being melodramatic, he told himself. On the other hand, there was no sense rushing in—Barton Stone was not a fool and he didn't want to become an angel.

He looked over the transom.

The loft was huge. A dusty skylight dominated the ceiling, and enough light filtered through to bathe the room in sickly luminance. Stone could see everything, everything.

He saw the books, stacked man-high, row after row of thick books. He saw the sheaves bulked between the books, pile after pile of sheaves. He saw the papers rising in solid walls from the floor. He saw the table in the center of the loft—the table, bulwarked on three sides by books and sheaves and papers all tossed together in toppling towers.

And he saw the man.

The man sat behind the table, back to the wall, surrounded on three sides by the incredible array of printed matter. He sat there, head down, and peered at the pages of an opened book. He never looked up, never made a sound, just sat there and stared.

Stone stared back. He understood the source of the noise now; one of the books had fallen from its stack. But nothing else made sense to him. His eyes sought clues; his mind sought meaning.

The man was short, fat, middle-aged. His hair was graying into white, his face lining into wrinkles. He wore a dirty khaki shirt and trousers and he might have been an ex-GI, a tramp, a fugitive from justice, an indigent bookdealer, an eccentric millionaire.

Stone moved from the realm of might-have-been to a consideration of what he actually saw. The little fat man was riffling through the pages of a fat, paperbound book which could easily be mistaken for a telephone directory. He turned the pages, apparently at random, with his left hand. Very well, then; he was left-handed.

Or was he? His right hand moved across the table, raised and poised so that the sunlight glittered in a thin line of silver against the object he held.

It was a pin, a long, silver pin. Stone stared at it. The man was staring at it too. Stone's gaze held curiosity. The little fat man's gaze held utter loathing and, more than that, a sort of horrified fascination.

Another sound broke the stillness. The little man sighed. It was a deep sight that became, with abrupt and hideous clarity, a groan.

Eyes still intent on the pin, the little man brought it down suddenly upon the opened pages of his book. He stabbed at random, driving the point home. Then he hurled the book to the floor, sat back, buried his face in his hands, and his shoulders shook with silent sobbing.

A second sped. Stone blinked. And beyond the door, in the loft, the little man straightened up, reaching for a long sheet of paper that might have been a polling list, and scanned its surface. The pin poised itself over the center of the sheet. Again the sigh, the stab, the sob.

Now the little man rose, and for a frantic moment Stone wondered if he'd been detected. But no, the pin wielder merely wandered down the row of books and pulled out another thick volume. He carried it back to the table and sat down, picking up the pin with his right hand as his left turned page after page. He scanned, scrutinized, then sighed, stabbed, sobbed.

Barton Stone descended from the top of the crate, replaced it carefully in the corner, and tiptoed down the stairs. He moved carefully and silently, and it was an effort to do so, because he wanted all the while to run.

His feeling was irrational, and he knew it, but he could not control himself. He had always experienced that sudden surge of fear in the presence of the demented. When he saw a drunk in a bar, he was afraid—because you never know what a drunk will do next, what will enter his mind and how he will act. He shied away from arguments, because of what happens to a man's reaction pattern when he sees red. He avoided the mumblers, the people who talk to themselves or to the empty air as they shuffle down the street.

Right now he was afraid of a little fat man, a little fat man with a long, sharp, silver needle. The needle was crooked at one end, Stone remembered—and he could see that needle sinking into his own throat, right up to the crooked angle. The fat man was crazy and Stone wanted no part of him. He'd go back to the rental agency, see Mr. Freed, tell him. Freed could evict him, get him out of there in a hurry. That would be the sensible way.

Before he knew it, Stone was back in his own walk-up flat, resting on the bed and staring at the wall. Although it wasn't the wall he was seeing. He was seeing the little fat man and studying him as he sat at his big table. He was seeing the books and the sheaves and the long rolls and scrolls of paper.

He could group them in the background, so. Just sketch them in lightly, in order to place the figure. The khaki shirt hung thusly—and the open collar draped in this fashion. Now the outlines of the head and shoulders; be sure to catch the intent intensity, the concentrated concentration of the pose.

Stone had his sketchpad out now, and his hands moved furiously. The sunlight would serve as a high light over the shoulder. It would strike the silver pin and the reflection would fleck the features of the face.

The features—the face—most important. He began to rough it in. If he could only capture the instant before the sob, if he could only fathom the secret of the eyes as the pin stabbed down, he'd have a painting.

What *was* that look? Stone had unconsciously catalogued and categorized the features. The proportions of nose to forehead, ears to head, chin to jaw; the relationship of brow and cheekbone to the eyes—he knew them and reproduced them. But the expression itself—particularly that look around the eyes—that was the key to it all.

And he couldn't get it down. He drew, erased, drew again. He made a marginal sketch and rubbed it out. The charcoal smeared his palm.

No, it was wrong, all wrong. He'd have to see him again. He was afraid to go, but he wanted that painting. He wanted to do it; he *had* to do it. There was a mystery here, and if he could only pin it down on canvas he'd be satisfied.

Pin it down. The pin was what frightened him, he knew it now. It wasn't the man so much. Granted, he was probably insane—without the pin he'd be harmless, deprived of weapons.

Stone stood up. He went out, down the stairs, walked. He should have gone to the rental agency first, he told himself, but the other need was greater. He wanted to see his subject once more. He wanted to stare into the face of the little fat man and read the secret behind the planes and angles.

And he did. He climbed the stairs silently, mounted the crate quietly, directed his soundless gaze over the transom.

The fat man was still at work. New books, new papers bulked high on the big table. But the left hand turned the pages, the right hand poised the pin. And the endless, enigmatic pantomime played on. Sigh, stab, sob. Stop and shudder, shuffle through fresh pages, scan and scrutinize again, and then— sigh, stab, sob.

The silver pin glared and glistened. It glowed and glittered and grew.

Barton Stone tried to study the face of the fat man, tried to impress the image of his eyes.

Instead he saw the pin. The pin and only the pin. The pin that poised, the pin that pointed, the pin that pricked the page.

He forced himself to concentrate on the little man's face, forced himself to focus on form and features. He saw sorrow, read resignation, recognized revulsion, found fear there. But there was neither sorrow nor resignation, revulsion nor fear in the hand that drove the pin down again and again. There was only a mechanical gesture, without pattern or meaning that Barton Stone could decipher. It was the action of a lunatic, the antic gesture of aberration.

Stone stepped down from the crate, replaced it in the corner, then paused before the loft door. For a moment he hesitated. It would be so simple merely to walk into the loft, confront the little man, ask him his business. The little man would look up, and Stone could stare into his eyes, single out and scrutinize the secrets there.

But the little man had his pin, and Stone was afraid. He was afraid of the pin that didn't sob or sigh but merely stabbed down. And made its point.

The point — what was it?

Well, there was another way of finding out, the sensible way. Stone sidled softly down the stairs, padded purposefully up the street.

Here it was, ACME RENTALS. But the door was locked. Barton Stone glanced at his watch. Only four o'clock. Funny he'd be gone so early, unless he'd left with a client to show some property or office space.

Stone sighed. Tomorrow, then. Time enough. He turned and strode back down the street. He intended to go to his flat and rest before supper, but as he rounded the corner he saw something that stopped him in his tracks.

It was only a brownish blur, moving very fast. His eye caught a glimpse of khaki, a suggestion of a bowed back, a white-thatched head disappearing into the doorway of a local restaurant. That was enough; he was sure now. His little fat man had taken time out to eat.

And that meant . . .

Stone ran the remaining blocks, clattered up the rickety stairs. He burst into the loft, raced over to the table. Then, and then only, he stopped. What was he doing here? What did he hope to find out? What was he looking for?

That was it. He was looking for something. Some clue, some intimation of the little fat man's perverted purpose.

The books and papers billowed balefully all about him. There were at least half a hundred presently on the table. Stone picked up the first one. It was a telephone directory, current edition, for Bangor, Maine. Beneath it was another — Yuma, Arizona. And below that, in a gaudy cover, the city directory of Montevideo. At one side a long list of names, sheet after sheet of them, in French. The town roll of Dijon. And over at one side the electoral rolls of Manila, P.I. Another city directory—Stone guessed it must be in Russian. And here was the phone book from Leeds, and the census sheets from Calgary, and a little photostat of the unofficial census of Mombasa.

Stone paged through them, then directed his attention to another stack on the right-hand side of the table. Here were opened books aplenty, piled one upon the other in a baffling miscellany. Stone glanced at the bottom of the collection. Another phone book, from Seattle. City directory of Belfast. Voting list from Bloomington, Illinois. Precinct polling list, Melbourne, Australia. Page after page of Chinese ideographs. Military personnel, USAF, Tokyo base. A book in Swedish or Norwegian—Stone wasn't sure which, but he recognized that it contained nothing but names; and like all the others it was recent or currently published and in use.

And here, right on top, was a Manhattan directory. It was open, like the others, and apparently the choice of page had been made on random impulse. Barton Stone glanced at the heading: FRE. Was there a pin mark? He stared, found it.

Freed, George A. And the address.

Wait a minute! Wasn't that *his* rental agency man? Something began to form and fashion, and then Stone pushed the book away and ran out of the room and down the stairs, and he rounded the corner and found the news-stand and bought his paper and clawed it open to the death notices, and then he read the name again.

Freed, George A. And the address. And on another page—Stone's hands were trembling, and it took him a while to find it—was the story. It had happened this morning. Accident. Hit by a truck crossing the street. Survived by blah, blah, blah.

Yes, blah, blah, blah, and this morning (perhaps while Stone has been watching him the first time) the pin had pointed and stabbed and a name in the directory was marked for destruction. For death.

For *Death!*

Nobody'd ever bother looking up there. You could hide out there for years without being caught. Yes, you could gather together all the lists, all the sources, all the names in the world and put them into that deserted loft. You could sit there, day after day and night after night, and stick pins into them the way the legends said witches stuck pins into effigies of their victims. You'd sit there and choose book after book at random, and the pin would point. And wherever it struck somebody died. You could do that, and you *would* do that. If you were the little fat man. The little fat man whose name was *Death.*

Stone almost laughed, although the sound didn't come out that way. He'd wondered why he couldn't get the little man's eyes right, wondered why he couldn't search out their secret. Now he knew. He'd encountered the final mystery—that of Death itself. Death *himself.*

And where was Death now? Sitting in a cheap restaurant, a local hash house, taking a breather. Death was dining out. Simple enough, wasn't it? All Stone need do now was find a policeman and take him into the joint.

"See that little fat guy over there, Officer? I want you to arrest him for murder. He's Death, you know. And I can prove it. I'll show you the pin point."

Simple. *Insanely* simple.

Maybe he was wrong. He *had* to be wrong. Stone riffled back to the death notices again. Kooley, Leventhaler, Mautz. He had to make sure.

Kooley, Leventhaler, Mautz.

Question: How long does it take for Death to dine?

Question: Does Death care to linger over a second cup of coffee?

Question: Does one dare go back and search that directory to find the pin points opposite the names of Kooley, Leventhaler, and Mautz?

The first two questions couldn't be answered. They constituted a calculated risk. The third question could be solved only by action.

Barton Stone acted. His legs didn't want to move; his feet rebelled every step of the way, and his hands shook as he climbed the stairs once more.

Stone almost fell as he peered over the transom. The loft was still empty. And it was shrouded now in twilight. The dusk filtering through the skylight provided just enough illumination for him to read the directory. To find the names of Kooley, Leventhaler, and Mautz. And the pin points penetrating each, puncturing the *o*, the *v*, the *u*. Puncturing their names, puncturing their lives, providing punctuation. The final punctuation—period.

How many others had died today, in how many cities, towns, hamlets, crossroads, culverts, prisons, hospitals, huts, kraals, trenches, tents, igloos? How many times had the silver pin descended, force by fatal fancy?

Yes, and how many times would it descend tonight? And tomorrow, and the next day, and forever and ever, time without end, amen?

They always pictured Death wielding a scythe, didn't they? And to think that it was really just a pin—a pin with a curve or a hook in it. A long, sharp, silver pin, like *that one there.*

The last rays of the dying sunset found it, set its length ablaze in a rainbow glow. Stone gasped sharply. It was here, right here on the table, where the little fat man had left it when he went out to eat—the silver pin!

Stone eyed the sparkling instrument, noted the hooked end, and gasped again. It *was* a scythe after all! A little miniature scythe of silver. The weapon of Death which cut down all mankind. Cut down mankind without rhyme or reason, stabbed senselessly to deprive men forever of sensation. Stone could picture it moving in frantic rhythm over the names of military personnel, pick, pick, picking away at lives; point, point, pointing at people; stick, stick, sticking into human hearts. The fatal instrument, the lethal weapon, smaller than any sword and bigger than any bomb.

It was *here*, on the table.

He had only to reach out and take it. . . .

For a moment the sun stood still and his heart stopped beating and there was nothing but silence in the whole wide world.

Stone picked up the pin.

He put it in his shirt pocket and stumbled out of the room, stumbled through darkness and tumbled down the flights of the night.

Then he was out on the street again and safe. He was safe, and the pin was safe in his pocket, and the world was safe forever.

Or was it? He couldn't be sure.

He couldn't be sure, and he wouldn't be sure, and he sat there in his room all night long, wondering if he'd gone completely mad.

For the pin was only a pin. True, it was shaped like a miniature scythe. True, it was cold and did not warm to the touch, and its point was sharper than any tool could ever grind.

But he couldn't be sure. Even the next morning there was nothing to show. He wondered if Death read the papers. He couldn't read *all* the papers. He couldn't attend *all* the funerals. He was too busy. Or, rather, he *had* been too busy. Now he could only wait, as Stone was waiting.

The afternoon editions would begin to provide proof. The home editions. Stone waited, because he couldn't be sure. And then he went down to the corner and bought four papers and he knew.

There were death notices still; of course there would be. Death notices from yesterday. *Only* from yesterday.

And the front pages carried further confirmation. The subject matter of the stories was serious enough, but the treatment was still humorous, quizzical, or, at best, speculative and aloof. Lots of smart boys on the wire services and the city desks; too hard-boiled to be taken in or commit themselves until they were certain. So there was no editorial comment yet, just story after story, each with its own "slant."

The prisoner up at Sing Sing who went to the chair last night — and was still alive. They'd given him plenty of juice, and the power worked all right. The man had fried in the hot seat. Fried, literally, but lived. Authorities were investigating.

Freak accident up in Buffalo — cables snapped and a two-ton safe landed squarely on the head and shoulders of Frank Nelson, forty-two. Broken back, neck, arms, legs, pelvis, skull completely crushed. But in Emergency Hospital, Frank Nelson was still breathing and doctors could not account for . . .

Plane crash in Chile. Eighteen passengers, all severely injured and many badly burned when engines caught fire, but no fatalities were reported and further reports . . .

City hospitals could not explain the sudden cessation of deaths throughout Greater New York and environs. .

Gas-main explosions, automobile accidents, fires and natural disasters; each item isolated and treated as a freak, a separate phenomenon.

That's the way it would be until perhaps tomorrow, when the hard-boiled editors and the hard-headed medical men and the hard-shelled Baptists and the hard-nosed military leaders and the hard-pressed scientists all woke up, pooled their information, and realized that Death had died.

Meanwhile, the torn and the twisted, the burned and the maimed, the tortured and the broken ones writhed in their beds—but breathed and lived, in a fashion.

Stone breathed and lived in a fashion too. He was beginning to see the seared body of the convict, the mangled torso of the mover, the agonized forms that prayed for the mercy of oblivion all over the world.

Conscience doth make cowards of us all and *no man is an island.* But on the other hand, Stone breathed and lived after a fashion. And as long as he had the pin, he'd breathe and live forever. Forever!

So would they all. And more would be born, and the earth would teem with their multitude—what then? Very well, let the editors and the doctors and the preachers and the soldiers and the scientists figure out solutions. Stone had done his part. He'd destroyed Death. Or at the least, disarmed him.

Barton Stone wondered what Death was doing right now. Death, in the afternoon. Was he sitting in the loft, pondering over his piles of useless papers, lingering over his lethal ledgers? Or was he out, looking for another job? Couldn't very well expect to get unemployment compensation, and he had no social security.

That was *his* problem. Stone didn't care. He had other worries.

The tingling, for example. It had started late that morning, around noon. At first Stone ascribed it to the fact that he hadn't eaten or slept for over twenty-four hours. It was fatigue. But fatigue gnaws. Fatigue does not bite. It doesn't sink its sharp little tooth into your chest.

Sharp. Chest. Stone reached up, grabbed the silver pin from his pocket. The little scythe was cold. Its sharp, icy point had cut through his shirt, pricked against his heart.

Stone laid the pin down very carefully on the table, and he even turned the point away from himself. Then he sat back and sighed as the pain went away.

But it came back again, stronger. And Stone looked down and saw that the pin pointed at him again. He hadn't moved it. He hadn't touched it. He hadn't even looked at it. But it swung around like the needle of a compass. And he was its magnetic pole. He was due north. North, cold and icy like the pains that shot through his chest.

Death's weapon had power—the power to stab him, stab his chest and heart. It couldn't kill him, for there was no longer any dying in the world. It would just stab him now, forever and ever, night and day for all eternity. He was a magnet, attracting pain. Unendurable, endless pain.

The realization transfixed him, just as the point of the pin itself transfixed him.

Had his own hand reached out and picked up the pin, driven it into his chest? Or had the pin itself risen from the table and sought its magnetic target? Did the pin have its own powers?

Yes. That was the answer, and he knew it now. Knew that the little fat man was just a man and nothing more. A poor devil who had to go out and eat, who slept and dozed as best he could while he still stabbed ceaselessly away. He was only a tool. *The pin itself was Death.*

Had the little man once looked over a transom or peered through a window in New York or Baghdad or Durban or Rangoon? Had he stolen the silver pin from yet another poor devil and then been driven by it, driven out into the street by the pin that pricked and pricked at his heart? Had he returned to the place where all the names in the world awaited their final sentencing?

Barton Stone didn't know. All he knew was that the pin was colder than arctic ice and hotter than volcanic fire and it was tearing at his chest. Every time he tore it free the point inexorably returned and his hand descended with it, forcing the pin into his chest. Sigh, stab, sob—the power of Death was in the pin.

And the power of Death animated Barton Stone as he ran through the nighted streets, panted up the midnight stairs, staggered into the loft.

A dim light burned over the table, casting its glow over the waiting shadows. The little fat man sat there, surrounded by his books, and when he saw Barton Stone he looked up and nodded.

His stare was impersonal and blank. Stone's stare was agonized and intent. There was something Stone had to find out, once and for all, a question which must be answered. He recognized its nature and the need, sought and found his solution in the little fat man's face.

The little fat man *was* a man and nothing more. He *was* merely the instrument, and the pin held all the power. That was enough for Barton Stone to know. It was all he could know, for the rest was only endless pain. He had to be relieved of the pain, had to be released from it, just as the poor devils all over the world had to be relieved and released. It was logic, cold logic, cold as the pin, cold as Death.

Stone gasped, and the little fat man stood up and moved around from behind the table.

"I've been waiting for you," he said. "I knew you'd come back."

Stone forced the words out. "I stole the pin," he panted. "I've come to give it back."

The little fat man looked at him, and for the first time Stone could read his eyes. In them he saw infinite compassion, limitless understanding, and an endless relief.

"What is taken cannot be returned," murmured the little man. "I think you know that. When you took the pin you took it forever. Or until—"

The little man shrugged and indicated the seat behind the table.

Silently Stone sat down. The books bulked before him; the books, the directories, the papers and scrolls and lists that contained all the names in the world.

"The most urgent are on top," whispered the little man. "I sorted them while I waited."

"Then you knew I'd be back?"

The little fat man nodded. "I came back once too. And I found—as you will find—that the pain goes away. You can remove the pin now and get to work. There's so much work to do."

He was right. There was no longer any stabbing sensation in Stone's chest. The little scythe-shaped pin came away quite easily and balanced in Stone's right hand. His left hand reached for the topmost book. A small piece of paper, bearing a single scribbled name, rested on the opened volume.

"If you don't mind," breathed the little fat man, "this name first, please."

Stone looked at the little fat man. He didn't look down at the scribbled name—he didn't have to, for he knew. And his right hand stabbed down, and the little man sighed and then he fell over and there was only a wisp of dust.

Old dust, gossamer-light dust, soon blows away. And there was no time to look at the dancing, dissipating motes. For Barton Stone was sighing, stabbing, shuddering, sobbing.

And the pin pointed and pricked. Pricked the convict up in Sing Sing and Frank Nelson in Buffalo Emergency and the crash victims in Chile. Pricked Chundra Lal of Bombay, Ramona Neilson of Minneapolis, Barney Yates in Glasgow, Igor Vorpetchzki in Minsk, Mrs. Minnie Haines and Dr. Fisher and Urbonga and Li Chan and a man named John Smith in Upper Sandusky.

It was day and it was night and it was summer and it was autumn and it was winter and it was spring and it was summer again, but you could hide out there for years without being caught.

All you did was keep shuffling the books, picking at random. That was the best you could do, the only fair way. Sometimes you got mad and took a lot from one place; sometimes you just kept going, plodding along and leaving it up to the pin.

You sighed, you stabbed, you shuddered, and you sobbed. But you never stopped. Because the pin never stopped; the scythe was always swinging.

Thus it was, and thus it would be forever. Until the day came, inevitably, when somehow, somewhere, someone would find out. . . .

THE GODDESS OF WISDOM

LET'S NOT PULL ANY PUNCHES.

The first thing that I wanted, after I landed at Skyport, was a female.

Yes, that's right. I didn't say "woman." I said "female." There aren't any women at Skyport, except for one or two of the officials, and there's no sense in wishful thinking.

But I'm not making any excuses for the way I felt. If you're one of the narrow-minded, earthbound kind, nothing I'd say would help to explain. But if you've ever been outside, you can understand. Particularly if you've been way outside.

That's where I'd been — way, way outside — for six long months. Simple little phrase, isn't it. "Six long months." But it doesn't mean to you what it means to me; it couldn't, unless you've spent that length of time in prison or any asylum on Earth, or in a floating prison or asylum outside.

Maybe you swallow all that stuff about the glamour of the Service; maybe you think of a stretch of patrol or exploratory duty in terms of a luxury cruise in a 60-passenger Moonliner. Well, you're wrong. And if you'd just gone through what I went through, you'd want female company and want it bad.

So here I was at Skyport, back again after my six long months. Six long months of imprisonment in an artificial cell, eating artificial food, breathing artificial air, living under artificial gravity. Six long months of monotony, of loneliness, of regular routine and enforced discipline. Six long months with nothing to see but the six long faces of your companions. You get so you know every possible thought in their heads, anticipate every possible word they can utter. Anticipate? You get so you *dread* the next thought, the next word.

Of course, there's some relief when you land—if you can call risking your neck on some science-forsaken asteroid a relief. If you enjoy wearing a protectelope against blazing heat or bitter cold or deadly gas, you can actually get out and stretch your legs, sometimes. All too often you have to stretch them pretty fast, when some new, unclassified denizen decides you'd make a good entree for dinner.

But I've got nothing to sell. All I say is that I had had six long months. Now I was back. I'd landed, taken the Decontamination routine, got my shots, my tests, my orders for the next trip out, and—almost as an afterthought—my five-day leave.

Five-day leave on Skyport! What a break that was!

I've already mentioned the absence of women. Now I can throw in a remark or two about the presence of Service officials, Service technicians, Service observers and Service police. Add a smattering of gouging, chiseling merchants and a good number of criminal riffraff, squeeze them all together into three square miles of tin-topped magnificence, and you have Skyport.

Think I'm griping? Well, let me tell you, right now, that it looked mighty good to me. Mighty good.

I stepped out of Barrack #5 and headed past the gates, down toward the center of town. Dark-hour was due, and the incs began to blaze in the streets. It was a sight for space-sore eyes, and no mistake. Just to see lights, any kind of lights, was momentarily enough. Just to breathe air, fresh air, all the air I wanted—wonderful! Just to feel marsth under my feet, to feel marsth and imagine it was earth—paradise!

New uniform on my back, a full exchange-clip in my pocket, and five full days of freedom; that was the setup. Five Mars-days, not Earth-days, but why quibble? This was no time for quibbling—I had a lot of things on my agenda.

I was going to hole up in one of the three Stopovers, just like a private citizen, and sleep in a real bed. A real bed, with soft silk sheets brought all the way from Earth. . . .

I was going to hit the best tavs and drink the best Earth beer; beer in cans, beer fresh from the pressurized reefer units, beer from a place called Milwoky, umpteen million miles away. . . .

I was going to look up Harley and some of the others, if they were around, and yarn about the good old days, and gripe about the Service. . . .

But first of all, and most important, I wanted a female.

I walked down the street into town, gawking and marveling the way I suppose the old "cowboys" did, five hundred years ago, when they entered some frontier post after a stretch on the "range."

Come to think of it, this *was* frontier. This was the jumping-off place; full of soldiers, Service people, crooks and gamblers and chiselers and brinkers and drifters. It was noise and bustle and cheating and drinking and it was tough as plutonium and crude as gerk—and I loved the sight and the sound of it at Dark-hour.

And more important still, I loved the thought of the contrast to come—the soft serenity, the palpable presence of an actual female. A man can relax, a man can lose his tensions, a man can find himself again, if there's a female around who can talk, who can listen, who can give him back those old illusions of grace and beauty. I wasn't seeking flesh, I was seeking spirit.

You get those ideas, outside. And when you come back, and you're in Skyport, you go to Ottar. You go to fat Ottar at his bar, the House of All Planets. You get yourself a room in his hotel upstairs and you go down to the bar and ask Ottar if he has any guests. Females, transients waiting to take the liners out again; females you can eat with, drink with, talk with.

You go to Ottar with hunger in your eyes, and you find him sitting at the downstairs desk next to the deserted bar and you say, "Long time."

And fat Ottar grins and holds out his hand. It isn't a nice hand—particularly it you believe that rumor about his having Marty blood—but you grasp it like a drowning man grasps a rope. And what fat Ottar could give me was much better than a rope.

I said, "I've got the shakes. I was wondering—"

He cut me off with a nod. "Too bad you weren't here about three months ago. A woman came here—"

"A *real woman?*"

"I wouldn't brink you. Young, too. With that yellow hair, what you call it?"

"Blonde."

"Yes. Like yours. Only longer. And she looked so." His fat hands made fat gestures.

"What happened?"

"Run off with a Chief."

I said something under my breath. Just my luck. Ottar shuffled to the reefer, got out a can of beer, pulled a posturchair up to the bar. He opened the can for me.

The beer was cold. Cold and *real.* I could actually taste it going down. That sense of reality was what I craved, now, more than anything else.

"Where's everybody?" I asked. "How's business?"

Ottar shrugged. "They're all like you," he said. "When the liners bring females, they come in to see them, to talk. Otherwise, no."

Then he leaned forward. "But there is a female here. For you to see. You, only."

"What do you mean?"

"Just arrived, off Harley's unit."

I starched my ears. "Harley? You mean the old so-and-so is in town?"

"Yes and no."

"Don't brink me, Ottar. Where is he?"

"Deathside."

"No!" I stood up. "Of all the rotten, lousy news—"

"He was your friend. I am sorry." Ottar shuffled away and came back with more beer. He opened the cans with his nails. "Poor, poor Harley." He lifted the cans, extending one to me, and we drank a toast. It wasn't much of a gesture, it was a grotesque way of showing sorrow and saying goodbye, but it was genuine. The beer, as I drank it, tasted sour. Poor old Harley gone deathside! Not good.

"You know what happened?" I asked.

Ottar nodded. "Part of it."

"Then tell me—what are you waiting for?"

"I can trust you?"

"I'm not in uniform now, Ottar. This is between friends, about a friend."

"All right. I'll level. Harley and I, we were partners. I put up the money for his unit. Prospecting, off-bounds. No permits."

"I thought he was freighting, all along."

"That was the front. But he wanted to wildcat. For metals on unstaked asteroids. I got him clearance through the Chiefs."

"Don't tell me how you did it," I cut in. "It's all right. There must be dozens in the same game."

"Whatever he brought back, we split. I sold it for him, each of us took our share. And he was paying off on the unit. You know the job? Brand-new, Foss model, auto-control." Ottar sighed. "You should see what it looks like now."

"Where is it?"

"Edge of the Private Strip. Right where it crash-landed two days ago. I got the signal on my tape, of course, when the unit hit grav. And I knew what that meant—something had gone very much wrong. I was out to the Strip in five *likhs*. Got there just as it came down. Lucky, there was no explosion. Sometime or other he'd set auto-control, and a Foss unit is tough. But the nose caved in, and everything buckled. The Emergency was on the way, and I had to do some fixing in order to get on board first. But as part-owner, I made out all right."

"What did you find?"

Ottar gulped beer. "Harley must have hit something, I dope-out. Maybe he had a heart attack, or a stroke. He must have just had time to set auto-control, and then he dropped. Dropped, and hit something at grav. It was—pretty bad. Worst I've ever seen."

"How can you be so sure?"

"What other answer is there?" Ottar didn't look at me. "There was blood all over the cabin. And he was ripped open, ripped apart, wedged there in the corner with his head blown wide, nothing above the neck—"

"Damned fool would go out in a solo unit," I grumbled, which meant I could see poor old Harley lying there mangled and I felt like crying.

"Here." Ottar pushed beer my way. "You wanted me to tell you about the female."

"She was on the unit?"

"Sitting there, strapped, and staring at him. She must have strapped herself when they hit grav. She was all spattered with—"

"Did she kill him?" I snapped it out.

"Impossible. No weapons. And nobody could have done a job like that on a man. He was torn apart, I tell you, with his head almost gone. Maybe he picked up something on the trip, something Emergency has never heard about—they're investigating, of course. Something to burst a man's head and insides wide open. Oh, forget it!"

"What did the female say about it?"

Ottar shrugged. "Nothing. She doesn't talk."

"You mean she doesn't understand? Or is it shock?"

"No shock. She just doesn't talk. Can't. No sound at all."

"Where'd Harley pick her up?"

"How would I know? The Service is decoding the tape-records, but they're faked. Harley always faked them so he could sneak off to unstaked asteroids. He told me where he'd been when he came in. But now, of course, I'll never find out.

"It must have been way off the course, wherever he went. No specimens or metal in the unit—which is lucky for me, of course, with the Service investigating."

"What about the female?"

"Don't ask too many questions. I got her off the unit without anyone seeing her."

"But that's impossible—"

"They looked the other way." Ottar grinned. "Understand?"

I understood. And it wasn't any of my business. If some of the officials took graft, that was their department. I was sick of the Service, sick of hearing about Harley's death. I had five days' leave, and time was wasting.

I stood up. "This female—what's she like?"

"I'll show you." Ottar rose, led the way. We went to the stairs and a little man came out of the back and took Ottar's place at the desk, in case any customers came in while he was away.

Then we climbed the stairs.

I don't know how many rooms Ottar has in his establishment—more than anyone would suspect, from the looks of the place. All I know is that they're on both sides of a long hall, and each one has a glass panel set in the top of the door. There's a blind which drops from inside, for privacy. But unless the need for privacy exists, the blinds stay up and you can look into the rooms as you pass.

"I knew you were scheduled back," Ottar was saying. "That's why I took her off the unit — also, because I figured she might talk and then the Service would find out what Harley and I had been doing. But mostly I was hoping you could see her and find out something about what had happened."

I nodded. We went down the corridor, rounded a corner, reached the room at the farther end of the hallway.

"Now, I do not know," Ottar said. "She cannot talk or will not talk to me. She will not smile. She will not eat. She merely sits and looks at me as if she didn't like what she saw. And it hurts me, because she is so lovely."

This was strange talk, coming from old Ottar. He wasn't usually susceptible to females, any females. Nor, for that matter, was Harley. There was something very odd here, and Ottar was right — I *did* want to find out what had happened to Harley.

"But what do you expect me to do?" I asked.

Ottar shook his head. "I do not know. All I ask is that you try."

He led me to a door, halted before the glass panel. I looked inside. And Ottar was right. Wherever she was from, whoever and whatever she was — she was lovely.

The female sat on the couch in the small room, sat to one side almost directly below my line of vision, so that I stared down at her from above. She was wearing some kind of sheer smock that Ottar must have provided, but I paid no attention to that. I looked at *her* — at the smooth sweep of her limbs, at the white slope of her shoulders, at the classic contours of a face I'd seen many times before in dreams.

Her hair was woven darkness and her eyes had never known anything but light. Her mouth was a molded magnet, and — Ottar was right. She was lovely.

"She looks like a woman," I whispered. "What's the catch here, Ottar? Is she dangerous, does she bite? A carnivore?"

Ottar shrugged. "I do not think so. She made no attempt to resist when I found her, brought her here. It is just that she will not communicate. Perhaps you cannot even make her understand. But you can try."

"I'll try," I said, and meant it.

"You are not afraid, then? Good. I see you are armed, in case she proves unexpectedly hostile. But I do not think she will trouble you in that way."

I didn't think she would trouble me in *that* way, either.

"Go ahead," Ottar said. "I'll be downstairs, at the bar. Somebody may come in. Call if you need me. And try to find out about Harley. It is important that I know."

He shuffled down the hall. I opened the door, stepped into the room, closed the door behind me. Locked myself in and locked reality out.

That was the feeling. Standing on the other side of the door, looking at her, everything had been real. And now the reality had gone. We faced each other as total strangers. She was a stranger to me, and I was suddenly a stranger to myself.

A stranger and afraid. Who said that? I used to read the classic tapes when I was Earthside. And I used to go out for six months at a time on Service assignments. I used to dream about females, I used to talk to Ottar about Harley's death, I used to look through a glass door at living dreams. . . .

That was reality, that was past. Now I stood in the present. In the room, with her. I looked down and she looked up. A moment, a minute, an hour, a century slipped by. The present didn't change.

A faint, foolish, far-off part of me was wondering, "Now what do you do? She doesn't talk, you know. She doesn't even understand what you're here for. And what are you here for, anyway?"

Yes. That made sense. What *was* I here for? My original purpose, my past purpose, was gone. She wasn't just a female. She was somehow less than that and somehow much, much more.

I can say that her hair was black and her skin was white and her lips were red, but that doesn't begin to describe the *intensity*, the pure depths of the colors that clashed and flamed and blended, the colors that offered the beauty of her body to my eyes.

I can say that she was proud, that her every attitude and gesture made a measure of that pride, but I cannot describe how that pride seemed justified in her very being.

And I can say that, sitting there, she lifted her head and looked into my eyes. Gazed into my eyes. Stared into my eyes. *Flowed* into my eyes.

Her eyes were like warm suns, far away. Her eyes were like blazing guns, close at hand. Her eyes burned inside me.

She was inside me, and she communicated.

"I am here. What do you wish of me?"

Telepathy? Perhaps. Whatever it was, it worked. She didn't talk, she communicated. And what *did* I wish of her?

"What'll I call you?"

"Minerva. That would be closest."

"Minerva?"

"The goddess of wisdom."

"Where did you learn that?"

"From your mind, now. I tried to find what would be most — equivalent." It wasn't a voice inside my head, it was a flowing. She did it with her eyes, I knew that now. They blazed with a sensitivity beyond all sight.

"Yes," she assented.

"Yes, what?"

"You may sit down. Closer, if you like."

I sat down, sat very close to Minerva on the sofa. Close to midnight, ice and fire.

"You wish to ask me — ?"

"Where are you from?"

The communication I got in return was not formed in words for me. Instead came a familiar picture. Grass, trees, clouds, flowers — it was Earthside!

"Earth?" I spoke aloud.

"No. Not there. I cannot tell you. There is nothing in your mind that would be a counterpart, nothing you could ever understand about where I came from."

At least she was honest. I framed my next question.

"Where did you meet Harley?"

"Harley?" She waited for me to form the concept of Harley.

Then she shook her head. The flow came. "I do not know this Harley."

"But you must. You came here with him on the unit." I thought of Harley, lying dead with his smashed head. I pushed the thought away quickly, but she caught it.

"Yes. There was such a one on the unit. Was that Harley?"

I nodded. "How did you get on the unit?"

In reply, blankness. Then, "I do not know. It happened before I was there."

"Before you were there? That doesn't make sense."

"It happened before I was there. I do not lie."

I believed her. But I did not understand.

"I am sorry," the flow came. "But there is no way of explaining."

"Then you can't tell me about Harley, and about the trip? About where he was going, where he'd been, how he died?"

Her eyes answered. "I am truly sorry. It all happened before I was there."

Suddenly I caught sight of myself — sitting here with the most beautiful female I'd ever known, asking questions with my mouth and getting answers from her eyes. It was unusual, it was interesting, it would have made somebody from Research Control very happy — but it was also a waste of time. A complete waste of time.

So she didn't know about Harley, and I believed her. So Harley was dead. Harley was dead and he'd stay deathside, while I was alive. Alive, after six months outside. I'd come here in the first place wanting the company of a female. Wanting more than that, but not daring to hope. Wanting love.

"Love?"

She'd read my thoughts, all of them. And she understood all of them — except the last.

"What is this love?"

All right. I thought about "love." About all kinds of "love." And I thought about her.

"No. It is not possible."

She was honest, this wasn't a brink-job, there must be a reason. I asked for it. "Why?"

"There can be nothing of what you think between you and myself. It is impossible. You are a *man* but I am not a—you call it—*woman*. You understand?"

I didn't. All I could understand was that I was suddenly in the presence of perfection; that woman or no, she was more completely and utterly female than anything or anyone I could ever imagine. She was the essence of everything I wanted and needed, and we were alone together and yet eternities apart.

There must be some way of bridging eternity. There had to be. I asked the only question I could ask.

"Are there other ways of expressing love for your kind?"

"Yes."

"And what are those ways?"

She hesitated a moment before communication came. It was as though she were learning, too. "With the eyes, I know. Or *through* the eyes. Mind to mind. Or my *being* to your mind."

"I do not understand." And a part of my mind said, "You're lying."

Her eyes answered. "I do not lie. It is an ancient way of love, the first way, which you of mankind have forgotten."

Mind to mind. Her being to my mind. "Then how do you—reproduce?"

The concept formed, the answer came swiftly. "Being to mind. Thought is the seed. But not as you know it. The male is the host."

"Host? You mean the male carries the child?"

"Not the way you understand. The male carries the seed within him for—your time—a week, perhaps. And we are born as you see me now."

"Full-grown? But how?"

"I cannot tell you. We are of a different order than mankind. *More.* I am today as I will be forever. I can communicate, learn if I desire, but it is not necessary. I am complete in myself without anything further."

It didn't make sense, but it was self-evident. Whatever she was trying to tell me I already knew. She *was* complete. I couldn't imagine her as she might be *before*, and I couldn't imagine her changing. She was past, present, future all incarnate. A beautiful statue holding life. But this gibberish about gestation, parturition—

"I cannot explain. You have no parallel concept to give me the words. There is my thought, which is seed to that part of you which accepts it. And the—cells, you'd call them, although they are not cells, multiply swiftly.

They grow in the warm, soft darkness. They feed and grow, feed and grow. And then—I am born. Always new, always the same. For ever and ever. This I know, although I was not told. There was no one to tell me."

She sounded like a class in metaphysics, or whatever they used to call it. But she looked like the most desirable woman ever created. And that's what she was to me, now. I moved closer; it was almost agony to be so close and not touch her.

"No," came the message. "It is not for you. You do not understand the danger, what it means—"

I didn't. All I understood was that I wanted her, wanted her in any way possible; wanted love with the eyes, the mind, anything. I once heard that there are times when the merest touch is worth ten nights in a harem, and I'd laughed. I wasn't laughing now. Looking at her, I knew it could be true. It would be true, must be true for me.

"There's more to love than lips and loins may learn."

Was that her thought or mine? I did not know. All I knew was the need. And was it her need or mine?

She was staring at me now, and suddenly I sensed that she shared my sensation. She understood what I wanted, what I desired, because she desired it, too. She'd warned me because she loved me. And because she loved me, she'd give herself in her own way.

"Yes."

Her eyes said that. And her hands sought mine, the hands of marble, the hands of fire. We sat there, silently, and our eyes met.

She gave me her eyes, and all that lay behind them. And the first gift was loneliness. All the loneliness of endless space, all the loneliness of endless time. It surged into me, surged through me, until I was filled with all that is empty. Now I understood why she held my hands—in some way, that was all she could do to keep my being from losing itself in the frozen void. As it was, I remained, retained my identity, and took the loneliness from her. It was her gift, and it became part of me.

Her second gift was memory. Not her memory, but the memory of all who had gone before her. It was not words, it was not images, it was not thoughts; it was a whirling, incredibly flashing blend and blur of sense impressions in which I found earth and marble columns, moons and craters, shattered stars and blazing suns set in a continuity which had nothing to do with time. It came to me swiftly, and incorporated without identifying. Again, it was only the touch of her hands that saved me.

"In love you are given more than you can ever know."

We *both* felt that. For we were one. And one was many. One was all.

Our eyes were inches apart. I could not *see*; that minor function had long since ceased. My eyes communicated and received directly from her being. They sought the third gift, now.

The third gift was warmth. Heat. Fire. Her warmth, her heat, her fire. It was love as I knew it, love as I had never known it, love as I'd never dared dream it. Worlds were split apart to make mountains, mountains ripped asunder to spew lava, and the molten mass of it flowed to fuse us into pure flame. This was the love of the gods, which is fire. And out of fire comes life.

"Out of fire comes life." She was telling me that, now, and ever so slowly I realized once again that there was a *she* and that I had my own identity.

Her hands fell away. I sat back, gasping, trying to focus my eyes and my thoughts. I felt exhausted beyond belief, but there was no feeling of emptiness. Quite the contrary; a new fullness had been added. The quite incredible conviction came to me that perhaps she had spoken the literal truth. That I might now be carrying the seed—

"Yes. Oh, yes! It is done now, as it was ever done, as it must always be done."

And what flowed from her eyes now was more than thought. It was pity. She, who was beyond emotion, had taken it from me. Two tears—her tears, my tears, our tears?—glistened in those glowing depths, then stained the beauty of immortal flesh.

I closed my eyes. There was a churning inside me. I had to sleep, sleep, sleep without dreams or desire. . . .

When I opened my eyes again, she was gone.

The key was missing from the table and the door was open. I peered into the emptiness of the dawn-gray hall.

Then, slowly, I found my way back through the corridor and down the stairs.

Ottar slept at his desk, his big head cradled in his arms. He jumped a bit when I poked him.

He did more than jump when I told him that she was gone.

"But how could she go? I was here, I didn't see anyone, I didn't hear a sound. All at once I was asleep and that's all I remember."

I smiled, or tried to smile. "That makes sense. She's a telepath, among other things. Which means she can probably use her mind as a hypnotic weapon, too. She put you to sleep and went on her way."

Ottar grabbed my shoulder. "What happened? What did you find out about Harley? Tell me."

"There's nothing to tell. She didn't know Harley. That's what she claims, and I believe her."

"How could that be? It doesn't make sense."

"Not our kind of sense." I sighed. "But there are other kinds of sense and other kinds of life in the universe."

I started to walk out.

"Where are you going? Will you look for her, bring her back?"

I nodded. There was no sense saying any more. No sense telling him that I'd never find her, never bring her back. Some man would see her soon, walking in the dawn, and gaze into her eyes, then take her for himself whatever the risk. Before the day was out, I knew, she'd be in a unit bound for another world. She, or those before her, had known many worlds and would know many more as long as there are men who dare to desire a dream come true.

I thought about it all through the day, after I'd taken a room here at the Unit-el. Now it's Dark-hour again, and I'm writing it all down. Writing helps to put everything in order, so that it makes sense. Sense, and more than sense.

Gradually, I've figured it out. About poor old Harley and what happened to him, and about what happened to me.

She didn't lie at all. She told me everything I needed to know. It's just that I wanted her too much and didn't stop to realize.

But I can realize, now. That's all I have left, the realization of how it must have been.

Harley hit some spot and landed, better than a week ago. And he met Minerva's mother, if you can call her that. And they loved, if you can call it that. *"It happened before I was there,"* she had said to me.

Then he took off again in the unit. Alone.

But he wasn't really alone. Because, *"the cells multiply swiftly. They grow in the soft, warm darkness. They feed and grow, feed and grow."*

She told the truth. She told the truth when she said that she didn't know Harley. Of course she didn't. And she didn't know her mother, because she never saw her.

When she was born, she was already on the unit, and Harley was already dead.

Harley died with his head ripped open incredibly, and she was born.

"You do not understand the danger —"

I understand, now.

I understand, how, in searching my mind for concepts, she found the name Minerva. The seeds travel from world to world, from universe to universe, and man is the carrier and the host. And in ancient times, a man who could make such a journey would be a god. His offspring would be a god or a goddess. It must have happened on Olympus, when Minerva was born. Yes, that's the way it was.

I remember the legend of the goddess of wisdom now, the legend of Minerva. Minerva, who *sprang fullblown from the head of Jupiter.*

But it wasn't a legend. *"My being meets your mind. The cells feed and grow, feed and grow. One week. Full-grown."*

And the seed grew in Harley's brain, where it had been planted to grow, and his head burst out there in space, and in a week it was all over and Minerva was born. My Minerva.

In a week, now, she'll reproduce again. But this time it's feeding and growing in *my* brain. It absorbs the bony parts of the skull and the skin expands incredibly. It drinks the blood and eats the soft gray nourishment and waxes fat in godliness as it sups on the wisdom of men. And then it springs, fullblown. In just one week.

I can't write any more. My head is beginning to ache. . . .

THE PAST MASTER

Statement of Debby Gross

HONESTLY, I could just die. The way George acts, you'd think it was my fault or something. You'd think he never even saw the guy. You'd think I stole his car. And he keeps asking me to explain everything to him. If I told him once, I told him a hundred times — and the cops too. Besides, what's there to tell him? He was there.

Of course, it doesn't make sense. I already know that. Honest to Pete, I wish I'd stayed home Sunday. I wish I'd told George I had another date when he called up. I wish I'd made him take me to the show instead of that old beach. Him and his convertible! Besides, your legs stick to those leather seats in hot weather.

But you should of seen me Sunday when he called. You'd think he was taking me to Florida or someplace, the way I acted. I had this new slack suit I bought at Sterns, with the plaid top sort of a halter, like. And I quick put on some more of that Restora Rinse. You know, George is the one down at the office who started everybody calling me "Blondie."

So anyhow he came around and picked me up about four, and it was still hot and he had the top down. I guess he just finished washing the car. It looked real snazzy, and he said, "Boy, it just matches your hair, don't it?"

First we drove along the Parkway and then out over the Drive. It was just packed, the cars, I mean. So he said how about it if we didn't go to the beach until after dinner.

That was all right by me, so we went to this Luigi's — it's a seafood place way south on the highway. It's real expensive and they got one of those big menus with all kinds of oozy stuff like pompanos and terrapins. That's a turtle, like.

I had a sirloin and french fries, and George had—I can't remember, oh, yes I do—he had fried chicken. Before we ate we had a couple drinks, and after we just sat in the booth and had a couple more. We were sort of kidding back and forth, you know, about the beach and all, and waiting until after dark so we could go swimming on account of not bringing any suits.

Anyways, I was kidding. That George, he'd just as soon do anything. And don't think I didn't know why he was feeding me all those drinks. When we went out he stopped over at the bar and picked up a pint.

The moon was just coming up, almost full, and we started singing while we drove, and I felt like I was getting right with it. So when he said let's not go to the regular beach—he knew this little place way off somewhere—I thought, why not?

It was like a bay, sort of, and you could park up on the bluff along this sideroad, and then walk down to the sand and see way out across the water.

Only that's not why George picked it. He wasn't interested in looking at water. First thing he did was to spread out this big beach blanket, and the second thing he did was open up his pint, and the third thing he did was to start monkeying around.

Nothing serious, you understand, just monkeying around, kind of. Well, he's not so bad-looking even with that busted nose of his, and we kept working on that pint, and it was kind of romantic. I mean, the moon and all.

It wasn't until he really began messing that I made him stop. And even then, I practically had to sock him one before he figured out I wasn't kidding.

"Cut it out," I said. "Now see what you've done! You tore my halter."

"Hell, I'll buy you a new one," he said. "Come on, baby." He tried to grab me again, and I gave him a good one, right on the side of his head. For a minute I thought he'd—you know—get tough about it. But he was pretty canned up, I guess. Anyhow, he just started blubbering about how sorry he was, and that he knew I wasn't that kind, but it was just that he was so crazy about me.

I almost had to laugh, they're so funny when they get that way. But I figured it was smarter to put on an act, so I made out like I was real sore, like I'd never been so insulted in all my life.

Then he said we should have another drink and forget about it, only the pint was empty. So he said how about him taking a run up to the road and getting some more? Or we could both go to a tavern if I liked.

"With all these marks on my neck?" I told him. "I certainly will not! If you want more, you get it "

So he said he would, and he'd be back in five minutes. And he went.

Anyhow, that's how I was alone, when it happened. I was just sitting there on the blanket, looking out at the water, when I saw this thing sort of moving. At first it looked sort of like a log or something. But it kept coming closer, and then I could see it as somebody swimming, real fast.

So I kept on watching, and pretty soon I made out it was a man, and he was heading right for shore. Then he got close enough so's I could see him stand up and start wading in. He was real tall, real tall, like one of those basketball players, only not skinny or anything. And so help me he didn't have any trunks on or anything. Not a stitch!

Well, I mean, what could I do? I figured he didn't see me, and besides, you can't go running around screaming your head off. Not that there was anyone to hear me. I was all alone there. So I just sat and waited for him to come out of the water and go away up the beach or someplace.

Only he didn't go away. He came out and he walked right over to me. You can imagine—there I was, sitting and there he was, all dripping wet and with no clothes. But he gave me a big hello, just like nothing was wrong. He looked real dreamy when he smiled.

"Good evening," he said. "Might I inquire my whereabouts, Miss?"

Dig that "whereabouts" talk!

So I told him where he was, and he nodded, and then he saw how I was staring and he said, "Might I trouble you for the loan of that blanket?"

Well, what else could I do? I got up and gave it to him and he wrapped it around his waist. That's the first I noticed he was carrying this bag in his hand. It was some kind of plastic, and you couldn't tell what was inside of it.

"What happened to your trunks?" I asked him.

"Trunks?" You'd of thought he never heard of such things the way he said it. Then he smiled again and said, "I'm sorry. They must have slipped off."

"Where'd you start from?" I asked. "You got a boat out there?" He was real tan, he looked like one of these guys that hang around the Yacht Basin all the time.

"Yes. How did you know?" he said.

"Well, where else would you come from?" I told him. "It just stands to reason."

"It does, at that," he said.

I looked at the bag. "What you got in there?" I asked.

He opened his mouth to answer me, but he never got a chance. Because all of a sudden George came running down from the bluff. I never even seen his lights or heard the car stop. But there he was, just tearing down, with a bottle in his hand, all ready to swing. Character!

"What the hell's going on here?" he yelled.

"Nothing," I told him.

"Who the hell is this guy? Where'd he come from?" George shouted.

"Permit me to introduce myself," the guy said. "My name is John Smith and—"

"John Smith, my foot!" yelled George, only he didn't say "foot." He was real mad. "All right, let's have it. What's the big idea, you two?"

"There isn't any big idea," I said. "This man was swimming and he lost his trunks, so he borrowed the blanket. He's got a boat out there and—"

"Where? Where's the boat? I don't see any boat." Neither did I, come to think of it. George wasn't waiting for any answers, though. "You there, gimme back that blanket and get the hell out of here."

"He can't," I told him. "He hasn't got any trunks on."

George stood there with his mouth open. Then he waved the bottle. "All right, then, fella. You're coming with us." He gave me a wise look. "Know what I think? I think this guy's a phony. He could even be one of those spies the Russians are sending over in submarines."

That's George for you. Ever since the papers got full of this war scare, he's been seeing Communists all over the place.

"Start talking," he said. "What's in that bag?"

The guy just looked at him and smiled.

"OK, so you want to do it the hard way, it's OK by me. Get up that bluff, fella. We're gonna take a ride over to the police. Come on, before I let you have it." And he waved the bottle.

The guy sort of shrugged and then he looked at George. "You have an automobile?" he asked.

"Of course, what do I look like, Paul Revere or something?" George said.

"Paul Revere? Is he alive?" The guy was kidding, but George didn't know it.

"Shut up and get moving," he said. "The car's right up there."

The guy looked up at the car. Then he nodded to himself and he looked at George.

That's all he did. So help me. He just looked at him.

He didn't make any of those funny passes with his hands, and he didn't say anything. He just looked, and he kept right on smiling. His face didn't change a bit.

But George—his face changed. It just sort of set, like it was frozen stiff. And so did everything. I mean, his hands got numb and the bottle fell and busted. George was like he couldn't move.

I opened my mouth but the guy kind of glanced over at me and I thought maybe I'd better not say anything. All of a sudden I felt cold all over, and I didn't know what would happen if he looked at me.

So I stood there, and then this guy went up to George and undressed him. Only it wasn't exactly undressing him, because George was just like one of those window dummies you see in the stores. Then the guy put all of George's clothes on himself, and he put the blanket around George. I could see he had this plastic bag in one hand and George's car keys in the other.

I was going to scream, only the guy looked at me again and I couldn't. I didn't feel stiff like George, or paralyzed, or anything like that. But I couldn't scream to save my neck. And what good would it of done anyhow?

Because this guy just walked right up the side of the bluff and climbed in George's car and drove away. He never said a word, he never looked back. He just went.

Then I could scream, but good. I was still screaming when George came out of it, and I thought he'd have a hemorrhage or something.

Well, we had to walk back all the way. It was over three miles to the highway patrol, and they made me tell the whole thing over and over again a dozen times. They got George's license number and they're still looking for the car. And this sergeant, he thinks George is maybe right about the Communists.

Only he didn't see the way the guy looked at George. Every time I think about it, I could just die!

Statement of Milo Fabian

I scarcely got the drapes pulled when he walked in. Of course, at first I thought he was delivering something. He wore a pair of those atrocious olive-drab slacks and a ready-made sports jacket, and he had on one of those caps that look a little like those worn by jockeys.

"Well, what is it?" I said. I'm afraid I was just a wee bit rude about it — truth to tell, I'd been in a perfectly filthy mood ever since Jerry told me he was running up to Cape Cod for the exhibit. You'd think he might at least have considered my feelings and invited me to go along. But no, I had to stay behind and keep the gallery open.

But I actually had no excuse for being spiteful to this stranger. I mean, he was rather an attractive sort of person when he took that idiotic cap off. He had black, curly hair and he was quite tall, really immense; I was almost afraid of him until he smiled.

"Mr. Warlock?" he asked.

I shook my head.

"This is the Warlock Gallery, isn't it?"

"Yes. But Mr. Warlock is out of the city. I'm Mr. Fabian. Can I help you?"

"It's rather a delicate matter."

"If you have something to sell, you can show me. I do all the buying for the gallery."

"I've nothing to sell. I want to purchase some paintings."

"Well, in that case, won't you come right back with me, Mr. —"

"Smith," he said.

We started down the aisle together. "Could you tell me just what you had in mind?" I asked. "As you probably know, we tend to specialize in moderns. We have a very good Kandinsky now, and an early Mondrian — "

"You don't have the pictures I want here," he said. "I'm sure of it."

We were already in the gallery. I stopped. "Then what was it you wished?"

He stood there, swinging this perfectly enormous plastic pouch. "You mean what kind of painting? Well, I want one or two good Rembrandts, a Vermeer, a Raphael, something by Titian, a Van Gogh, a Tintoretto. Also a Goya, an El Greco, a Breughel, a Hals, a Holbein, a Gauguin. I don't suppose there's a way of getting 'The Last Supper'—that was done as a fresco, wasn't it?"

It was positively weird to hear the man. I'm afraid I was definitely piqued, and I showed it. "Please!" I said. "I happen to be busy this morning. I have no time to—"

"You don't understand," he answered. "You buy pictures, don't you? Well, I want you to buy me some. As my—my agent, that's the word, isn't it?"

"That's the word," I told him. "But surely you can't be serious. Have you any idea of the cost involved in acquiring such a collection? It would be simply fabulous."

"I've got money," he said. We were standing next to the deal table at the entrance, and he walked over to it and put his pouch down. Then he zipped it open.

I have never, but simply never, seen such a fantastic sight in my life. The pouch was full of bills, stack after stack of bills, and every single one was either a five- or ten-thousand dollar bill. Why, I'd never even seen one before!

If he'd been carrying twenties or hundreds, I might have suspected counterfeits, but nobody would have the audacity to dream of getting away with a stunt like this. They looked genuine, and they were. I know, because—but, that's for later.

So there I stood, looking at this utterly mad heap of money lying there, and this Mr. Smith, as he called himself, said, "Well, do you think I have enough?"

I could have just passed out, thinking about it.

Imagine, a perfect stranger, walking in off the street with ten million dollars to buy paintings. And my share of the commission is five percent!

"I don't know," I said. "You're really serious about all this?"

"Here's the money. How soon can you get me what I want?"

"Please," I said. "This is all so unusual, I hardly know where to begin. Do you have a definite list of what you wish to acquire?"

"I can write the names down for you," he told me. "I remember most of them."

He knew what he wanted, I must say. Velásquez, Gorgione, Cézanne, Degas, Utrillo, Monet, Toulouse-Lautrec, Delacroix, Ryder, Pissarro—

Then he began writing titles. I'm afraid I gasped. "Really," I said. "You can't actually expect to buy the 'Mona Lisa'!"

"Why not?" He looked perfectly serious.

"It's not for sale at any price, you know."

"I didn't know. Who owns it?"

"The Louvre. In Paris."

"I didn't know." He was serious, I'd swear he was. "But what about the rest?"

"I'm afraid many of these paintings are in the same category. They're not for sale. Most of them are in public galleries and museums here and abroad. And a number of the particular works you request are in the hands of private collectors who could never be persuaded to sell."

He stood up and began scooping the money back into his pouch. I took his arm.

"But, we can certainly do our best," I said. "We have our sources, our connections. I'm sure we can at least procure some of the lesser, representative pieces by every one of the masters you list. It's merely a matter of time."

He shook his head. "Won't do. This is Tuesday, isn't it? I've got to have everything by Sunday night."

Did you ever hear of anything so ridiculous in all your life? The man was stark staring.

"Look," he said. "I'm beginning to understand how things are, now. These paintings I want, they're scattered all over the world. Owned by public museums and private parties who won't sell. And I suppose the same thing is true of manuscripts. Things like the Gutenberg Bible, Shakespeare first folios, the Declaration of Independence — "

Stark staring. I didn't trust myself to do anything but nod at him.

"How many of the things I want are here?" he asked. "Here, in this country?"

"A fair percentage, well over half."

"All right. Here's what you do. Sit down over there and make me up a list. I want you to write me down the names of the paintings I've noted, and just where they are. I'll give you $10,000 for the list."

Ten thousand dollars for a list he could have acquired free of charge at the public library! Ten thousand dollars for less than an hour's work!

I gave him his list. And he gave me the money and walked out.

By this time, I was just about frantic. I mean, it was all so shattering. He came and he went, and there I stood — not knowing his real name, or anything. Talk about your eccentric millionaires! He went, and there I stood with $10,000 in my hand.

Well, I'm not one to do anything rash. He hadn't been gone three minutes before I locked up and stepped over to the bank. I simply hopped all the way back to the gallery.

Then I said to myself, "What for?"

I didn't have to go back now, really. This was my money, not Jerry's. I'd earned it all by my little self. And as for him, he could stay up at the Cape and rot. I didn't need his precious job.

I went right down and bought a ticket to Paris. All this war scare talk is simply a lot of fluff, if you ask me. Sheer fluff.

Of course, Jerry is going to be utterly furious when he hears about it. Well, let him. All I have to say is, he can get himself another boy.

Statement of Nick Krauss

I was dead on my feet. I'd been on the job ever since Tuesday night and here it was Saturday. Talk about living on your nerves!

But I wasn't missing out on this deal, not me. Because this was the payoff. The payoff to the biggest caper that was ever rigged.

Sure, I heard of the Brink's job. I even got a pretty good idea who was in on it. But that was peanuts, and it took better'n a year to set up.

This deal topped 'em all. Figure it for yourself, once. Six million bucks, cash. In four days. Get that, now. I said six million bucks in four days. That's all, brother!

And who did it? Me, that's who.

Let me tell you one thing: I earned that dough. Every lousy cent of it. And don't think I didn't have to shell out plenty in splits. Right now I can't even remember just how many was in on it from the beginning to end. But what with splits and expenses—like hiring all them planes to fly the stuff down—I guess it cost pretty near a million and a half, just to swing it.

That left four and a half million. Four and a half million—and me going down to the yacht to collect.

I had the whole damn haul right in the truck. A hundred and forty pieces, some of 'em plenty heavy, too. But I wasn't letting nobody else horse around with unloading. This was dynamite. Only two miles from the warehouse where I got everything assembled. Longest two miles I ever drove.

Sure, I had a warehouse. What the hell, I bought the thing! Bought the yacht for him, too. Paid cash. When you got six million in cash to play with, you don't take no chances on something you can just as well buy without no trouble.

Plenty of chances the way it was. Had to take chances, working that fast Beat me how I managed to get through the deal without a dozen leaks.

But the dough helped. You take a guy, he'll rat on you for two–three grand. Give him twenty or thirty, and he's yours. I'm not just talking syndicate, either. Because there was plenty guys in on it that weren't even in no mob—guys that never been mugged except maybe for these here college annual books where they show pictures of all the professors. I paid off guards and I paid off coppers and I paid off a bunch of curators, too. Not characters, curators. Guys that run museums.

I still don't know what this joker wanted with all that stuff. Only thing I can figure is maybe he was one of these here Indian rajahs or something. But he didn't look like no Hindu—he was a big, tall, youngish guy. Didn't talk like one, either. But who else wants to lay out all that lettuce for a bunch of dizzy paintings and stuff?

Anyways, he showed up Tuesday night with this pouch of his. How he got to me, how he ever got by Lefty downstairs I never figured out.

But there he was. He asked me if it was true, what he heard about me, and he asked me if I wanted to do a job. Said his name was Smith. You know the kind of con you get when they want to stay dummied up on you.

I didn't care if he dummied up or not. Because, like the fella says, money talks. And it sure hollered Tuesday night. He opens this pouch of his and spills two million bucks on the table.

So help me, two million bucks! Cash!

"I've brought this along for expenses," he said. "There's four million more in it if you can cooperate."

Let's skip the rest of it. We made a deal, and I went to work. Wednesday I had him on that yacht, and he stayed there all the way through. Every night I went down and reported.

I went to Washington myself and handled the New York and Philadelphia end, too. Also Boston, on Friday. The rest was by phone, mostly. I kept flying guys out with orders and cash to Detroit, Chicago, St. Louis and the Coast. They had the lists and they knew what to look for. Every mob I contacted set up its own plans for the job. I paid whatever they asked, and that way nobody had any squawks coming. No good any of 'em holding out on me—where could they sell the stuff? Those things are too hot.

By the time Thursday come around, I was up to my damn neck in diagrams and room plans and getaway routes. There was six guys just checking on alarm systems and stuff in the joints I was supposed to cover. We had maybe fifty working in New York, not counting from the inside. You wouldn't believe it if I told you some of the guys who helped. Big professors and all, tipping us off on how to make a heist, or cutting wires and leaving doors unlocked. I hear a dozen up and lammed after it was over. That's what real dough can buy you.

Of course, I run into trouble. Lots of it. We never did get a haul out of L.A. The fix wasn't in the way it was supposed to be, and they lost the whole load trying for a getaway at the airport. Lucky thing the cops shot up all four of the guys, the ones who made the haul. So they couldn't trace anything.

All told, must of been seven or eight cashed in; the four in L.A., two in Philly, one guy in Detroit and one in Chicago. But no leaks. I kept the wires open, and I had my people out there, sort of supervising. Every bit of the stuff we did get came in by private plane, over in Jersey. Went right to the warehouse.

And I had the whole works, 143 pieces, on the truck when I went down for the payoff.

It took me three hours to cart that stuff onto the yacht. This guy, this Mr. Smith, he just sat and watched the whole time.

When I was done I said, "That's the works. You satisfied now or do you want a receipt?"

He didn't smile or anything. Just shook his head. "You'll have to open them," he said.

"Open 'em up? That'll take another couple hours," I told him.

"We've got time," he said.

"Hell we have! Mister, this stuff's hot and I'm hotter. There's maybe a hundred thousand honest johns looking for the loot—ain't you read the papers or heard the radio? Whole damn country's in an uproar. Worse than the war crisis or whatever you call it. I want out of here, fast."

But he wanted them crates and boxes open, so I opened 'em. What the hell, for four million bucks, a little flunkey work don't hurt. Not even when you're dead for sleep. It was a tough job, though, because everything was packed nice. So as not to have any damage, that is.

Nothing was in frames. He had these canvases and stuff all over the floor, and he checked them off in a notebook, every one. And when I got the last damn picture out and hauled all the wood and junk up on deck and put it over the side in the dark, I come back to find him in the forward cabin.

"What's the pitch?" I asked. "Where you going?"

"To transfer these to my ship," he told me. "After all, you didn't expect I'd merely sail off in this vessel, did you? And I'll need your assistance to get them on board. Don't worry, it's only a short distance away."

He started the engines. I came right up behind him and stuck my Special in his ribs.

"Where's the bundle?" I asked.

"In the other cabin, on the table." He didn't even look around.

"You're not pulling anything, are you?"

"See for yourself."

I went to see. And he was leveling.

Four million bucks on the table. Five- and ten-thousand dollar bills, and no phony geetus either. Wouldn't be too damn easy passing this stuff—the Feds would have the word out about big bills—but then, I didn't count on sticking around with the loot. There's plenty countries where they like them big bills and don't ask any questions. South America, such places. That part didn't worry me too much, as long as I knew I'd get there.

And I figured on getting there all right. I went back to the other cabin and showed him my Special again. "Keep going," I said. "I'll help you, but the first time you get cute I'm set to remove your appendix with a slug."

He knew who I was. He knew I could just let him have it and skid out of there any time I wanted. But he never even blinked at me—just kept right on steering.

He must of gone about four–five miles. It was pitch-dark and he didn't carry any spot, but he knew where he was going. Because all at once we stopped and he said, "Here we are."

I went up on deck with him and I couldn't seen nothing. Just the lights off on shore and the water all around. I sure as hell didn't see no boat any-wheres.

"Where is it?" I asked him.

"Where is what?"

"Your boat?"

"Down there." He pointed over the side.

"What the hell you got, a submarine or something?"

"Something." He leaned over the side. His hands was empty, he didn't do anything but lean. And so help me, all of a sudden up comes this damn thing. Like a big round silver ball, sort of, with a lid on top.

I didn't even notice the lid until it opened up. And it floated alongside, so's he could run the gangplank out to the rest on the lid.

"Come on," he said. "I'll help you. It won't take long this way."

"You think I'm gonna carry stuff across that lousy plank?" I asked him. "In the dark?"

"Don't worry, you can't fall. It's magnomeshed."

"What the hell does that mean?"

"I'll show you."

He walked across that plank and climbed right down into the thing before I thought to try and stop him. The plank never moved an inch.

Then he was back out. "Come on, there's nothing to be afraid of."

"Who's afraid?"

But I was scared, plenty. Because now I knew what he was. I'd been reading the papers a lot these days, and I didn't miss none of the war talk. Them Commies with all their new weapons and stuff—well, this was one of them. It is no wonder he was tossing around millions of bucks like that.

So I figured on doing my patriotic duty. Sure, I'd haul these lousy pictures on board for him. I wanted to get a look inside that sub of his. But when I finished, I made up my mind he wasn't gonna streak out for Russia or some-place. I'd get him first.

That's the way I played it. I helped him cart the whole mess down into the sub.

Then I changed my mind again. He wasn't no Russian. He wasn't any-thing I ever heard of except an inventor, maybe. Because that thing he had was crazy.

It was all hollow inside. All hollow, with just a thin wall around. I could tell there wasn't space for an engine or anything. Just enough room to stack the stuff and leave space for maybe two or three guys to stand.

There wasn't any electric light in the place either, but it was light. And daylight. I know what I'm talking about—I know about neon and fluorescent lights too. This was something else. Something new.

Instruments? Well, he had some kind of little slots on one part, but they was down on the floor. You had to lay down next to them to see how they'd work. And he kept watching me, so I didn't want to take a chance on acting too nosy. I figured it wasn't healthy.

I was scared because he wasn't scared.

I was scared because he wasn't no Russian.

I was scared because there ain't any round balls that float in water, or come up from under water when you just look at 'em. And because he come from nowhere with his cash and he was going nowhere with the pictures. Nothing made any sense any more, except one thing. I wanted out! I wanted out bad.

Maybe you think I'm nuts, but that's because you never was inside a shiny ball floating in water, only not bobbing around or even moving when the waves hit it, and all daylight with nothing to light it with. You never saw this Mr. Smith who wasn't named Smith and maybe not even Mr.

But if you had, you would of understood why I was so glad to get back on that yacht and go down in the cabin and pick up the dough.

"All right," I said. "Let's go back."

"Leave whenever you like," he said. "I'm going now."

"Going yourself? Then how the hell do I get back?" I yelled.

"Take the yacht," he told me. "It's yours." Just like that he said it.

"But I can't run no yacht, I don't know how."

"It's very simple. Here, I'll explain—I picked it up myself in less than a minute. Come up to the cabin."

"Uh uh." I got the Special out. "You're taking me back to the dock right now."

"Sorry, there isn't time. I want to be on my way before—"

"You heard me," I said. "Get this boat moving."

"Please. You're making this difficult. I must leave now."

"First you take me back. Then you go off to Mars or wherever it is."

"Mars? Who said anything about—"

He sort of smiled and shook his head. And then he looked at me.

He looked—right—at—me. He looked—into—me. His eyes were like two of those big round silver balls, rolling down into slots behind my eyeballs and crashing right into my skull. They came toward me real slow and real heavy, and I couldn't duck. I felt them coming, and I knew if they ever hit I'd be a goner.

I was out on my feet. Everything was numb. He just smiled and stared and sent his eyes out to get me. They rolled and I could feel them hit. Then I was — gone.

The last thing I remember was pulling the trigger.

Statement of Elizabeth Rafferty, M.D.

At 9:30 Sunday morning, he rang the bell. I remember the time exactly, because I'd just finished breakfast and I was switching on the radio to get the war news. Apparently they'd found another Soviet boat, this one in Charleston harbor, with an atomic device aboard. The Coast Guard and the Air Force were both on emergency, and it —

The bell rang, and I opened the door.

There he stood. He must have been six-foot-four at the very least. I had to look up at him to see his smile, but it was worth it.

"Is the doctor in?" he asked.

"I'm Dr. Rafferty."

"Good. I was hoping I'd be lucky enough to find you here. I just came along the street, taking a chance on locating a physician. You see, it's rather an emergency — "

"I gathered that." I stepped back. "Won't you come inside? I dislike having my patients bleed all over the front stoop."

He glanced down at his left arm. He was bleeding, all right. And from the hole in his coat, and the powdermarks, I knew why.

"In here," I said. We went into the office. "Now, if you'll let me help you with your coat and shirt, Mr. — "

"Smith," he said.

"Of course. Up on the table. That's it. Now, easy — let me do it — there. Well! A nice neat perforation, upper triceps. In again, out again. It looks as if you were lucky, Mr. Smith. Hold still now. I'm going to probe. . . . This may hurt a bit. . . . Good! . . . We'll just sterilize, now — "

All the while I kept watching him. He had a gambler's face, but not the mannerisms. I couldn't make up my mind about him. He went through the whole procedure without a sound or a change of expression.

Finally, I got him bandaged up. "Your arm will probably be stiff for several days. I wouldn't advise you to move around too much. How did it happen?"

"Accident."

"Come now, Mr. Smith." I got out the pen and looked for a form. "Let's not be children. You know as well as I do that a physician must make a full report on any gunshot wound."

"I didn't know." He swung off the table. "Who gets the report?"

"The police."

"No!"

"Please, Mr. Smith! I'm required by law to—"

"Take this."

He fished something out of his pocket with his right hand and threw it on the desk. I stared at it. I'd never seen a five-thousand dollar bill before, and it was worth staring at.

"I'm going now," he said. "As a matter of fact, I've never really been here."

I shrugged. "As you will," I told him. "Just one thing more, though."

I stooped, reached into the left-hand upper drawer of the desk, and showed him what I kept there.

"This is a .22, Mr. Smith," I said. "It's a lady's gun. I've never used it before, except on the target range. I would hate to use it now, but I warn you that if I do you're going to have trouble with your right arm. As a physician, my knowledge of anatomy combines with my ability as a marksman. Do you understand?"

"Yes, *I* do. But *you* don't. Look, you've got to let me go. It's important. I'm not a criminal!"

"Nobody said you were. But you will be, if you attempt to evade the law by neglecting to answer my questions for this report. It must be in the hands of the authorities within the next twenty-four hours."

He chuckled. "They'll never read it."

I sighed. "Let's not argue. And don't reach into your pocket, either."

He smiled at me. "I have no weapon. I was just going to increase your fee."

Another bill fluttered to the table. Ten thousand dollars. Five thousand plus ten thousand makes fifteen. It added up.

"Sorry," I said. "This all looks very tempting to a struggling young doctor—but I happen to have old-fashioned ideas about such things. Besides, I doubt if I could get the change from anyone, because of all this excitement in the newspapers over—"

I stopped, suddenly, as I remembered. Five-thousand and ten-thousand dollar bills. They added up, all right. I smiled at him across the desk.

"Where are the paintings, Mr. Smith?" I asked.

It was his turn to sigh. "Please, don't question me. I don't want to hurt anyone. I just want to go, before it's too late. You were kind to me. I'm grateful. Take the money and forget it. This report is foolishness, believe me."

"Believe you? With the whole country in an uproar, looking for stolen art masterpieces, and Communists hiding under every bed? Maybe it's just feminine curiosity, but I'd like to know." I took careful aim. "This isn't conversation, Mr. Smith. Either you talk or I shoot."

"All right. But it won't do any good." He leaned forward. "You've got to believe that. It won't do any good. I could show you the paintings, yes. I could give them to you. And it wouldn't help a bit. Within twenty-four hours they'd be as useless as that report you wanted to fill out."

"Oh, yes, the report. We might as well get started with it," I said. "In spite of your rather pessimistic outlook. The way you talk, you'd think the bombs were going to fall here tomorrow."

"They will," he told me. "Here, and everywhere."

"Very interesting." I shifted the gun to my left hand and took up the fountain pen. "But now, to business. Your name, please. Your real name."

"Kim Logan."

"Date of birth?"

"November 25th, 2903."

I raised the gun. "The right arm," I said. "Medial head of the triceps. It will hurt, too."

"November 25th, 2903," he repeated. "I came here last Sunday at 10 P.M., your time. By the same chronology I leave tonight at nine. It's a 169-hour cycle."

"What are you talking about?"

"My instrument is out there in the bay. The paintings and manuscripts are there. I intended to remain submerged until the departure moment tonight, but a man shot me."

"You feel feverish?" I asked. "Does your head hurt?"

"No. I told you it was no use explaining things. You won't believe me, any more than you believed me about the bombs."

"Let's stick to facts," I suggested. "You admit you stole the paintings. Why?"

"Because of the bombs, of course. The war is coming, the big one. Before tomorrow morning your planes will be over the Russian border and their planes will retaliate. That's only the beginning. It will go on for months, years. In the end— shambles. But the masterpieces I take will be saved."

"How?"

"I told you. Tonight, at nine, I return to my own place in the time continuum." He raised his hand. "Don't tell me it's not possible. According to your present-day concepts of physics it would be. Even according to our science, only forward movement is demonstrable. When I suggested my project to the Institute they were skeptical. But they built the instrument according to my specifications, nevertheless. They permitted me to use the money from the Historical Foundation at Fort Knox. And I received an ironic blessing prior to my departure. I rather imagine my actual vanishment caused raised eyebrows. But that will be nothing compared to the reaction upon my return. My triumphant return, with a cargo of art masterpieces presumably destroyed nearly a thousand years in the past!"

"Let me get this straight," I said. "According to your story, you came here because you knew war was going to break out and you wanted to salvage some old masters from destruction. Is that it?"

"Precisely. It was a wild gamble, but I had the currency. I've studied the era as closely as any man can from the records available. I knew about the linguistic peculiarities of the age — you've had no trouble understanding me, have you? And I managed to work out a plan. Of course I haven't been entirely successful, but I've managed a great deal in less than a week's time. Perhaps I can return again — earlier — maybe a year or so beforehand, and procure more." His eyes grew bright. "Why not? We could build more instruments, come in a body. We could get everything we wanted, then."

I shook my head. "For the sake of argument, let's say for a minute that I believe you, which I don't. You've stolen some paintings, you say. You're taking them back to 29-something-or-other with you, tonight. You hope. Is that the story?"

"That's the truth."

"Very well. Now you suggest that you might repeat the experiment on a larger scale. Come back to a point a year before this in time and collect more masterpieces. Again, let's say you do it. What will happen to the paintings you took with you?"

"I don't follow you."

"Those paintings will be in your era, according to you. But a year ago they hung in various galleries. Will they be there when you come back? Surely they can't coexist."

He smiled. "A pretty paradox. I'm beginning to like you, Dr. Rafferty."

"Well, don't let the feeling grow on you. It's not reciprocal, I assure you. Even if you were telling the truth, I can't admire your motives."

"What's wrong with my motives?" He stood up, ignoring the gun. "Isn't it a worthwhile goal — to save immortal treasures from the senseless destruction of a tribal war? The world deserves the preservation of its artistic heritage. I've risked my existence for the sake of bringing beauty to my own time — where it can be properly appreciated and enjoyed by minds no longer obsessed with the greed and cruelty I find here."

"Big words," I said. "But the fact remains. You stole those paintings."

"Stole? I saved them! I tell you, before the year is out they'd be utterly destroyed. Your galleries, your museums, your libraries — everything will go. Is it stealing to carry precious articles from a burning temple?" He leaned over me. "Is that a crime?"

"Why not stop the fire, instead?" I countered. "You know — from historical records, I suppose — that war breaks out tonight or tomorrow. Why not take advantage of your foresight and try to prevent it?"

"I can't. The records are sketchy, incomplete. Events are jumbled. I've been unable to discover just how the war began — or will begin, rather. Some trivial incident, unnamed. Nothing is clear on that point."

"But couldn't you warn the authorities?"

"And change history? Change the actual sequence of events, rather? Impossible!"

"Aren't you changing them by taking the paintings?"

"That's different."

"Is it?" I stared into his eyes. "I don't see how. But then, the whole thing is impossible. I've wasted too much time in arguing."

"Time!" He looked at the wall clock. "Almost noon. I've got just nine hours left. And so much to do. The instrument must be adjusted."

"Where is this precious mechanism of yours?"

"Out in the bay. Submerged, of course, I had that in mind when it was constructed. You can conceive of the hazards of attempting to move through time and alight on a solid surface; the face of the land alters. But the ocean is comparatively unchanging. I knew if I departed from a spot several miles offshore and arrived there, I'd eliminate most of the ordinary hazards. Besides, it offers a most excellent place of concealment. The principle, you see, is simple. By purely mechanical means, I shall raise the instrument above the stratospheric level tonight and then intercalculate dimensionally when I am free of Earth's orbit. The gantic-drive will be — "

No doubt about it. I didn't have to wait for the double-talk to know he was crazier than a codfish. A pity, too; he was really a handsome specimen.

"Sorry," I said. "Time's up. This is something I hate to do, but there's no other choice. No, don't move. I'm calling the police, and if you take one step I'll plug you."

"Stop! You mustn't call! I'll do anything. I'll even take you with me. That's it, I'll take you with me! Wouldn't you like to save your life? Wouldn't you like to escape?"

"No. Nobody escapes," I told him. "Especially not you. Now stand still, and no more funny business. I'm making that call."

He stopped. He stood still. I picked up the phone, with a sweet smile. He smiled back. He looked at me.

Something happened.

There has been a great dispute about the clinical aspects of hypnotic therapy. I remember, in school, an attempt being made to hypnotize me. I was entirely immune. I concluded that a certain degree of cooperation or conditioned suggestibility is required of an individual in order to render him susceptible to hypnosis.

I was wrong.

I was wrong, because I couldn't move now. No lights, no mirrors, no voices, no suggestion. It was just that I couldn't move. I sat there holding the gun. I sat there and watched him walk out, locking the door behind him. I could see and I could feel. I could even hear him say "Goodbye."

But I couldn't move. I could function, but only as a paralytic functions. I could, for example, watch the clock.

I watched the clock from noon until almost seven. Several patients came during the afternoon, couldn't get in, and went away. I watched the clock until its face was lost in darkness. I sat there and endured hysteric rigidity until — providentially — the phone rang.

That broke it. But it broke me. I couldn't answer that phone. I merely slumped over on the desk, my muscles tightening with pain as the gun fell from my numb fingers. I lay there, gasping and sobbing, for a long time. I tried to sit up. It was agony. I tried to walk. My limbs rejected sensation. It took me an hour to gain control again. And even then, it was merely a partial control — a physical control. My thoughts were another matter.

Seven hours of thinking. Seven hours of true or false? Seven hours of accepting and rejecting the impossibly possible.

It was after eight before I was on my feet again, and then I didn't know what to do.

Call the police? Yes — but what could I tell them? I had to be sure, I had to know.

And what did I know? He was out in the bay, and he'd leave at nine o'clock. There was an instrument which would rise above the stratosphere —

I got in the car and drove. The dock was deserted. I took the road over to the Point, where there's a good view. I had the binoculars. The stars were out, but no moon. Even so, I could see pretty clearly.

There was a small yacht bobbing on the water, but no lights shone. Could that be it?

No sense taking chances. I remembered the radio report about the Coast Guard patrols.

So I did it. I drove back to town and stopped at a drugstore and made my call. Just reported the presence of the yacht. Perhaps they'd investigate, because there were no lights. Yes, I'd stay there and wait for them if they wished.

I didn't stay, of course. I went back to the Point. I went back there and trained my binoculars on the yacht. It was almost nine when I saw the cutter come along, moving up behind the yacht with deadly swiftness.

It was exactly nine when they flashed their lights — and caught for an incredible instant, the gleaming reflection of the silver globe that rose from the water, rose straight up toward the sky.

Then came the explosion and I saw the shattering before I heard the echo of the report. They had portable anti-aircraft, something of the sort. It was effective.

One moment, the globe roared upward. The next moment, there was nothing. They blew it to bits.

And they blew me to bits with it. Because if there was a globe, perhaps he was inside. With the masterpieces, ready to return to another time. The story was true, then, and if that was true, then—

I guess I fainted. My watch showed 10:30 when I came to and stood up. It was 11:00 before I made it to the Coast Guard Station and told my story.

Of course, nobody believed me. Even Dr. Halvorsen from Emergency— he said he did, but he insisted on the injection and they took me here to the hospital.

It would have been too late, anyway. That globe did the trick. They must have contacted Washington immediately with their story of a new secret Soviet weapon destroyed offshore. Coming on the heels of finding those bomb-laden ships, it was the final straw. Somebody gave the orders and our planes were on their way.

I've been writing all night. Outside in the corridor they're getting radio reports. We've dropped bombs over there. And the alert has gone out, warning us of possible reprisals.

Maybe they'll believe me now. But it doesn't matter any more. It's going to be the way he said it was.

I keep thinking about the paradoxes of time travel. This notion of carrying objects from the present to the future—and this other notion, about altering the past. I'd like to work out the theory, only there's no need. The old masters aren't going into the future. Any more than he, returning to our present, could stop the war.

What had he said? "I've been unable to discover just how the war began —or will begin, rather. Some trivial incident, unnamed."

Well, this was the trivial incident. His visit. If I hadn't made that phone call, if the globe hadn't risen—but I can't bear to think about it any more. It makes my head hurt. All that buzzing and droning noise. . . .

I've just made an important discovery. The buzzing and droning does not come from inside my head. I can hear the sirens sounding, too. If I had any doubts about the truth of his claims, they're gone now.

I wish I'd believed him. I wish the others would believe me now. But there just isn't any time. . . .

WHERE THE BUFFALO ROAM

MAY HAVE BEEN TWO SEASONS ago, may have been three. This child don't shine at figures much. Doc, now—he's got a passel of books up to his lodge, and even Iron Head keeps a few in his *tipi*. But I never did hold with book talk, not even for a white, let alone Injuns.

This child's happy and sassy as long as he's got his hide in one piece, with plenty of fleece fat to fill it, and a good gun and a few traps to set for the getting of plews. A rifle's all the company you need beyond the Platte. Come winter, of course, I push back to the river with my catch, and then I allow it's slick to hole up in a lodge of my own with a squaw for the fixing and the making of robes. But there's always a might to do and no need for books even then—spite of all Doc's talk.

Books won't skin a painter for you or cure you of the flux. And books weren't handy agin' *them*, either. It was books caused all the misery in the first place, I figger. *They* have books aplenty.

But it was *them* I aimed to tell about, to begin with. Like I say, might have been two, could be three seasons back. It was fixing summer anyways, that I know. That's when *they* come.

I recollect the night it happened. Doc and Iron Head and I had headed back to the river to see if the team had come with the new guns and the ammunition. It was in, all right, and I got me a brand-new rifle—along with a lot of blankets and such, and even some fancy folderol for Taffy. Taffy was my squaw; still would be, but she died birthing. Taffy had yellow hair, same as me. I guess she was more white than Injun, but they're all squaws.

Anyways, we'd had a regular powwow for a couple days after the team pulled in, like always, and Jed and Huck did a heap of bragging about the trip.

They always fetch some tall stories about the places back Across the River. Doc holds the yarns are true, but I figger they stretch a mite.

Then we set out again, four party of us. Two headed upriver for the traps; one hit downriver with the team—to trade extry guns and shot with the next camp. Me and Doc and Iron Head struck out west to buffalo country. The grass was in now, and we figgered they'd be ranging this way. We aimed to strike a big herd and drive it back to the river. Then the hull camp'd come out—boys and squaws and old folk alike—and just blaze away until we snagged a smart passel, enough for meat and skinning and curing to hold us through winter.

That was the scheme of it, and we reckoned on working our way for maybe two, three days.

But we struck it pretty the afternoon of the first day out. Coming up over a rise, just up from the plains, with the sun scorching our eyeballs fit to fry, and we looked down onto the level with the tall grass stretching for a hundred miles off.

But we didn't see any grass. Everything was black. Black and moving.

"Huh!" Iron Head let out a grunt. "Buffler!"

"Buffalo?" said Doc, squinting through those spectacles he wears. "Sure enough. But look at the size of that herd! You ever see so many, Jake?"

I had to allow as I hadn't. In all my born days, and I knowed this country ever since I was big enough to tote a rifle, I never did see a sight to match this one.

There was buffalo as far as sight would stretch, like a big black cloud settled over the land. Cows and calves and yearlings, young bulls with their horns still black and old bulls just lording it over the harems.

"Reckon we better circle behind?" I asked. But Iron Head grinned. "Walk along," he said. "Take us two days to go around."

"What if they get riled up?" Doc said.

"Make noise," Iron Head told him. I allowed as he was right—buffalo always scatter if you fetch them a start. That's how we aimed to stampede them to the river, by shooting guns. But right now we wanted to get on the other side of the herd, so as to drive them in the right direction.

So we walked down, moving close together, and headed straight for the herd. And Doc told us to sing.

That's what we did. We traipsed along, singing fit to bust—the old songs, anything that come into our head. Tunes like "Tea for Two" and "Roll Out the Barrel" and "The Sweetheart of Sigma Chi"—all them songs with the crazy words. Made a powerful ruckus too.

And you know, it worked. It got us into the herd all right, but come a time when this child wondered if we'd ever get out again. Wondered if there *was* an end to it or if we'd just go wandering and singing along until our voice boxes plumb wore out.

Because it was a herd the likes of which a hump-hungry old hoss dreams about. Doc's the head for figures, so I asked him. "How many you reckon? A million head?"

"Easy," Doc said. "We been walking close to three hours now. Seems to be no end to it."

"Strikes me mighty odd," I told him. "I don't allow as I ever saw more'n two–three thousand at a crack before."

"The herds grow every year," Doc came back. "It's like the old days. Remind me tonight and I'll tell you about it. But something must have happened to force them together this way."

"Dry," said Iron Head. "Powerful dry ahead. Dust storm, so they move. Buffler heap migratory ruminant."

He was right. Way off to the west the sun was going down, and from the clouds I reckoned haze. The plains were dry, so the herds came together and moved east to graze. Now, hoofing it through the center, this child could see that it wasn't one big herd at all. Instead, it was thousands of little herds, each one ranging from twenty to two–three hundred head. Old bulls heading their cows and the calves. Young bulls bunched together, hanging on at the fringes and waiting for a chance. And here and there the strays and the cripples.

We didn't dast break off singing to talk much. I tell you it gave me a might crawly feeling to scrunch along through that grass, with hundreds of thousands of sharp-horned critters less than a holler away from us. They was making their own racket, too—calves a-bawling and them bulls roaring and tossing horn at any cow out of line. We spotted a few fights, too, and every once in a while a bull'd rear up for a mount. They smelled powerful strong that day, but the flies wasn't so bad around account of the wind. That was a fancy fix, because at times you can't nigh breathe for the clouds of flies pestering a herd.

We kept moving and singing and staring. "Look at those spike bulls," Doc said. "They get bigger every year." It was true. Some of the young ones were crowding six feet, maybe ten long. And I spotted some whopping big full-grown critters with a spread of maybe three feet; them horns run a good two feet long, and I allow as a couple topped a ton weight. That's two thousand pounds, a ton.

Close up this way I made notice of the robes—regular brown aplenty, but here and there a black, a beaver, a buckskin, and even a blue. Iron Head squinted too; I knew what he was fixing for. He wanted a whitey if he could find one. Them whiteys are the rarest; you can fetch most anything you want with a white, from stale firewater to a fresh squaw.

But he wouldn't snag one even if he saw it, because a shot might set the whole passel off. It was best we keep on a-singing and a-walking, and so we did until it was raising a powerful dark.

Then we got through and oozed out the other side, onto a little dried-over crick bed. We didn't figger the herd'd move in the night, and come morning we could start the drive back. So we bedded down.

But first we made us a fire and broke out supplies.

Iron Head stuck a pipe in his craw and curled up in his bag, closing his eyes and looking like a hoss gone under for sure—it was always his way, come night at a camp.

Me and Doc just set there for a spell.

"I can't shake it," I said. "All them critters, more than this child could count."

"Nature is fecund," Doc said.

"Wouldn't know about that," I told him. "But there's a powerful lot of breeding. Beaver, deer, elk, fish. And the flies and skeeters and chiggers too. Even up there." I pointed at the sky. "Look at that big white herd, forever roaming and twinkling down. Doc, do you reckon stars mate too?"

"I wouldn't know," Doc mumbled. "And I don't want to find out."

"One thing's mighty dark to this child," I said. "And I been meaning to ask. Seeing that we're animals, too, in a way—how is it that we never breed strong?"

"There's fifty-five of us on the Platte," Doc said. "And forty downriver, and another forty beyond. It's that way all over, Jake. Thousands of us, really."

"But that's just a smidgen compared to the others," I said. "You'd figger maybe there'd be millions."

Doc sort of sighed. "There were once."

"You mean like in the book stories? About the cities and all?" I let out a bark. "Don't tell me you put stock in that talk too."

"It's true, Jake. Where do you think the books came from? And don't Jed and the others take the team back to the ruins to get us guns and ammunition from the arsenals? You heard him tell about it with his own lips."

"I just can't swaller," I said. "I always figgered he aimed to stuff us with his talk. Thousands of stone *tipis* in one place, wagons that used to run without a team—it don't hold with nature."

"That's why everything turned out this way," Doc told me. "Men didn't hold with nature. Jake, I've read it in the books. And my father told me what *his* father told him—*he* was alive and saw it when he was a boy. Once there were cities and towns and villages everywhere."

"What happened?" I asked. "What became of the people, and why?"

Iron Head opened his eyes for a spell. "People go under," he grunted. "Heap bad medicine called nuclear fission."

"That's right," Doc said. "They got to fighting, and they had weapons. Atomic bombs, nerve gas. The cities were razed, the survivors scattered. And most of them didn't last long. They couldn't live in the open. They couldn't cope with the wilderness. They died of disease and plague. They froze in the winter, and they starved—"

"I don't rightly make out the meaning of the words," I told him. "But I'll allow you're talking straight about the fighting and maybe rough ways of killing. Only that part about the starving, now—how could they starve, with all this game here for the taking?"

Doc smiled. "You'd find it all in the books if you'd only be willing to learn," he said. "Iron Head knows the story, don't you?"

The Injun opened his eyes again. "No story," he said. "Only biological inevitability to restore the balance of nature."

Sometimes that Injun talk, or book talk, whichever it is, gets me down. But Doc set up a hoot and a holler.

"Probably right at that," he said. "Here's the way it was, Jake. Originally all this land was much the way you see it now. Then men came and settled. They killed the beaver. They fished the streams. They hunted buffalo and game until many animals were almost extinct. That means there were hardly any left.

"When the last wars were fought, there were only a few deer, a few buffalo, a few bear left roaming out here in the wilderness. There wasn't a wild creature east of the Big River at all. And the gas and the bombs and the plague killed off most of the domestic animals in the East—cows and sheep and pigs and horses. We've got a few horses here, but we're lucky, and you know we're trying to breed more because we need them. Some day we might try plowing."

"Plowing for squaw men," Iron Head muttered. "Agricultural perversion."

"Don't worry," Doc said. "It wouldn't be for a long time yet—and then only if we have to." He turned to me again. "But I was telling you about what happened. There was no game, and people died. Only a few of us managed to survive, out here in the open. A few hunters, trappers, Indians."

Doc always talked like that—he never did learn how to say "Injun" rightly but stuck to book talk. Only I knew what he palavered anyhow.

"Gradually they came together, in little groups, for protection. The old crafts came into their own, the old speech ways and folkways that had somehow survived through two centuries of so-called civilization."

"You mean city life?" I asked.

"City death," Iron Head said. And Doc nodded again.

"We managed. We survived. And the remaining animals bred again, unrestricted and unmolested. They multiplied quickly, so that for the past generation it's been like old times once more. Plenty of game, and the timber's come back up north too. There's nothing left of the cities but ruins, and not even ruins where most of the villages and homesteads were. Life is simple again. Crude, perhaps, but—peaceful."

Sometimes I get the savvy of what Doc says, even if I can't understand the foferaw lingo. I knew what he meant now when I lay back and looked up at all the stars, blazing away.

Doc lay back too. It was quiet and easy, 'cept for a coyote howling off on the ridge.

"You never did say about the stars, Doc," I told him. "Reckon they mate? Reckon anybody's ever hit out to take a look?"

Doc frowned. "What made you say that?"

"Nothing. Only I was figgering maybe if they had some of them contraptions you showed me once in the books—what they call them, rackets?"

"Rockets," Doc said. "No, men didn't reach the stars. But there at the last they were ready to try for the moon. Some said that when war began they actually took off and—"

He closed lip, fast. Then he sat up.

I sat up too. Iron Head was already standing with his rifle cocked at the ready.

So it was no mistake. We'd all seen it and heard it at the same time.

It was like a big orange flash in the sky, over to the east. And like a big thunder. Only it wasn't lightning and it wasn't a storm. Something had hit, back there, near the river.

"Meteor!" Doc muttered.

"What's that?" I asked.

"I can't tell you now. Come on."

"Where you aiming to sashay to?"

"I want to see if I can find it." He was folding his pack. Iron Head stamped out the fire.

"All right," I said. "Reckon this child's not bent on rumping it far behind. But that thunder's getting nigher."

"Wait." Doc held up his hand. "He's correct."

"Correct, hell," I said. "I'm right! Just you clean the grubs out of your ears."

We could all hear it then, roaring closer and closer. And now Iron Head was squinting off aways, and he turned back and yelled, "Buffler! The noise —they're stampeding this way!"

No mistake, the herd was pounding prairie. I could see them plain now, black moving on black, in a crazy wave.

Nobody had to tell this hoss what to do, or the others, either. We spread out and got to our knees. Then we started pumping lead.

"Fire together!" Doc hollered. "Else they can't hear you!" So we fired together, or tried to. And the wave come on, faster and faster, and I could see horns tossing in the starlight, and I could hear the bawling and panting and the drumming, and it did something to me inside so that I sort of tightened up all over, because I knowed for a fact now that we were going under. Unless they heard and stopped.

They did, and not a mite too soon, either. The lead bulls reared up, and then they crashed back against the cows, and for a minute they was milling around, raising dust. Then it was like a wave dying off into ripples that stretched way back, far as eye could see. And then they quieted down again, ready to graze.

Doc stood up, rubbing his knees. "That was close," he said. "Think we're safe to walk through?"

Iron Head nodded. "Come," he said. "We sing 'Onward Christian Soldiers.'"

So we walked back through the herd, and we sang "Onward Christian Soldiers" and "Roll Me Over in the Clover" and "No Business Like Show Business" and everything Doc could remember teaching us from the books at the rendezvous sings at springtime.

It was even worse in the dark, with the eyes and the horns sort of glittering and skittering all around us, but we went on. And on. And on.

Until we got back to the top of the ridge, where we'd come over in the afternoon, and looked down and saw it.

"God!" said Doc.

"The devil!" said Iron Head.

"What is it?" I asked.

But neither answered me, just stared. I stared too. This hoss has seen a heap of sights but never nothing like this. Never nothing like this big shiny shape setting there on the prairie, bigger'n all the lodges and *tipis* put together.

We stared, and that's how it happened—how he fixed it so's he snuck up behind us. And we not noticing until the light come.

It like to of blinded me, at first, and I could scarce make out to aim. Then the voice come, and I knowed it was a man.

"Don't shoot," he said. "We're friends."

Iron Head was drawing a bead, too; he's got Injun eyes.

"Put it down," said the man. "We're friends, don't you understand?" He sort of jerked his head away, and it come over me he was talking to other men behind him. "Maybe they don't understand English."

All at once I could see. The light was coming from a little stick he held in his hand. It wasn't a torch, and it wasn't any kind of oil lamp I ever heard tell of. But the light was bright as day, and he stood there with three others behind him, all alike as chips under a buffalo. Wearing floppy duds all of one piece, but with bare heads; the hair cut short the way tads wear it, and not a beard to be seen. That's the truth of it—four overgrown nippers is what they shined up to be.

This child's not one to run from tads, and neither is Iron Head. We dropped our guns.

"That's better," said the one with the light. "Maybe they do understand after all."

"Of course we understand," Doc told him. "It's just that you startled us."

"*We* startled *you*?" The man grinned. "That's a good one. But look, this is no way to meet. After all, it's a historic occasion. The every least it rates is a 'Doctor Livingstone, I presume,' or something similar."

"Then you say it," Doc told him. "My name happens to *be* Doctor Livingstone."

It was book talk, but I got the hang of it, enough to remember every word, even what I couldn't rightly reckon out. Because it was strange I set store by it.

Doc pointed to us. "This is Iron Head," he said. "And that's Jake."

"I'm Captain Buckton," the big tad told us. "And this is Lieutenant Thorne, Ensign Winters, Ensign Taylor." He nodded our way. "These Indians understand English?"

"Dry your gap," I spoke up. "I ain't no Injun. Iron Head here's a true Cree, but I allow as he can palaver better'n you hosses."

"No offense," Captain Buckton said. He took Doc by the arm. "It's wonderful to find you here. We didn't know what to expect—whether there'd be any life at all, for that matter. I presume you realize we've just landed. You can see the rocket down there."

Doc nodded. "We noticed it. But I could scarcely believe my eyes—there are still rumors preserved, of course, yet I never knew if anyone had succeeded in taking off."

"Tell you anything you want to know," Buckton said. "But come on, let's go down to the ship and make ourselves comfortable."

I looked at Doc and he nodded, so we trailed along. We let him and this Captain Buckton do all the jawing.

Now here's the meat, without hide or fat or guts or lights—according to the way Buckton skinned it. What Doc used to tell about was gospel true, about the war and all. Seems there had been men that were set on hitting the sky trail, and they'd built these rockets out in the desert. When things got bad, they decided it was time to get shut of Earth, and the whole kit and kaboodle took off for the moon.

Some made her; some went under. According to this Buckton—and Doc, he didn't make him out a liar—things on the moon ain't natural-like. He allowed as how your weight changes, and it's hard to breathe, and there's no critters up there. But the ships that landed brought means of making air which I don't rightly comprehend, and they dug lodges underground. From the talk I figger they made regular cities like the old ones down here, only all underneath, living like prairie dogs. For a while it was all leather and no fleece for them, until they got the hang of how to live that way. Then they got so's they could mine metals and make things and set up a way of making their air and raised a bellyful by some means—the word for it is "hydroponics," whatever that is. They knew how to get water, too. Doc asked a powerful lot of questions, but it's of no nevermind to me. Main thing is, they done it.

All this time they figgered Earth for a goner. But they were breeding up again and wanted to fan out, and for some seasons there was a heap of talk about coming back.

It weren't easy to ready a rocket for the trip, from all Buckton said, and they only hoped to make do with it once they got her.

Doc asked aplenty about that part, but I got lost in the brush right off—anyhow, they pieced it out and took off for Earth. Buckton and six others, there were, come to scout and see what had happened back here. They were a month on the way, and here they were.

"But where are we?" Buckton asked.

"Just west of the Platte," Doc told him. "Our group is located across the river, to the east of here."

And he told him how many we were, and about the other lodges we knew or reckoned tell of, and how we made out. And about the game, and how we lived, the hunting and fishing and trapping and trading and all.

Buckton kept asking the questions now, and no matter what Doc told him, he said, "Incredible," which means, near as I can figger from the way he said it, "Well, I'll be goddamned."

Then it was *our* turn to say it, because we come to the rocket ship. Called it a ship, but it was no more a proper boat than it was anything else. Didn't even look like the *pictures* of the ships in Doc's books. More like a big bullet with fins on, stood up on end with a metal door to it that opened up so's you could mosey into a lodge. No sense fixing to tell what was inside—reckon nobody'd believe it anyway. But this child saw it, and he's not making brag.

Anyways, we met up with the other three in the rocket and all of us settled down for a palaver. They didn't squat rightly; had some metal contraptions to ease their rumps into. Didn't talk rightly, either, and as for chawing! They passed out what they called coffee and I couldn't go it. Had the taste of hot painter-water, and even Doc set it aside.

But Doc seemed to know about most of this doing, and so did Iron Head, even if he froze over. I kept waiting for the game to flush, and it did.

Buckton said, "This is wonderful! From what you tell us, we'll have no trouble at all. We've got light cruising gear, and of course we intend to survey as much of the area as we can. But if things are as you say, that's almost unnecessary. We can return, make a report, and implement other ships for a full-scale landing."

"Don't know as I follow you," Doc said.

"Isn't it obvious? We're coming back! Look—according to the latest survey, we number in excess of forty thousand. We've got technicians and can train more. Excellent data on microfilm covering the field. All we need to do is go into the ruins and rebuild. We can set up the factories again, get transportation in order—communications too. We'll use your group, every group we can find. We need plenty of manpower. Of course, we're prepared to set up a fiscal system and restore governmental control. I presume there are other men like yourself scattered around the country, men who have sufficient intelligence and elementary education to assist us. You'll be a great help."

"Will we?" Doc asked.

"Why not? Surely you can see the advantages. It's going to be like pioneering days all over again for a while, but modern technology is on our side. In a generation or so we should be able to restore the world to where it was before the war."

"Suppose our people don't want it that way?" Doc spoke out. "Suppose they like things this fashion?"

"Don't worry, we'll educate them to the advantages," Buckton said. "And there's more than one way of dealing with savages. We've no atomic weapons, of course, but we're well-armed. And the next ships can bring the necessary bacterial cultures—just in case of emergency, you understand."

"I understand," Doc said. And he fetched a sigh.

"Well, don't look so down in the mouth about it," Buckton told him. "This is a great day. It's the beginning of a fresh start for Earth. You should be proud, as I am proud, of an opportunity to participate."

The book talk made my skull bones ache, and Doc wasn't looking sassy either. "Only a generation or so until we're back to where we were before the war," he muttered. "But what assurance have you we can just stop there? This country's rich again—rich in natural resources. Timber, game, minerals. There'll be trouble."

Lieutenant Thorne laughed. "Not under proper control," he said. "We won't repeat our mistakes. We've learned the errors of democracy. Men have become civilized at last."

"Strange." Buckton shook his head. "We've gone so far in three generations on the moon. And you have relapsed into such barbarism. Living like mountain men and Indians." He cocked an eye at Iron Head. "I mean—"

"You mean no races," Iron Head said. "No creeds, No money. No taxes. No war. No economic problems. No greed, no intolerance, no worship of dollars or machines. Just freedom and plenty for all. That's barbarism. Also happiness."

"He talks!" Lieutenant Thorne said.

"Sure, I talk. I talk book English and I talk heap plenty pidgin too. I live in one world, but I've read about the other. Enough to be sure that I prefer the world I live in."

Buckton nodded at me. "And you?" he asked. "What do you think? Remember, you're a white man—not a savage."

I scratched my thatch. "Ain't much difference atween the two, I figger. Anyways, Iron Head's right. We got all we can ever use. No ruckus, nothing this child's agin'."

Buckton shrugged. "I can't understand it," he said. He looked at Doc. "How could you permit such a state to exist? You say there are others like you in settlements scattered all over. Men with books, men with background and comprehension. Surely you could have done something to keep things going. Education, reclamation. What became of the railroads, the telegraph, telephone, radio? Why haven't you gone down into the cities, rebuilt? Why this—this—"

He got so red, looked as if he'd swallowed a hornet. Doc sort of grinned.

"I talk to other men from other settlements," he said. "Iron Head and Jake don't know this, but we get together for meetings regularly, once a season or so. And we've considered a lot of possibilities. The railroad tracks are still here, but they're overgrown. Telegraph and telephone poles went down a generation ago. The cities are ruins. We send in to the arsenals from time to time for ammunition, and that's about all."

"Now I understand," Buckton said. "You lack the equipment, the engineering facilities. Well, we'll provide that. You'll be surprised how quickly we can get things running again."

"But the education," Lieutenant Thorne busted in. "Why didn't you combat this savagery?"

"Because it survived," Doc told him. "When the educated men took the world into war, they died. The strays, the outcasts, the remnants of atavistic social orders proved their fitness then. They lived in harmony with nature. We've encouraged that since then. If a man like Iron Head wants to read, we let him read. If a man like Jake prefers illiteracy, that's his business. The important thing is that Iron Head and Jake and I, and all those like us or unlike us, have managed to exist in peace together. To me that's true progress."

Buckton stood up. "Then I take it you're not in sympathy with our plans? You have no intention of collaborating in reclaiming the world?"

"Nobody reclaims the world," Doc said. "Because nobody had a right to claim it in the first place. Not governments or priests or moneylenders or scientists or engineers. It belongs to everyone. That's the way I think, and Iron Head and Jake and all of us. And so do the others in our settlement and all the settlements. You'll find that out."

"We intend to." Buckton nodded at Lieutenant Thorne and the others. "Tomorrow we'll cross the river and talk to your people. Then we'll head on and visit elsewhere. We'll survey the cities, go east. Maybe we'll find sentiment as you say it is. But it doesn't matter. Because we'll come back. We'll come back with the right men and the right weapons.

"You can't turn back the clock, you know. Once before this was a wild frontier until progress came. You know what happened then."

"Yes." Iron Head stood up too. "Buffler died. My people died. Everything died but white men. So they ended up killing each other. Progress stinks!"

Buckton got riled then. "All right. I guess we know where we stand then. And under the circumstances you'll realize it will be necessary for me to detain you here until we've investigated your settlement. . . ."

Doc shrugged. "I expected as much."

"What does he mean, Doc?" I asked.

"He means we're prisoners," Doc told me.

Then I got the drift of it. Buckton gave a signal and the men eased around behind us, two to each. They all had these pesky little guns out.

Doc looked at me and I looked at Iron Head, and he said, "Let's raise hair."

So I tromped out and caught the nearest tad on the shinbone, and then I twisted the gun up and like to blast his head off. Other one let fire but only singed me, and I took and threw him up agin' Lieutenant Thorne. Doc was clubbing with his rifle when Buckton come nigh, but he didn't have to stop — Iron Head broke him in half over one of them metal rump holders. That left two, and we just took aim and let the rifles chaw guts.

It was powerful smoky in there when we finished, and Iron Head didn't really get riled when Doc stopped him from lifting scalps.

So we left them with hair after all and just hightailed it out of there.

The ship, or rocket, or whatever it was, looked mighty peaceful in the moonlight. I squinted up.

"Reckon they really come from there?" I asked Doc.

"That's right, Jake."

"Allow as they'll ever send another ship down?"

"Doubt it, if this one doesn't come back."

"Wonder what them hosses from across river will say when they set eyes on this contraption. Figger any of them will get ornery on account of thinking we did wrong?"

Iron Head grunted. "Maybe they no see it."

Doc and I looked at each other. That was Injun talk, for fair, and straight talk too.

We knew what to do.

We headed west again and come to the buffalo herd. It was a long hike back, singing all the way. Songs like "When Irish Eyes Are Smiling" and "Alexander's Ragtime Band" and the only one that ever makes sense to me, the one with the words a man can understand — "Home on the Range." I guess we sang that one pretty near all the way.

Then we got through the herd, rumbling and restless-like in the dark, and come out the other side.

We fanned.

Then we let fly. We loaded and reloaded, and we kept it up until they were on the run. All of them, a million of them, heading east away from the guns and the noise.

We run after.

But you couldn't keep up, not with a million buffalo, a million of them roaring and charging and pouring over the ridge and down into the valley. Into the valley where the rocket pointed at the sky.

All we could do was get to the top of the ridge in time to see it happen. They didn't stop for the rocket, of course. They kept on going. The moon was bright now, and this child could see everything plain. This child saw them hit the rocket.

Their hoofs made powerful thunder, and then there was a crash when a thousand hit the side of the rocket and a hundred thousand came on behind, driving them through.

One minute the rocket stood there, like a big bullet—and the next minute the bullet exploded. This child's never seen sight or heard sound to match. It was something to shake the sky.

Doc and Iron Head and me, we dropped in our tracks and closed our eyes agin' the light. It rained buffalo meat and hunks of metal.

"They brought explosives," Doc said.

"Sure," Iron Head grunted. "The white man's burden."

I stood up again, watching the critters wheel and fan out for the river.

"Come on," I hollered. "They'll make for the river from the lodges to get meat now. We better hump along and help."

So we did, and that was the end of it

Doc and Iron Head and this child let on that it was one of them meteors that fell and exploded, and there weren't a contrariwise notion, ever. Because the rocket was gone. Nothing but a big burned-out hole in the prairie.

Like I say, that was two–three seasons back. I been across just lately, and I see the grass is coming in again. It'll be right pretty in another season or so.

Meantimes the buffalo are grazing over the plain, like they used to in the old days.

It's a mighty peaceful sight.

I LIKE BLONDES

OF COURSE, it's all a matter of taste, nothing more. It's a weakness with me, I suppose. My friends have their own opinions: some are partial to brunettes or redheads, and I suppose that's all right. I certainly don't criticize them in the least.

But blondes are my favorites. Tall ones, short ones, fat ones, thin ones, brilliant ones, dumb ones—all sorts, sizes, shapes, and nationalities. Oh, I've heard all the objections: their skin ages faster, they have peculiar personalities; they're giddy and mercenary and conceited. None of which bothers me a bit, even if it's true. I like blondes for their special qualities and I'm not alone in my weakness. I notice Marilyn Monroe hasn't done too badly in general favor. Nor Kim Novak.

Enough of this; after all, I'm not apologizing. What I do is my own business. And if I wanted to stand on the corner of Reed and Temple at eight o'clock at night and pick up a blonde, I owed no apologies to anyone.

Perhaps I was a bit obvious and overdressed for the occasion. Perhaps I shouldn't have winked, either. But that's a matter of opinion, too, isn't it?

I have mine. Other people have theirs. And if the tall girl with the page-boy cut chose to give me a dirty look and murmur, "Disgusting old man," that was her affair. I'm used to such reactions, and it didn't bother me a bit.

A couple of cute young things in blue jeans came sauntering along. Both of them had hair like Minnesota wheat, and I judged they were sisters. Not for me, though. Too young. You get into trouble that way, and I didn't want trouble.

It was a nice, warm, late-spring evening. Lots of couples out walking. I noticed one blonde in particular—she was with a sailor, I recall—and I

267

remember thinking to myself that she had the most luscious calves I've ever seen. But she was with a sailor. And there was one with a child and one with a party of stenographers out on the town for a night, and one I almost spoke to, until her boyfriend came up suddenly after parking the car.

Oh, it was exasperating, I can tell you! It was beginning to seem as though everybody had his blonde but me. Sometimes it's like that for weeks, but I'm philosophical about such things.

I glanced up at the clock, around nine, and concluded that I'd best be on my way. I might be a "disgusting old man" but I know a trick or two. Blondes are where you find them.

Right now, I knew, the best place to find them would be over at Dreamway. Sure, it's a dime-a-dance hall. But there's no law against that.

There was no law against my walking in and standing there at the back before I bought tickets. There was no law to prevent me from looking, from sorting out and selecting.

Ordinarily I didn't much care for these public dance halls. The so-called "music" hurts my ears, and my sensibilities are apt to be offended by the spectacle of dancing itself. There is a vulgar sexual connotation which dismays me, but I suppose it's all a part of the game.

Dreamway was crowded tonight. The "operators" were out in force: filling-station attendants with long sideburns, middle-aged dandies incongruous in youthfully styled "sharp" suits, wistful little Filipinos and lonesome servicemen on leave. And mixing and mingling with them, the girls.

Those girls, those hostesses! Where did they get their dresses — the crimson Day-Glow gowns, the orange and cerise abominations, the low-cut black atrocities, the fuchsia horrors? And who did their hair — poodle cuts and pony cuts and tight ringlets and loose maenad swirls? The garish, slashing, red-and-white makeup, the dangling, bangling cheap jewelry gave the effect of pink ribbons tied to the horns of a prize heifer.

And yet there were some prize heifers here. I don't mean to be crude in the least; merely honest. Here, in the reeking cheap-perfume-deodorant-cigarette-smoke-talcum-scented mist of music and minglement, strange beauty blossomed.

Poor poetry? Rich truth! I saw a tall girl with the body of a queen, whose eyes held true to a far-off dream. She was only a brunette, of course, but I'm not one to adhere to blind prejudice. There was a redhead whose dancing was stiff and stately; she held her body like a white candle surmounted by a scarlet flame. And there was a blonde —

Yes, *there* was a blonde! Quite young, a bit too babyishly plump, and obviously a prey to fatigue, but she had what I was looking for. The true, fair-haired type, bred blondely to the bone. If there's one thing I can't stand, it's a fake blonde. Dyed hair, or the partial blonde who becomes a "brownette" in her late twenties. I've been fooled by them before and I know.

But this was a real blonde, a harvest goddess. I watched her as she swept, in unutterable boredom, around the floor. Her dancing partner was a clod—visiting rancher, I'd guess. Expensively dressed, but with that telltale red neck rising out of the white collar of his shirt. Yes—and unless my eyes deceived me, he was chewing on a toothpick as he danced!

I made my decision. This was it. I went up and bought myself three dollars' worth of tickets. Then I waited for the number to end.

They play short numbers at Dreamway, of course. In about a minute the clamor ceased. My blonde was standing on the edge of the floor. The rancher broke away, apparently determined to buy more tickets.

I walked over to her, displayed my handful. "Dance?" I asked. She nodded, scarcely looking at me. She *was* tired. She wore an emerald-green gown, low-cut and sleeveless. There were freckles on her plump arms and —intriguingly enough—on her shoulders and down the neckline to the V. Her eyes seemed green, but that was probably the dress. No doubt they were actually gray.

The music started. Now I may have given the impression that, since I dislike dance halls and dancing, I am not particularly adept at the ballet of the ballroom. In all modesty, this is far from the case. I have made it my business to become an expert dancer. I find it inevitably to be of help to me in establishing contacts.

Tonight was no exception.

We weren't out on the floor thirty seconds before she glanced up and looked at me—really looked at me, for the first time.

"Gee, you're a good dancer!"

That "Gee" was all I needed. Together with her rather naive tone of voice, it gave me an immediate insight into her character and background. Small-town girl, probably, who quit school and came to the city. Perhaps she came with some man. If not, she met one shortly after her arrival. It ended badly, of course. Maybe she took a job in a restaurant or a store. And then she met another man, and the dance hall seemed easier. So here she was.

Quite a lot to adduce from a single exclamation? Yes, but then I've met so many blondes in similar situations, and the story is always the same; that is, if they're the "Gee!" type. And I'm not deprecatory in the least. I happen to like the "Gee!" type best of all.

She could tell that I liked her, of course, from the way I danced. I almost anticipated her next remark. "There's life in the old boy yet."

I smiled, not at all resentful. "I'm younger than I look." I winked. "You know, I could dance with you all night—and something tells me that's not a bad idea."

"You flatter me." But she looked worried. That was the whole idea. She believed me.

ˈ gave her just under a minute for the thought to take hold. Then I pulled the switch. "I wouldn't fool you," I told her. "I'm like all the other men you meet—just lonely. I'm not going to ask if we couldn't go somewhere and talk, because I know the answer. You're paid to dance. But I happen to know that if I buy, say, ten dollars' more worth of tickets, you can get off. And we can sneak off for a few drinks." I winked again. "Sitting down."

"Well, I don't know—"

"Of course you don't. But I do. Look, if you have any worries about me pulling a fast one, I'm old enough to be your grandfather."

It was obvious, and she considered it. She also considered the delightful prospect of sitting down. "I guess it's OK," she murmured. "Shall we go, Mr. —?"

"Beers," I said.

"What?" She checked a giggle. "Not really?"

"Really. Beers is the name. Not the drink. You can drink anything you like, Miss—"

"Shirley Collins." Now the giggle came out. "Sort of a coincidence, don't you think? Beers and Collins."

"Come on, what are we waiting for?" I steered her over to the edge of the floor, went to buy my tickets, and made the necessary arrangements with the manager while she got her coat. It cost me an extra five for his tip, but I didn't begrudge him the money. We all have to eat, you know.

She didn't look bad at all, once she had some of that mascara washed off. Her eyes *were* gray, I discovered. And her arms were soft and rounded. I escorted her quite gallantly to the bar down the street and hung up her coat when we found a nice quiet back booth.

The waitress was one of those scrawny, sallow-faced brunettes. She wore slacks and chewed gum; I'd never consider her for a moment. But she served her purpose—drinks, rather. I ordered rye on the rocks and she brought the two glasses.

I paid her, not forgetting to tip, because I'd be wanting prompt service. She snapped her gum in friendly acknowledgment and left us alone. I pushed my drink over to Shirley.

"What's the matter?" she said.

"Nothing. It's just that I don't indulge."

"Now, wait a minute, Mr. Beers. You aren't trying to get a girl loaded, are you?"

"My dear young lady—please!" I sounded for all the world like an elderly college professor admonishing his class. "You don't have to drink if you don't want to."

"Oh, that's OK. Only you know, a girl has to be careful." The way she downed the first rye belied her words. She toyed with the second glass. "Say, this can't be much fun for you, sitting and watching me drink."

"If you only knew," I said. "Didn't I tell you I was lonely? And wanted someone to talk to?"

"A girl hears some funny lines, but I guess you're on the level. What'll we talk about?"

That was an easy one. "You." From now on I didn't even need to think about what I was saying. Everything proceeded automatically. My mind was free to consider her blondeness, her ripe and ample richness. Why should anyone insist on the presence of a brain in a body like that?

I certainly didn't. I was content to let her ramble on, ordering drinks for her whenever the glass was empty. "And honest, you have no idea what that grind does to your feet —"

"Excuse me a moment," I said. "I must say hello to an old friend."

I walked down to the other end of the bar. He had just come in and was standing there with a lovely black girl. Ordinarily I wouldn't have known him, but something about the way he kept staring at her tipped me off.

"Hello," I said softly. "See you're up to your old tricks."

"Look here!" He tried to appear arrogant, but he couldn't hide the fright. "I don't know you."

"Yes, you do," I told him. "Yes, you do." I pulled him away and put my mouth to his ear. When he heard what I had to say he laughed.

"Dirty trick, trying to scare me, but I forgive you. It's just that I didn't expect to see you here. Where you located?"

"Something called the Shane Apartments. And you?"

"Oh, I'm way outside town. How do you like her?" He nudged me and indicated his girl.

"Nice. But you know my weakness."

We both laughed.

"Well," I concluded, "I won't disturb you any longer. I just wondered if you were making out all right."

"Perfectly. No trouble at all."

"Good," I said. "We've got to be extra careful these days, with all that cheap publicity going around."

"I know." He waved me along. "Best of luck."

"Same to you," I said and walked back to the booth. I felt fine.

Shirley Collins felt fine too. She'd ordered another drink during my absence. I paid and tipped the waitress.

"My, my!" the blonde gushed. "You certainly do throw your dough around."

"Money means nothing to me," I said. I fanned five twenties from the roll. "Here — have some."

"Why, Mr. Beers! I couldn't, really."

She was positively drooling. "Go ahead," I urged. "Plenty more where that come from. I like to see you happy."

So she took the money. They always do. And, if they're as high as Shirley was, their reactions are always the same.

"Gee, you're a nice old guy." She reached for my hand. "I've never met anyone quite like you. You know, kind and generous. And no passes, either."

"That's right." I drew my hand away. "No passes."

This really puzzled her. "I dunno, I can't figure you out, Mr. Beers. Say, by the way, where'd you get all this money?"

"Picked it up," I told her. "It's easy if you know how."

"Now you're kidding me. No fooling, what do you do for a living?"

"You'd be surprised." I smiled. "Actually you might say I'm retired. I devote all my time to my hobbies."

"You mean, like books or paintings or something? Are you a collector?"

"That's right. Come to think of it, maybe you'd like to get acquainted with my collection."

She giggled. "Are you inviting me up to see your etchings?"

I went right along with the gag. "Certainly. You aren't going to pretend that you won't come, are you?"

"No. I'll be glad to come."

She put the five twenty-dollar bills in her purse and rose. "Let's go, Pappy."

I didn't care for that "Pappy" stuff at all—but she was such a luscious blonde. Even now, slightly tipsy, she was wholly delectable. What the young folks call "a real dish."

A half-dozen stares knifed my back as we walked past the bar on our way outside. I knew what they were thinking. "Old dried-up fossil like that with a young girl. What's the world coming to nowadays?"

Then, of course, they turned back to their drinks, because they really didn't want to know what the world was coming to nowadays. Bombs can drop, saucers can fly, and still people will sit at bars and pass judgments between drinks. All of which suits me perfectly.

Shirley Collins suited me perfectly, too, at the moment. I had no difficulty finding a cab or bundling her inside. "Shane Apartments," I told the driver. Shirley snuggled up close to me.

I pulled away.

"What's the matter, Pappy—don't you like me?"

"Of course I do."

"Then don't act as if I was gonna bite you."

"It's not that. But I meant it when I said I had no—er—intentions along such lines."

"Sure, I know." She relaxed, perfectly content. "So I'll settle for your etchings."

We pulled up and I recognized the building. I gave the driver a ten-dollar bill and told him to keep the change.

"I can't figure you out, Mr Beers," Shirley said—and meant it "Way you toss that moola around."

"Call it one last fling. I'm leaving town shortly." I took her arm and we stepped into the lobby. The self-service elevator was empty. I pressed the button for the top floor. We rose slowly.

On the way up Shirley sobered suddenly. She faced me and put her arms on my shoulders. "Look here, Mr. Beers. I just got to thinking. I saw a movie once and—say, what I mean is, way you hand out dough and talking about leaving town and all—you aren't sick, are you? I mean, you haven't just come from the doctor and heard you're gonna die from some disease?"

Her solicitude was touching, and I didn't laugh. "Really," I said, "I can assure you that your fears are groundless. I'm very much alive and expect to stay that way for a long time to come."

"Good. Now I feel better. I like you, Mr. Beers."

"I like you, too, Shirley." I stepped back just in time to avoid a hug. The elevator halted and we got out. I led her down the hallway to the stairs.

"Oh, you have the penthouse!" she squealed. Now she was really excited.

"You go first," I murmured.

She went first. At the top of the stairs she halted, puzzled. "But there's a door here—it's the roof or something."

"Keep going," I directed.

She stepped out on the rooftop and I followed. The door closed behind us, and everything was still.

Everything was still with a midnight stillness. Everything was beautiful with a midnight beauty. The dark body of the city stretched below us, wearing its neon necklaces, its bracelets and rings of incandescence. I've seen it many times from the air, many times from rooftops, and it's always a thrilling spectacle to me. Where I come from things are different. Not that I'd ever care to trade—the city's a nice place to visit, but I wouldn't want to live there.

I stared, and the blonde stared. But she wasn't staring at the streets below.

I followed her gaze to the shadow of the building abutment, to the deep shadows where something shimmered roundly and iridescently in the darkness. It was completely out of sight from the surrounding buildings, and it couldn't be seen at first glance from the doorway here on the roof. But she saw it now, and she said, "Gee!"

She said, "Gee! Mr. Beers—look at that!"

I looked.

"What is it, a plane? Or—could it be one of those saucer things?"

I looked.

"Mr. Beers, what's the matter?—you aren't even surprised."

I looked.

"You—you knew about this?"

"Yes. It's mine."

"Yours? A saucer? But it can't be. You're a man and—"

I shook my head slowly. "Not exactly, Shirley. I don't really look like this, you know. Not where I came from." I gestured down toward the tired flesh. "I borrowed this from Ril."

"Ril?"

"Yes. He's one of my friends. He collects, too. We all collect, you know. It's our hobby. We come to Earth and collect."

I couldn't read her face, because as I came close she drew away.

"Ril has a rather curious hobby, in a way. He collects nothing but *B*s. You should see his trophy room! He has a Bronson, three Bakers, and a Beers— that's the body I'm using now. Its name was Ambrose Beers, I believe. He picked it up in Mexico a long time ago."

"You're crazy!" Shirley whispered, but she listened as I went on. Listened and drew away.

"My friend Kor has a collection of people of all nations. Mar you saw in the tavern a while ago—Melanesian types are his hobby. Many of us come here quite often, you know, and in spite of the recent publicity and the danger, it's an exhilarating pastime." I was quite close to her now, and she didn't step back any farther. She couldn't—she stood on the edge of the roof.

"Now, take Vis," I said. "Vis collects redheads, nothing but redheads. He has a magnificent grouping, all of them stuffed. Ril doesn't stuff his specimens at all—that's why we can use them for our trips. Oh, it's a fascinating business, I can tell you! Ril keeps them in preservative tanks and Vis stuffs them—his redheads, I mean. Now as for me, I collect blondes."

Her eyes were wide, and she could scarcely get the words out for panting. "You're—going to—stuff me?"

I had to chuckle. "Not at all, dear. Set your mind at rest. I neither stuff nor preserve. I collect for different reasons entirely." She edged sideways, toward the iridescent bubble. There was nowhere else to go, and I followed closely, closely.

"You're—fooling me—" she gasped.

"No. Oh, my friends think I have peculiar ideas, but I enjoy it this way. There's nothing like a blonde, as far as I'm concerned. And I ought to know. I've collected over a hundred so far since I started. You are number one hundred and three."

I didn't have to do anything. She fainted, and I caught her, and that made things just perfect—no need to make a mess on the roof. I merely carried her right into the ship and we were off in a moment.

Of course people would remember the old man who picked up Shirley Collins in the dance hall, and I'd left a trail of money all over town. There'd be an investigation and all that. There almost always was an investigation.

But that didn't bother me. Ril has many bodies for use besides old Beers, whoever he might have been. Next time I'd try a younger man. Variety is the spice of life.

Yes, it was a very pleasant evening. I sang to myself almost all the way back. It had been good sport, and the best was yet to come.

But then, I like blondes. They can laugh at me all they please — I'll take a blonde any time. As I say, it's a matter of taste.

And blondes are simply delicious.

You Got to Have Brains

MUST HAVE BEEN about a year ago, give or take a month, when Mr. Goofy first showed up here on the street.

We get all kinds here, you know — thousands of bums and winos floating in and out every day of the year. Nobody knows where they come from and nobody cares where they go. They sleep in flophouses, sleep in bars, and in doorways — sleep right out in the gutter if you let 'em. Just so's they get their kicks. Wine jags, shot-an'-beers, canned heat, reefers — there was one guy, he used to go around and bust up thermometers and drink the juice, so help me!

When you work behind the bar, like me, you get so you hardly notice people any more. But this Mr. Goofy was different.

He come in one night in winter, and the joint was almost empty. Most of the regulars, right after New Year's, they get themselves jugged and do ninety. Keeps 'em out of the cold.

So it was quiet when Mr. Goofy showed up, around supper time. He didn't come to the bar, even though he was all alone. He headed straight for a back booth, plunks down, and asked Ferd for a couple of hamburgers. That's when I noticed him.

What's so screwy about that? Well, it's because he was lugging about ten or fifteen pounds of scrap metal with him, that's why. He banged it down in the booth alongside him and sat there with his hands held over it like he was one of them guards at Fort Knock or wherever.

I mean, he had all this here dirty scrap metal — tin and steel and twisted old engine parts covered with mud. He must have dug it out of the dumps around Canal Street, some place like that. So when I got a chance I come down to this end of the bar and looked this character over. He sure was a sad one.

He was only about five feet high and weighed about a hunnerd pounds, just a little dried-up futz of a guy. He had a kind of a bald head and he wore old twisted-up glasses with the earpieces all bent, and he had trouble with the hamburgers on account of his false choppers. He was dressed in them War Surplus things — leftovers from World War I, yet. And a cap.

Go out on the street right now and you'll see plenty more just like him, but Mr. Goofy was different. Because he was clean. Sure, he looked beat-up, but even his old duds was neat.

Another thing. While he waited for the hamburgers he kept writing stuff. He had this here pencil and notebook out and he was scribbling away for dear life. I got the idea he was figuring out some kind of arithametics.

Well, I was all set to ask him the score when somebody come in and I got busy. It happens that way; next thing I know the whole place was crowded and I forgot all about Mr. Goofy for maybe two hours. Then I happened to look over and by gawd if he ain't still sitting there, with that pencil going like crazy!

Only by this time the old juke is blasting, and he kind of frowns and takes his time like he didn't care for music but was, you know, concentrated on his figures, like.

He sees me watching him and wiggles his fingers like so, and I went over there and he says, "Pardon me — but could you lower the volume of that instrument?"

Just like that he says it, with a kind of funny accent I can't place. But real polite and fancy for a foreigner.

So I says, "Sure, I'll switch it down a little." I went over and fiddled with the control to cut it down, like we do late at night.

But just then Stakowsky come up to me. This Stakowsky used to be a wheel on the street — owned two–three flophouses and fleabag hotels, and he comes in regular to get loaded. He was kind of mean, but a good spender.

Well, Stakowsky come up and he stuck his big red face over the bar and yelled. "Whassa big idea, Jack? I puts in my nickel, I wanna hear my piece. You wanna busted nose or something?"

Like I say, he was a mean type.

I didn't know right off what to tell him, but it turned out I didn't have to tell him nothing. Because the little guy in the booth stood up and he tapped Stakowsky on the shoulder and said, real quiet, "Pardon me, but it was I who requested that the music be made softer."

Stakowsky turned around and he said, "Yeah? And who in hell you think you are — somebody?"

The little guy said, "You know me. I rented the top of the loft from you yesterday."

Stakowsky looks at him again and then he says, "Awright. So you rent. So you pay a month advance. Awright. But that ain't got to do with how I play music. I want it should be turned up, so me and my friends can hear it good."

By this time the number is over and half the bar has come down to get in on the deal. They was all standing around waiting for the next pitch.

The little guy says, "You don't understand, Mr. Stakowsky. It happens I am doing some very important work and require freedom from distraction."

I bet Stakowsky never heard no two-dollar words before. He got redder and redder and at last he says, "You don't understand so good, neither. You wanna figure, go by your loft. Now I turn up the music. Are you gonna try and stop me?" And he takes a swipe at the little futz with his fist.

Little guy never batted an eye. He just sort of ducked, and when he come up again he had a shiv in his hand. But it wasn't no regular shiv, and it wasn't nothing he found in no junk-heap.

This one was about a foot long, and sharp. The blade was sharp and the tip was sharp, and the little guy didn't look like he was just gonna give Stakowsky a shave with it.

Stakowsky, he didn't think so either. He whitened up fast and backed away to the bar and he says, "All right, all right," over and over again.

It happened all in a minute, and then the knife was gone and the little guy picked up his scrap metal and walked out without even looking back once.

Then everybody was hollering, and I poured Stakowsky a fast double, and then another. Of course he made off like he hadn't been scared and he talked plenty loud — but we all knew.

"Goofy," he says. "That's who he is. Mr. Goofy. Sure, he rents from me. You know, by the Palace Rooms, where I live. He rents the top — a great big loft up there. Comes yesterday, a month rent in advance he pays too. I tell him, 'Mister, you're goofy. What do you want with such a big empty loft? A loft ain't no good in winter, unless you want to freeze. Why you don't take a nice warm room downstairs by the steam heat?' But no, he wants the loft, and I should put up a cot for him. So I do, and he moves in last night."

Stakowsky got red in the face. "All day today that Mr. Goofy, he's bringing up his crazy outfits. Iron and busted machinery. Stuff like that. I ask him what he's doing and he says he's building. I ask him what he's building and he says — well, he just don't say. You saw how he acted tonight? Now you know. He's goofy in the head. I ain't afraid of no guys, but those crazy ones you got to watch out for. Lofts and machinery and knives — you ever hear anything like that Mr. Goofy?"

So that's how he got his name. And I remembered him. One of the reasons was, I was staying at the Palace Rooms myself. Not in the flops, but a nice place on the third floor, right next to Stakowsky's room. And right upstairs from us was this loft. An attic, like. I never went up there, but there were stairs in back.

The next couple of days I kept my eyes open, figuring on seeing Mr. Goofy again. But I didn't. All I did was hear him. Nights, he kept banging and pounding away, him and his scrap metal or whatever it was, and he moved stuff across the floor. Me, I'm a pretty sound sleeper and Stakowsky was always loaded when he turned in, so it didn't bother him neither. But Mr. Goofy never seemed to sleep. He was always working up there. And on what?

I couldn't figure it out. Day after day he'd come in and out with some more metal. I don't know where he got it all, but he must have lugged up a couple of thousand pounds, ten or fifteen each trip. It got to bothering me because it was the sort of a mystery you feel you've got to know more about.

Next time I saw him was when he started coming into the place regular, to eat. And always he had the pencil and notebook with him. He took the same booth every night—and nobody bothered him with loud music after the story got around about him and his shiv.

He'd just sit there and figure and mumble to himself and walk out again, and pretty soon they were making up all kinds of stories about the guy.

Some said he was a Red on account of that accent, you know, and he was building one of them there atomic bombs. One of the winos says no, he passed the place one night about four A.M. and he heard a big clank like machinery working. He figured Mr. Goofy was a counterfitter. Which was the kind of crazy idea you'd expect from a wino.

Anyways, the closest anybody come was Manny Schreiber from the hock shop, and he guessed Goofy was a inventor and maybe he was building a rowbot. You know, a rowbot, like in these scientist magazines. Mechanical men, they run by machinery.

One day, about an hour before I went on shift, I was sitting in my room when Stakowsky knocked on the door. "Come on," he says. "Mr. Goofy just went out. I'm gonna take a look around up there."

Well, I didn't care one way or the other. Stakowsky, he was the landlord, and I figured he had a right. So we sneaked up and he used his key and we went inside the loft.

It was a big barn of a place with a cot in the corner. Next to the cot was a table with a lot of notes piled up, and maybe twenty-five or thirty books. Foreign books they were, and I couldn't make out the names. In the other corners there were piles of scrap metal and what looked like a bunch of old radio sets from a repair shop.

And in the center of the room was this machine. At least, it looked like a machine, even though it must have been thirty feet long. It was higher than my head, too. And there was a door in it and you could get inside the machinery that was all tangled up on the sides and sit down in a chair. In front of the chair was a big board with a lot of switches on it.

And everywhere was gears and pistons and coils and even glass tubes. Where he picked up all that stuff, I dunno. But he'd patched it all together somehow and when you looked at it — it made sense. I mean, you could tell the machine would do something, if you could only figure out what.

Stakowsky looked at me and I looked at him and we both looked at the machine.

"That Mr. Goofy!" says Stakowsky. "He does all this in a month. You know something, Jack?"

"What?" I says.

"You tell anybody else and I'll kill you. But I'm scared to even come near Mr. Goofy. This machine of his, I don't like it. Tomorrow his month is up. I'm going to tell him he should move. Get out. I don't want crazy people around here."

"But how'll he move this thing out?"

"I don't care how. Tomorrow he gets the word. And I'm going to have Lippy and Stan and the boys here. He don't pull no knife on me again. Out he goes."

We went downstairs and I went to work. All night long I tried to figure that machine of his. There wasn't much else to do, because there was a real blizzard going and nobody came in.

I kept remembering the way the machine looked. It had a sort of framework running around the outside, and if it got covered over with some metal it would be like a submarine or one of them rockets. And there was a part inside, where a big glass globe connected up to some wires leading to the switchboard, or whatever it was. And a guy could sit in there. It all made some kind of crazy sense.

I sat there, thinking it over, until along about midnight. Then Mr. Goofy came in.

This time he didn't head for his booth. He come right up to the bar and sat down on a stool. His face was red, and he brushed snow off his coat. But he looked happy.

"Do you have any decent brandy?" he asked.

"I think so," I told him. I found a bottle and opened it up.

"Will you be good enough to have a drink with me?"

"Sure, thanks." I looked at him. "Celebrating?"

"That's right," says Mr. Goofy. "This is a great occasion. My work is finished. Tonight I put on the sheaths. Now I am almost ready to demonstrate."

"Demonstrate what?"

Well, he dummied up on me right away. I poured him another drink and another, and he just sat there grinning. Then he sort of loosened up. That brandy was plenty powerful.

"Look," he says. "I will tell you all about it. You have been kind to me, and I can trust you. Besides, it is good to share a moment of triumph."

He says, "So long I have worked, but soon they will not laugh at me any more. Soon the smart Americans, the men over here who call themselves Professors, will take note of my work. They did not believe me when I offered to show them my plans. They would not accept my basic theory. But I knew I was right. I knew I could do it. Part of it must be mechanical, yes. But the most important part is the mind itself. You know what I told them? To do this, and to do it right, you've got to have brains."

He sort of chuckled, and poured another drink. "Yes. That is the whole secret. More than anything else, you need brains. Not mechanical formula alone. But when I spoke of harnessing the mind, powering it with metal energy rather than physical, they laughed. Now we'll see."

I bought myself a drink, and I guess he realized I wasn't in on the pitch, because he says, "You don't understand, do you?"

I shook my head.

"What would you say, my friend, if I told you I have just successfully completed the construction of the first practical spaceship?"

Oh-oh, I thought to myself. Mr. Goofy!

"But not a model, not a theory in metal — an actual, practical machine for travel to the moon?"

Mr. Goofy and his knife, I thought. Making a crazy thing out of old scrap iron. Mr. Goofy!

"If I wish, I can go tonight," he said. "Or tomorrow. Any time. No astronomy. No calculus. Mental energy is the secret. Harness the machinery to a human brain and it will be guided automatically to its destination in a moment, if properly controlled. That's all it takes — a single instant. Long enough to direct the potential energy of the cortex."

Maybe you think it's funny the way I can remember all those big words, but I'll never forget anything Mr. Goofy said.

And he told me, "Who has ever estimated the power of the human brain — its unexploited capacity for performance? Using the machine for autohypnosis, the brain is capable of tremendous effort. The electrical impulses can be stepped up, magnified ten millionfold. Atomic energy is insignificant in comparison. Now do you see what I have achieved?"

I thought about it for a minute or so — him sitting there all steamed up over his dizzy junk heap. Then I remembered what was happening to him tomorrow.

I just didn't have the heart to let him go on and on about how his life-work was realized, and how he'd be famous in Europe and America and he'd reach the moon and all that crud. I didn't have the heart. He was so little and so whacky. Mr. Goofy!

So I says, "Look, I got to tell you something. Stakowsky, he's bouncing you out tomorrow. That's right. He's gonna kick you and your machine into the street. He says he can't stand it around."

"Machine?" says Mr. Goofy. "What does he know of my machine?"

Well, I had to tell him then. I had to. About how we went upstairs and looked.

"Before the sheath was on, you saw?" he asked.

"That's the way it was," I told him. "I saw it, and so did Stakowsky. And he'll kick you out."

"But he cannot! I mean, I chose this spot carefully, so I could work unobserved. I need privacy. And I cannot move the ship now. I must bring people to see it when I make the announcement. I must make the special arrangements for the tests. It is a very delicate matter. Doesn't he understand? He'll be famous, too, because of what happened in his miserable hole of a place —"

"He's probably famous tonight," I said. "I'll bet he's down the street somewheres right now, blabbing about you and your machine, and how he's gonna toss you out."

Mr. Goofy looked so sad I tried to make a joke. "What's the matter with you? You say yourself it works by brain power. So use your brain and move it someplace else. Huh?"

He looked even sadder. "Don't you realize it is designed only for space travel? And properly, my brain must be free to act as the control agent. Still, you are right about that man. He is a wicked person, and he hates me. I must do something. I wonder if —"

Then you know what he does, this Mr. Goofy? He whips out his pencil and notebook and starts figuring. Just sits there and scribbles away. And he says, "Yes, it is possible. Change the wires leading to the controls. It is only a matter of a few moments. And what better proof could I ask than an actual demonstration? Yes. It is fated to be this way. Good."

Then he stood up and stuck out his mitt. "Goodbye, Jack," he says. "And thank you for your suggestion."

"What suggestion?"

But he doesn't answer me, and then he's out the door and gone.

I closed up the joint about one-thirty. The boss wasn't around and I figured what the hell, it was a blizzard.

There was nobody out on the street this time of night, not with the wind off the lake and the snow coming down about a foot a minute. I couldn't see in front of my face.

I crossed the street in front of the Palace Rooms—it must have been quarter to two or thereabouts—and all of a sudden it happened.

Whoom!

Like that it goes, a big loud blast you can hear even over the wind and the blizzard. On account of the snow being so thick I couldn't see nothing. But let me tell you. I sure heard it.

At first I thought maybe it was some kind of explosion, so I quick run across to the Palace and up the stairs. All the winos in the flops was asleep —those guys, they get a jag on and they'll sleep even if you set fire to the mattress. But I had to find out if anything was wrong.

I didn't smell no smoke and my room was okay, and it was all quiet in the hall. Except that the back door leading to the attic was open, and the air was cold.

Right away I figured maybe Mr. Goofy had pulled something off, so I ran up the stairs. And I saw it

Mr. Goofy was gone. The junk was still scattered all over the room, but he'd burned all his notes and he was gone. The great big machine, or space-ship, or whatever it was—that was gone, too.

How'd he get it out of the room and where did he take it? You can search me, brother.

All I know is there was a big charred spot burned away in the center of the floor where the machine had stood. And right above there was a big round hole punched smack through the roof of the loft.

So help me, I just stood there. What else could I do? Mr. Goofy said he built a spaceship that could take him to the moon. He said he could go there in a flash, just like that. He said all it took was brains.

And what do I know about this autohypnosis deal, or whatever he called it, and about electricity-energy, and force fields, and all that stuff?

He was gone. The machine or ship was gone. And there was this awful hole in the roof. That's all I knew.

Maybe Stakowsky would know the rest. It was worth a try, anyhow. So I run down to Stakowsky's room.

After that, things didn't go so good.

The cops started to push me around when they got there, and if it hadn't been for my boss putting the old pressure on, they'd have given me a real rough time. But they could see I was sorta like out of my head—and I was, too, for about a week.

I kept yelling about this Mr. Goofy and his crazy invention and his big knife and his trip to the moon, and it didn't make no sense to the cops. Of course, nothing ever made any sense to them, and they had to drop the whole case—hush it up. The whole thing was too screwy to ever let leak out.

Anyhow, I felt rugged until I moved out of the Palace Rooms and got back to work. Now I scarcely ever think about Mr. Goofy any more, or Stakowsky —or the whole cockeyed mess.

I don't like to think about the mess.

The mess was when I ran down the stairs that night and looked for Stakowsky in his room. He was there all right, but he didn't care about Goofy or the trip to the moon or the hole in his loft roof, either.

Because he was very, very dead.

And Mr. Goofy's foot-long knife was laying right next to him on the bed. So that part was easy to figure out. Mr. Goofy come right back there from the tavern, and he killed him.

But after that?

After that, your guess is as good as mine. The cops never found out a bit—not even Mr. Goofy's real name, or where he came from, or where he got this here theory about spaceships and power to run them.

Did he really have a invention that would take him to the moon? Could he change some wires and controls and just scoot off through the roof with his mental energy hooked up?

Nobody knows. Nobody ever will know. But I can tell you this.

There was a mess, one awful mess, in Stakowsky's room. Mr. Goofy must have taken his knife and gone to work on Stakowsky's head. There was nothing left on top but a big round hole, and it was empty.

Stakowsky's head was empty.

Mr. Goofy took out what was inside and fixed his machine and went to the moon.

That's all.

Like Mr. Goofy says, you got to have brains. . . .

A Good Imagination

I MAY HAVE MY FAULTS, but lack of imagination isn't one of them.

Take this matter of George Parker, for example. It finally came to a head today, and I flatter myself that I handled it very well. That's where imagination counts.

If it hadn't been for my imagination I probably never would have noticed George in the first place. And I certainly wouldn't have been prepared to deal with him properly. But as it was, I had everything worked out.

He showed up, right on schedule, just after lunch. I was down in the basement, mixing cement, when I heard him rap on the back door.

"Anybody home?" he called.

"Down here," I said. "All ready to go."

So he walked through the kitchen and came down the cellar stairs, clumping. George, the eternal clumper, banging his way through life; about as subtle as a steamroller. And with a steamroller's snug belief in its own power, in its ability to crush anything that didn't get out of its way.

He had to stoop a bit here in the basement because he was so tall. Tall and heavyset, with the thick neck and broad shoulders that are the common endowment of outdoor men, movie stars, and adult male gorillas.

Of course I'm being a bit uncharitable. George Parker couldn't be compared to a gorilla. Not with that boyish haircut and amiable grin of his. No self-respecting gorilla would affect either.

"All alone?" he asked. "Where's Mrs. Logan?"

"Louise?" I shrugged. "She's gone over to Dalton to close up the bank account."

The grin vanished. "Oh. I was sort of hoping I'd get a chance to say goodbye to her."

I'll bet he was. It almost killed him, realizing that he wasn't going to see her again. I knew. I knew why he'd come scratching on the door with his "Anybody home?" routine. What he really meant was, "Is the coast clear, darling?"

How many times had he come creeping around this summer? I wondered. How many times had he called her "darling"? How many times during the long weekdays when I wasn't home—when I was slaving away in town, and she was alone up here at the summer house?

Alone with George Parker. The steamroller. The gorilla. The ape in the t-shirt.

In June, when we first came up, I had thought we were lucky to find somebody like George to fix things around the place. The house needed repairs and carpentry work, and a fresh coat of paint. The lawn and garden demanded attention, too. And since I could only get away on weekends, I congratulated myself on finding a willing worker like George.

Louise had congratulated me too. "It was wonderful of you to discover such a jewel. This place needs a handyman."

Well, George must have been handy. All summer long, Louise kept finding new things for him to do. Putting in a walk to the pier. Setting up trellises. The neighbors got used to seeing him come in three or four days a week. I got used to it, too. For better than two months, you'd have thought I didn't have any imagination at all. Then I began to put two and two together. Or one and one, rather. George and Louise. Together up here, day after day. And night after night?

Even then, I couldn't be sure. It took a great deal of imagination to conceive of any woman allowing herself to become enamored of such an obvious ape. But then, perhaps some women like apes. Perhaps they have a secret craving for hairy bodies and crushing weight and panting animalism. Louise always told me she hated that sort of thing. She respected me because I was gentle and understanding and controlled myself. At least, that's what she said.

But I saw the way she looked at George. And I saw the way he looked at her. And I saw the way they both looked at me, when they thought I wasn't aware.

I was aware, of course. Increasingly aware, as the weeks went by. At first I contemplated getting rid of George, but that would have been too obvious. Firing him in midsummer, with work to be done, didn't make sense. Unless I wanted to force a showdown with Louise.

That wasn't the answer, either. All I'd have gotten from her would've been a tearful denial. And before she was through, she'd have twisted things around so that I was to blame. I'd be the brute who penned her up here in the country all summer long and left her alone to suffer. After all, I couldn't really prove anything.

So then I decided to sell. It wasn't difficult. Getting the place fixed up was a good idea; it added a couple of thousand to the value of the property. All I had to do was pass the word around to the realtor over at Dalton, and he did the rest. By the end of August there were three offers. I chose the best one, and it gave me a tidy profit.

Of course, Louise was heartbroken when she heard about the deal. She loved it here, she was just getting settled, she looked forward to coming back next year—why, she had even meant to talk to me about having a furnace put in so we could stay the year round.

She played the scene well, and I enjoyed it. All except the part about staying up here permanently. Did the little fool really think I was stupid enough to go for that? Staying in town alone all week, slaving away at the business, and then dragging up here weekends in the dead of winter to hear her excuses? "No, really, I'm just too bushed, honey. If you only knew how much work I've been doing around the place! I just want to sleep forever."

I wanted to shout at her, then. I wanted to curse her. I wanted to spit it all out, tell her that I knew, then take her in my arms and shake her until her silly head spun. But I couldn't. Louise was too delicate for such brutality. Or so she had always intimated to me. She demanded gentle treatment. Gentle George, the gorilla.

So I was gentle with her. I told her that selling the place was merely a matter of good business. We had a chance to realize a handsome profit. And next year we'd buy another. In fact, I had already arranged a little surprise for her. After Labor Day, on our way back to town, I'd show it to her, even though it was a day or so out of our way.

"Out of our way?" She gave me that wide-eyed stare. "You mean you've got another place picked out, not around here?"

"That's right."

"Where? Tell me. Is it far?"

I smiled. "Quite far."

"But I—I'd like to stay here, on the river."

"Wait until you see it before you decide," I said. "Let's not talk about it any more now. I imagine you're tired."

"Yes. I think I'll sleep on the day bed, if you don't mind."

I didn't mind. And we didn't talk about it any more. I just completed the sale and got Louise to start packing. There wasn't much to pack, because I'd sold the furniture, too.

Then I waited. Waited and watched. Louise didn't know about the watching, of course. Neither did George.

And now it was the last day, and George stood in the cellar with me and looked at the mixing trough.

"Say, you do a pretty good job," he said. "Never knew you was so handy."

"I can do anything if I set my mind to it." I gave him back his grin.

"Is this the hole you want me to plug up?" he asked. He pointed to the opening underneath the cellar steps. It was a black shelf about two feet high and three feet wide, between the top of the basement blocks and the ceiling beams.

"That's it," I told him. "Goes clear back to the shed, I think. Always bothered me to see it, and I'd like to cement it up for the new owners before I go."

"Keep the mice out, eh?"

"And the rats," I said.

"Not many rats around here," George muttered.

"You're wrong, George." I stared at him. "There are rats everywhere. They creep in when you're not around to see them. They destroy your property. If you're not careful, they'll eat you out of house and home. And they're cunning. They try to work silently, unobserved. But a smart man knows when they're present. He can detect the signs of their handiwork. And a smart man gets rid of them. I wouldn't want to leave any opening for rats here, George. I'd hate to think of the new owner going through the same experience I did."

"You never told me about the rats," George said, looking at the hole in the wall. "Neither did Lou — Mrs. Logan."

"Perhaps she didn't know about them," I answered. "Maybe I should have warned her."

"Yeah."

"Well, it doesn't matter now. The cement will take care of them." I stepped back. "By the way, George, this is some new stuff that I got in town. I don't know if you've ever worked with it before. It's called Fast-seal. Understand it dries hard in less than an hour."

"You got the instructions?" George stared at the coagulating mass.

"Nothing to it. You use it the same way as the regular cement." I handed him the trowel and the boards. "Here, might as well get started. I'm going to dismantle this target range."

He went to work then and I stepped over to the other side of the basement and took down my targets. Then I got the pistols out of their case and packed them. After that I took up the revolvers. I did a little cleaning before I laid them away.

George worked fast. He had the energy for tasks like this; energy, coupled with lack of imagination. Physical labor never troubles people like George, because they're not plagued by thoughts while they work. They live almost entirely in the world of sensation, responding aggressively to every challenge. Show them a hole in the wall and they'll cement it, show them a woman and they'll—

I steered my thoughts away from that and concentrated on oiling the last revolver. It was a big Colt. one I'd never used down here. Odd, that I collected weapons and used them so seldom. I liked to handle them, handle them and speculate upon their potential power. See, here in this tiny hole lurks death; from this minute opening comes a force big enough to burst the brain of idiot and emperor alike, to shatter the skull of sinner and of saint. With such a weapon one could even kill a gorilla at close range.

I held the revolver and stared at George's broad back. He was working swiftly with the trowel, closing off the opening entirely and smoothing it over.

I loaded the revolver, cocked it, and stared again. Ten feet away from me was a perfect target. It was an easy shot. The fool would never know what hit him.

That was the whole trouble, of course. He'd never know what hit him.

And I wanted him to know. Somewhere, deep down inside, even an ape like George had the ability to think, to realize. The trick lay in finding a method that would stimulate his imagination.

So I put down the revolver and walked over to him.

"Looks like you're finished," I said.

He nodded and wiped the perspiration from his forehead. An animal odor came from his armpits.

"Yeah. This stuff sure does a swell job. It's getting hard already. I just got to smooth it off a little more."

"Never mind." I stepped back. "You look as if you could use a beer."

He grinned and followed me over to the portable refrigerator in the corner. I took out a bottle of beer and opened it for him. He gulped gratefully. The bottle was empty before he bothered to look up and remark, "Aren't you drinking?"

I shook my head.

"Not around firearms, George." I pointed to the cases on the table.

"Say, Mr. Logan, I always meant to ask you something. How come a fella like you collects guns?"

"Why not? It's a fairly common hobby."

"But I never seen you shoot one."

I walked over and fished out another beer, uncapped it and handed it to him.

"Perhaps I don't collect them to shoot, George," I told him. "Perhaps I just collect them as symbols. Take this Colt, for example." I held it up. "My admiration for the black barrel has nothing to do with ballistics. When I look at it, I see a thousand stories. A story for every bullet fired. Scenes of violence and danger, of high drama and low melodrama."

"Sort of appeals to your imagination, is that it?"

"Precisely." I handed him another beer. "Go ahead, George," I said. "I've got to clean out the refrigerator anyway. This is our last day, you know. Might as well celebrate."

He nodded. But he didn't look as though he was in a mood for celebrating our departure. The ice-cold beer, downed rapidly, was beginning to take effect. Just a few bottles on a hot day will do the trick—particularly after violent exertion. I saw to it that another was ready before he had finished this one. He drank quickly, noisily, his neck bulging, his thick lips greedily encircling the mouth of the bottle. On his face was the absorbed look of an animal oblivious to everything except the immediate satisfaction of his appetite.

I picked up the Colt again and walked over to the cemented portion of the wall. With my left hand I rubbed the solidifying surface. "Marvelous stuff," I said. "Why, it's hard already. And perfectly dry."

He grunted. He put down the empty bottle and reached for the full one, his fifth. I waited until he had taken a healthy swig. Then I bent down and put my head next to the wall.

"What's that sound?" I asked.

He looked up. "I don't hear no sound."

"Mice," I said. "Back in there."

"Or rats, like you told me." He nodded.

"No, I rather think this is a mouse. The squeaking is so shrill. Can't you hear it?"

"I don't hear nothing."

He came over and stooped. His hand brushed the Colt and I drew it away. "I still can't hear nothing."

"Well, it doesn't matter. This job is airtight, isn't it?"

"Sure."

"Then whatever's inside will suffocate in a few minutes or so." I smiled at him. "You must be deaf to the high tones, George. I heard that sound all during the time you were cementing the wall."

"What's the matter, it bother you, thinking about the mouse?"

"Not particularly, George."

"Anyways, there won't be no more getting through. This wall is really solid, now."

He thumped it with his fist.

"I done a pretty good job."

"Yes, you certainly did. And it's your last one, too." I went over to the refrigerator. "Which reminds me, it's time we settled up. But first, let's have another drink."

George glanced at his wristwatch. "Well, I dunno, Mr. Logan. Maybe I better be running along. I got some business over to Dalton. . . ."

Yes, he had business in Dalton, all right. He wanted to run over and see Louise. Maybe they'd have time to say goodbye again, the way they had last night before I'd arrived. Or before they knew I had arrived. But I saw them then, and I could see them now in my imagination.

It took a lot of effort for me to shut out the picture of what I had seen, but I did it. I even grinned back at George. And I held out the bottle and said, "Just one more, for old times' sake. And if you don't mind, I'll join you."

I took out a bottle for myself, opened it, raised it. With my left hand I picked up the Colt again.

He lifted his beer and belched. The sound echoed through the cellar like a revolver shot.

"A little toast might be in order," I said.

"Go ahead."

I smiled. "Here's to freedom."

He started to drink, then pulled the bottle away from his lips. I watched the crease form in his sweating forehead. "Freedom?"

I shrugged. "There's no sense trying to keep any secrets," I said. "After all, you're almost like one of the family, in a way."

"I don't get it."

"You will."

"What's this business about freedom?"

"Mrs. Logan," I said. "Louise."

He put the beer down on the table. "Yeah?"

"We've separated."

"Sep—"

"That's right, George." I turned my head. "Do you hear anything from behind the wall?"

"No. But what's all this about separating? You have a fight or something?"

"Nothing like that. It was all very sudden. You might say it was completely unexpected, at least as far as she was concerned. But I thought you might like to know."

"Isn't she over to Dalton, then?"

"I'm afraid not."

"You mean she went away already today?"

"You might say that."

"Look here, Logan, just what are you driving at? What's the big idea of—"

I cocked my head toward the wall. "Are you sure you don't hear anything, George?"

"What's there to hear?"

"I thought she might be telling you goodbye."

He got it, then.

"Jesus, no! Logan, you're kidding me!"

I smiled.

His eyes began to bulge. I watched his hand curl around the mouth of the beer bottle. And I brought the muzzle of the Colt up until he could see it.

"Put it down, George. It won't do you any good. I've killed a mouse. What makes you think I'd be afraid to kill a rat?"

He put the bottle down. The minute he let go, his hands started to tremble. "Logan, you couldn't've done it, not you. You wouldn't—"

I inched the revolver up higher, and he flinched back. "That's right," I said. "I couldn't have. You and Louise were so certain about me, weren't you? You decided I couldn't do anything. I couldn't suspect, couldn't see what was going on right under my eyes. And if I did find out, I couldn't do anything about it, because I'm a poor weak fool. Well, you were wrong, George. And Louise was wrong. I wonder if she can hear me now, eh?" I raised my voice. "Are you listening, Louise?"

George moved back against the wall, his mouth twitching. "You're lying," he said. "You didn't kill her."

"That's right. I didn't kill her. She was quite alive when I was finished. I merely saw to it that her arms and legs were bound tightly, so that she couldn't thresh around, and that the gag was firmly in place. Then I lifted her up into the hole and waited for you to come."

His face was whiter than the wall.

"You can understand why, can't you, George? Even an ape has enough imagination to appreciate the situation. Quite a joke, isn't it? You cementing up the wall, and all the while I knew you were killing her. And to make it even funnier, *she* knew it too, of course. She lay in that black hole, trying to cry out to you, while you sealed her up in a airless tomb, in a darkness that is worse than night, in the darkness of death—"

"You're crazy!"

I saw his muscles flex, his neck tighten. "Take one step," I said, "and I'll blow your face off."

He moved then, but away from me. He went to the wall and he began to pound on it. The cement held.

"No use," I said. "It's solid. You did a good job, George. Your last job, and your best. Besides, it wouldn't be any use now. The air couldn't have lasted this long. She's gone."

He turned, panting. He held up his hands, and they were red. "Crazy!" he gasped. "No wonder she was scared of you, hated you. No human being could think of a thing like that."

I smiled. "Yes they could, George. Haven't you ever read any books? Did you ever hear of Edgar Allan Poe? *The Black Cat*, or *Cask of Amontillado*? I guess not, George. You've always been too busy living, haven't you? And Louise was the same way. You believe in action, and you despise people like me. You say we've always got our noses buried in a book, while you're the practical ones, the go-getters. You're proud because you take what you want from life. And you laugh at us. I'll bet you and Louise laughed at me a lot. Now it's my turn."

"You—you can't get away with it!"

"Why not?"

"I'll tell. I'll get the sheriff on you!"

"No you won't. You're an accessory, George. Don't forget, you walled her up. And if you go to the sheriff I'll have my story. I'll tell him we were both in on it together, that I'd promised you half of her insurance. She has quite a lot of insurance, George. I'll tell the sheriff how you walled her up alive, while she writhed and kicked and tried to scream, knowing you were killing her. Not me, George. You!"

He almost rushed me, then. I took the first step forward and at the sight of the Colt he wilted. When I laughed, he put his hands over his ears.

"A pity she didn't listen to you last night, George, when you kept urging her not to wait until I came. You wanted her to drop everything and run away right then and there. You could get a ranger's job in Montana, wasn't that it? And nobody would ever know. Only she had to be practical. She wanted to stick around and draw the money out of the bank first. Wasn't that it?"

"You heard us?"

"Of course. I parked down the road and came up under the window. Then I went back and drove in, the way I always do. You didn't even have time to plan how you two would meet and arrange for your getaway, did you, George? You couldn't even say goodbye properly. Well, do it now. There's a chance in a thousand that she can still hear you."

His eyes were glassy. It wasn't the heat and it wasn't the beer. He was shaking, whimpering.

"Hurry up, George. Tell the lady goodbye. Tell the lovely lady goodbye before she takes her last breath, before she gasps the last gulp of air into her lungs and feels them burn and shrivel. She'll die fast, George, if she isn't dead already. And then she'll crumble. She won't rot, because it's dry in there. There'll be no odor. She'll just mummify. Her limbs will turn to brown leather, and her hair will become brittle and drop out, and her skin will flake and her eyes will finally coagulate in their sockets. But on what's left of her face you'll still be able to see an expression. You'll be able to see how she was at the moment when she died—with that last silent scream for mercy. She's screaming at you now. Can't you hear her? She's screaming, 'George, help me! Get me out of here, get me out of here, get me out—' "

George made a sound deep in his chest. Then he blinked and ran for the stairs. I didn't try to stop him. I let him thud up the steps, listened as he thundered through the kitchen, slammed the door.

It was very quiet in the cellar after that. I put the Colt away in its case, but first I took the precaution of unloading it and wiping off the barrel and the butt.

Then I took the empty bottles and stacked them neatly in the corner.

I finished George's beer and drank my own. And after that, I went upstairs.

There was nothing left to do now but wait.

I must have had two or three more beers while I was waiting. I got them from the big refrigerator in the kitchen and carried them into the front room so that they'd be handy while I read. I picked up my copy of Poe, and not by accident. I wondered if his treatment of the situation was as melodramatic as mine had been. Perhaps not, but then, I had my reasons. In retrospect, what I had said to George seemed a bit silly and overdrawn, but it served a purpose.

After a while, I got absorbed in my reading. Say what you will, Poe had a wonderful imagination, and I can appreciate that.

It was almost dusk when I heard a tapping on the door. I thought of Poe's raven, and put the book aside.

"Come in," I said.

It wasn't Poe's raven, of course.

"Hello, Louise." I smiled up at her. "Did you get everything accomplished?"

"Yes, darling." She sat down, and I noticed just the hint of a frown on her face.

"What's wrong?"

"Nothing. But something odd happened to me on the way back."

"So?"

"I was coming along the County Trunk, just about opposite the Beedsley place, when a state trooper pulled up alongside me."

"Speeding?"

"Of course not, silly. You know I never do over fifty. But he asked for my driver's license, and then he did a funny thing. He made me get out of the car and come over to the motorcycle. And he had me talk into the squawk-box. I think that's what he called it, anyway."

"What on earth for?"

"He didn't tell me. All I know is I had to give my name to the sheriff. And then he said he was sorry to trouble me, but I'd saved him a trip out here for nothing. And he let me go. I asked him what this was all about, and he just shrugged and said there'd been a little misunderstanding but this cleared everything up. Can you figure it out, darling?"

I smiled. "Perhaps," I said. "But maybe we'd better talk about it some other time. I don't want you getting all upset over nothing on our last night here."

"Darling, tell me. I insist!"

"Well, we had a little excitement around here, too," I told her. "Remember George Parker was supposed to come over and put in that cement?"

"Yes, that's right." She hesitated. I watched her. It was pleasant to watch her, to sense the way she was waiting for what I'd say next. If I could have, I'd been willing to prolong that particular moment forever. But finally I let it go.

"Well, he never showed up," I said.

I could almost *feel* the way she sighed with relief.

"So finally I went ahead and did it myself."

"Poor dear. You must be tired."

"You don't understand. That isn't the excitement I was talking about."

"N-no?"

Again I let her wait, savoring the moment. Then I went on, knowing there was a better moment to come. "But along about four, Sheriff Taylor called up, wanting to know where you were. Of course I told him, and I imagine that's why the troopers were out trying to locate you."

"But whatever for?"

"Are you sure you want to hear the rest?"

"Please."

"It's a rather unpleasant situation, apparently. It seems our friend George has suffered some sort of nervous breakdown."

"George?"

"Rather incredible, isn't it? Always seemed like such a stolid, unimaginative fellow, too. You've seen a bit more of him than I did, and I'm sure you wouldn't say he was the sensitive type, would you?"

"Tell me what's wrong, what's happened —"

"If you wish. As I get it, friend George came bursting into the sheriff's office with an utterly fantastic story. At first they thought he'd been drinking, but apparently he was in a state of actual hysteria. It seems he was accusing me of murdering you and walling your body up in the cellar."

"You're joking!"

"That's what the sheriff told George, at first. Until he realized the poor fellow was almost out of his head with fear. Naturally, the sheriff called me and I told him to try and locate you. I'm glad he did. I'd hate to have us involved in any trouble just as we're ready to leave."

I couldn't see her face in the dusk, so I got up and went over to her. She tried to turn away, but I held her and patted her shoulder. "There, there," I murmured. "I didn't want to upset you. Nothing to worry about. It's all over."

"George!" Her voice started to break, but she controlled it. "How is he?"

I sighed. "Stark staring, according to the sheriff. They called Doc Silvers right away. Unless he snaps out of it, he'll be committed. A pity, too — somebody said he was planning to take a ranger's job in Montana."

Louise was shaking, but her voice was firm. "Did he say anything else?"

"No. What more is there to say?"

"Why did he think you'd try to kill me?"

"I haven't the faintest idea. Funny about these strong, silent types. Once their imagination runs away with them, they can't seem to control it. They get keyed up to a certain pitch and then snap, all at once. I'm just glad it didn't happen when he was out here with you. There's no telling what he might have attempted." I laughed. "It may sound far-fetched to you, darling, but he could even have tried to assault you. Can you imagine being made love to by a lunatic?"

She shuddered and buried her head against me.

"Let's talk about something more cheerful," I said. "Here, have a beer."

I could feel her sob.

"Don't cry," I told her. "We're going away tomorrow, remember? Back to town. Just you and I. You needn't worry about George—they'll take care of him. You'll never have to see him again. Why, in a little while you'll forget all about him."

"Y-yes . . ."

"We're going to have a lot of fun together," I murmured. "That's a promise. I've got it all planned."

And I have, of course.

I wasn't lying to her.

I intend to have quite a lot of fun with Louise, tonight. She's in the bedroom right now as I write this, sleeping. I gave her quite a strong sedative, but it will wear off in another half hour or so. Then she'll be wide awake again. And I want her to be wide awake.

I want her to be wide awake when I take her in my arms, and I want her to be wide awake afterwards, when I hold her ever so gently, but ever so firmly, and tell her just what really happened. I want her to know how clever I am, and how strong, and how wise. I want her to know that I'm stronger and wiser than George could ever be.

She must realize the cleverness that brought everything to perfection. She must come to appreciate that I'm the better man after all. And of course I am.

It would have been stupid to confront them both with their guilt; what could I possibly have gained? And it would have been equally stupid for me to kill George and run the risk of discovery. As things worked out, as I *planned* them to work out, George is disposed of forever. I've sealed *him* up behind the walls of a madhouse for life. He'll live on and suffer, thinking Louise is dead and that he killed her. And of course the sheriff and the folks around here know differently. They know she's alive, and that there's nothing behind the cement wall. They'll remember talking to her and to me, and that she was to go away with me. Neither the new owners nor anyone else will ever tear down that wall.

I'm going to make all this very plain to Louise. I'm going to tell her exactly what happened. In fact, that's why I'm writing this. I don't trust myself to find the exact word to convey the meaning of the moment.

I'll let her read what I've written.

Have you read this far, Louise?

Do you understand now? Do you understand what I've done?

And do you understand what I'm going to do, in just another moment?

That's right, Louise.

I'm going to bind and gag you. And I'm going to carry you down into the cellar, and tear the wall open once again. I'm going to thrust you into the darkness and let you scream away your life and your sanity while I wall you up again with fresh cement—wall you up forever, until your body rots to match your rotten soul.

I'll be standing right behind you when you've read this far, so you won't have a chance to scream. And you won't have a chance to beg, or plead, or try any of your stupid feminine tricks with me. Not that they would do any good. No use telling me I'll be caught, either. You know better than that.

The alibi is already set. I'll leave here alone in the morning. And you'll stay here forever.

That's because everything was planned, Louise. Because, you see, I *am* a better man than George. He was only an animal, really. And the difference between an animal and a man is really very simple.

It's all a matter of knowing how to use your imagination.

DEAD-END DOCTOR

THE LAST PSYCHIATRIST ON EARTH sat alone in a room. There was a knock on the door.

"Come in," he said.

A tall robot entered, the electronic beam of its single eye piercing the gloom and focusing on the psychiatrist's face.

"Dr. Anson," the robot said, "the rent is due today. Pay me."

Dr. Howard Anson blinked. He did not like the harsh light, nor the harsh voice, nor the harsh meaning of the message. As he rose, he attempted to conceal his inner reactions with a bland smile, then remembered that his facial expression meant nothing to the robot.

That was precisely the trouble with the damned things, he told himself; you couldn't use psychology on them.

"Sixty tokens," the robot chanted, and rolled across the room toward him.

"But—" Dr. Anson hesitated, then took the plunge. "But I haven't got sixty tokens at the moment. I told the manager yesterday. If you'll only give me a little time, a slight extension of credit—"

"Sixty tokens," the robot repeated, as if totally unmindful of the interruption, which, Dr. Anson assured himself, was exactly the case. The robot was unmindful. It did not react to unpredictable factors; that was not its function. The robot didn't see the rental figures in this office building and had no power to make decisions regarding credit. It was built to collect the rent, nothing more.

But that was enough. More than enough.

The robot rolled closer. Its arms rose and the hooklike terminals slid back the panels in its chest to reveal a row of push buttons and a thin, narrow slot.

"The rent is due," repeated the robot. "Please deposit the tokens in the slot."

Anson sighed. "Very well," he said. He walked over to his desk, opened a drawer and scooped out half a dozen shiny disks.

He slipped the disks into the slot. They landed inside the robot's cylindrical belly with a series of dull plops. Evidently the robot had been making the rounds of the building all day; it sounded more than half full.

For a wild moment, Dr. Anson wondered what would happen if he kidnapped the robot and emptied its cashbox. His own medical specialty was psychiatry and neurosurgery, and he was none too certain of a robot's anatomical structure, but he felt sure he could fool around until he located the jackpot. He visualized himself standing before the operating table, under the bright lights. "Scalpel—forceps—blowtorch—"

But that was unthinkable. Nobody had ever dared to rob a robot. Nobody ever robbed anything or anyone today, which was part of the reason Dr. Anson couldn't pay his rent on time.

Still, he had paid it. The robot's terminals were punching push buttons in its chest and now its mouth opened. "Here is your receipt," it said and a pink slip slid out from its mouth like a paper tongue.

Anson accepted the slip and the mouth said, "Thank you."

The terminals closed the chest panels, the electronic beam swept the corners as the wheels turned, and the robot rolled out of the room and down the corridor.

Anson closed the door and mopped his brow.

So far, so good. But what would happen when the robot reached the manager? He'd open his walking cash register and discover Anson's six ten-token disks. Being human, he'd recognize them for what they were—counterfeit.

Dr. Anson shuddered. To think that it had come to this, a reputable psychiatrist committing a crime!

He considered the irony. In a world totally devoid of antisocial activity, there were no antisocial tendencies which required the services of psychiatry. And that was why he, as the last living psychiatrist, had to resort to antisocial activity in order to survive.

Probably it was only his knowledge of antisocial behavior, in the abstract, which enabled him to depart from the norm and indulge in such actions in the concrete.

Well, he was in the concrete now and it would harden fast—unless something happened. At best, his deception would give him a few days' grace. After that, he could face only disgrace.

Anson shook his head and sat down behind the desk. Maybe this was the beginning, he told himself. First counterfeiting and fraud, then robbery and embezzlement, then rape and murder. Who could say where it would all end?

"Physician, heal thyself," he murmured and glanced with distaste at the dust-covered couch, where no patient reposed; where, indeed, no patient had ever reposed since he'd opened his office almost a year ago.

It had been a mistake, he realized. A big mistake ever to listen to his father and—

The visio lit up and the audio hummed. Anson turned and confronted a gigantic face. The gigantic face let out a gigantic roar, almost shattering the screen.

"I'm on my way up, Doctor!" the face bellowed. "Don't try to sneak out! I'm going to break your neck with my bare hands!"

For a few seconds Anson sat there in his chair, too numb to move. Then the full import of what he had seen and heard reached him. The manager was coming to kill him!

"Hooray!" he said under his breath and smiled. It was almost too good to be true. After all this time, at last, somebody was breaking loose. A badly disturbed personality, a potential killer, was on his way up— he was finally going to get himself a patient. If he could treat him before being murdered, that is.

Tingling with excitement, Anson fumbled around in his files. Now where in thunder was that equipment for the Rorschach test? Yes, and the Porteus Maze and—

The manager strode into the room without knocking. Anson looked up, ready to counter the first blast of aggression with a steely professional stare.

But the manager was smiling.

"Sorry I blew up that way," he said. "Guess I owe you an apology."

"When I found those counterfeit tokens, something just seemed to snap for a moment," the manager explained. "You know how it is."

"Yes, I do," said Anson eagerly. "I understand quite well. And it's nothing to be ashamed of. I'm sure that with your cooperation, we can get to the roots of the trauma. Now if you'll just relax on the couch over there—"

The red-faced little man continued to smile, but his voice was brusque. "Nonsense! I don't need any of that. Before I came up here, I stopped in at Dr. Peabody's office, down on the sixth floor. Great little endocrinologist, that guy. Gave me some kind of a shot that fixed me up in a trice. That's three times faster than a jiffy, you know."

"I don't know," Anson answered vaguely. "Endocrinology isn't my field."

"Well, it should be. It's the only field in medicine that really amounts to anything nowadays. Except for diagnosis and surgery, of course. Those gland-handers can do anything. Shots for when you feel depressed, shots for when you're afraid, shots for when you get excited, or mad, the way I was. Boy, I feel great now. At peace with the world!"

"But it won't last. Sooner or later, you'll get angry again."

"So I'll get another shot," the manager replied. "Everybody does."

"That's not a solution. You're merely treating the symptom, not the basic cause." Anson rose and stepped forward. "You're under a great deal of tension. I suspect it goes back to early childhood. Did you suffer from enuresis?"

"It's my turn to ask questions. What about those fake tokens you tried to palm off on me?"

"Why, it was all a joke. I thought if you could give me a few more days to dig up—"

"I'm giving you just five minutes to dig down," the manager said, smiling pleasantly, but firmly. "You ought to know that you can't pull a trick like that with a cash collector; these new models have automatic tabulators and detectors. The moment that robot came back to my office, it spat up the counterfeits. It couldn't stomach them. And neither can I."

"Stomach?" asked Anson hopefully. "Are you ever troubled with gastric disturbances? Ulcers? Psychosomatic pain in the—"

The manager thrust out his jaw. "Look here, Anson, you're not a bad sort, really. It's just that you're confused. Why don't you clever up and look at the big picture? This witch doctor racket of yours, it's atomized. Nobody's got any use for it today. You're like the guys who used to manufacture buggy whips; they sat around telling themselves that the automobile would never replace the horse, when any street cleaner could see what was happening to business.

"Why don't you admit you're licked? The gland-handers have taken over. Why, a man would have to be crazy to go to a psychiatrist nowadays and you know there aren't any crazy people any more. So forget about all this. Take a course or something. You can be an End-Doc yourself. Then open up a real office and make yourself some big tokens."

Anson shook his head. "Sorry," he said. "Not interested."

The manager spread his hands. "All right. I gave you a chance. Now there's nothing left to do but call in the ejectors."

He walked over and opened the door. Apparently he had been prepared for Anson's decision, because two ejectors were waiting. They rolled into the room and, without bothering to focus their beams on Anson, commenced to scoop books from the shelves and deposit them in their big open belly-hampers.

"Wait!" Anson cried, but the ejector robots continued inexorably and alphabetically: there went Adler, Brill, Carmichael, Dunbar, Ellis, Freud, Gresell, Horney, Isaacs, Jung, Kardiner, Lindner, Moll—

"Darling, what's the matter?"

Sue Porter was in the room. Then she was in his arms and Dr. Anson had a difficult time remembering what the matter was. The girl affected him that way.

But a look at the manager's drugged smile served as a reminder. Anson's face reddened, due to a combination of embarrassment and lipstick smudges, as he told Sue what had happened.

Sue laughed. "Well, if that's all it is, what are you so upset about?" Without waiting for a reply, she advanced upon the manager, her hand digging into her middle bra-cup. "Here's your tokens," she said. "Now call off the ejectors."

The manager accepted the disks with a smile of pure euphoria, then strode over to the robots and punched buttons. The ejectors halted their labors between Reich and Stekel, then reversed operations. Quickly and efficiently, they replaced all the books on the shelves.

In less than a minute, Anson faced the girl in privacy. "You shouldn't have done that," he said severely.

"But darling, I wanted to. After all, what are a few tokens more or less?"

"A few tokens?" Anson scowled. "In the past year, I've borrowed over two thousand from you. This can't go on."

"Of course not," the girl agreed. "That's what I've been telling you. Let's get a Permanent and then Daddy will give you a nice fat job and—"

"There you go again! How often must I warn you about the Elektra situation? This unnatural dependency on the father image is dangerous. If only you'd let me get you down on the couch—"

"Why, of course, darling!"

"No, no!" Anson cried. "I want to analyze you!"

"Not now," Sue answered. "We'll be late for dinner. Daddy expects you."

"Damn dinner and damn Daddy, too," Anson said. But he took the girl's arm and left the office, contenting himself by slamming the door.

"Aren't you going to put up that DOCTOR WILL RETURN IN TWO HOURS sign?" the girl asked, glancing back at the door.

"No," Anson told her. "I'm not coming back in two hours. Or ever."

Sue gave him a puzzled look, but her eyes were smiling.

Dr. Howard Anson's eyes weren't smiling as he and Sue took off from the roof. He kept them closed, so that he didn't have to watch the launching robots, or note the 'copter's progress as it soared above the city. He didn't want to gaze down at the metallic tangle of conveyors moving between the factories or the stiffly striding figures which supervised their progress on the ramps and loading platforms. The air about them was filled with 'copters, homeward bound from offices and recreation areas, but no human figures moved in the streets. Ground level was almost entirely mechanized.

"What's the matter now?" Sue's voice made him look at her. Her eyes held genuine concern.

"The sins of the fathers," Anson said. "Yours and mine." He watched the girl as she set the 'copter on autopilot for the journey across the river. "Of course it really wasn't my father's fault that he steered me into psychiatry. After all, it's been a family tradition for a hundred and fifty years. All my paternal ancestors were psychiatrists, with the exception of one or two renegade Behaviorists. When he encouraged my interest in the profession, I never stopped to question him. He trained me — and I was the last student to take up the specialty at medical school. The last, mind you!

"I should have known then that it was useless. But he kept insisting this state of affairs couldn't last, that things were sure to change. 'Cheer up,' he used to tell me, whenever I got discouraged. 'The pendulum is bound to swing in the other direction.' And then he'd tell me about the good old days when he was a boy and the world was still full of fetishism and hebephrenia and pyromania and mixoscopic zoophilia. 'It will come again,' he kept telling me. 'Just you wait and see! We'll have frottage and nympholepsy and compulsive exhibitionism — everything your little heart desires.'

"Well, he was wrong. He died knowing that he had set me up in a dead-end profession. I'm an anachronism, like the factory worker or the farmer or the miner or the soldier. We don't have any need for them in our society any more; robots have replaced them all. And the End-Docs have replaced the psychiatrists and neurosurgeons. With robots to ease the physical and economic burden and gland-handers to relieve mental tension, there's nothing left for me. The last psychiatrist should have disappeared along with the last advertising man. Come to think of it, they probably belong together. My father was wrong, Sue, I know that now. But most of the real blame belongs to your father."

"Daddy?" she exclaimed. "How can you possibly blame him?"

Anson laughed shortly. "Your family has been pioneering in robotics almost as long as mine has worked in psychiatry. One of your ancestors took out the first basic patent. If it weren't for him and those endocrine shots, everything would still be normal — lots of incest and scoptophilia, plenty of voyeurism for everybody — "

"Why, darling, what a thing to say! You know as well as I do what robots have done for the world. You said it yourself. We don't have any more manual or menial labor. There's no war, plenty of everything for everybody. And Daddy isn't stopping there."

"I suppose not," Anson said bitterly. "What is the old devil dreaming up now?"

Sue flushed. "You wouldn't talk like that if you knew just how hard he's been working. He and Mr. Mullet, the engineering chief. They're just about ready to bring out the new pilot models they've developed for space travel."

"I've heard that one before. They've been announcing those models for ten years."

"They keep running into bugs, I guess. But sooner or later, they'll find a way to handle things. Nothing is perfect, you know. Every once in a while, there's still some trouble with the more complicated models."

"But they keep trying for perfection. Don't you see where all this leads to, Sue? Human beings will become obsolescent. First the workers, now the psychiatrists and other professions. But it won't end there. Inside of another generation or two, we won't need anyone any more. Your father, or somebody like him, will produce the ultimate robot—the robot that's capable of building other robots and directing them. Come to think of it, he's already done the first job; your factories are self-perpetuating. All we need now is a robot that can take the place of a few key figures like your father. Then that's the end of the human race. Oh, maybe they'll keep a few men and women around for pets, but that's all. And thank God I won't be here to see it."

"So why worry?" Sue replied. "Enjoy yourself while you can. We'll apply for a Permanent and Daddy will give you a job like he promised me—"

"Job? What kind of job?"

"Oh, maybe he'll make you a vice-president or something. They don't have to do anything."

"Fine! A wonderful future!"

"I don't see anything wrong with it. You ought to consider yourself lucky."

"Listen, Sue." He turned to her earnestly. "You just don't understand the way I feel. I've spent eighteen years of my life in school, six of it in training for my profession. That's all I know and I know it well. And what have I to show for it? I'm a psychiatrist who's never had a patient, a neurosurgeon who's never performed anything but an experimental topectomy or lobotomy. That's my work, my life, and I want a chance to function. I don't intend to sit around on a fat sinecure, raising children whose only future is oblivion. I don't want a Permanent with you under those conditions."

She sniffed petulantly. "A Permanent with me isn't good enough, is that it? I suppose you'd rather have a lot of repression and guilt complexes and all that other stuff you're always talking about."

"It isn't that," Anson insisted. "I don't really want the world to revert to neurotic or psychotic behavior just so I can have a practice. But damn it, I can't stand to see the way things are going. We've done away with stress and privation and tension and superstition and intolerance, and that's great. But we've also done away with ourselves in the process. We're getting to the point where we, as human beings, no longer have a function to perform. We're not needed."

The girl gave him an angry glance. "What you're trying to say is that you don't need me, is that it?"

"I do need you. But not on these terms. I'm not going to lead a useless existence, or bring children into a world where they'll be useless. And if your father brings up that vice-president deal at dinner tonight, I'm going to tell him to take his job and—"

"Never mind!" Sue flipped the switch from autopilot back to manual and the 'copter turned. "You needn't bother about dinner. I'll take you back to your office now. You can put yourself down on the couch and do a little practicing on your own mind. You need it! Of all the stupid, pig-headed—"

The sound of the crash reached them even at flying level. Sue Porter broke off abruptly and glanced down at the riverfront below. Anson stared with her.

"What was that?" he asked.

"I don't know—can't make it out from here." Sue spun the controls, guiding the 'copter down until it hovered over a scene of accelerating confusion.

A huge loading barge was moored against one of the docks. Had been moored, rather; as they watched, it swung erratically into the current, then banged back against the pier. Huge piles of machinery, only partially lashed to the deck, now tumbled and broke free. Some of the cranes splashed into the water and others rolled across the flat surface of the barge.

"Accident," Sue gasped. "The cable must have broken."

Anson's eyes focused on the metallic figures which dotted the deck and stood solidly on the dock. "Look at the robots!"

"What about them?" asked Sue.

"Aren't they supposed to be doing something? That one with the antenna —isn't it designed to send out a warning signal when something goes wrong?"

"You're right. They beam Emergency in a case like this. The expediters should be out by now."

"Some of them look as if they're paralyzed," Anson noted, observing a half-dozen of the metallic figures aboard the barge. They were rigid, unmoving. Even as he watched, a round steel bell bowled across the deck. None of the robots moved—the sphere struck them like a ball hitting the pins and hurtled them into the water.

On the pier, the immobilized watchers gave no indication of reaction.

"Paralyzed," Anson repeated.

"Not that one!"

Sue pointed excitedly as the 'copter hovered over the deck. Anson looked and found the cause of her consternation.

A large, fully articulated robot with the humanoid face of a controller clattered along in a silvery blur of motion. From one of its four upper appendages dangled a broad-bladed axe.

It bumped squarely against an armless receptacle-type robot in its loading compartment. There was crash as the victim collapsed.

And the controller robot sped on, striking at random, in a series of sped-up motions almost impossible to follow—but not impossible to understand.

"That's the answer!" said Anson. "It must have cut the cable with the axe. And attacked the others, to immobilize them. Come on, let's land this thing."

"But we can't go down there! It's dangerous! Somebody will send out the alarm. The expediters will handle it—"

"Land!" Anson commanded. He began to rummage around in the rear compartment of the 'copter.

"What are you looking for?" Sue asked as she maneuvered the machine to a clear space alongside a shed next to the dock.

"The rope ladder."

"But we won't need it. We're on the ground."

"I need it." He produced the tangled length and began to uncoil it. "You stay here," he said. "This is my job."

"What are you going to do?"

"Yes, what are you going to do?" The deep voice came from the side of the 'copter. Anson and Sue looked up at the face of Eldon Porter.

"Daddy! How did you get here?"

"Alarm came through."

The big, gray-haired man scowled at the dock beyond where the expediter robots were already mopping up with flamethrowers.

"You've got no business here," Eldon Porter said harshly. "This area's off limits until everything's under control." He turned to Anson. "And I'll have to ask you to forget everything you've seen here. We don't want word of accidents like this to leak out—just get people needlessly upset."

"Then this isn't the first time?" asked Anson.

"Of course not. Mullet's had a lot of experience; he knows how to handle this."

"Right, Chief." Anson recognized the thin, bespectacled engineer at Eldon Porter's side. "Every time we test out one of these advanced models, something goes haywire. Shock, overload, some damned thing. Only thing we can do is scrap it and try again. So you folks keep out of the way. We're going to corner it with the flamethrowers and—"

"No!"

Anson opened the door and climbed out, dragging the long rope ladder behind him.

"Where in hell do you think you're going?" demanded Eldon Porter.

"I'm after that robot," Anson said. "Give me two of your men to hold the ends of this ladder. We can use it like a net and capture the thing without destroying it. That is, put it in restraint."

"Restraint?"

"Technical term we psychiatrists use." Anson smiled at the two men and then at the girl. "Don't worry," he said. "I know what I'm doing. I've got a case at last. Your robot is psychotic."

"Psychotic," grumbled Eldon Porter, watching the young man move away. "What's that mean?"

"Nuts," said Sue sweetly. "A technical term."

Several weeks passed before Sue saw Dr. Howard Anson again.

She waited anxiously outside in the corridor with her father until the young man emerged. He peeled off his gloves, smiling.

"Well?" rumbled Eldon Porter.

"Ask Mullet," Anson suggested.

"He did it!" the thin engineer exulted. "It works, just like he said it would! Now we can use the technique wherever there's a breakdown. But I don't think we'll have any more. Not if we incorporate his suggestions in the new designs. We can use them on the new space pilot models, too."

"Wonderful!" Eldon Porter said. He put his hand on Anson's shoulder. "We owe you a lot."

"Mullet deserves the credit," Anson replied. "If not for him and his schematics, I'd never have made it. He worked with me night and day, feeding me the information. We correlated everything—you know, I'd never realized how closely your engineers had followed the human motor-reaction patterns."

Eldon Porter cleared his throat. "About that job," he began. "That vice-presidency—"

"Of course," Anson said. "I'll take it. There's going to be a lot of work to do. I want to train at least a dozen men to handle emergencies until the new models take over. I understand you've had plenty of cases like this in the past."

"Right. And we've always ended up by junking the robots that went haywire. Hushed it up, of course, so people wouldn't worry. Now we're all set. We can duplicate the electronic patterns of the human brain without worrying about breakdowns due to speed-up or overload. Why didn't we think of the psychiatric approach ourselves?"

"Leave that to me," Anson said. And as the two men moved off, he made a psychiatric approach toward the girl.

She finally stepped back out of his arms. "You owe me an explanation. What's the big idea? You're taking the job, after all!"

"I've found I can be useful," Anson told her. "There is a place for my profession—a big one. Human beings no longer go berserk, but robots do."

"Is that what this is all about? Have you been psychoanalyzing that robot you caught?"

Anson smiled. "I'm afraid psychoanalysis isn't suitable for robots. The trouble is purely mechanical. But the brain is a mechanism, too. The more I worked with Mullet, the more I learned about the similarities."

"You cured that robot in there?" she asked incredulously.

"That's right." Anson slipped out of his white gown. "It's as good as new, ready to go back on the job at once. Of course it will have slower, less intense reactions, but its judgment hasn't been impaired. Neurosurgery did the trick. That's the answer, Sue. Once you open them up, you can see the cure's the same."

"So that's why you were wearing a surgical gown," she said. "You were operating on the robot."

Anson grinned triumphantly. "The robot was excited, in a state of hysteria. I merely applied my knowledge and skill to the problem."

"But what kind of an operation?"

"I opened up the skull and eased the pressure on the overload wires. There used to be a name for it, but now there's a new one." Anson took her back into his arms. "Darling, congratulate me! I've just successfully performed the first prefrontal robotomy!"

TERROR IN THE NIGHT

IT MUST HAVE BEEN ABOUT two o'clock when Barbara started shaking me.

She kept saying "Wake up!" over and over again, and tugging at my shoulder. Since I'm generally a pretty sound sleeper, it took me almost a minute to come to.

Then I noticed she had the lights on and she was sitting up in her bed.

"What's the matter?" I asked.

"There's somebody downstairs, pounding on the door. Can't you hear?"

I listened and I heard. It certainly sounded like the door was getting a workout.

"Who the devil would be showing up here at this hour?" I asked.

"Get up and find out," Barbara told me. Which was a sensible suggestion.

So I walked over to the window and looked down. Sure enough, I could see someone standing down there, but in the shadows it was hard to make out any details. I got the funniest notion that whoever it was, was wearing a white sheet.

Now the doorbell began to ring, insistently.

Barbara said, "Well?"

"I don't know," I told her. "Can't make out anything from up here. You stay where you are. I'll go down and see"

I went out of the bedroom and almost tripped on the stairs, because I forgot about turning on the light. I still wasn't used to staying here in the summer place.

Of course I remembered where the hall light was, and when I got down there I switched it on. All the while the doorbell kept ringing.

Then I opened the door.

There was a woman standing on the porch. She wasn't wearing a sheet, but she had on the next thing to it — some kind of long white nightgown. Not lingerie, but a real old-fashioned nightgown that came way down to her ankles. Or used to. Now it was torn and there were stains on it; dirt or grease. Her hair hung down over her eyes and she was crying or panting, or both. For a minute I didn't recognize her, and then she said, "Bob!"

"Marjorie! Come in."

I turned my head and called up to Barbara, "Come on down, honey. It's Marjorie Kingston."

There wasn't time to say anything more. Marjorie was off the porch in nothing flat, and she hung onto me as if she were afraid of drowning. Her head was right against my chest, so that I could feel her shaking, and all the while she kept mumbling something I couldn't make out. At last I got it.

She was saying, "Shut the door, please. Shut the door!"

I closed the door and steered her into the front room. I turned on one of the lamps, and she looked at me and said, "Pull the shades, Bob."

She'd stopped crying and her breathing was a little more relaxed by the time Barbara came downstairs.

Barbara didn't say anything. She just walked over to Marjorie and put her arms around her, and that was the signal for her to really let go.

I finished pulling the shades and then ducked out to the kitchen. I couldn't find any soda, but when I came back I had three glasses and the bottle of Scotch I'd bought when I went into town on Monday.

The two of them were sitting on the sofa now, and Marjorie had calmed down a little. I didn't ask if anyone wanted a drink, just poured three stiff slugs. I gave Marjorie her glass first, and she put the shot down like water.

Barbara took a sip as I sat down in the armchair, and then she looked at Marjorie and said, "What happened?"

"I ran away."

"Ran away?"

Marjorie brushed the hair out of her eyes and looked straight at her. "Oh, you needn't worry about pretending. You must have heard where I've been. At the asylum."

Barbara gave me a look but I didn't say anything. I remembered the day I bumped into Freddie Kingston at lunch in town and he told me about Marjorie. Said she'd had a nervous breakdown at school and they were sending her up to this private sanatorium at Elkdale. That must have been about three months ago. I hadn't see him since to get any further details.

I stood up. Marjorie sucked in her breath. "What's the matter?" I asked.

"Don't go," she said. "Don't call anyone. Please, Bob. I'm begging you."

"How about Freddie? Shouldn't he know?"

"Not Freddie. Not anybody, but most of all not Freddie. You don't understand, do you?"

"Suppose you tell us," Barbara suggested.

"All right." Marjorie held out her glass. "Can I have another drink, first?" I poured for her. When she lifted the glass up I could see her fingers. The nails had been bitten all the way down.

She drank, and then all at once she was talking, even before she took the glass away from her lips.

"You see, it wouldn't do any good to tell Freddie, because he sent me there in the first place and he must have known what it was like. He has this Mona Lester, and he thought they'd kill me and then he'd be free. I had plenty of time to figure things out and I can see that now. I mean, it makes sense, doesn't it?"

I tried to catch Barbara's eye but she wasn't looking at me. She kept staring at Marjorie. And then she said, very softly, "We heard you had a nervous breakdown, dear."

Marjorie nodded. "Oh, that part's true enough. It's been coming on for a long time, only nobody knew it. That's my fault, really. I was too proud to tell anyone. About Freddie, I mean."

"What about Freddie?"

"Freddie and this Mona Lester. She's a model. He met her last year, down at the studio. They've been living together ever since. When I found out, he just laughed. He said he wanted a divorce and he'd furnish me with all the evidence I needed. Glad to. But of course I don't believe in divorce. I tried everything—I argued with him, I pleaded with him, I went down on my hands and knees to him. Nothing did any good.

"He started to stay away night after night, and weekends, too. Then he'd come back and tell me about what he'd been doing with Mona, in detail, everything. You can't imagine the things he said, and the way he'd watch me while he told me. And he used to watch me at parties, too, when we had to go out together. He said he got a kick out of seeing me pretend that everything was all right. Because nobody knew about Mona. You didn't, did you? Freddie was too smart for that. Even then he must have been planning the whole thing. Yes, I know he must, because I remember now what he said that one time—if I didn't divorce him he'd keep on until I went crazy and then he could do what he pleased." She paused for breath.

Barbara bit her lip. "Are you sure you want to talk about this?" she asked. "You mustn't get excited. . . ."

Marjorie made a sound. It took me a second to realize she was laughing, or trying to laugh. "Quit talking like a doctor," she said. "You don't have to humor me. I'm not crazy and I'm not psychotic. That's the word the doctors use, you know. Psychotic. Or when they talk to the relatives they say, 'mentally disturbed.' It isn't that way with me at all. When I broke down in class that day—English IV, my last afternoon class—it was just nerves. I had hysterics. God knows what the pupils thought. The principal had to come in and quiet me down. They sent me home and gave me a sedative, and the doctor came and he left some pills. Then Freddie came. He doped me up. I mean it. I was supposed to take two pills at the most. He gave me six. He kept on feeding me the stuff, all through the next week. When the other doctor came, and when he took me to see Corbel, and when we went to court. I was shot. By the time I came to, I was committed. He'd gotten the papers signed and everything. And I woke up in Corbel's little private asylum."

I didn't look at her. I couldn't. She went on talking, louder and louder.

"That was three months ago. I've kept track of the days. The hours, even. What else was there to do? Freddie has never come to see me. And nobody else has come, either. He has it fixed with Corbel not to let them. I tried to write, until I realized the letters weren't being mailed. And if I got any letters, Corbel saw to it they weren't allowed to reach me. That's the way he runs the place. That's why they pay him so much—to keep anyone from getting in, to keep anyone from getting out. It must be costing Freddie a fortune to have me there, but it's worth it to him. And to the others."

"What others?" Barbara asked.

"The other relatives. Of the other patients, I mean. Most of them are wealthy, you know. We've got some alcoholics and some drug addicts out there, but I wouldn't say any of them were really mental cases. At least they weren't when they arrived. But Corbel does his best to drive them crazy. You can have all the liquor and shots you want. He calls it therapy. What he's really trying to do is kill them off as fast as he can. Maybe he gets an extra fee that way. He must. Particularly with the old people. The sooner they die, the sooner the relatives inherit."

"This Corbel," I said. "He's a psychiatrist?"

"He's a murderer!" Marjorie leaned forward. "Go ahead, laugh at me— it's true! I can hear. I stay awake all night and listen. I heard him and Leo beating old Mr. Scheinfarber to death two weeks ago in the hydrotherapy room. They never use it for hydrotherapy at all, you know. But when he was done screaming they dumped his body in the water and left him there. The next morning they said he'd been taking a treatment and slipped under— committed suicide. Corbel signed the certificate. I know what's going on! Poor old Mr. Scheinfarber, who only wanted to be left alone. . . . And now that sneaky son and daughter-in-law of his get all the money. Leo almost admitted as much to me."

"Who is Leo?" Barbara asked.

"One of the orderlies. Leo and Hugo. Leo's the worst; he's on night duty. He was after me from the beginning."

"What for?"

"Can't you guess?" Marjorie made that laughing sound again. "He's after most of the women patients there. Once he locked Mrs. Matthews in isolation and stayed with her for two days. She couldn't dare do anything about it; he said he'd see to it she starved to death if she wouldn't let him."

"I see," I said.

Marjorie looked at me. "You don't see. You think I'm lying to you. I can tell. But it's all true. I can prove it. That's why I ran away—to prove it. I want to get to the police. Not the sheriff or anyone around here; I think they're in cahoots with Corbel. Otherwise, how would he be able to fix things with the coroner and everyone so there isn't any fuss? But when I get to town maybe somebody will listen. We could force an investigation. That's all I want, Bob. Really it is. I don't even want to punish Freddie. I'm past that stage. I just want to help those people, those poor, hopeless people stuck away to rot and die. . . ."

Barbara reached over and patted her on the shoulder. "It's all right," she said. "It's all right. We believe you, don't we, Bob?"

"I know what it sounds like," Marjorie said, and she was calmer now. "You tell yourself such things can't happen in this day and age. And you see Doctor Corbel in town and he's such a kind, brilliant man. You go for a drive past the sanatorium and look at the building up on the hill, in among all those trees—you think it's a beautiful place, a wonderful rest home for those who can afford it. You don't notice the bars, and you never get inside the soundproof part where you could hear the screams and the moans, or see the stains on the floor in isolation. The stains that won't wash off, the stains that never wash off—"

"Another drink?" I interrupted. I didn't want to give her another drink, but I had to stop her someway.

"No thanks. I'm all right now, really I am. You'll see. It's just all this running—"

"You need rest," Barbara nodded. "A good night's sleep before we decide anything."

"There's nothing to decide," Marjorie said. "I've made up my mind. I want you to drive me into the city tonight so that I can make a statement right away. I don't care if they believe me or not, just so they come out and investigate. Once they get inside, they'll find proof. I'll show them. All I'm asking you to do is drive me."

"I can't," I said. "The car's in the garage but the battery's out of whack. I'm having the garage man out to fix it in the morning."

"It may be too late then," Marjorie said. "They'll cover things up once they realize I'm liable to go to the authorities."

I took a deep breath. "How did you manage to get away?" I asked her.

Marjorie put her hands down in her lap and looked at them. Her voice was very low.

"For a long while I didn't even think about escaping. Everyone said it was impossible, and besides, even if I did, where could I go? Certainly not to

Freddie or the local police. And how could I get to town safely without any money? Then I happened to remember that you folks had this summer place, and you'd be up here. It isn't too far from Elkdale. All I needed was a good start. So I knew the thing to do, then.

"I told you about this Leo, the night orderly — the one who was always after me? I kept fighting him off all the time; I'd never take sleeping pills or even doze off while he was on duty.

"Well, tonight Leo was drinking a little. I heard him coming around in the hall, and I asked him in. I even took a drink from him, just to get him started again. He had quite a few. And then . . . I let him."

She didn't say anything for almost a minute. Barbara and I waited.

"After he fell asleep, I got his keys. The rest was easy. At first I couldn't get my bearings, but then I remembered the creek running next to the highway. I kept close to the creek and waded in it at first. That was to throw them off the scent."

"Throw *who* off the scent?" Barbara asked.

Marjorie's eyes widened. "The bloodhounds."

"What?"

"Didn't you know? Corbel keeps bloodhounds out there. To track down the patients, in case they ever escape."

I stood up.

"Where are you going?"

"To fix your bed," I said.

"I won't sleep," Marjorie told me. "I can't. What if Leo woke up? What if he got Corbel and they called out the bloodhounds to look for me?"

"Don't you worry about a thing," I answered. "No bloodhounds can get in here. We won't let anyone harm you, Marjorie. You're overtired. You've got to rest and forget about — "

"The asylum! You're going to call Corbel!"

"Marjorie, please try — "

"I knew it! I knew it when you stood up, from the look on your face! You're going to send me back; you're going to let them kill me!"

She jumped up. Barbara reached for her and I started forward, but not in time. She hit Barbara in the face and ran. I tried to head her off from the hall, but she got there first and tugged the front door open. Then she was running, jumping off the porch and circling through the trees in back. I could see her white nightgown waving behind her. I called, but she didn't answer.

If the car had been working, I would have tried to follow her. But even so, there wouldn't have been much chance of catching up, because she wouldn't stick to the roads.

After a couple of minutes, I went back into the house and closed the door. Barbara took the glasses into the kitchen, but she didn't say anything, not even when we went upstairs. It wasn't until we switched off the light and settled down in bed that she spoke to me.

"Poor Marjorie," Barbara said. "I felt so sorry for her."

"Me, too."

"You know, for a while she almost had me believing her. Sometimes those crazy stories turn out to be true after all."

I grunted. "I know. But all that medieval stuff about killing patients in asylums—that's just delusions of persecution."

"Are you sure, Bob?"

"Of course I'm sure. I admit I had my doubts for a while, too. But you know what tipped the scales?"

"What?"

"When she got to that part about the bloodhounds. That did it for me. Only a nut would dream up an idea like that."

"It bothers me, though. Don't you think we ought to call the sheriff after all? Or this Doctor Corbel, or Freddie?"

"Why get mixed up in it?" I asked. "I mean, look at the mess we'd get into."

"But the poor girl, running around out there all alone . . ."

"Don't worry, they'll get her. And she'll be taken care of."

"I can't help thinking about what she said, though. Do you think the part about this Leo was true?"

"I told you, it's delusions of persecution, Barbara. The whole works; about Freddie and his woman, about the killings—everything. Now just forget it."

She was quiet for a minute and I was quiet for a minute, and then we heard the noise. Faint and far away it was, but I recognized it.

"What's that?" Barbara asked.

I sat up in bed, listening to it, listening to it get closer and closer. I was still listening to it when it faded off in the distance again.

"What's that?" Barbara asked, again.

"Oh, just some damned dogs on the loose," I told her. "Lots of strays out here, you know."

But I was lying.

I'm a Southerner, born and bred, and if there's one thing I can recognize, it's the sound of bloodhounds. Bloodhounds, unleashed and on the scent.

ALL ON A GOLDEN AFTERNOON

1

THE UNIFORMED MAN at the gate was very polite, but he didn't seem at all in a hurry to open up. Neither Dr. Prager's new Cadillac nor his old goatee made much of an impression on him.

It wasn't until Dr. Prager snapped, "But I've an appointment—Mr. Dennis said it was urgent!" that the uniformed man turned and went into the little guard booth to call the big house on the hill.

Dr. Saul Prager tried not to betray his impatience, but his right foot pressed down on the accelerator and a surrogate of exhaust did his fuming for him.

Just how far he might have gone in polluting the air of Bel Air couldn't be determined, for after a moment the man came out of the booth and unlocked the gate. He touched his cap and smiled.

"Sorry to keep you waiting, Doctor," he said. "You're to go right up."

Dr. Prager nodded curtly and the car moved forward.

"I'm new on this job and you got to take precautions, you know," the man called after him, but Dr. Prager wasn't listening. His eyes were fixed on the panorama of the hillside ahead. In spite of himself he was mightily impressed.

There was reason to be—almost half a million dollars' worth of reason. The combined efforts of a dozen architects, topiarists, and landscape gardeners had served to create what was popularly known as "the Garden of Eden." Although the phrase was a complimentary reference to Eve Eden, owner of the estate, there was much to commend it, Dr. Prager decided.

That is, if one can picture a Garden of Eden boasting two swimming pools, an eight-car garage, and a corps of resident angels with power mowers.

This was by no means Dr. Prager's first visit, but he never failed to be moved by the spectacle of the palace on the hill. It was a fitting residence for Eve, the First Woman. The First Woman of the Ten Box-Office Leaders, that is.

The front door was already open when he parked in the driveway, and the butler smiled and bowed. He was, Dr. Prager knew, a genuine English butler, complete with accent and sideburns. Eve Eden had insisted on that, and she'd had one devil of a time obtaining an authentic specimen from the employment agencies. Finally she'd managed to locate one—from Central Casting.

"Good afternoon," the butler greeted him. "Mr. Dennis is in the library, sir. He is expecting you."

Dr. Prager followed the manservant through the foyer and down the hall. Everything was furnished with magnificent taste—as Mickey Dennis often observed, "Why not? Didn't we hire the best inferior decorator in Beverly Hills?"

The library itself was a remarkable example of calculated decor. Replete with the traditional overstuffed chairs, custom-made by a firm of reliable overstuffers, it boasted paneled walnut walls, polished mahogany floors, and a good quarter mile of bookshelves rising to the vaulted ceiling. Dr. Prager's glance swept the shelves, which were badly in need of dusting anyway. He noted a yard of Thackeray in green, two yards of brown Thomas Hardy, complemented by a delicate blue Dostoevski. Ten feet of Balzac, five feet of Dickens, a section of Shakespeare, a mass of Molière. Complete works, of course. The booksellers would naturally want to give Eve Eden the works. There must have been two thousand volumes on the shelves.

In the midst of it all sat Mickey Dennis, the agent, reading a smudged and dog-eared copy of *Variety*.

As Dr. Prager stood, hesitant, in the doorway, the little man rose and beckoned to him. "Hey, Doc!" he called. "I been waiting for you!"

"Sorry," Dr. Prager murmured. "There were several appointments I couldn't cancel."

"Never mind the appointments. You're on retainer with us, ain'cha? Well, sweetheart, this time you're really gonna earn it."

He shook his head as he approached. "Talk about trouble," he muttered —although Dr. Prager had not even mentioned the subject. "Talk about trouble, we got it. I ain't dared call the studio yet. If I did there'd be wigs floating all over Beverly Hills. Had to see you first. And you got to see *her*."

Dr. Prager waited. A good fifty percent of his professional duties consisted of waiting. Meanwhile he indulged in a little private speculation. What would it be this time? Another overdose of sleeping pills—a return to narcotics—an attempt to prove the old maxim that absinthe makes the heart grow fonder? He'd handled Eve Eden before in all these situations and topped it off with more routine assignments, such as the time she'd wanted to run off with the Japanese chauffeur. Come to think of it, that hadn't been exactly routine. Handling Eve was bad; handling the chauffeur was worse, but handling the chauffeur's wife and seven children was a nightmare. Still, he'd smoothed things over. He always smoothed things over, and that's why he was on a fat yearly retainer.

Dr. Prager, as a physician, generally disapproved of obesity, but when it came to yearly retainers he liked them plump. And this was one of the plumpest. Because of it he was ready for any announcement Mickey Dennis wanted to make.

The agent was clutching his arm now. "Doc, you gotta put the freeze on her, fast! This time it's murder!"

Despite himself, Dr. Prager blanched. He reached up and tugged reassuringly at his goatee. It was still there, the symbol of his authority. He had mastered the constriction in his vocal chords before he started to speak. "You mean she's killed someone?"

"No!" Mickey Dennis shook his head in disgust. "*That* would be bad enough, but we could handle it. I was just using a figger of speech, like. She wants to murder herself, Doc. Murder her career, to throw away a brand-new seven-year noncancelable no-option contract with a percentage of the gross. She wants to quit the industry."

"Leave pictures?"

"Now you got it, Doc. She's gonna walk out on four hundred grand a year."

There was real anguish in the agent's voice—the anguish of a man who is well aware that ten percent of four hundred thousand can buy a lot of convertibles.

"You gotta see her," Dennis moaned. "You gotta talk her out of it, fast."

Dr. Prager nodded. "Why does she want to quit?" he asked.

Mickey Dennis raised his hands. "I don't know," he wailed. "She won't give any reasons. Last night she just up and told me. Said she was through. And when I asked her politely just what the hell's the big idea, she dummied up. Said I wouldn't understand." The little man made a sound like trousers ripping in a tragic spot. "Damned right I wouldn't understand! But I want to find out."

Dr. Prager consulted his beard again with careful fingers. "I haven't seen her for over two months," he said. "How has she been behaving lately? I mean, otherwise?"

"Like a doll," the agent declared. "Just a living doll. To look at her you wouldn't of thought there was anything in her head but sawdust. Wrapped up the last picture clean, brought it in three days ahead of schedule. No blowups, no goofs, no nothing. She hasn't been hitting the sauce or anything else. Stays home mostly and goes to bed early. Alone, yet." Mickey Dennis made the pants-ripping sound again. "I might of figgered it was too good to be true."

"No financial worries?" Dr. Prager probed.

Dennis swept his arm forward to indicate the library and the expanse beyond. "With *this*? All clear and paid for. Plus a hunk of real estate in Long Beach and two oil wells gushing like Lolly Parsons over a hot scoop. She's got more loot than Fort Knox and almost as much as Crosby."

"Er—how old is Eve, might I ask?"

"You might ask, and you might get some funny answers. But I happen to know. She's thirty-three. I can guess what you're thinking, Doc, and it don't figger. She's good for another seven years, maybe more. Hell, all you got to do is look at her."

"That's just what I intend to do," Dr. Prager replied. "Where is she?"

"Upstairs, in her room. Been there all day. Won't see me." Mickey Dennis hesitated. "She doesn't know you're here either. I said I was gonna call you and she got kinda upset."

"Didn't want to see me, eh?"

"She said if that long-eared nanny goat got within six miles of this joint she'd—" The agent paused and shifted uncomfortably. "Like I mentioned, she was upset."

"I think I can handle the situation," Dr. Prager decided.

"Want me to come along and maybe try and soften her up a little?"

"That won't be necessary." Dr. Prager left the room, walking softly.

Mickey Dennis went back to his chair and picked up the magazine once more. He didn't read, because he was waiting for the sound of the explosion.

When it came he shuddered and almost gritted his teeth until he remembered how much it would cost to buy a new upper plate. Surprisingly enough, the sound of oaths and shrieks subsided after a time, and Dennis breathed a deep sigh of relief.

The doc was a good headshrinker. He'd handle her. He was handling her. So there was nothing to do now but relax.

2

"Relax," Dr. Prager said. "You've discharged all your aggression. Now you can stretch out. That's better."

The spectacle of Eve Eden stretched out in relaxation on a chaise longue was indeed better. In the words of many eminent lupine Hollywood authorities, it was the best.

Eve Eden's legs were long and white and her hair was long and blonde; both were now displayed to perfection, together with a whole series of coming attractions screened through her semitransparent lounging pajamas. The face that launched a thousand close-ups was that of a petulant child, well-versed in the more statutory phases of juvenile delinquency.

Dr. Prager could cling to his professional objectivity only by clinging to his goatee. As it was, he dislodged several loose hairs and an equal number of loose impulses before he spoke again.

"Now," he said, "tell me all about it."

"Why should I?" Eve Eden's eyes and voice were equally candid. "I didn't ask you to come here. I'm not in any jam."

"Mr. Dennis said you're thinking of leaving pictures."

"Mr. Dennis is a cockeyed liar. I'm not thinking of leaving. I've left, period. Didn't he call the lawyers? Hasn't he phoned the studio? I told him to."

"I wouldn't know," Dr. Prager soothed.

"Then he's the one who's in a jam," Eve Eden announced happily. "Sure, I know why he called you. You're supposed to talk me out of it, right? Well, it's no dice, Doc. I made up my mind."

"Why?"

"None of your business."

Dr. Prager leaned forward. "But it is my business, Wilma."

"Wilma?"

Dr. Prager nodded, his voice softening. "Wilma Kozmowski. Little Wilma Kozmowski. Have you forgotten that I know all about her? The little girl whose mother deserted her. Who ran away from home when she was twelve and lived around. I know about the waitress jobs in Pittsburgh, and the burlesque show, and the B-girl years in Calumet City. And I know about Frank, and Eddie, and Nino, and Sid, and—all the others." Dr. Prager smiled. "You told me all this yourself, Wilma. And you told me all about what happened after you became Eve Eden. When you met me you weren't Eve Eden yet, not entirely. Wilma kept interfering, didn't she? It was Wilma who drank, took the drugs, got mixed up with the men, tried to kill herself. I helped you fight Wilma, didn't I, Eve? I helped you *become* Eve Eden, the movie star. That's why it's my business now to see that you stay that way. Beautiful, admired, successful, happy—"

"You're wrong, Doc. I found that out. If you want me to be happy, forget about Eve Eden. Forget about Wilma, too. From now on I'm going to be somebody else. So please, just go away."

"Somebody else?" Dr. Prager leaped at the phrase. An instant later he leaped literally.

"What's that?" he gasped.

He stared down at the floor, the hairs in his goatee bristling as he caught sight of the small white furry object that scuttled across the carpet.

Eve Eden reached down and scooped up the creature, smiling.

"Just a white rabbit," she explained. "Cute, isn't he? I bought him the other day."

"But—but—"

Dr. Prager goggled. It was indeed a white rabbit which Eve Eden cradled in her arms, but not *just* a white rabbit. For this rabbit happened to be wearing a vest and a checkered waistcoat, and Dr. Prager could almost swear that the silver chain across the vest terminated in a concealed pocket watch.

"I bought it after the dream," Eve Eden told him.

"Dream?"

"Oh, what's the use?" She sighed. "I might as well let you hear it. All you headshrinkers are queer for dreams anyway."

"You had a dream about rabbits?" Dr. Prager began.

"Please, Doc, let's do it my way," she answered. "This time *you* relax and I'll do the talking. It all started when I fell down this rabbit hole. . . ."

3

In her dream, Eve Eden said, she was a little girl with long golden curls. She was sitting on a riverbank when she saw this white rabbit running close by. It was wearing the waistcoat and a high collar, and then it took a watch out of its pocket, muttering, "Oh dear, I shall be too late." She ran across the field after it, and when it popped down a large rabbit hole under a hedge, she followed.

"Oh no!" Dr. Prager muttered. "Not *Alice*!"

"Alice who?" Eve Eden inquired.

"Alice in Wonderland."

"You mean that movie Disney made, the cartoon thing?"

Dr. Prager nodded. "You saw it?"

"No. I never waste time on cartoons."

"But you know what I'm talking about, don't you?"

"Well—" Eve Eden hesitated. Then from the depths of her professional background an answer came. "Wasn't there another movie, way back around the beginning of the Thirties? Sure, Paramount made it, with Oakie and Gallagher and Horton and Ruggles and Ned Sparks and Fields and Gary Cooper. And let's see now, who played the dame—Charlotte Henry?"

Dr. Prager smiled. *Now* he was getting somewhere. "So that's the one you saw, eh?"

Eve Eden shook her head. "Never saw that one either. Couldn't afford movies when I was a brat, remember?"

"Then how do you know the cast and—"

"Easy. Gal who used to work with Alison Skipworth told me. She was in it too. And Edna May Oliver. I got a good memory, Doc. You know that."

"Yes." Dr. Prager breathed softly. "And so you must remember reading the original book, isn't that it?"

"Was it a book?"

"Now look here, don't tell me you've never read ALICE IN WONDERLAND, by Lewis Carroll. It's a classic."

"I'm no reader, Doc. You know that too."

"But surely as child you must have come across it. Or had somebody tell you the story."

The blonde curls tossed. "Nope. I'd remember if I had. I remember everything I read. That's why I'm always up on my lines. Best sight reader in the business. I not only haven't read ALICE IN WONDERLAND, I didn't even know there was such a story, except in a screenplay."

Dr. Prager gave an irritable tug at his goatee. "All right. You *do* have a remarkable memory, I know. So let's think back now. Let's think back very carefully to your earliest childhood. Somebody must have taken you on their lap, told you stories."

The star's eyes brightened. "Why, sure!" she exclaimed. "That's right! Aunt Emma was always telling me stories."

"Excellent." Dr. Prager smiled. "And can you recall now the first story she ever told you? The very first?"

Eve Eden closed her eyes, concentrating with effort. When her voice came it was from far away. "Yes," she whispered. "I remember now. I was only four. Aunt Emma took me on her lap and she told me my first story. It was the one about the drunk who goes in this bar, and he can't find the john, see, so the bartender tells him to go upstairs and—"

"No," said Dr. Prager. "No, no! Didn't she ever tell you any fairy tales?"

"Aunt Emma?" Eve Eden laughed. "I'll say she didn't. But stories—she had a million of 'em! Did you ever hear the one about the young married couple who wanted to—"

"Never mind." The psychiatrist leaned back. "You are quite positive you have never read or heard or seen ALICE IN WONDERLAND?"

"I told you so in the first place, didn't I? Now, do you want to hear my dream or not?"

"I want to very much," Dr. Prager answered, and he did. He took out his notebook and uncapped his fountain pen. In his own mind he was quite certain that she had heard or read ALICE, and he was interested in the reasons for the mental block which prevented her from recalling the fact. He was also interested in the possible symbolism behind her account. This promised to be quite an enjoyable session. "You went down the rabbit hole," he prompted.

"Into a tunnel," Eve continued. "I was falling, falling very slowly."

Dr. Prager wrote down *tunnel—womb fixation?* And he wrote down *falling dream.*

"I fell into a well," Eve said. "Lined with cupboards and bookshelves. There were maps and pictures on pegs."

Forbidden sex knowledge, Dr. Prager wrote.

"I reached out while I was still falling and took a jar from a shelf. The jar was labeled 'Orange Marmalade.'"

Marmalade—Mama? Dr. Prager wrote.

Eve said something about "Do cats eat bats?" and "Do bats eat cats?" but Dr. Prager missed it. He was too busy writing. It was amazing, now that he thought of it, just how much Freudian symbolism was packed into ALICE IN WONDERLAND. Amazing, too, how well her subconscious recalled it.

Eve was now telling how she had landed in the long hall with the doors all around and how the rabbit disappeared, muttering, "Oh, my ears and whiskers, how late it's getting." She told about approaching the three-legged solid-glass table with the tiny golden key on it, and Dr. Prager quickly scribbled *phallic symbol*. Then she described looking through a fifteen-inch door into a garden beyond and wishing she could get through it by shutting up like a telescope. So Dr. Prager wrote *phallic envy*.

"Then," Eve continued, "I saw this little bottle on the table, labeled 'Drink Me.' And so I drank, and do you know something? I did shut up like a telescope. I got smaller and smaller, and if I hadn't stopped drinking I'd have disappeared! So of course I couldn't reach the key, but then I saw this glass box under the table labeled 'Eat Me,' and I ate and got bigger right away."

She paused. "I know it sounds silly, Doc, but it was real interesting."

"Yes indeed," Dr. Prager said. "Go on. Tell everything you remember."

"Then the rabbit came back, mumbling something about a Duchess. And it dropped a pair of white gloves and a fan."

Fetishism, the psychiatrist noted.

"After that it got real crazy." Eve giggled. Then she told about the crying and forming a pool on the floor composed of her own tears. And how she held the fan and shrank again, then swam in the pool.

Grief fantasy, Dr. Prager decided.

She went on to describe her meeting with the mouse and with the other animals, the caucus race, and the recital of the curious poem about the cur, Fury, which ended, "I'll prosecute you, I'll be judge, I'll be jury—I'll try the whole cause and condemn you to death."

Superego, wrote Dr. Prager and asked, "What are you afraid of, Eve?"

"Nothing," she answered. "And I wasn't afraid in the dream either. I liked it. But I haven't told you anything yet."

"Go on."

She went on, describing her trip to the rabbit's house to fetch his gloves and fan and finding the bottle labeled "Drink Me" in the bedroom. Then followed the episode of growth, and being stuck inside the house (*Claustrophobia*, the notebook dutifully recorded), and her escape from the animals who pelted her with pebbles as she ran into the forest.

It was ALICE all right, word for word, image for image. *Father image* for the caterpillar, who might (Dr. Prager reasoned wisely) stand for himself as the psychiatrist, with his stern approach and enigmatic answers. The *Father William* poem which followed seemed to validate this conclusion.

Then came the episode of eating the side of the mushroom, growing and shrinking. Did this disguise her drug addiction? Perhaps. And there was a moment when she had a long serpentine neck and a pigeon mistook her for a serpent. A viper was a serpent. And weren't drug addicts called "vipers"? Of course. Dr. Prager was beginning to understand now. It was all symbolic. She was telling about her own life. Running away and finding the key to success—alternating between being very "small" and insignificant and trying every method of becoming "big" and important. Until she entered the garden—her Garden of Eden here—and became a star and consulted him and took drugs. It all made sense now.

He could understand as she told of the visit to the house of the Duchess (*mother image*) with her cruel "Chop off her head." He anticipated the baby who turned into a pig and wrote down *rejection fantasy* quickly.

Then he listened to the interview with the Cheshire cat, inwardly marveling at Eve Eden's perfect memory for dialogue.

" 'But I don't want to go among mad people,' I said. And the crazy cat came back with, 'Oh, you can't help that. We're all mad here. I'm mad. You're mad.' And I said, 'How do you know I'm mad?' and the cat said, 'You must be—or you wouldn't have come here.' Well, I felt plenty crazy when the cat started to vanish. Believe it or not, Doc, there was nothing left but a big grin."

"I believe it," Dr. Prager assured her.

He was hot on the trail of another scent now. The talk of madness had set him off. And sure enough, now came the tea party. With the March Hare and the Mad Hatter, of course—the *Mad* Hatter. Sitting in front of their house (*asylum*, no doubt) with the sleeping dormouse between them. *Dor*mouse—*dor*mant sanity. She was afraid of going insane, Dr. Prager decided. So much so did he believe it that when she quoted the line, "Why is a raven like a writing desk?" he found himself writing down, *Why is a raving like a Rorschach test?* and had to cross it out.

Then came the sadistic treatment of the poor dormouse and another drug fantasy with mushrooms for the symbol, leading her again into a beautiful garden. Dr. Prager heard it all: the story of the playing-card people (*club* soldiers and *diamond* courtiers and *heart* children were perfectly fascinating symbols too!).

And when Eve said, "Why, they're only a pack of cards after all—I needn't be afraid of them," Dr. Prager triumphantly wrote *paranoid fantasies: people are unreal.*

'Now I must tell you about the croquet game," Eve went on, and so she told him about the croquet game and Dr. Prager filled two whole pages with notes.

He was particularly delighted with Alice-Eve's account of the conversation with the ugly Duchess, who said among other things, "Take care of the sense and the sounds will take care of themselves," and "Be what you seem to be—or more simply, never imagine yourself not to be otherwise than what it might appear to others that what you were or might have been was not otherwise than what you had been who have appeared to them to be otherwise."

Eve Eden rattled it off, apparently verbatim. "It didn't seem to make sense at the time," she admitted. "But it does now, don't you think?"

Dr. Prager refused to commit himself. It made sense all right. A dreadful sort of sense. This poor child was struggling to retain her identity. Everything pointed to that. She was adrift in a sea of illusion, peopled with Mock Turtles—*Mock* Turtle, very significant, that—and distorted imagery.

Now the story of the Turtle and the Gryphon and the Lobster Quadrille began to take on a dreadful meaning. All the twisted words and phrases symbolized growing mental disturbance. Schools taught "reeling and writhing" and arithmetic consisted of "ambition, distraction, uglification, and derision." Obviously fantasies of inferiority. And Alice-Eve growing more and more confused with twisted, inverted logic in which "blacking" became "whiting"—it was merely an inner cry signifying she could no longer tell the difference between black and white. In other words, she was losing all contact with reality. She was going through an ordeal—a trial.

Of course it was a trial! Now Eve was telling about the trial of the Knave of Hearts, who stole the tarts (*Hadn't Eve once been a "tart" herself?*) and Alice-Eve noted all the animals on the jury (*another paranoid delusion: people are animals*) and she kept growing (*delusions of grandeur*) and then came the white rabbit reading the anonymous letter.

Dr. Prager picked up his own ears, rabbit fashion, when he heard the contents of the letter.

> "My notion was that you had been
> (before she had this fit)
> An obstacle that came between
> Him, and ourselves, and it.
> Don't let him know she liked them best
> For this must ever be
> A *secret* kept from all the rest
> Between yourself and me."

Of course. A *secret*, Dr. Prager decided. Eve Eden had been afraid of madness for a long time. That was the root of all her perverse behavior patterns, and he'd never probed sufficiently to uncover it. But the dream, welling up from the subconscious, provided the answer.

"I said I didn't believe there was an atom of meaning in it." Eve told him. "And the Queen cried, 'Off with her head,' but I said, 'Who cares for *you*? You're nothing but a pack of cards.' And they all rose up and flew at me, but I beat them off, and then I woke up fighting the covers."

She sat up. "You've been taking an awful lot of notes," she said. "Mind telling me what you think?"

Dr. Prager hesitated. It was a delicate question. Still, the dream content indicated that she was perfectly well aware of her problem on the subliminal level. A plain exposition of the facts might come as a shock but not a dangerous one. Actually a shock could be just the thing now to lead her back and resolve the initial trauma, whatever it was.

"All right," Dr. Prager said. "Here's what I think it means." And in plain language he explained his interpretation of her dream, pulling no punches but, occasionally, his goatee.

"So there you have it," he concluded. "The symbolic story of your life — and the dramatized and disguised conflict over your mental status which you've always tried to hide. But the subconscious is wise, my dear. It always knows and tries to warn. No wonder you had this dream at this particular time. There's nothing accidental about it. Freud says —"

But Eve was laughing. "Freud says? What does he know about it? Come to think of it, Doc, what do you know about it either? You see, I forgot to tell you something when I started. I didn't just *have* this dream." She stared at him, and her laughter ceased. "I bought it," Eve Eden said, "I bought it for ten thousand dollars."

4

Dr. Prager wasn't getting anywhere. His fountain pen ceased to function and his goatee wouldn't respond properly to even the most severe tugging. He heard Eve Eden out and waved his arms helplessly, like a bird about to take off. He felt like taking off, but on the other hand he couldn't leave this chick in her nest. Not with a big nest egg involved. But why did it have to be so involved?

"Go over that again," he begged finally. "Just the highlights. I can't seem to get it."

"But it's really so simple," Eve answered. "Like I already told you. I was getting all restless and keyed up, you know, like I've been before. Dying for a ball, some new kind of kick. And then I ran into Wally Redmond and he told me about this Professor Laroc."

"The charlatan," Dr. Prager murmured.

"I don't know what nationality he is," Eve answered. "He's just a little old guy who goes around selling these dreams."

"Now wait a minute—"

"Sure, it sounds screwy. I thought so, too, when Wally told me. He'd met him at a party somewhere and got to talking. And pretty soon he was spilling his—you'll pardon the expression—guts about the sad story of his life and how fed up he was with everything, including his sixth wife. And how he wanted to get away from it all and find a new caper.

"So this Professor Laroc asked him if he'd ever been on the stuff, and Wally said no, he had a weak heart. And he asked him if he'd tried psychiatry, and Wally said sure, but it didn't help him any."

"Your friend went to the wrong analyst," Dr. Prager snapped in some heat. "He should have come to a Freudian. How could he expect to get results from a Jungian—"

"Like you say, Doc, relax. It doesn't matter. What matters is that Professor Laroc sold him this dream. It was a real scary one, to hear him tell it, all about being a burglar over in England someplace and getting into a big estate run by a little dwarf with a head like a baboon. But he liked it; liked it fine. Said he was really relaxed after he had it: made him feel like a different person. And so he bought another, about a guy who was a pawnbroker, only a long time ago in some real gone country. And this pawnbroker ran around having himself all kinds of women who—"

"JURGEN," Dr. Prager muttered. "And if I'm not mistaken, the other one was from LUKUNDOO. I think it was called *The Snout*."

"Let's stick to the point, Doc," Eve Eden said. "Anyway, Wally was crazy about these dreams. He said the professor had a lot more to peddle, and even though the price was high, it was worth it. Because in the dream you felt like somebody else. You felt like the character you were dreaming about. And, of course, no hangover, no trouble with the law. Wally said if he ever tried some of the stuff he dreamed about on real women they'd clap him into pokey, even here in Hollywood. He planned to get out of pictures and buy more. Wanted to dream all the time. I guess the professor told him if he paid enough he could even *stay* in a dream without coming back."

"Nonsense!"

"That's what I told the man. I know how you feel, Doc. I felt that way myself before I met Professor Laroc. But after that it was different."

"You met this person?"

"He isn't a person, Doc. He's a real nice guy, a sweet character. You'd like him. I did when Wally brought him around. We had a long talk together. I opened up to him, even more than I have to you, I guess. Told him all my troubles. And he said what was wrong with me was I never had any childhood. That somewhere underneath there was a little girl trying to live her life with a full imagination. So he'd sell me a dream for that. And even though it sounded batty it made sense to me. He really seemed to understand things I didn't understand about myself.

"So I thought here goes, nothing to lose if I try it once, and I bought the dream." She smiled. "And now that I know what it's like I'm going to buy more. All he can sell me. Because he was right, you know. I don't want the movies. I don't want liquor or sex or H or gambling or anything. I don't want Eve Eden. I want to be a little girl, a little girl like the one in the dream, having adventures and never getting hurt. That's why I made up my mind. I'm quitting, getting out while the getting is good. From now on, me for dreamland."

Dr. Prager was silent for a long time. He kept staring at Eve Eden's smile. It wasn't *her* smile—he got the strangest notion that it belonged to somebody else. It was too relaxed, too innocent, too utterly seraphic for Eve. It was, he told himself, the smile of a ten-year-old girl on the face of a thirty-three-year-old woman of the world.

And he thought *hebephrenia* and he thought *schizophrenia* and he thought *incipient catatonia* and he said, "You say you met this Professor Laroc through Wally Redmond. Do you know how to reach him?"

"No, he reaches me." Eve Eden giggled. "He sends me, too, Doc."

She was really pretty far gone, Dr. Prager decided. But he had to persist. "When you bought this dream, as you say, what happened?"

"Why, nothing. Wally brought the professor here to the house. Right up to this bedroom actually. Then he went away and the professor talked to me and I wrote out the check and he gave me the dream."

"You keep saying he 'gave' you this dream. What does that mean?" Dr. Prager leaned forward. He had a sudden hunch. "Did he ask you to lie down, the way I do?"

"Yes. That's right."

"And did he talk to you?"

"Sure. How'd you guess?"

"And did he keep talking until you went to sleep?"

"I—I think so. Anyway, I did go to sleep, and when I woke up he was gone."

"Aha."

"What does that mean?"

"It means you were hypnotized, my dear. Hypnotized by a clever charlatan, who sold you a few moments of prepared patter in return for ten thousand dollars."

"But—but that's not true!" Eve Eden's childish smile became a childish pout. "It was *real*. The dream, I mean. It *happened*."

"Happened?"

"Of course. Haven't I made that clear yet? The dream *happened*. It wasn't like other dreams. I mean, I could feel and hear and see and even taste. Only it wasn't *me*. It was this little girl. Alice. I was Alice. That's what makes it worthwhile, can't you understand? That's what Wally said, too. The dream place is real. You *go* there, and you *are* somebody else."

"Hypnotism," Dr. Prager murmured.

Eve Eden put down the rabbit. "All right," she said. "I can prove it." She marched over to the big bed—the bed large enough to hold six people, according to some very catty but authenticated reports. "I didn't mean to show you this," she said, "but maybe I'd better."

She reached under her pillow and pulled out a small object which glittered beneath the light. "I found this in my hand when I woke up," she declared. "Look at it."

Dr. Prager looked at it. It was a small bottle bearing a white label. He shook it and discovered that the bottle was half-filled with a colorless transparent liquid. He studied the label and deciphered the hand-lettered inscription which read simply, "Drink Me."

"Proof, eh?" he mused. "Found in your hand when you woke up?"

"Of course. I brought it from the dream."

Dr. Prager smiled. "You were hypnotized. And before Professor Laroc stole away—and *stole* is singularly appropriate, considering that he had your check for ten thousand dollars—he simply planted this bottle in your hand as you slept. That's my interpretation of your proof." He slipped the little glass container into his pocket. "With your permission, I'd like to take this along," he said. "I'm going to ask you now to bear with me for the next twenty-four hours. Don't make any announcements about leaving the studio until I return. I think I can clear everything up to your satisfaction."

"But I am satisfied," Eve told him. "There's nothing to clear up. I don't want to—"

"Please." Dr. Prager brushed his brush with authority. "All I ask is that you be patient for twenty-four hours. I shall return tomorrow at this same time. And meanwhile, try to forget about all this. Say nothing to anyone."

"Now wait a minute, Doc—"

But Dr. Prager was gone. Eve Eden frowned for a moment, then sank back on the chaise longue. The rabbit scampered out from behind a chair and she picked it up again. She stroked its long ears gently until the creature fell asleep. Presently Eve's eyes closed and she drifted off to slumber herself. And the child's smile returned to her face.

5

There was no smile, childish or adult, on Dr. Prager's face when he presented himself again to the gatekeeper on the following day.

His face was stern and set as he drove up to the front door, accepted the butler's greeting, and went down the hall to where Mickey Dennis waited.

"What's up?" the little agent demanded, tossing his copy of *Hollywood Reporter* to the floor.

"I've been doing a bit of investigating," Dr. Prager told him. "And I'm afraid I have bad news for you."

"What is it, Doc? I tried to get something out of her after you left yesterday, but she wasn't talking. And today—"

"I know." Dr. Prager sighed. "She wouldn't be likely to tell you, under the circumstances. Apparently she realizes the truth herself but won't admit it. I have good reason to believe Miss Eden is disturbed. Seriously disturbed."

Mickey Dennis twirled his forefinger next to his ear. "You mean she's flipping?"

"I disapprove of that term on general principles," Dr. Prager replied primly. "And in this particular case the tense is wrong. *Flipped* would be much more correct."

"But I figgered she was all right lately. Outside of this business about quitting, she's been extra happy—happier'n I ever seen her."

"Euphoria," Dr. Prager answered. "Cycloid manifestation."

"You don't say so."

"I just did," the psychiatrist reminded him.

"Level with me," Dennis pleaded. "What's this all about?"

"I can't until after I've talked to her," Dr. Prager told him. "I need more facts. I was hoping to get some essential information from this Wally Redmond, but I can't locate him. Neither his studio nor his home seems to have information as to his whereabouts for the past several days."

"Off on a binge," the agent suggested. "It figgers. Only just what did you want from him?"

"Information concerning Professor Laroc," Dr. Prager answered. "He's a pretty elusive character. His name isn't listed on any academic roster I've consulted, and I couldn't find it in the City Directory of this or other local communities. Nor could the police department aid me with their files. I'm almost afraid my initial theory was wrong and that Professor Laroc himself is only another figment of Eve Eden's imagination."

"Maybe I can help you out there, Doc."

"You mean you met this man, saw him when he came here with Wally Redmond that evening?"

Mickey Dennis shook his head. "No. I wasn't around then. But I been around all afternoon. And just about a half hour ago a character named Professor Laroc showed up at the door. He's with Eve in her room right now."

Dr. Prager opened his mouth and expelled a gulp. Then he turned and ran for the stairs.

The agent sought out his overstuffed chair and riffled the pages of his magazine.

More waiting. Well, he just hoped there wouldn't be any explosions this afternoon.

6

There was no explosion when Dr. Prager opened the bedroom door. Eve Eden was sitting quietly on the chaise longue, and the elderly gentleman occupied an armchair.

As Dr. Prager entered, the older man rose with a smile and extended his hand. Dr. Prager felt it wise to ignore the gesture. "Professor Laroc?" he murmured.

"That is correct." The smile was a bland blend of twinkling blue eyes behind old-fashioned steel-rimmed spectacles, wrinkled creases in white cheeks, and a rictus of a prim, thin-lipped mouth. Whatever else he might be, Professor Laroc aptly fitted Mickey Dennis's description of a "character." He appeared to be about sixty-five, and his clothing seemed of the same vintage, as though fashioned in anticipation at the time of his birth.

Eve Eden stood up now. "I'm glad you two are getting together," she said. "I asked the professor to come this afternoon so we could straighten everything out."

Dr. Prager preened his goatee. "I'm very happy that you did so," he answered. "And I'm sure that matters can be set straight in very short order now that I'm here."

"The professor has just been telling me a couple of things," Eve informed him. "I gave him your pitch about me losing my buttons and he says you're all wet."

"A slight misquotation," Professor Laroc interposed. "I merely observed that an understanding of the true facts might dampen your enthusiasm."

"I think I have the facts," Dr. Prager snapped. "And they're dry enough. Dry, but fascinating."

"Do go on."

"I intend to." Dr. Prager wheeled to confront Eve Eden and spoke directly to the girl. "First of all," he said, "I must tell you that your friend here is masquerading under a pseudonym. I have been unable to discover a single bit of evidence substantiating the identity of anyone named Professor Laroc."

"Granted," the elderly man murmured.

"Secondly," Dr. Prager continued, "I must warn you that I have been unable to ascertain the whereabouts of your friend Wally Redmond. His wife doesn't know where he is, or his producer. Mickey Dennis thinks he's off on an alcoholic fugue. I have my own theory. But one fact is certain—he seems to have completely disappeared."

"Granted," said Professor Laroc.

"Third and last," Dr. Prager went on. "It is my considered belief that the man calling himself Professor Laroc did indeed subject you to hypnosis and that, once he had managed to place you in a deep trance, he deliberately read to you from a copy of ALICE IN WONDERLAND and suggested to you that you were experiencing the adventures of the principal character. Whereupon he placed the vial of liquid labeled 'Drink Me' in your hand and departed."

"Granted in part." Professor Laroc nodded. "It is true that I placed Miss Eden in a receptive state with the aid of what you choose to call hypnosis. And it is true that I suggested to her that she enter into the world of ALICE, as Alice. But that is all. It was not necessary to read anything to her, nor did I stoop to deception by supplying a vial of liquid, as you call it. Believe me, I was as astonished as you were to learn that she had brought back such an interesting souvenir of her little experience."

"Prepare to be astonished again then," Dr. Prager said grimly. He pulled the small bottle from his pocket and with it a piece of paper.

"What's that, Doc?" Eve Eden asked.

"A certificate from Haddon and Haddon, industrial chemists," the psychiatrist told her. "I took this interesting souvenir, as your friend calls it, down to their laboratories for analysis." He handed her the report. "Here, read for yourself. If your knowledge of chemistry is insufficient, I can tell you that H_2O means water." He smiled. "Yes, that's right. This bottle contains nothing but half an ounce of water."

Dr. Prager turned and stared at Professor Laroc. "What have you to say now?" he demanded.

"Very little." The old man smiled. "It does not surprise me that you were unable to find my name listed in any registry or directory of activities, legal or illegal. As Miss Eden already knows, I chose to cross over many years ago. Nor was 'Laroc' my actual surname. A moment's reflection will enable you to realize that 'Laroc' is an obvious enough anagram for 'Carroll,' give or take a few letters."

"You don't mean to tell me—"

"That I am Lewis Carroll, or rather, Charles Lutwidge Dodgson? Certainly not. I hold the honor of being a fellow alumnus of his at Oxford, and we did indeed share an acquaintance—"

"But Lewis Carroll died in 1898," Dr. Prager objected.

"Ah, you *were* interested enough to look up the date." The old man smiled. "I see you're not as skeptical as you pretend to be."

Dr. Prager felt that he was giving ground and remembered that attack is the best defense. "Where is Wally Redmond?" he countered.

"With the Duchess of Towers, I would presume," Professor Laroc answered. "He chose to cross over permanently, and I selected PETER IBBETSON for him. You see, I'm restricted to literature which was directly inspired by the author's dream, and there's a rather small field available. I still have Cabell's SMIRT to sell, and *The Brushwood Boy* of Kipling, but I don't imagine I shall ever manage to dispose of any Lovecraft — too gruesome, you know." He glanced at Eve Eden. "Fortunately, as I told you, I've reserved something very special for you. And I'm glad you decided to take the step. The moment I saw you my heart went out to you. I sensed the little girl buried away beneath all the veneer, just as I sensed the small boy in Mr. Redmond. So many of you Hollywood people are frustrated children. You make dreams for others but have none of your own. I am glad to offer my modest philanthropy — "

"At ten thousand dollars a session!" Dr. Prager exploded.

"Now, now," Professor Laroc chided. "That sounds like professional jealousy, sir! And I may as well remind you that a permanent crossover requires a fee of fifty thousand. Not that I need the money, you understand. It's merely that such a fee helps to establish me as an authority. It brings about the necessary transference relationship between my clients and myself, to borrow from your own terminology. The effect is purely psychological."

Dr. Prager had heard enough. This, he decided, was definitely the time to call a halt. Even Eve Eden in her present disturbed state should be able to comprehend the utter idiocy of this man's preposterous claims.

He faced the elderly charlatan with a disarming smile. "Let me get this straight," he began quietly. "Am I to understand that you are actually selling dreams?"

"Let us say, rather, that I sell experiences. And the experiences are every bit as real as anything you know."

"Don't quibble over words." Dr. Prager was annoyed. "You come in and hypnotize patients. During their sleep you suggest they enter a dream world. And then — "

"If you don't mind, let us quibble a bit over words, please," Professor Laroc said. "You're a psychiatrist. Very well, as a psychiatrist, please tell me one thing. Just what *is* a dream?"

"Why, that's very simple," Dr. Prager answered. "According to Freud, the dream phenomenon can be described as — "

"I didn't ask for a description, Doctor. Nor for Freud's opinion. I asked for an exact definition of the dream state, as you call it. I want to know the etiology and epistemology of dreams. And while you're at it, how about a definition of 'the hypnotic state' and of 'sleep'? And what is 'suggestion'? After you've given me precise scientific definitions of these phenomena, as you love to call them, perhaps you can go on and explain to me the nature of 'reality' and the exact meaning of the term 'imagination.' "

"But these are only figures of speech," Dr. Prager objected. "I'll be honest with you. Perhaps we can't accurately describe a dream. But we can observe it. It's like electricity: nobody knows what it *is*, but it's a measurable force which can be directed and controlled, subject to certain natural laws."

"Exactly," Professor Laroc said. "That's just what I would have said myself. And dreams are indeed like electrical force. Indeed, the human brain gives off electrical charges, and all life—matter—energy—enters into an electrical relationship. But this relationship has never been studied. Only the physical manifestations of electricity have been studied and harnessed, not the psychic. At least, not until Dodgson stumbled on certain basic mathematical principles, which he imparted to me. I developed them, found a practical use. The dream, my dear doctor, is merely an electrically charged dimension given a reality of its own beyond our own space-time continuum. The individual dream is weak. Set it down on paper, as some dreams have been set down, share it with others, and watch the charge build up. The combined electrical properties tend to create a *permanent* plane—a dream dimension, if you please."

"I don't please," answered Dr. Prager.

"That's because you're not receptive," Professor Laroc observed smugly. "Yours is a negative charge rather than a positive one. Dodgson—Lewis Carroll—was positive. So was Lovecraft and Poe and Edward Lucas White and a handful of others. Their dreams live. Other positive charges can live in them, granted the proper method of entry. It's not magic. There's nothing supernatural about it at all, unless you consider mathematics as magic. Dodgson did. He was a professor of mathematics, remember. And so was I. I took his principles and extended them, created a practical methodology. Now I can enter dream worlds at will, cause others to enter. It's not hypnosis as you understand it. A few words of non-Euclidean formula will be sufficient—"

"I've heard enough," Dr. Prager broke in. "Much as I hate to employ the phrase, this is sheer lunacy."

The professor shrugged. "Call it what you wish," he said. "You psychiatrists are good at pinning labels on things. But Miss Eden here has had sufficient proof through her own experience. Isn't that so?"

Eve Eden nodded, then broke her silence. "I believe you," she said. "Even if Doc here thinks we're both batty. And I'm willing to give you the fifty grand for a permanent trip."

Dr. Prager grabbed for his goatee. He was clutching at straws now. "But you can't," he cried. "This doesn't make sense."

"Maybe not your kind of sense," Eve answered. "But that's just the trouble. You don't seem to understand there's more than *one* kind. That crazy dream I had, the one you say Lewis Carroll had first and wrote up into a book—it makes sense to you if you really *live* it. More sense than Hollywood, than this. More sense than a little kid named Wilma Kozmowski growing up to live in a half-million-dollar palace and trying to kill herself because she can't be a little kid any more and never had a chance to be one when she was small. The professor here, he understands. He knows everybody has a right to dream. For the first time in my life I know what it is to be happy."

"That's right," Professor Laroc added. "I recognized her as a kindred spirit. I saw the child beneath, the child of the pure unclouded brow, as Lewis Carroll put it. She deserved this dream."

"Don't try and stop me," Eve cut in. "You can't, you know. You'll never drag me back to your world, and you've got no reason to try—except that you like the idea of making a steady living off me. And so does Dennis, with his lousy ten percent, and so does the studio with its big profits. I never met anyone who really liked me as a person except Professor Laroc here. He's the only one who ever gave me anything worth having. The dream. So quit trying to argue me into it, Doc. I'm not going to be Eve any more or Wilma either. I'm going to be Alice."

Dr. Prager scowled, then smiled. What was the matter with him? Why was he bothering to argue like this? After all, it was so unnecessary. Let the poor child write out a check for fifty thousand dollars—payment could always be stopped. Just as this charlatan could be stopped if he actually attempted hypnosis. There were laws and regulations. Really, Dr. Prager reminded himself, he was behaving like a child himself: taking part in this silly argument just as if there actually was something to it besides nonsense words.

What was really at stake, he realized, was professional pride. To think that this old mountebank could actually carry more authority with Eve Eden than he did himself!

And what was the imposter saying now, with that sickening, condescending smile on his face?

"I'm sorry you cannot subscribe to my theories, Doctor. But at least I am grateful for one thing, and that is that you didn't see fit to put them to the test."

"Test? What do you mean?"

Professor Laroc pointed his finger at the little bottle labeled "Drink Me" which now rested on the table before him. "I'm happy you merely analyzed the contents of that vial without attempting to drink them."

"But it's nothing but water."

"Perhaps. What you forget is that water may have very different properties in other worlds. And this water came from the world of Alice."

"You planted that," Dr. Prager snapped. "Don't deny it."

"I do deny it. Miss Eden knows the truth."

"Oh, does she?" Dr. Prager suddenly found his solution. He raised the bottle, turning to Eve with a commanding gesture. "Listen to me now. Professor Laroc claims, and you believe, that this liquid was somehow transported from the dream world of ALICE IN WONDERLAND. If that is the case, then a drink out of this bottle would cause me either to grow or to shrink. Correct?"

"Yes," Eve murmured.

"Now wait—" the professor began, but Dr. Prager shook his head impatiently.

"Let me finish," he insisted. "All right. By the same token, if I took a drink from this bottle and nothing happened, wouldn't it prove that the dream-world story is a fake?"

"Yes, but—"

"No 'buts.' I'm asking you a direct question. Would it or wouldn't it?"

"Y-yes. I guess so. Yes."

"Very well, then." Dramatically, Dr. Prager uncorked the little bottle and raised it to his lips. "Watch me," he said.

Professor Laroc stepped forward. "Please!" he shouted. "I implore you —don't—"

He made a grab for the bottle, but he was too late.

Dr. Prager downed the half ounce of colorless fluid.

7

Mickey Dennis waited and waited until he couldn't stand it any longer. There hadn't been any loud sounds from upstairs at all, and this only made it worse.

Finally he got the old urge so bad he just had to go on up there and see for himself what was going on.

As he walked down the hall he could hear them talking inside the bedroom. At least he recognized Professor Laroc's voice. He was saying something about, "There, there, I know it's quite a shock. Perhaps you'd feel better if you didn't wait—do you want to go now?"

That didn't make too much sense to Mickey, and neither did Eve's reply. She said, "Yes, but don't I have to go to sleep first?"

And then the professor answered, "No, as I explained to him, it's just a question of the proper formulae. If I recite them we can go together. Er— you might bring your checkbook along."

Eve seemed to be giggling. "You too?" she asked.

"Yes. I've always loved this dream, my dear. It's a sequel to the first one, as you'll discover. Now if you'll just face the mirror with me—"

And then the professor mumbled something in a very low voice, and Mickey bent down with his head close to the door but he couldn't quite catch it. Instead his shoulder pushed the door open.

The bedroom was empty.

That's right, empty.

FOUNDING FATHERS

1

EARLY ON THE MORNING of July 4th, 1776, Thomas Jefferson poked his peruked head into the deserted chamber of what was to be known as Independence Hall and yelled, "Come on, you guys, the coast is clear!"

As he stepped into the big room he was followed by John Hancock, who puffed nervously on a cigarette.

"All right," Jefferson said. "Ditch the butt, will ya? You wanna louse us up, creep?"

"Sorry, boss." Hancock glanced around the place, then addressed a third man who entered behind him. "Dig this," he murmured. "Not an ashtray in the joint. What kind of a setup we got here anyway, Nunzio?"

The third man scowled. "Don't call me Nunzio," he growled. "The name's Charles Thomson, remember?"

"Okay, Chuck."

"Charles!" The third man dug John Hancock in the ribs. "Straighten that wig of yours. Ya look like somethin' out of a Boy Scout pageant yet."

John Hancock shrugged. "Well, whaddya expeck? Guy can't even smoke, and these here britches are so tight I'm scared to sit down in 'em."

Thomas Jefferson turned and confronted him. "You ain't gonna sit down," he said. "All you gotta do is sign and keep your yap shut. Let Ben do the talking, remember?"

"Ben?"

"Benjamin Franklin, schmoe," said Thomas Jefferson.

"Somebody mention my name?" The short, fat, balding man hurried into the room, carefully adjusting square-lensed spectacles to the bridge of his nose.

"What took you so long?" Thomas Jefferson demanded. "You run into trouble back there?"

"No trouble," Benjamin Franklin replied. "They're out cold, and the gags are holding. It's just these glasses—the lenses distort my vision. I'd forgotten I'd have to wear them."

"Can't you ditch 'em?"

"No. Somebody might get suspicious." Franklin peered at his companions over the tops of the spectacles. "They're likely to get suspicious anyway, if you don't do what I told you." He glanced around the room. "What time is it?"

Thomas Jefferson fumbled with the ruffles at his sleeves and gazed down at the face of his wristwatch. "Seven-thirty," he announced.

"You're sure?"

"Checked it with Western Union."

"Never mind that Western Union talk. And take off that thing—put it in your pocket. It's stuff like that can get us into trouble."

"Trouble." John Hancock groaned. "These here shoes are killin' me. They ain't nearly my size."

"Well, wear them and be quiet," Benjamin Franklin told him. "I wish to God you'd remembered to shave, too. Fine thing—the President of the Continental Congress on the most important day of our history, coming in without shaving."

"I forgot. Also they was no place to plug in an electric shaver."

"Well, never mind now. The main thing is just to be quiet and remember what you're supposed to do. Mr. Jefferson, do you have the Declaration?"

Nobody answered. Franklin strode up to the tall man in the peruke. "Jefferson, that's you I'm talking to."

"I forgot." The big man smiled sheepishly.

"You'd better not forget. Now, where is it?"

"Right here in my pocket."

"Well, get it out. We've got to sign right away, before anybody else shows up. I expect they'll start drifting in around eight at the latest."

"Eight?" Jefferson sighed. "Do you mean to tell me they go to work that early here?"

"Our friends in the back room looked as if they'd been working all night," Franklin reminded him.

"Ain't they never heard of union hours?"

"No, and don't you mention it, either." Franklin surveyed his companions earnestly. "That goes for all of you. Watch your tongues. We can't afford a slip-up."

"Telling me?" Charles Thomson took the parchment from Thomas Jefferson and unfolded it.

"Careful with that," Franklin warned.

"Pipe down, will ya? I just wanna take a look at it," Thomson replied. "I ain't never seen that there thing." He glanced at the manuscript curiously. "Hey, dig this crazy hanwriting. It's all lettering, like."

He spread the Declaration on a table and squinted down at it, mumbling aloud.

"When inna course a human events, it becomes necessary for one people to dissolve the political bands which have connecked them with another, and to assume among the powers of the earth the separate—hey, what kinda double-talk is this, anyway? Whyn't these guys write English, huh?"

"Never mind." Ben Franklin took the parchment from him and strode to a desk. "I'm going to revise it right now." He rummaged around in the drawer, finding fresh parchment and a quill pen. "I'm not up to copying the lettering style, I'm afraid, but I can explain that to the Congress easily enough. I'll tell them that Jefferson here made his last-minute changes in a hurry. The hurry part of it is no lie."

He bent over the blank parchment and studied the Declaration as it rested alongside. "Got to keep the style," he said. "Very important. But the main thing is to add the provisions at the end."

"Provisions?" John Hancock brightened. "We gonna have some grub, hey? I'm starved."

"That can wait," Jefferson snapped. "Now keep still and let the guy work. This is the most important part of the whole caper, understand?"

Then there was silence in the room—silence except for the busy scratching of the quill pen as Benjamin Franklin wrote.

Jefferson stood over his shoulder, nodding from time to time. "Don't forget to put in that part about me being temporary boss," he said. "And stick in that we need a treasurer."

Franklin nodded impatiently. "I've got it all down here," he answered. "Nothing to worry about."

"Think they'll sign?"

"Sure they'll sign. It's only logical. Right after the part about being free and independent states there should be a mention of a temporary governing arrangement. They can't object to that. Wonder why it was left out in the first place."

"Search me." Jefferson shrugged. "How would I know?"

"Well, you're supposed to have written it."

"Oh, yeah, that's right."

Franklin finished, sat back, and poked at Jefferson's chest with his quill. "Cough," he said.

Jefferson coughed.

"Again. Louder."

"What's the big idea?"

"You've got laryngitis," Franklin told him. "A bad case. That's why you're not talking. Anybody asks you any questions, you just cough. Right?"

"Okay. I didn't want to talk anyway."

Franklin gazed at Hancock and Thomson. "You two better sign and disappear. When the gang arrives, you go in the back room and keep an eye on our buddies there. I'll make up some excuse why you're not around—can't take the risk of having you cornered and questioned. Got it?"

The two men nodded. Franklin extended the quill pen. "Here. You two are supposed to sign first." As John Hancock reached for the pen, Franklin chuckled. "Just put your John Hancock right here."

Hancock signed with a flourish. He gave the pen to Charles Thomson.

"Remember, you're the secretary," Franklin said, as Thomson dipped the quill in the inkwell. "What's the matter, that quill too clumsy for you?"

"Sure it's clumsy," Thomson said. "And these clothes are murder, and none of us guys knows how to talk. We can't get away with this, Thinker. We're gonna make mistakes."

Benjamin Franklin stood up. "We're going to make history," he declared. "Just follow orders and everything will be all right." He paused and lifted his hand. "In the immortal words of myself—Benjamin Franklin—we must all hang together, or assuredly we shall all hang separately."

2

They had hung together for a long time in Philly—Sammy, Nunzio, Mush and Thinker Tomaszewski. They shoved a little queer, peddled a few decks, but mostly they made book.

It was a nice setup for all of them, particularly since the Thinker came into the deal. The Thinker was a genuine shyster, with a degree and an office and everything, and he fronted for the outfit. The funny part of it was, Thinker Tomaszewski had a regular law practice too, and he could have made a pretty nice piece of change without cutting corners.

But he worked with them for kicks, at first.

"The only way I can explain it," he told them, "is that I don't seem to have a superego." Always with the two-dollar words, that was the Thinker.

And it was his two-dollar words that finally got them into trouble. In the beginning, everything was fine. Using his law office as a front, he had no difficulty in getting acquainted with a better class of mark—not the two-bucks-on-the-nose working stiff, but heavy bettors. He steered them to Sammy or Nunzio or Mush, and they made a big book.

They made a big buck, too. So big that they just had to place a few bets of their own, with some of the top wheels like Mickey Tarantino. Playing it smart, of course, and working only on inside tips, when they were sure of a horse getting the needle.

Came an afternoon when the needle stuck. And they were stuck for twenty grand. Mickey Tarantino held out his hand and smiled. But the smile vanished when Sammy went to him and said he needed time to pay up.

"Whaddya mean?" Mr. Tarantino had inquired. "You guys are loaded. Look at all the rich suckers you make book with."

"All we got to show for it is markers," Sammy confessed. "It's like your old man's delicatessen. The poor guys pay and the high-class trade puts it on the cuff. You know how those big operators work. Well it's the same in our line. You can't collect from them."

"You damn well better collect," Mr. Tarantino advised. "Because you got until tomorrow morning. Or else you wind up in Plotter's Field, or wherever."

So Sammy went away and called a meeting at Thinker Tomaszewski's office and broke the news.

Thinker had news for them too. "Tarantino isn't the only one who thinks we're rolling in the stuff," he announced. "Uncle Sam is looking down our throats for a little matter of back income taxes."

"Great!" Sammy groaned. "Tarantino's hoods in front of us and the Federal finks behind us. Which way do we turn?"

"I suggest you turn to our clients," Thinker answered. "Call on some of our investors and ask them to redeem their markers."

So Sammy and Nunzio and Mush called. And early that evening they assembled and pooled results.

"Three grand!" Sammy snorted. "Three lousy grand!"

"Is that all?" The Thinker was genuinely mystified. "I should have thought you'd get more than that."

"Sure we got more. Excuses we got, promises we got, brush-offs we got. But here's the moola. Three grand, period."

"How about Cobbett?" Thinker asked.

"Professor Cobbett? He's your baby, isn't he?"

The Thinker nodded. Professor Cobbett was indeed his baby. One of the upper crust.

"What's he into us for?" Sammy demanded.

"About eight, I think."

"Eight and three is eleven. Not so hot. But if we could get it fast, maybe Tarantino would hold off for a while."

"Let's get it fast," Mush suggested. "Let's go out and see old Cobbett right now."

So they all piled into Sammy's car and went out to see old Cobbett. The Professor had a country place — a nice layout for a man who lived all alone —

and he was cordial and pleasant when he greeted the Thinker on the front porch.

He was not quite so cordial or pleasant when he learned what the Thinker wanted, and he was downright inhospitable when the Thinker beckoned and his three companions appeared out of the darkness.

They had to stick their feet in the door and they had to stick their heaters in his ribs.

"No foolin'," Nunzio told him. "We want our loot."

"Oh dear!" said Professor Cobbett, as they marched him backwards into his own parlor. "But I have no money."

"Don't con us," Mush told him. "Look at this joint, all this fancy furniture."

"Mortgaged," the Professor sighed. "Mortgaged to the hilt, and past it."

"What about this here school where you teach at?" Mush asked. "You could maybe brace them for some advance dough on your salary, huh?"

"I am no longer connected with the university."

"What gives here?" Sammy wanted to know.

"Yes," Thinker added. "I thought you were a wealthy man."

The Professor shrugged and ran his hand through his graying hair. "Things are not always what they seem," he said. "For example, I considered you to be a reputable professional man. And when I innocently inquired about the possibilities of placing a small bet on the races, I never dreamed you were associated with these ruffians."

"Watch that talk," Sammy warned. "We ain't no more ruffians than eight grand is a small bet. Now whaddya mean about things ain't always what they seem?"

"Well, it's like this," the Professor answered. "I did have a certain sum of money set aside—yes. And I did have a position of some eminence at the university. The fact that both money and position are gone today can be attributed to one thing—my private research project.

"The cost of experimental models reduced my savings. The revelation of my theories cost me my faculty position. An attempt to raise funds to continue my work led me to the last resort—betting on the races. Now I have nothing."

"You can say that again," Sammy told him. "In about three minutes you're gonna have nothing with lace around it."

"Wait a moment," the Thinker interrupted. "Experimental models, you said. What have you been building?"

"I'll show you, if you like."

"Come on," Sammy ordered. "Boys, keep the heaters warm, in case he pulls a funny."

But the Professor didn't pull a funny. He led them downstairs to what had been the basement, and was now an ornate private laboratory. He led them up to the large rectangular metal structure, covered with coils and tubing. It had a vague resemblance to an outhouse designed by Frank Lloyd Wright.

"Jeez," Nunzio commented. "Watchoo doin', buildin' one of them there Frankensteens?"

"I bet it's a spaceship," Mush hazarded. "Was you gonna make a getaway to Mars?"

"Please," the Professor sighed. "You're making sport of me."

"We're making hamburger of you in another minute," Sammy corrected him. "This doojigger ain't no use to us. Couldn't get twenty bucks for it, at a junkyard."

Thinker Tomaszewski shook his head. "Just what is this object, Professor?"

Professor Cobbett blushed. "I hesitate to designate it as such, after the rebuffs I received at the hands of supposed authorities, but there is no other intelligible term for it. It is a time machine."

"Oof!" Sammy put his hand to his forehead. "And this is what we let get into us for eight grand. A nutty scientist, yet!"

The Thinker frowned at him. "A time machine, you say? An instrument capable of transporting one forward or backwards in time?"

"Backwards only," the Professor answered. "Forward travel is manifestly impossible, since the future is nonexistent. And travel is not the best word. Transit more closely approximates the meaning, insofar as time possesses no material or spatial characteristics, being bound to a three-dimensional universe by the single observable phenomenon which manifests itself as duration. Now if duration is designated as X, and—"

"Shuddup!" Nunzio suggested. "Let's kiss off this joker and scram outta here. We're wastin' time."

"Wasting time." The Thinker nodded. "Professor Cobbett, is this a working model?"

"I'm practically positive. It has never been tested. But I can show you formulae which—"

"Never mind that now. Why haven't you tested it?"

"Because I'm not sure of the past. Or rather, our present relationship to it. If any person or object in present time were sent to the past, alterations would occur. What is here now would be absent, and something added to what was there, then. This addition would alter the past. And if the past were altered, then it would not be the same past we know." He frowned. "It's hard to state without recourse to symbolic logic."

"You mean you're afraid that by time travel you'd change the past? Or come out in a different past—a past made different because you traveled into it?"

"That's an oversimplification, but you have the general idea."

"Then what good is your work on this?"

"No good, I'm afraid. But I wanted to prove a point. It became an almost monomaniacal obsession. I have no excuses."

"So." Sammy stepped forward. "Thanks for the lecture, but like you say, you got no excuses. And we got no time. This here basement looks like a nice soundproof place for target practice—"

The Thinker grabbed Sammy's arm. "What's the sense?" he asked.

"The guy welshed."

"So he welshed. Will murder change that? Will murder help us now?"

"No." Sammy bit his lip. "But what we gonna do? We got no dough. We got Tarantino after us, and also the govmint. We can't go back to town."

The Thinker looked around. "Why not stay here, then? We're safe, isolated with a nice big roof over our heads. Let's enjoy the Professor's hospitality for a while."

"Yeah," Mush said. "But how long? We're gonna run out of dough, or food, or somethin'. We'd just be stallin' for time."

The Thinker smiled. "Stalling for time." He gazed intently at the complicated structure in the center of the cellar. "But here is the logical vehicle for a getaway."

"You mean jump in that dizzy outfit and beat it?" Sammy demanded. "You're kidding."

"I'm serious," the Thinker replied. "Some time in the near future we'll be safe in the past."

3

It took a lot of figuring. That was the Thinker's job, working with the Professor during the next few days.

"How do you set the controls up? Is this for steering?"

"You do not steer—you press the computers. Here, I'll show you again."

"And you can choose any time in the past, any time at all?" asked the Thinker.

"Theoretically. The main problem is accurate computation. Remember, we and our Earth are not static. We do not occupy the same position in space that we did an instant ago, let alone a longer period. We must consider the speed of light, planetary motion, inclination, and—"

"That's going to be your department. But you can establish past position mathematically and set up a guiding plan for the computers accordingly?"

"I'm reasonably certain of it."

"Then all that remains is to determine where—or rather, when—we're going to."

Sammy and Nunzio and Mush tacked that problem on their own.

"Jeez, mebbe alls we gotta do is go back a couple weeks to before when the Professor made his bets. Then we ain't out no dough."

"Yeah? What about them there back taxes?"

"So we go to before when we owed 'em."

"That's when we went into business, stupid. We was broke."

"Well, if we can go anywheres we want in time, how's about way back, to the Egypians, like? I seen one of them there pitchers, they had all these hot broads runnin' around in their unnerwear—"

"You talk Egypian, stupid? Besides, we don't wanna stay back someplace forever. Way I figger, we go to some time where we can lay our mitts on some loot, real fast-like. And then come back."

"Now you got it. That's the angle. Hey, how about that there Gold Rush?"

The Professor interrupted them. "I'm afraid the Gold Rush wouldn't be of much use to you gentlemen. After all, it occurred in the year eighteen hundred and forty-nine."

"But you can send us to eighteen forty-nine, can't you?"

"Conceivably, if my theory is correct. But you would not be in California. You would still be right here in Philadelphia, in the field which stood here before this house was built."

"Then we gotta find our loot in Philly, huh? Somewheres in the past?"

"I'm afraid so."

"Jeez. And we can't show up in no vacant field with that machine, either."

Then the Thinker took over. "I am beginning to pinpoint our problem," he announced. "Professor, I am going to utilize your library for a day or so. Perhaps I can discover when gold was available in Philadelphia."

"There's always the Mint "

"Too well-guarded. We'd never be able to loot it, any more than it could have been looted by past efforts."

"Banks?" Sammy brightened. "With our heaters, we could knock over one of them big jugs easy—say, a hunnert years ago."

"And come out with what? Old-fashioned greenbacks? We wouldn't be able to use currency of that era today. Arouse suspicion. No, I'm looking for gold."

Finally, in a copy of Berkeley's HISTORY OF THE REVOLUTION, the Thinker found it. He broke in upon the others as they sat guarding Professor Cobbett.

"Here's the answer!" he exulted. "Remember what happened in Philadelphia on July fourth, seventeen seventy-six?"

"That's a holiday, ain't it?" Nunzio brightened. "Must be the Phillies took on the Giants in a doubleheader."

"Seventeen seventy-six, stupid!" Sammy scowled. "Yeah, I remember. They made Washington the President."

"Nah. It was the Decoration of Independence," Mush corrected.

"Right. The Declaration of Independence was presented to the Continental Congress assembled at what is now Independence Hall. And so forth.

But here's another little-known fact. At the same place, on the same day, the Revolutionary treasury was turned over to a small group for temporary storage. It consisted of upwards of thirty thousand pounds sterling in smelted ingots. That's about a hundred and fifty thousand dollars in gold."

"Brother!" Sammy whistled. "What a way to celebrate the Fourth!" Then he frowned. "I'll bet they had plenny guards around."

"No, that's just the point. It was all a secret—few people know of it to this day. Troops brought it in a wagon, around noon. They thought they were hauling documents. It was carted upstairs, and no guards were posted lest suspicion be aroused. Its presence was known only to Benjamin Franklin, Thomas Jefferson, and one or two others—probably John Hancock and maybe Charles Thomson, the Secretary of the Congress. It was to be used to pay troops and buy supplies."

"It sure could help to pay off old Mickey Tarantino and the Feds. And leave us plenny to spare."

"That is exactly what I had in mind, gentlemen." The Thinker smiled. "Now all that remains is to work out the details. I shall concentrate on the historical aspect and the Professor here can work out the mathematical computations."

Professor Cobbett blanched. "Mathematical computations? But you're asking the impossible. Why, that was over a hundred and eighty light-years ago; we'll be faced with the problem of billionfold magnitudes, and the slightest error or variation can have serious consequences."

"Ain't gonna be no errors," Sammy told him. "Or consequences will be really serious. For you." He showed the Professor his heater. "Now get to work. We're going places."

"Going places." Mush looked at him. "All this here stuff was at Independence Hall. The machine's here in the cellar. We gonna come out on July fourth inna cow-pasture or somethin'?"

"That's your job," Sammy decided. "Case this joint. See how it's set up for guards at night. Alarm system, the works. Look it over like you would a bank job. I think we can take over. Nobody's gonna think a mob would break into a Hysterical Shrine or whatever. We get things set, we hire us a truck and cart the machine right down to the Hall and take off from there some night soon. Right?"

"Hey, that's a tough deal."

"Things are tough all over," Sammy said. "Now get going."

So Mush got going and the Professor got going and the Thinker got going too. And before the first week was up they were organized.

Mush made his report. The invasion of Independence Hall could be made without too much trouble. Of course, it would cost money for the truck, and there might be repercussions, but they could try to pull it off.

And in view of their present hopeless situation—and in view of the possible gain—it was worth the gamble, Sammy decided.

The Professor presented them with the working manual, based on his computations.

"Are you sure this gets us there?" Sammy demanded. "And back, too?"

"Look it over," the Professor said. "See for yourself."

"It's all right," the Thinker told him. "I've checked it. See, we have no set time for return. Our plans call for us to get the gold and come back as soon after the noon hour as possible. So the Professor has worked out return-variations based on five-minute intervals throughout the early afternoon. It's as foolproof as we can hope to make it."

"All right, if you say so." Sammy shrugged. "But what I want to know is, what do we do when we get there?"

"I've been working on that angle," the Thinker said. "Checking all the source books and references I could muster. History texts. Biographical data on Franklin and Jefferson in particular. And I've got a plan. Apparently the first ones to arrive that morning were Jefferson and Thomson. Franklin and John Hancock came in early, too.

"It's not quite clear whether any of them spent part of the night there. The important thing is that the four men conceivably held an early morning meeting, discussing the Declaration before Congress convened on the fourth. So if we arrive early enough we'll be dealing with just four men. The four men who knew about the gold, by the way."

"Got it," Sammy said. "We come in, flash our heaters, and take over."

"Not quite so simple," the Thinker answered. "Remember, Congress will be gathering that morning. We can't hope to hold our guns on these four key figures from that time until noon, any more than we can hope to pass unnoticed in the crowd for such a period."

He paused as Sammy started to open his mouth, then hastily continued. "I know what you're thinking, and that won't work either. We can't show up at noon and just hijack the shipment. Not in front of fifty or more men, with troops just outside the door."

"Then what do you figger on us doing?"

The Thinker took a deep breath, and then he told them.

"Oh no!" cried Sammy.

"Me, making like John Hancock?" Mush gasped.

"I should run around in one of them wigs like a big-shot politician?" Nunzio scoffed.

The Thinker was calm. "Don't you see, it's the only way? The wigs are perfect disguises. Look I've got pictures of all these men, and we can buy a makeup kit. I'm fortunately bald and approximately Franklin's build. Physically, we'll get by. And don't worry about playing the role of a politician."

"Yeah." Mush was thoughtful. "After all, what's a politician, anyhow? Just a crook that's learned how to kiss babies."

"But we won't be kissing no babies that morning," Sammy reminded him. "Me, I been reading up a little on that stuff, too. Them four guys did a lot of things on the fourth. Made speeches, tried to get the rest of the Congress to sign, all kinds of stuff. And they knew everybody, everybody knew them. We'd fluff it for sure, trying to do what they did."

"That's just the point." Thinker Tomaszewski was triumphant. "We don't have to do what they did! Because we're going back in time, we're changing what happened. I think I'm familiar enough with Franklin's personality. I can talk, if necessary. Sammy, I'll coach you. The other two boys can be absent, if need be—and it may well be necessary to guard our machine and our captives in the rear room. We're not going to merely reenact history. We're going to change it, to suit ourselves. Now do you get it?"

They got it, eventually, because the Thinker rammed it down their throats.

And so they got their coaching, got their truck, got their plan, and actually transported the machine bodily into the rear of the vehicle on the evening arranged for departure.

It wasn't until they stood for the last time in the now open expanse of the cellar that Professor Cobbett voiced a final, timid protest.

"I hesitate to bring this up," he said, "because you'll very likely suspect my motives. You'll think it's because you're preempting my property, and because you are unwittingly involving me as an accomplice to your crime. You'll think it's because I have patriotic objections to your plans for desecrating our history."

"Well, haven't you?" Sammy asked.

"Yes, I admit it."

Sammy glanced significantly at Nunzio, then back to the Professor as he continued.

"But what I have to say to you now, I say in my capacity as a scientist. In that capacity I warn you, as I did on the first evening here. Time travel is hazardous. The possibility of alteration of the past due to your invasion cannot be discounted. You may well find yourselves up against unforeseen factors, unexpected problems. That's why I never dared make the attempt myself; not even a journey of one minute, let alone almost two centuries. Should you fail, I must absolve myself of any responsibility. I shall await your return with the utmost trepidation."

"Don't bother," Sammy told him. "We got that all figgered, too. You plan on waiting for our return with a gang of coppers, don't you?"

The Professor turned pale. "Don't tell me you gentlemen expect me to come along?" he murmured. "I couldn't do that. I couldn't. I'd—I'd be afraid.

Frankly, the dangers of dislocation or alteration in the past frighten me worse than the prospect of death itself."

"I'm glad," Sammy said slowly. "On account of it's either-or. And you just made up our minds for us."

The Thinker was already out in the truck, but Mush and Nunzio stood beside Sammy in the cellar.

Nunzio took out his heater and Mush smiled. "Well," he said. "Looks like we're starting off our trip with a bang."

4

And a bang-up journey it was. There was a route to travel, and guards to knock out and bind, and a heavy machine to cart up into the rear chambers of Independence Hall. Then came the nerve-wracking business of setting it up, and the Thinker's frantic rescanning of the Professor's charts and directions as he set the computers. By the time they were ready to take off— 1:45 A.M. on the dot—the transition itself was almost an anticlimax.

Anticlimax it proved to be. They huddled in the machine, the vacuum-lock set and the vacuum-lined walls enclosing them, and a generator hummed and their fluorescent light above the dials dimmed and the Thinker pressed his finger down after endless adjustment of tab-buttons and then—

Nothing happened.

Or seemed to happen, until the moment—or century, or eternity—of darkness elapsed. None of them were conscious of a change at all. It was when they opened the compartment and stepped out that the change occurred, or they were aware of its prior occurrence.

"Thinker!" Nunzio said, blinking in the bright morning sunlight that streamed through the high windows. "We made it!"

Sammy and the Thinker and Mush didn't even look at him. They were staring at the four men on the other side of the room—four men who stared, in turn, at them.

Then things happened fast. Things happened with orders and heaters and ropes and gags. Things happened with wigs and shoes and clothing.

Four writhing figures squirmed on the floor, then calmed to quiescence as Mush used the butt of his heater.

"Fancy this!" he sighed. "Me knocking out old Ben Franklin hisself!"

"Never mind fancying it now," the Thinker told him. "We've got to get ready for more action."

And so they'd gone into their act.

Altering the text of the Declaration itself was an inspiration on the Thinker's part.

"Give 'em something to argue about all morning," he said. "Keep them talking, then we don't have to. And if they accept the business about temporary governing powers and a treasurer, there'll be no questions asked when the gold arrives and we take charge of it."

He glanced at Mush and Nunzio. "You two go in the back room right now. Watch the machine, keep the Founding Fathers company. And don't forget to watch the windows—maybe the gold will arrive early. Professor Cobbett was no fool. I respect his judgment. If he said things might be a bit different in the past because our coming changed it, maybe he's right."

"Nothing different so far," Sammy said.

"Well, one never knows."

Mush and Nunzio vanished and the Thinker turned to his companion. "Remember your laryngitis. They call it quinsy in these times, and that's how I'll refer to it. And when I do, you cough."

"Got it," Sammy said. "But hey, when's the gang showing up?" He pulled his watch out of his pocket and studied. "Must be after eight by now." He frowned. "That's funny, it stopped. Still says seven-thirty."

"Let me take a look outside," the Thinker suggested. He strode to the window. "Crowd down there all right. But—wait a minute—" He tugged Sammy's arm. "Look at those soldiers!"

"I see 'em. You mean the ones in the tall hats, with the red uniforms?"

"Red uniforms mean British troops."

"British?"

The Thinker didn't answer. He rushed to the door of the hall, flung it open. Two grenadiers in scarlet coats confronted him. He stared at the white piping on the coats, stared at the silvery steel of their bayonets.

"Halt!" cried the taller of the two. "In the name of His Majesty."

"His Majesty?"

"Yes, His Majesty, you pesky rebel."

"What kind of a gag is this?" Sammy muttered.

"No gag," the Thinker whispered. "Professor Cobbett knew. We changed the past by coming here. The British occupy Philadelphia."

"Enough of your blabbing, sirrah," the soldier shouted. "Save your protests for General Burgoyne. When he enters the city today you and your fellow traitors can explain at a drumhead court-martial."

The Thinker paled. "Changed history," he whispered. "Burgoyne the victor. The Congress scattered. The four men we came upon in the back room weren't waiting for it to meet today. They've been trapped here without warning. They're prisoners. Which means we're prisoners, too!"

"Oh no we ain't!" Sammy drew out his heater and pulled the trigger. There was an almost inaudible click. He tried to fire again, but the Thinker slammed the door.

"What good is that?" he murmured. "The place is surrounded."

"Gun jammed," Sammy was grumbling. "Can't figure how—" Then he blinked. "Surrounded. And we're stuck, huh? Now what?"

"Obviously we get back in the machine and get out of here."

"But don't you have to wait until noon, anyway?"

"I'll worry about that. Let's get the boys. And hurry. Those soldiers may decide to come in after us at any time."

So they retreated to the rear room and they got the boys and explained. And in a surprisingly short time they were huddled in the time machine once more; huddled in the incongruous flummery of their Colonial costumes; huddled and trembling and perspiring as the Thinker hastily checked his data and then reached for the computer levers.

Reached and pressed.

Or tried to press.

"What's happening?" Sammy shouted, the echo of his voice almost deafening them in the cramped confines of the metal chamber.

"Nothing," the Thinker groaned. "Nothing's happening. That's just the trouble."

"It don't work?" Nunzio wailed.

"No. And Sammy's watch doesn't work, and your guns don't work, because all of the principles are wrong, altered the way everything is altered."

"Let me try!" Mush pawed at the levers, the buttons, the dials. Then they were all clawing and scrabbling at once, and still nothing happened.

The Thinker stopped them. "Might as well give up," he muttered. "Professor Cobbett was right. We've changed the past."

"But even in seventeen seventy-six, guns and watches and machinery worked, didn't they?" Sammy demanded.

"In our seventeen seventy-six," the Thinker said. "In our past. But this isn't our past any more. It's our present. And by making the past the present we've violated a fundamental law. Or tried to. Actually, fundamental laws can't be violated."

"But we came here."

"Yes. Here. But here isn't our past. It couldn't be. It would have to be somewhere else."

"Where else could it be?" Mush wanted to know.

"A place where modern mechanisms don't work, not having been perfected yet. A place where the British defeated the forces of the Revolution and captured the Founding Fathers. And that could only be in an alternate universe."

"Alternate universe?"

The Thinker was still trying to explain the concept of an alternate universe to them when the soldiers finally came in to drag them away.

He had time only for a final warning as the troops seized them. They were very rough about it.

"Remember, like Franklin said, we must all hang together," he whispered.

Even there the Thinker was wrong.

They were hanged separately.

STRING OF PEARLS

Jerry Gibson was sitting at the bar when she came in. He turned to stare at her. Five minutes later he was still staring.

"Exquisite, isn't she?" said Sweet William. "So tall, so slender. She carries herself like a sword sheathed in white silk."

Sweet William talked like that when he was a little high, and Jerry was used to it. Besides, what he said was true. She was a luxurious hunk of fluff, with black hair and eyes to match, and the kind of figure that made you want to whistle, except that your throat went dry when you looked at her.

Only that wasn't what made Jerry stare. He was looking at her throat, and what was around it.

It wasn't exactly a necklace and it wasn't a pendant, because it was drawn up tightly—just a string of perfectly matched pearls.

But such pearls! Ten of them, almost the size of marbles. They shone brightly under the light, and so did Jerry's eyes. He did a little quick appraisal job. Say five banners apiece, at least, if they were perfect—and genuine. Nobody could touch them without breaking the string up, so the best he could get might be three for each. But three times ten still added up to thirty—thirty thousand dollars.

And she was wearing other stuff, too: an emerald ring and a fancy gold bracelet with smaller emeralds set in it. No use figuring on them, though. Emeralds were out of style, and you just had to take whatever a fence would cough up for them.

But there was probably more stuff where this came from. Maybe Sweet William would know.

Sweet William knew, all right. He sat down at the bar next to Jerry and nodded. "Just got in yesterday." he murmured. "The Ranee."

"The what?"

"Ranee, old boy. Female of the species. Male title, Rajah. Only in this case there is no Rajah. Deceased. Suicide, last year—Rajah of Gwolapur. You must have read about it."

Jerry shook his head. How could he have read about it? They didn't print that kind of news in the *Racing Form*. But trust an operator like Sweet William to be up on such stuff. That was his specialty—moving in on rich widows, and rich women who wished they were widows.

They watched the Ranee of Gwolapur as she settled herself at a table. It was quite an interesting setup, because she had a lot of help. Two little characters in turbans were doing a brother act for her—pulling out the chair, taking the menu from the waiter and holding it so that she could look it over without unladylike haste.

"Her servants, huh?" Jerry asked.

Sweet William nodded. "Loaded," he said. And then, as his eyes narrowed, "Stacked, too. This might be interesting. I wonder if the oriental taste includes poetry?"

"I saw her first," Jerry said. "I got a right."

"The pearls?"

"What else?"

Sweet William put his head down and talked softly, so the bartender wouldn't hear. "Child's play," he said. "Crude, too. This calls for the delicate touch, old boy. Finesse."

Jerry scowled. "You got a one-track mind. You want to finesse everything in skirts. Me, I'll settle for the loot."

"You misunderstand. I'm thinking of the same thing. But we differ on ways and means."

"I'll handle the ways and means," Jerry told him. "I saw her first, remember? I'm gonna case this job good, find out if she keeps the stuff up in her room or puts it in the safe. Then—"

Sweet William dug his fingers into Jerry's arm and the two of them dummied up until the bartender passed down the line. Then he shook his head again.

"It would never do," he said. "Not here, old boy. Too plushy. There'd be a proper row. Suggestions in order? Deal me in. You know how I function. The subtle approach. I'll get the gumdrops for you. May take a bit longer, but no fuss. Clean. And we'll cut the cake two ways."

Jerry thought it over. Sweet William was right. Pulling off a caper in a big resort hotel was enough to make you sweat. With the fix in and the gambling wide open, the management kept its own stable of hoods. And they were on the lookout for loners like Jerry Gibson. They didn't like any funny business because it knocked their good name. So even if he got the pearls his way, he'd be certain to have the hoods on his tail as well as lots of law.

"Rough show, old boy," Sweet William said, like he was reading his mind.

Jerry bit his lip. It added up. Ten to one, the doll kept her ice stashed in the safe anyway, and he'd never get it there. He'd have to jump her or those flunkeys she kept around. Plenty rough, all right. But Sweet William would just move in and take over, without any trouble. He could do it, too; Jerry had seen him operate before. A real pussy-cat.

Jerry swallowed the rest of his drink. "All right," he said. "You got yourself a deal."

Sweet William started to smile, then stopped. Jerry saw that he was looking over at the table again.

"Perhaps not," Sweet William said. "We have company for dinner."

It was true. The Ranee wasn't alone any more. A tall, gray-haired man had just joined her. He was sitting across the table, smiling and talking, and from the way she smiled and talked back it looked as if neither of them worried much about using the same toothbrush.

In a minute the Ranee said something and the two flunkeys bowed and went away.

Jerry decided to do the same thing. He and Sweet William walked outside together.

"How dumb can you get?" Jerry asked. "It's crazy to figure a queen like that floating around without a jack in the pack. We'll have to do it my way after all."

"Cool's the word, old boy. Let me check on the gentleman first. Tomorrow morning, right off. Now, if you'll excuse me, I have an engagement."

Jerry let him go. He knew what Sweet William meant by an engagement. He needed another fix. That was Sweet William's little problem—he was on the stuff. Once he'd told Jerry that if it wasn't for the fixes he'd be sitting pretty in Hollywood right now. And Jerry believed him. Sweet William wasn't a liar—just a hophead blackmail artist who lived off women. Jerry could trust him.

And he would, until tomorrow.

Meanwhile, there might be some action at the tables.

There was, too. Jerry had a good night and he went to bed happy. Funny thing, he kept dreaming about the Ranee. Not about the pearls, but about the dame herself. In the dream she wasn't even wearing pearls.

It was a good dream, and when Jerry woke up he found himself envying Sweet William. Or the gray-haired gent who had already moved in.

He got up early, before lunch, and was just going to phone Sweet William's room when the character knocked on the door. He was all togged out in gray flannels and he looked great.

"Good morning, merry sunshine," he said.

"What's so good about it?" Jerry wanted to know. "You been checking up on the Ranee's boyfriend, is that it?"

Sweet William nodded. "Precisely," he said. "No trouble at all. Sylvan Lemo. Formerly of Athens. Shipping interests. Here on a sabbatical, as it were. As nearly as I can determine, he spent part of it in the Ranee's suite last night."

"So what's so good about that you should hold up an applause card?"

"Farewell appearance, old boy. The gentleman checked out at midnight. Bag and baggage. In fact, he did a bunk."

"Bunk?"

"Didn't pay his bill."

"Hey!" Jerry stood up. "You think he maybe got to her first? Maybe it was a phony name, and he had the same idea—"

Sweet William put his hand on Jerry's shoulder. "He didn't get the pearls, if that's what's worrying you. She's still wearing them this morning."

"How do you know?"

Sweet William grinned like a skunk eating bumblebees. "I saw them when we had breakfast together."

"Brother! You're not handing me a line—"

"Quite the contrary. She is the recipient. I happened to bump into her in the lobby and strike up an acquaintance. By the way, she speaks English beautifully. Does everything beautifully." Sweet William backed toward the door.

"Hey, where you going?"

"I've a luncheon engagement with the Ranee."

"You sure move fast."

"That's the specialty of the house."

"What do you want me to do?"

"Nothing, old boy. Absolutely nothing." Sweet William was serious now. "You understand the situation. From now on I don't know you. We don't speak to one another, or call one another."

"But—"

"I'll see to it that you get a progress report. And it won't take long. Trust me. This is the best way."

Jerry nodded.

But when Sweet William left, he went over and sailed a pillow across the room. Hell of a note. He was going to have to sweat it out alone while Sweet William had all the kicks. Did he understand the situation, like Sweet William said? Damned right he did—meaning, Sweet William couldn't afford to let a babe like this Ranee think he knew a ratty-faced little scrut like Jerry. It might queer the act.

A beautiful doll like the Ranee didn't have anything to do with ratty-faced little scruts, or even people who associated with them. In her book, he stunk.

"All right," Jerry told himself. "All right. Take it easy."

Or rather, sit tight, and let Sweet William take it easy. And when he took it, they'd cut up the loot and then there'd be plenty of moola. Enough moola so that Jerry could go out and buy himself a doll—a tall, ritzy-looking doll with black hair like the Ranee who would think him the playboy type. Or at least, she'd pretend she thought so, as long as the moola held out.

But damn it—

Jerry got hold of himself and went down to the bar. Two drinks later he was ready for the track. Going out he saw Sweet William coming in, steering the Ranee by the arm. She wasn't wearing the pearls now, but the two stooges were right behind her.

Jerry stared, but nobody stared back. Sweet William didn't even notice him. He was busy talking to the Ranee, and she was looking up at him and smiling and showing her teeth, and they were almost as good as the pearls. Jerry wondered what it would be like to feel those teeth digging into a guy's shoulder and—

The hell with it. He went out to the track.

He stayed in the bar out there after the last beetle crawled in, and met a couple of dealers he knew from K.C. They went out to eat and ended up in a joint on the highway. Highway was right: Jerry was plenty high when they finally poured him into the hotel about two A.M.

He flopped right on the bed without shedding his threads, and sort of passed out. But he dreamed about the Ranee, and her teeth and her eyes and her white arms reaching—

Jerry woke up at noon and it was rugged. A shower helped. He went downstairs, hoping to bump into Sweet William, but no dice.

By the time he finished eating it was too late to go out to the track, and he didn't feel like it anyway. He went into the bar and sobered up on beer.

It must have been almost five when somebody tapped him on the arm, and it was Sweet William. He didn't sit down.

"Only have a minute," he said. "Meeting the dear girl for dinner, you know."

"How's it going?"

"Splendidly, old boy. Couldn't be better. She's crackers over me, absolutely. Last night—"

Jerry didn't want to hear about last night.

"What about the deal?" he asked.

Sweet William wasn't even listening to him. "Would you believe it, she's on the stuff, too. The genuine. *Yen shee gow*. Smokes a pipe. You've never had a bang until you've tried the pure quill. Of course, the orientals were always great ones for opium. How she manages to maintain her supply I don't know, but I'll find out tonight."

"Is that all you're going to find out?" Jerry couldn't help sounding off.

"Of course not. I've been trying to get to you all day, but I couldn't shake off Her Highness. And those two attendants of hers watch me like narks. Bit of a problem, getting her alone. When she's gone they keep their eyes open, let me tell you."

"Bodyguards, huh?"

"In a manner of speaking. But don't worry—I'll get rid of them tonight."

"You got plans?"

"Don't underestimate me, dear boy. Certainly I have plans. The time is ripe for a bit of a rendezvous in her suite. She'll see to it that we're alone, I'm sure. Then we'll pad down a bit, with a pipe or two for company. The pipe sets her off; she's a proper caution, then. And so am I."

Sweet William smiled reminiscently, then sobered. "But tonight I'll indulge in a bit of duplicity. I won't really hit the stuff. When she's out, I'll take up a collection."

"Are you sure the pearls will be there?"

"I'll make sure. Usually she keeps them in the safe—you were right about that. But they'll be around her neck tonight, until I remove them. By the way, there happen to be eleven of them, not ten. You miscounted, old boy. But I forgive you since it's in our favor."

Jerry frowned. "Okay, then what?"

"Then we travel. In your car, naturally. We throw them off the scent. Nothing could be simpler. I'll check out now. You check out before midnight. Drive around to the parking lot of the Golden Wheel. Look out for me about two at the latest. I'll have a cab drop my luggage in the lobby checkroom and you can pick it up. No sense chancing someone seeing the baggage going into your car. Right?"

"Right."

Jerry wanted to say more, but Sweet William was gone. And now there was nothing to do but wait. Wait and sweat.

He waited and he sweated through supper. Then he went out and took a walk around. No sense drinking—not if he was going to drive tonight. They'd have to at least clear the state line by morning before holing up in a motel.

He walked around until eleven or so, then went back to the hotel and checked out. He got the car and took it to the parking lot and sat there. Just sat there, waiting and sweating.

Waiting and sweating was bad enough, but thinking was worse. Funny thing, he wasn't thinking about what might go wrong with the deal. Sweet William could swing it all right, and there was no sense in getting antsy over something he couldn't help either way.

What bothered him was thinking about the Ranee. The Ranee and Sweet William together, alone up in her suite. He wondered what they were doing and then he knew what they were doing and that was the worst part of it.

So he tried thinking about something else. He tried wondering what went with a dame like that. Husband committed suicide last year—was that the story? Guy must be nuts, killing himself when he had a dame like that.

Maybe she hit the pipe too hard, though. Maybe she was too much for him to handle. Maybe that's why she went around now, alone, moving from Miami to Vegas to Reno to Colorado Springs—the Big Circuit—picking up guys and getting her kicks on the way. Funny she hadn't been taken before. Asking for it, really. Unless those two stooges of hers protected her.

If that was the way it worked, then perhaps Sweet William would run into trouble. But no, no use figuring like that. Got to trust Sweet William. He'd get the pearls.

Wait and sweat.

Jerry glanced at his watch. Holy hellsmoke, two-thirty! And where was the joker?

He tried to hold it down, tried to bury it in his mind, but it kept popping up in other places—his stomach, for instance. His stomach began to jump up and down. At three o'clock he was ready to flip.

Maybe the two little guys, those servants, were knife artists. Sweet William might be up there with a shiv in his back. You couldn't trust foreigners anyhow. He'd wait another half hour, and then—

And then it was three-thirty, and no Sweet William. So what could he do? He could barge up to the Ranee's suite and knock on the door. But maybe he'd better go back to the hotel and check.

So he went back, and he checked.

The clerk on the desk was very polite. Yes, Mr. Henderson had left, about ten o'clock.

It was funny to think of Sweet William as "Mr. Henderson," but the rest wasn't so funny. Because while the clerk was explaining that no, Mr. Henderson hadn't left a message, somebody bumped into Jerry at the desk.

He looked around and there was one of the little guys—one of the Ranee's servants.

"You wish news of Mr. Henderson, sir?" he asked.

Jerry could hardly understand him, but he understood enough to nod and listen close.

"It is as the clark says. You friend go away, in his car."

"His car?"

"I know. I assist him with his bags."

Jerry nodded again. There was nothing else to say to the little character. He went away, and Jerry walked over to the lounge and sat down.

Sweet William was gone. Sweet William the joker, the guy who was so sure he'd get the pearls. Well, that's exactly what he'd done — and how easy it had been! Set Jerry up to wait for him, then skip out with a good four or five hours' start.

Almost six hours now, and no telling which direction he'd taken off in. There'd be no way of catching up with him. It was a clean getaway. So clean the Ranee probably didn't even know about it yet; the little guy in the turban didn't sound upset. Hell, the trick was so slick Sweet William even had him carry out his bags!

Jerry had to hand it to the joker. He wished he *could* hand him something, right now. Playing the Ranee for a mark was one thing — but playing him, too!

But there wasn't a damned thing he could do about it. Not a damned thing to do, now. Except to get his own bags, check in again, and try to figure out what could be done tomorrow.

All at once Jerry was very bushed. He needed a drink, and remembered the pint in his bag.

So he went up to the clerk, got himself a room again, let the bellboy haul in his stuff, and then he was set. The pint helped. He sat on the bed and drank it straight, drank it fast. Every time he felt like cursing Sweet William he shoved the old bottle into his mouth. It was almost light when he fell back across the bed and passed out.

It was almost dark when he woke up again. No hangover, but then he'd slept the clock around.

Jerry got up, shaved, dressed, and went downstairs. He was hungry, but the rage in his stomach kept him from eating. A drink would be better. Damn it, there must be something he could do to copper his bets. He'd counted on those pearls. He'd counted on a lot of things, including that lousy, double-crossing —

He was just walking into the bar when she stopped him.

"I beg your pardon," she said.

He'd never heard her voice before, and it did something to him. It made his stomach churn faster, but not with rage, not with hunger, not with thirst.

The Ranee was standing there in the corridor leading from the bar, and she was smiling at him.

"Aren't you the gentleman who was asking for Mr. Henderson last night? Ghopal spoke to me about it."

Jerry didn't know what to say. If she was trying to get a lead on her missing ice, he'd better dummy up fast.

Then he blinked. He'd been so busy watching her smile he'd never looked at her throat.

And she was still wearing the pearls. There they were! She had on the ring and the bracelet, too. And matching earrings. So Sweet William hadn't snatched the loot after all.

Jerry smiled. "Why, yes," he said. "We had a business matter to discuss."

"I happen to know where Mr. Henderson is," the Ranee told him. "He had an urgent call yesterday evening—something about an appointment in the city. But he told me he expected to be back before six. In fact, we had a dinner engagement."

It sounded phony as hell. But there was just an off-chance it might be true. Sweet William was a smoothie; he always had a couple of deals cooking. Could he have gotten a fast blast from town and scooted off to take care of it? There was no way he could have gotten in touch with Jerry beforehand, and maybe he was too smart to leave a note that would tie them together later.

So he'd checked out and planned to come back tonight. It was worth thinking about, anyway. And meanwhile, the Ranee was still here. The Ranee and that necklace, or whatever it was, with the big pearls. Big pearls, big eyes, big—

"I was on my way in to dinner," the Ranee was saying, "in hopes that your friend might join me later."

"Good idea," Jerry said. "How's about us waiting together?"

It was crude, and he could have kicked himself, but she didn't seem to mind. That smile of hers hit him hard. Maybe he'd been underestimating himself. She didn't seem to object when he introduced himself, and then they were sitting together and the two stooges were going through their routine with the chairs and the menu.

They poured the champagne, too, and it was easy to talk, and pretty soon Jerry didn't give a damn whether Sweet William showed or not.

What the hell, he could handle this. Sweet William wasn't the only one who could work the rich-bitch racket. Just because he was a smoothie, and easy on the eyes, that didn't mean guys like Jerry Gibson were good for nothing but that wait and sweat routine. Come to think of it, worse-looking guys than him managed to get places with the broads.

And he was certainly getting places with this one. The way the champagne hit on an empty stomach, he was talking a blue streak. And here it was—must have been—nine o'clock already, and they were still sitting here, eating and living it up. She was telling him all about Gwolapur, and how she and the Rajah used to go on shoots—which meant tiger-hunting, with elephants, just like in those movies—and about how she missed all that.

Then they talked about traveling and about how beautiful she was and what a shame it was that Sweet William had stood her up, and somehow he let it slip out how much he admired her ice. Of course he didn't call it ice, and she didn't get sore. She just said she had a lot more of it up in her suite. And would he like to see the collection?

That's when Jerry sobered up.

Here he'd been running off at the mouth, letting himself get half-crocked, and all the while he should have been figuring angles.

Now, when his chance came, he wasn't ready. He'd have to watch himself.

But he wanted to go up to the suite, all right. It would be a good chance to case the setup. He wouldn't pull anything off tonight, anyway—just take a look around. If he played it close to the chest he might be able to come back. And next time he'd have a plan.

So he stood up and she stood up and the turbans pulled out the chairs, and they took the elevator.

The elevator hesitated after the twelfth floor and for a second Jerry was afraid they'd stop at thirteen. Not that he was superstitious or anything, but he just didn't like thirteen. But of course that was a lot of malarkey. Hotels didn't have thirteenth floors any more. The elevator left them off at fourteen.

Then he was in the suite. There was a plush layout for you—big rooms, all dim lights, and lots of fancy cloths hung over the furniture and draped on the walls; she must have brought the stuff with her. It looked like one of those harems you see in the movies.

Funny smell, incense or something. Jerry remembered what Sweet William had said about *yen shee gow*, and it was funny to think of this gorgeous dish being a hophead. But then it was funny that she could go for him, too; sitting him down on one of the big sofas and bringing him a drink with her own hands. Because the two servants had disappeared.

They were all alone in the dim coolness, and the drink wasn't strong. He know he could take it without feeling it. He could take anything, he could take her if she just moved a little closer. The way she smiled, and her soft voice going through him, and talking to him about how lonely it was to live like this, traveling from place to place with nothing but memories—

Then Jerry saw the guy standing in the corner and he wanted to jump. He was big and black and he had six arms.

The Ranee laughed at him. "Do not be afraid," she said. "She will not do you harm."

"She?"

"The statue. Durga, the goddess of our household. Kali."

Jerry stared at the statue before leaning back again. She had six arms, all right, and looked plenty mean. There was a string of white things around the statue's neck, and it took Jerry less than five seconds to make out what they were. Little ivory skulls. Human skulls. A hell of a necklace.

Thinking of necklaces made him think of the pearls. The Ranee was sitting next to him now, and something about the way she rested her head on his shoulder told him he could take her in his arms, if he wanted to. If he wanted to? Just feeling her near him, feeling the whiteness and the redness and the blackness all blending in heat and perfume was enough to stone him. But before he reached out, he had to look at the pearls.

They were there, resting against her throat, moving up and down—big and round and perfect. Eight, nine, ten, eleven, twelve of them.

Twelve?

He'd counted ten, and Sweet William told him there were eleven. But that was before Sweet William went away.

There were ten the first day, and then the gray-haired man had gone away. After that, there were eleven. Then Sweet William went away, and now there were twelve—

She must have seen him jump, and he tried to smile and cover it up. He said, "You've got a better taste in jewelry than that statue of yours, if you don't mind my saying so."

And she smiled too, and said, "Kali is the goddess of the Thugs, you know. Each skull represents one of her victims."

Jerry stood up. She didn't try to hold him.

"The Thugs are stranglers, you know. They kill as a sacrifice. The cult was supposedly stamped out many years ago, but it still has its devotees. My late husband was a believer. He chose me as a bride because he looked upon me as a reincarnation of the goddess. Quaint, isn't it?"

Jerry looked at the necklace. She was close enough for him to make a grab for her, so he wasn't afraid. Besides, the servants were gone.

"So you killed him, huh? And you've been going around ever since, knocking guys off and adding to your string of pearls. That's what you did to the Greek, and to Sweet William. You're crazy as a bedbug."

The Ranee laughed. "How utterly absurd!" she said.

"Like hell it is," Jerry said. "You just got me up here because you were scared I'd kick up a fuss if Sweet William didn't come back. And maybe you had some loony idea of making me number thirteen in your necklace. Well, let me tell you—"

But Jerry Gibson never got a chance to tell her. Because all at once the servants were back, and one of them was holding his arms and the other one was wrapping something tight around his neck, something that squeezed and squeezed.

Jerry's eyes began to bulge. The last thing he saw was the string of pearls around the Ranee's neck. It wasn't really a necklace, of course. He knew that now.

It was more like a choker.

Notes for FINAL RECKONINGS

FINAL RECKONINGS